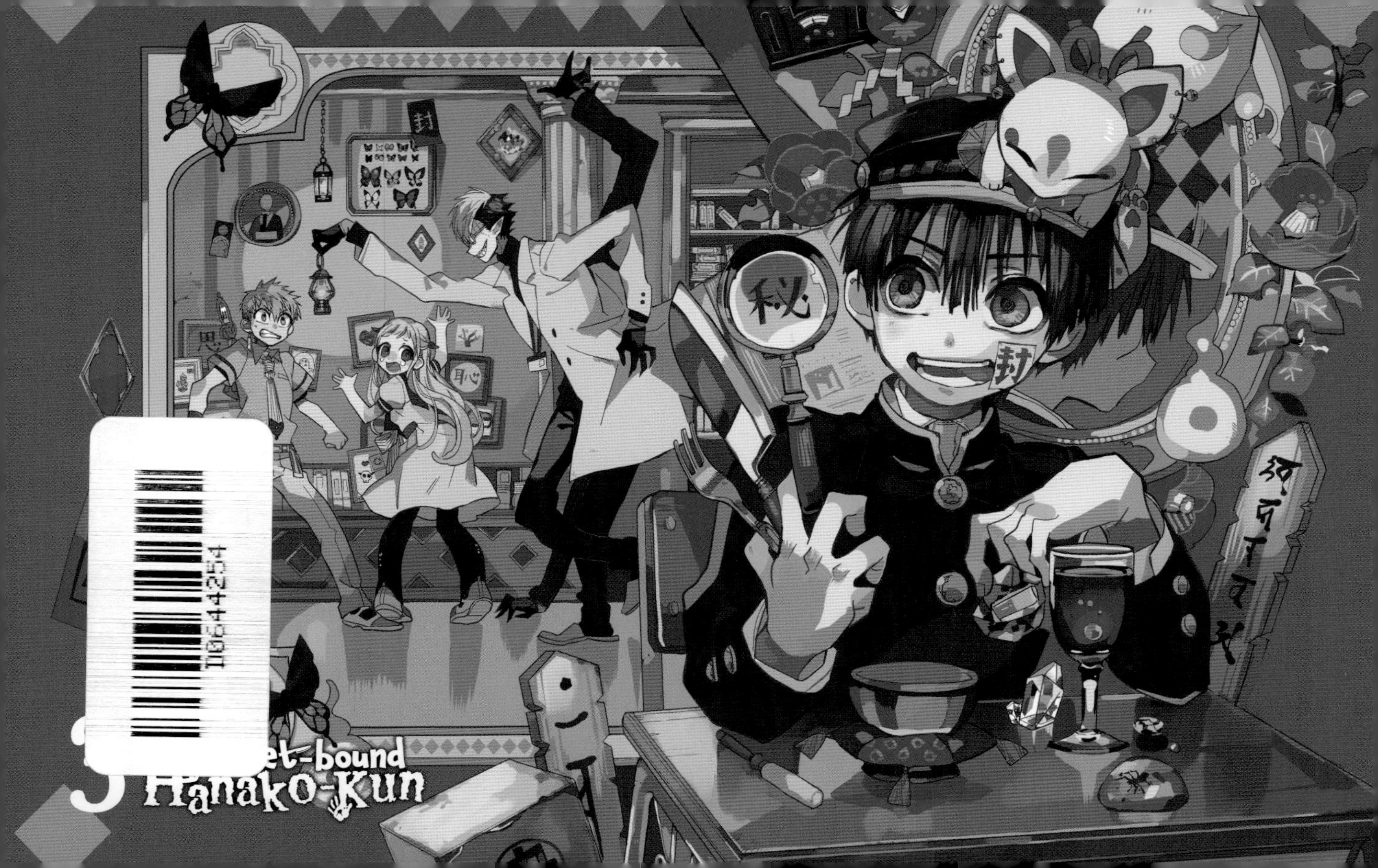
3
et-bound
Hanako-Kun
秘
封

Contents

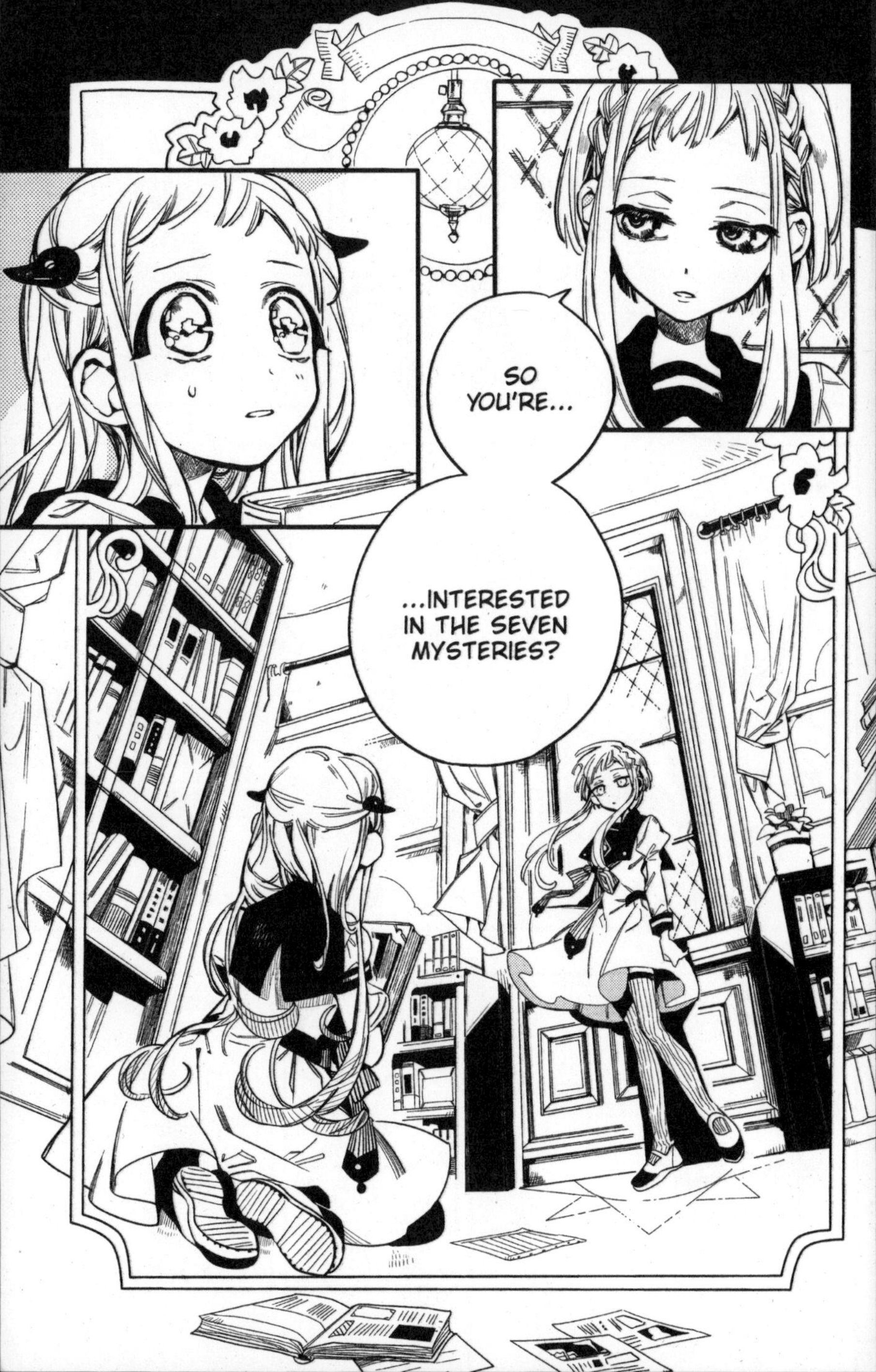
SO YOU'RE...
...INTERESTED IN THE SEVEN MYSTERIES?

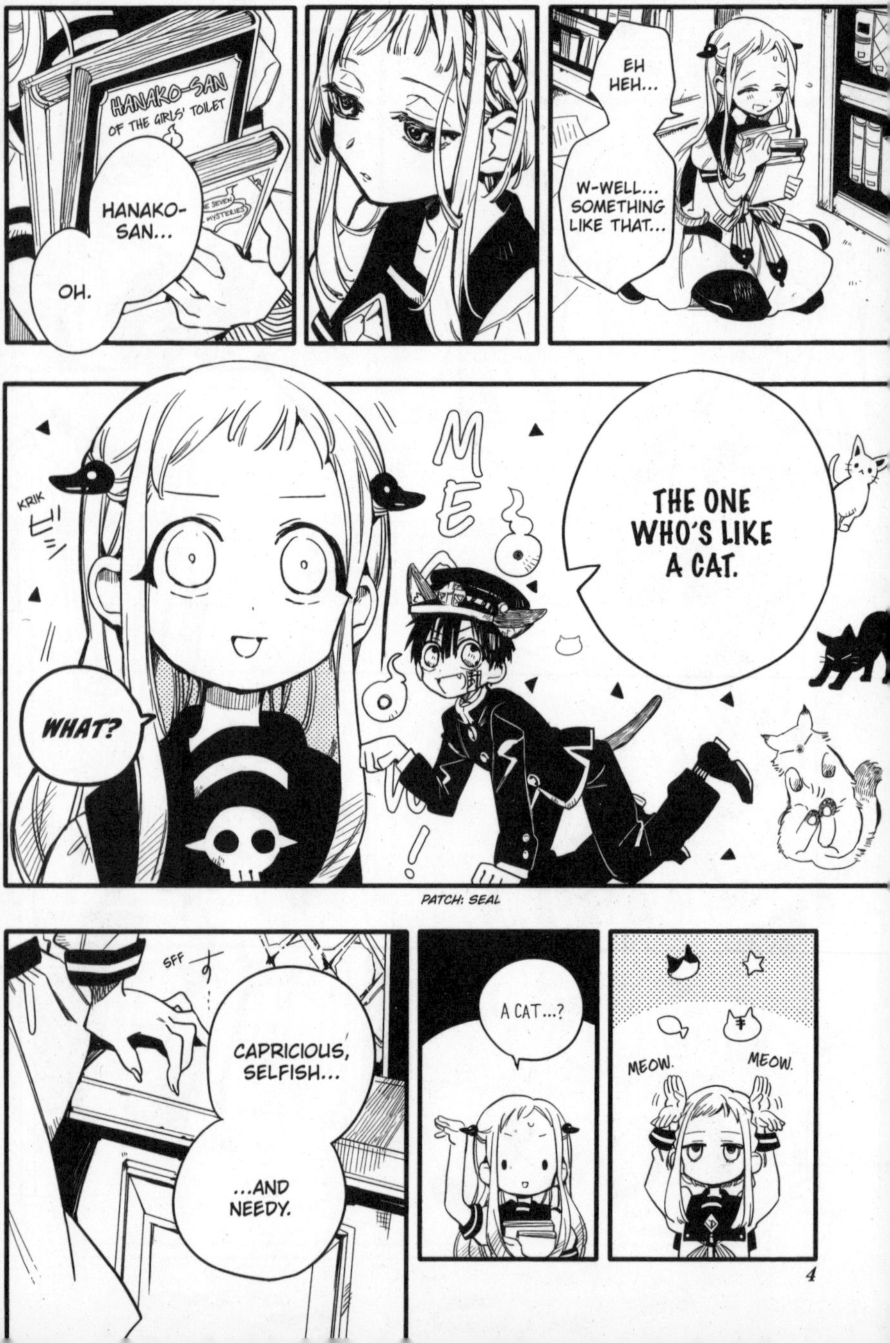
EH HEH...
W-WELL... SOMETHING LIKE THAT...
HANAKO-SAN OF THE GIRLS' TOILET
HANAKO-SAN...
OH.
THE ONE WHO'S LIKE A CAT.
MEOW!
KRIK
WHAT?
PATCH: SEAL
MEOW.
MEOW.
A CAT...?
SFF
CAPRICIOUS, SELFISH...
...AND NEEDY.

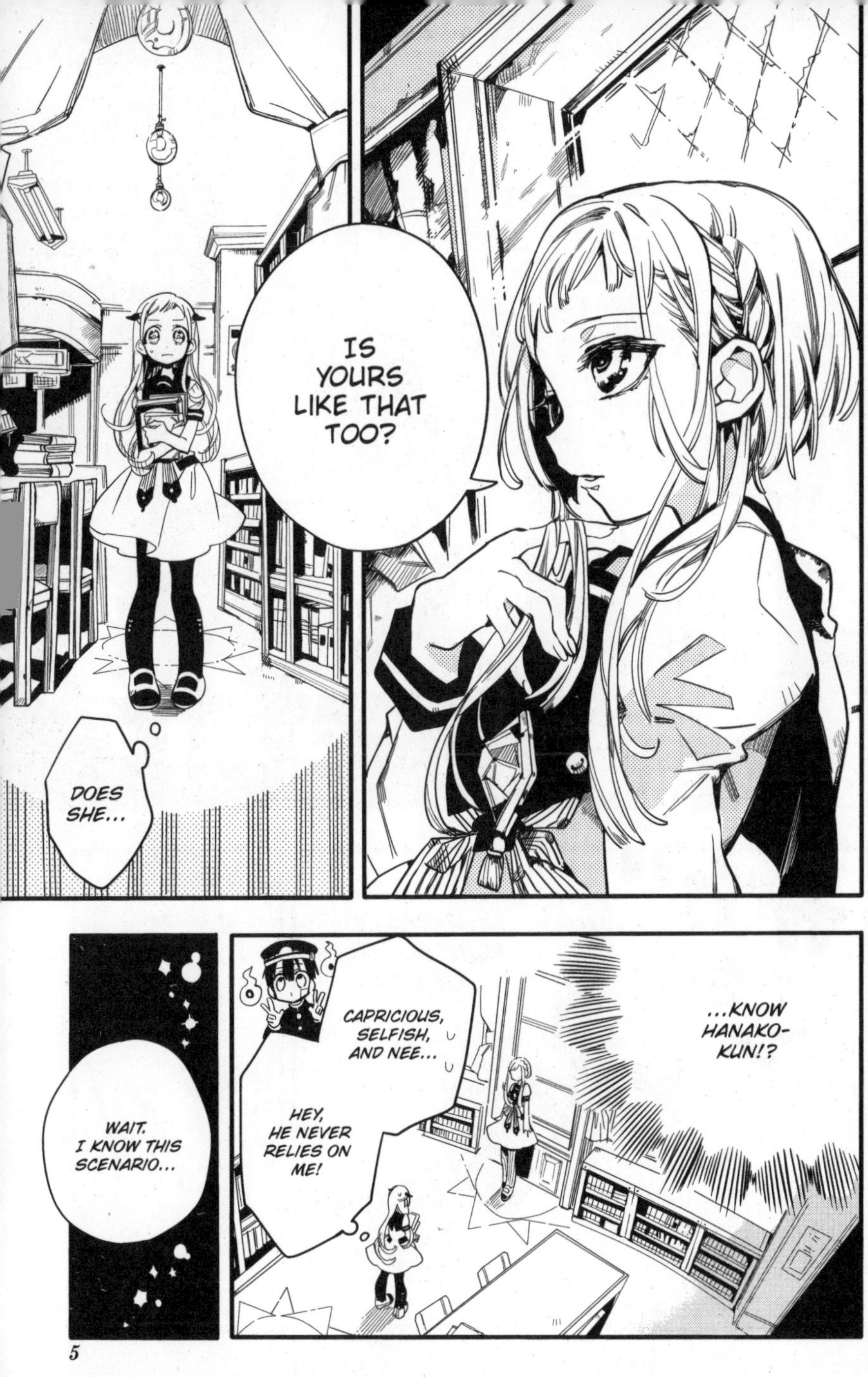
IS YOURS LIKE THAT TOO?
DOES SHE...
...KNOW HANAKO-KUN!?
CAPRICIOUS, SELFISH, AND NEE...
HEY, HE NEVER RELIES ON ME!
WAIT. I KNOW THIS SCENARIO...

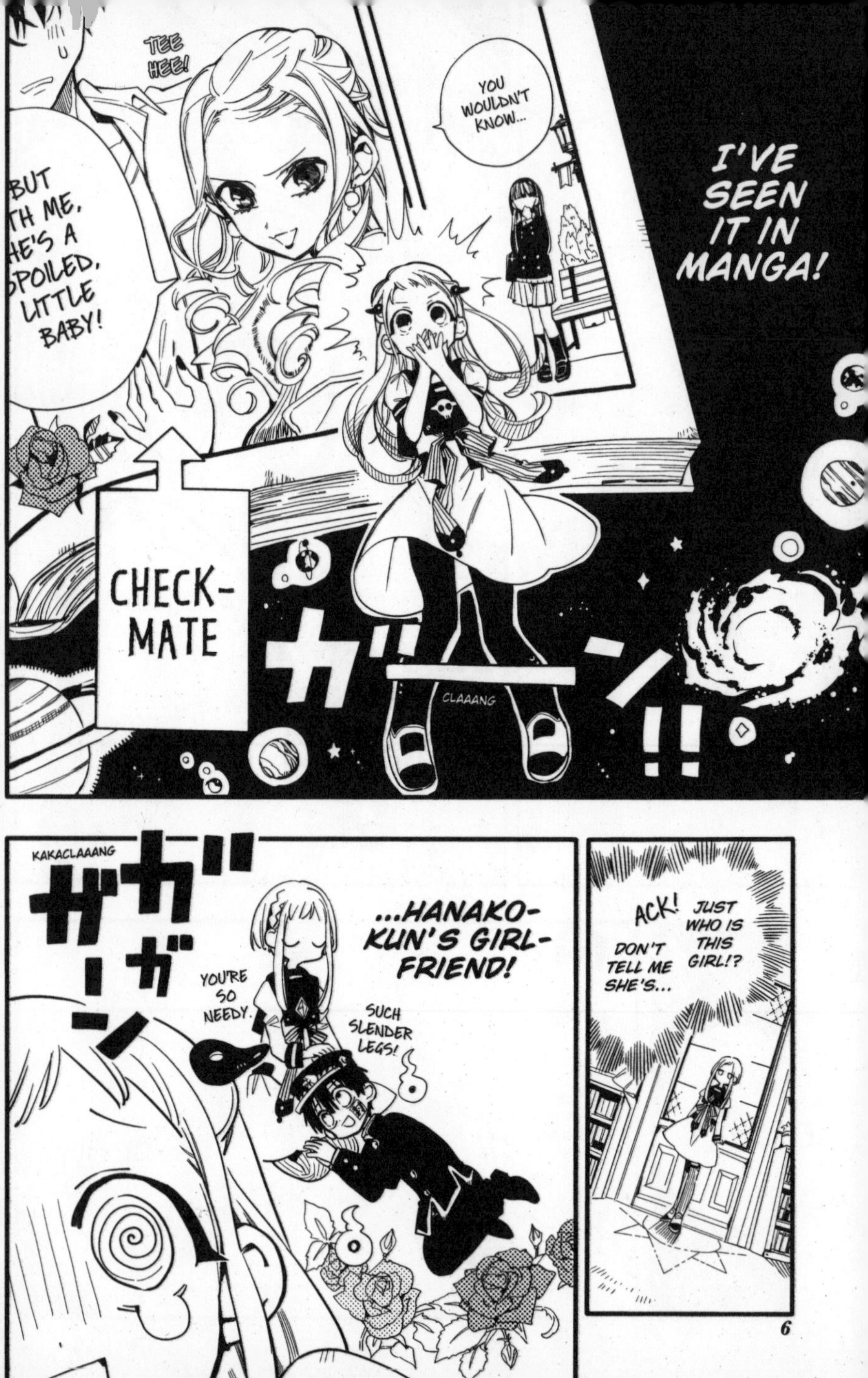
I'VE SEEN IT IN MANGA!
YOU WOULDN'T KNOW...
TEE HEE!
BUT TH ME, HE'S A SPOILED, LITTLE BABY!
CHECK-MATE
CLAAANG
ACK!
JUST WHO IS THIS GIRL!?
DON'T TELL ME SHE'S...
...HANAKO-KUN'S GIRL-FRIEND!
SUCH SLENDER LEGS!
YOU'RE SO NEEDY.
KAKACLAAANG

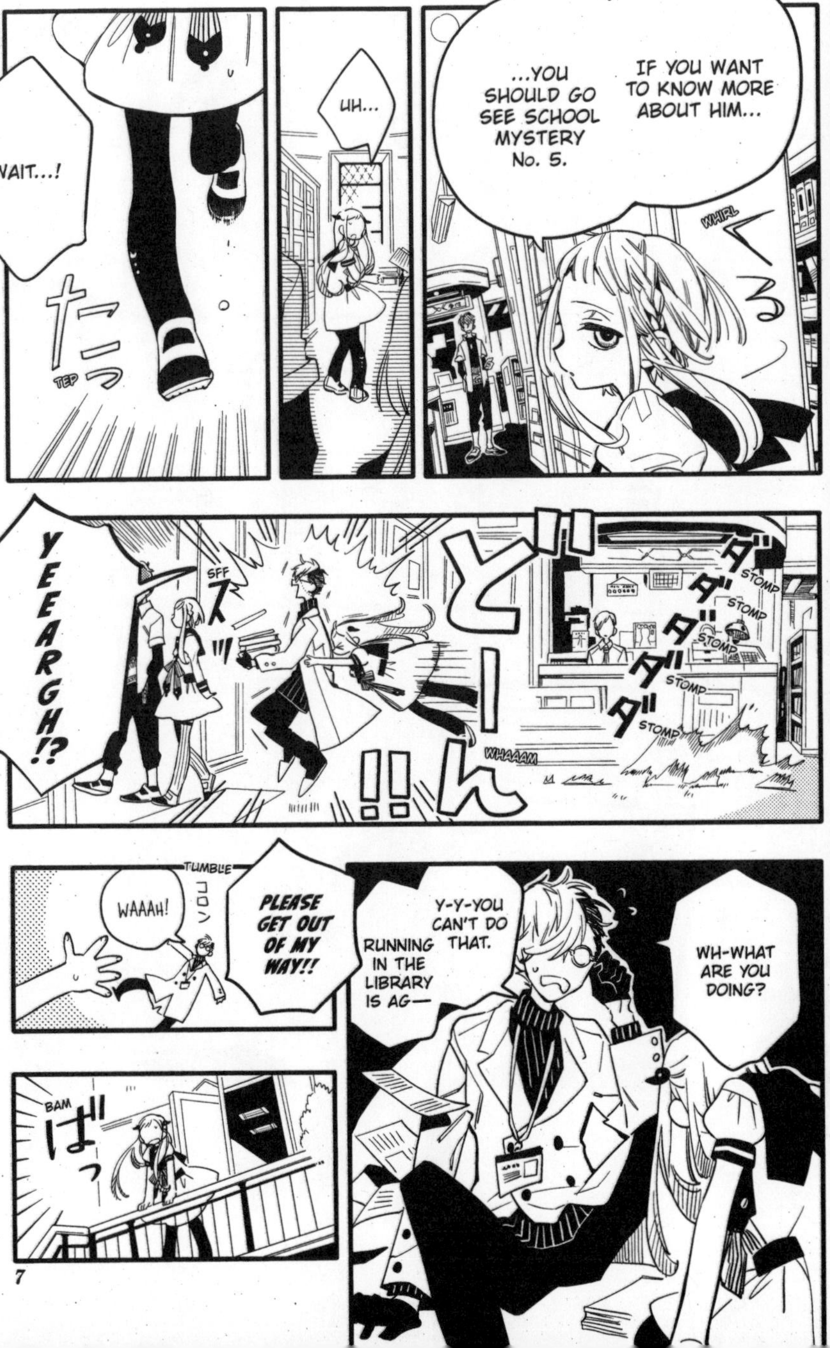
IF YOU WANT TO KNOW MORE ABOUT HIM...
...YOU SHOULD GO SEE SCHOOL MYSTERY No. 5.
WHIRL
UH...
WAIT...!
TEP
WHAAAM
STOMP
STOMP
STOMP
STOMP
STOMP
SFF
YEEARGH!?
WH-WHAT ARE YOU DOING?
Y-Y-YOU CAN'T DO THAT.
RUNNING IN THE LIBRARY IS AG—
PLEASE GET OUT OF MY WAY!!
WAAAH!
TUMBLE
BAM

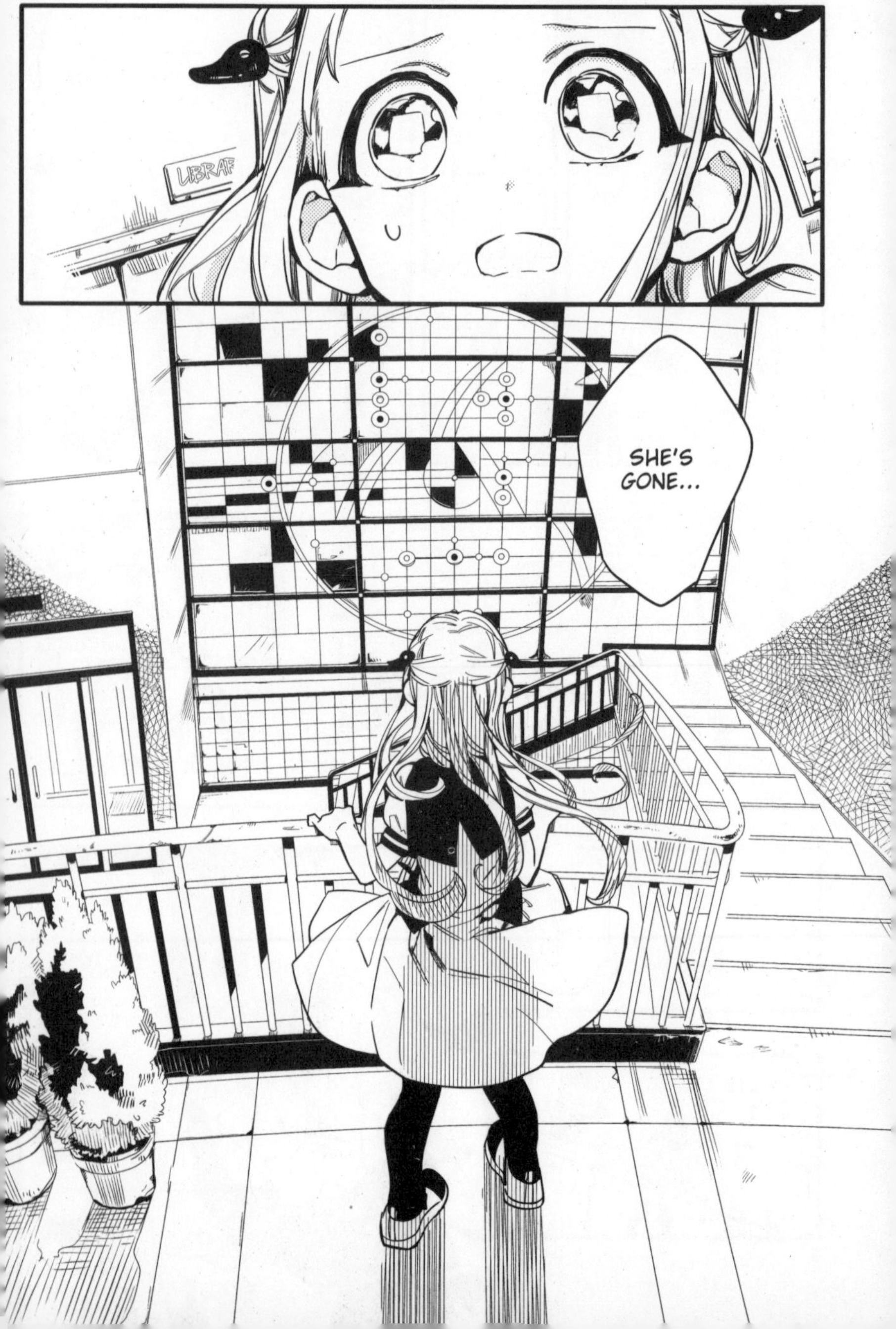
LIBRAR
SHE'S GONE...

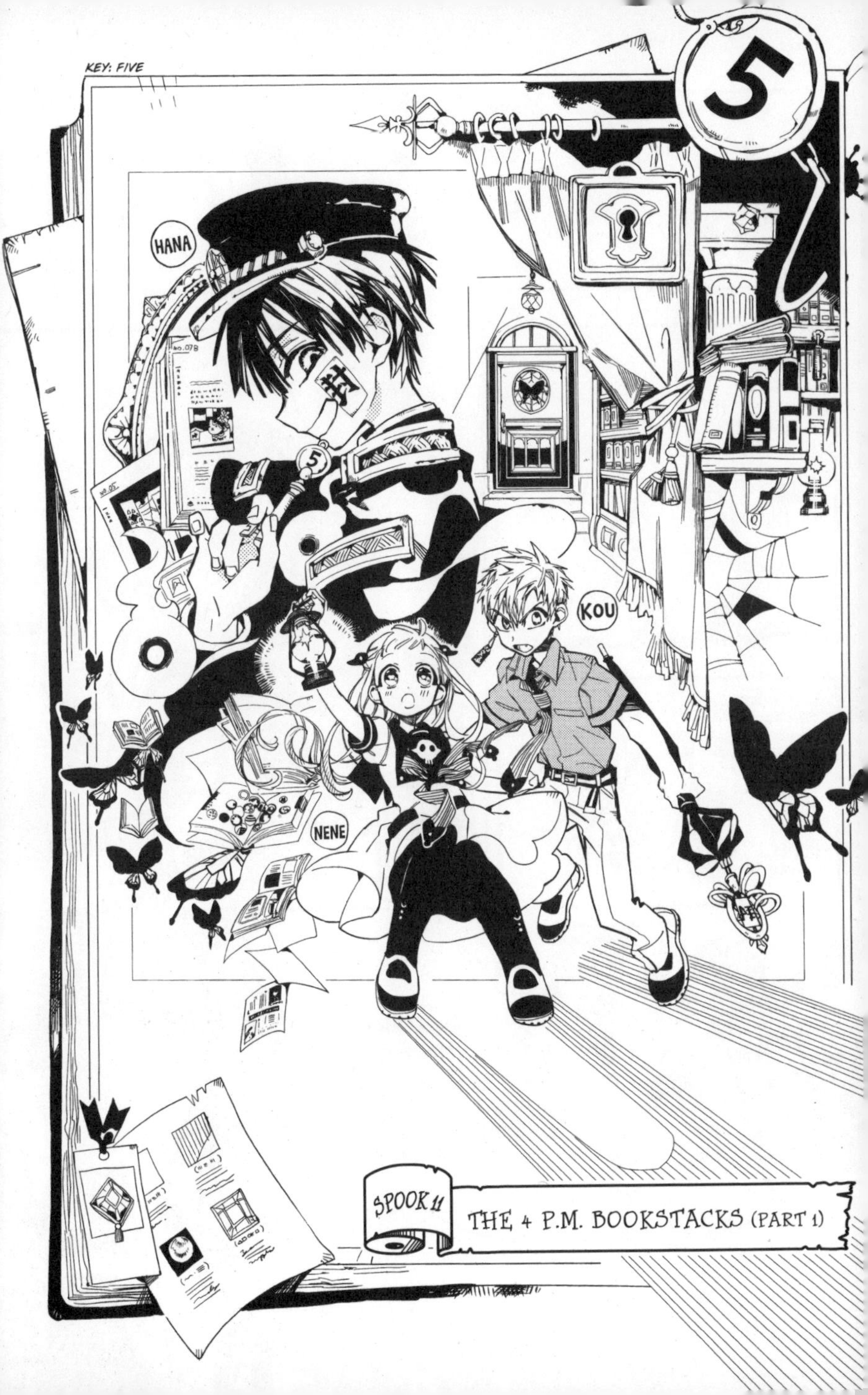
KEY: FIVE
5
HANA
KOU
NENE
SPOOK 11
THE 4 P.M. BOOKSTACKS (PART 1)

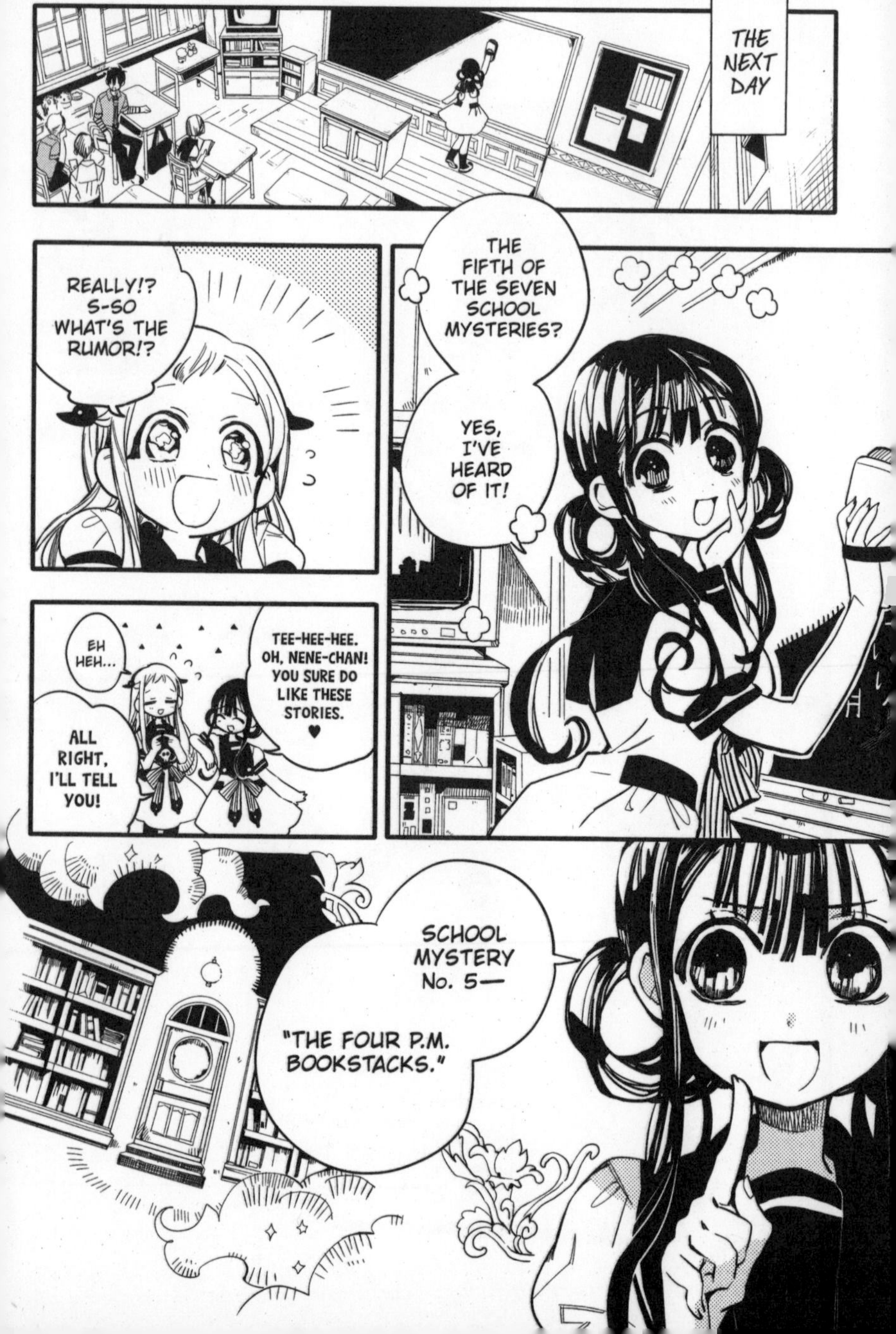
THE NEXT DAY
THE FIFTH OF THE SEVEN SCHOOL MYSTERIES?
YES, I'VE HEARD OF IT!
REALLY!? S-SO WHAT'S THE RUMOR!?
TEE-HEE-HEE. OH, NENE-CHAN! YOU SURE DO LIKE THESE STORIES. ♥
EH HEH...
ALL RIGHT, I'LL TELL YOU!
SCHOOL MYSTERY No. 5—
"THE FOUR P.M. BOOKSTACKS."

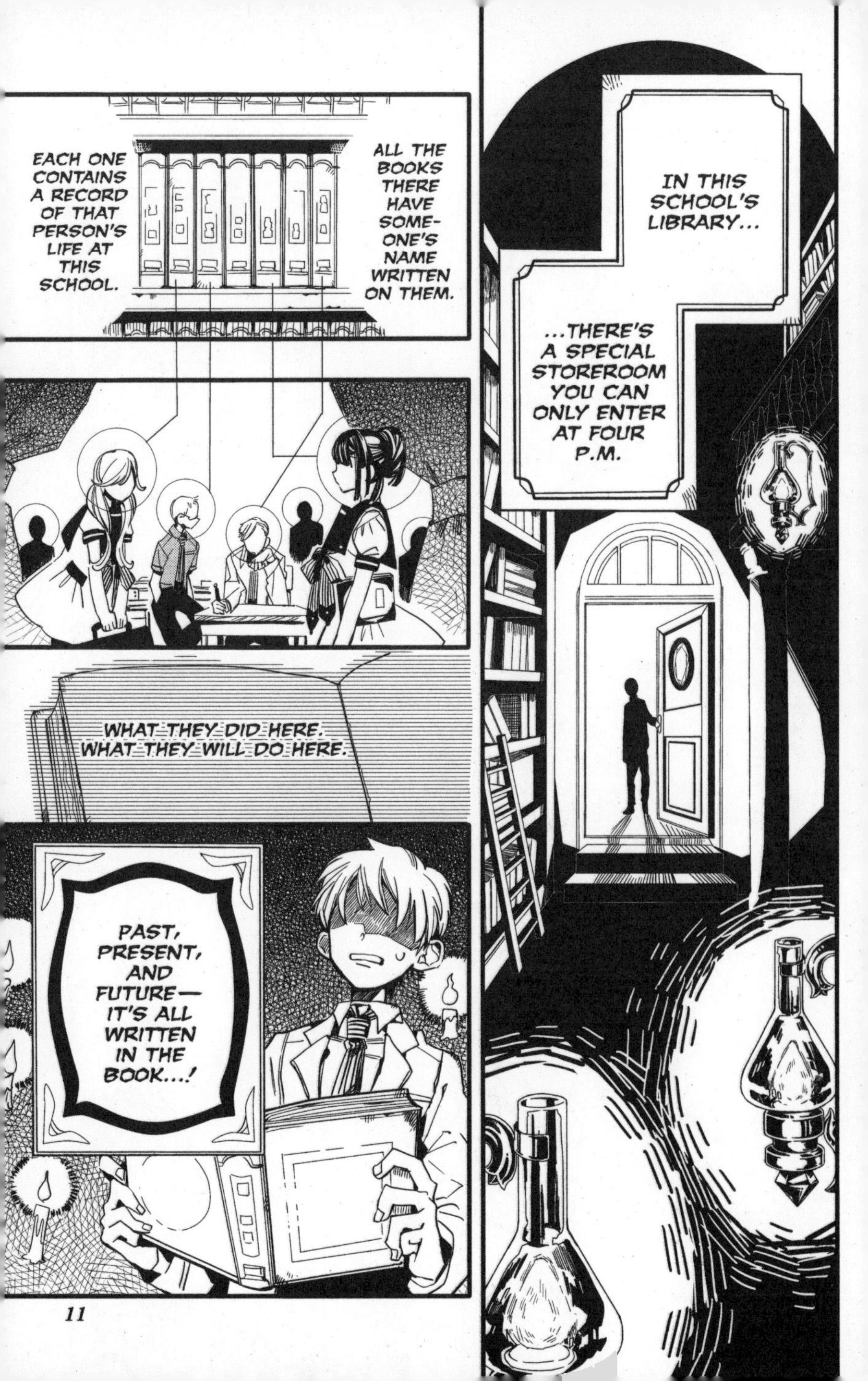
IN THIS SCHOOL'S LIBRARY...
...THERE'S A SPECIAL STOREROOM YOU CAN ONLY ENTER AT FOUR P.M.
ALL THE BOOKS THERE HAVE SOME-ONE'S NAME WRITTEN ON THEM.
EACH ONE CONTAINS A RECORD OF THAT PERSON'S LIFE AT THIS SCHOOL.
WHAT THEY DID HERE. WHAT THEY WILL DO HERE.
PAST, PRESENT, AND FUTURE—IT'S ALL WRITTEN IN THE BOOK...!

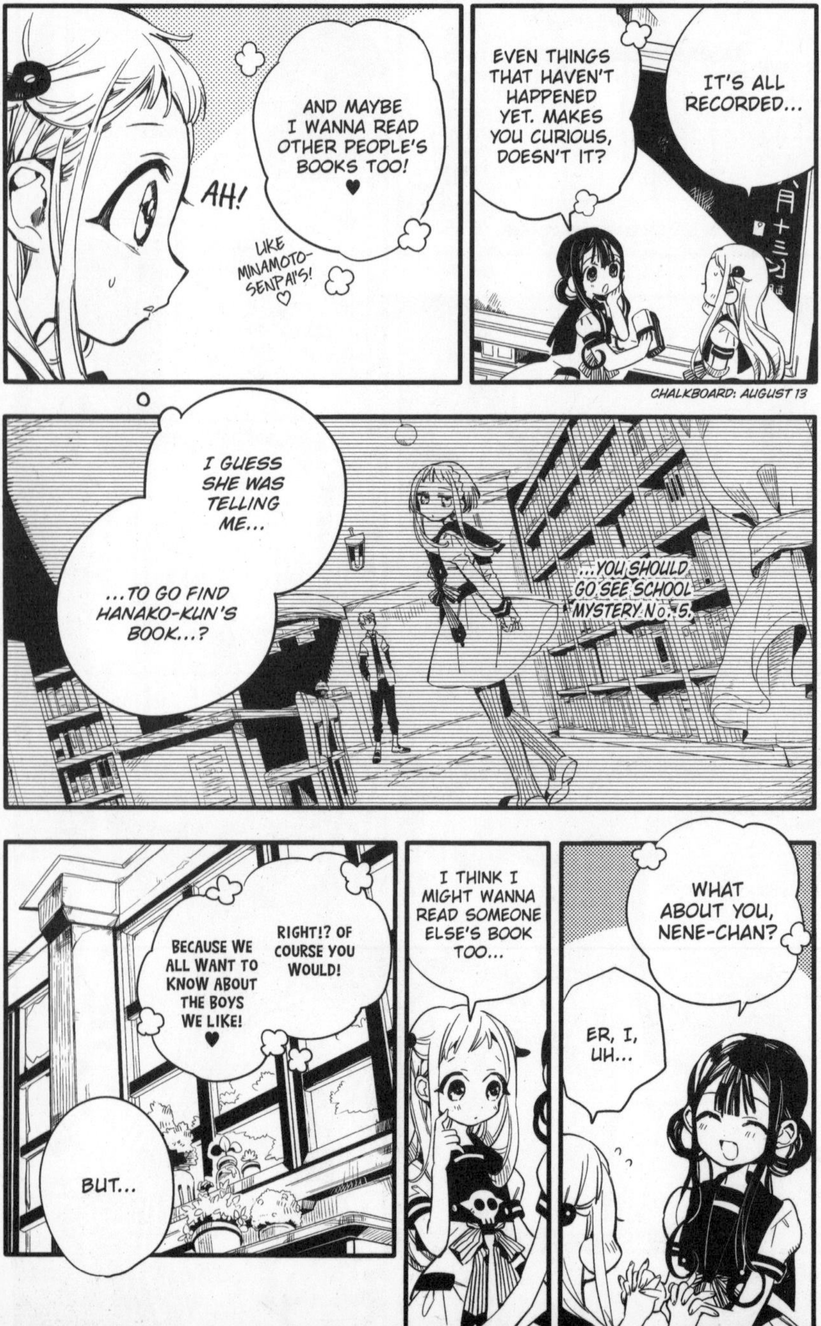
IT'S ALL RECORDED...
EVEN THINGS THAT HAVEN'T HAPPENED YET. MAKES YOU CURIOUS, DOESN'T IT?
CHALKBOARD: AUGUST 13
AND MAYBE I WANNA READ OTHER PEOPLE'S BOOKS TOO! ♥
AH!
LIKE MINAMOTO-SENPAI'S! ♡
...YOU SHOULD GO SEE SCHOOL MYSTERY No. 5.
I GUESS SHE WAS TELLING ME...
...TO GO FIND HANAKO-KUN'S BOOK...?
WHAT ABOUT YOU, NENE-CHAN?
ER, I, UH...
I THINK I MIGHT WANNA READ SOMEONE ELSE'S BOOK TOO...
RIGHT!? OF COURSE YOU WOULD!
BECAUSE WE ALL WANT TO KNOW ABOUT THE BOYS WE LIKE! ♥
BUT...

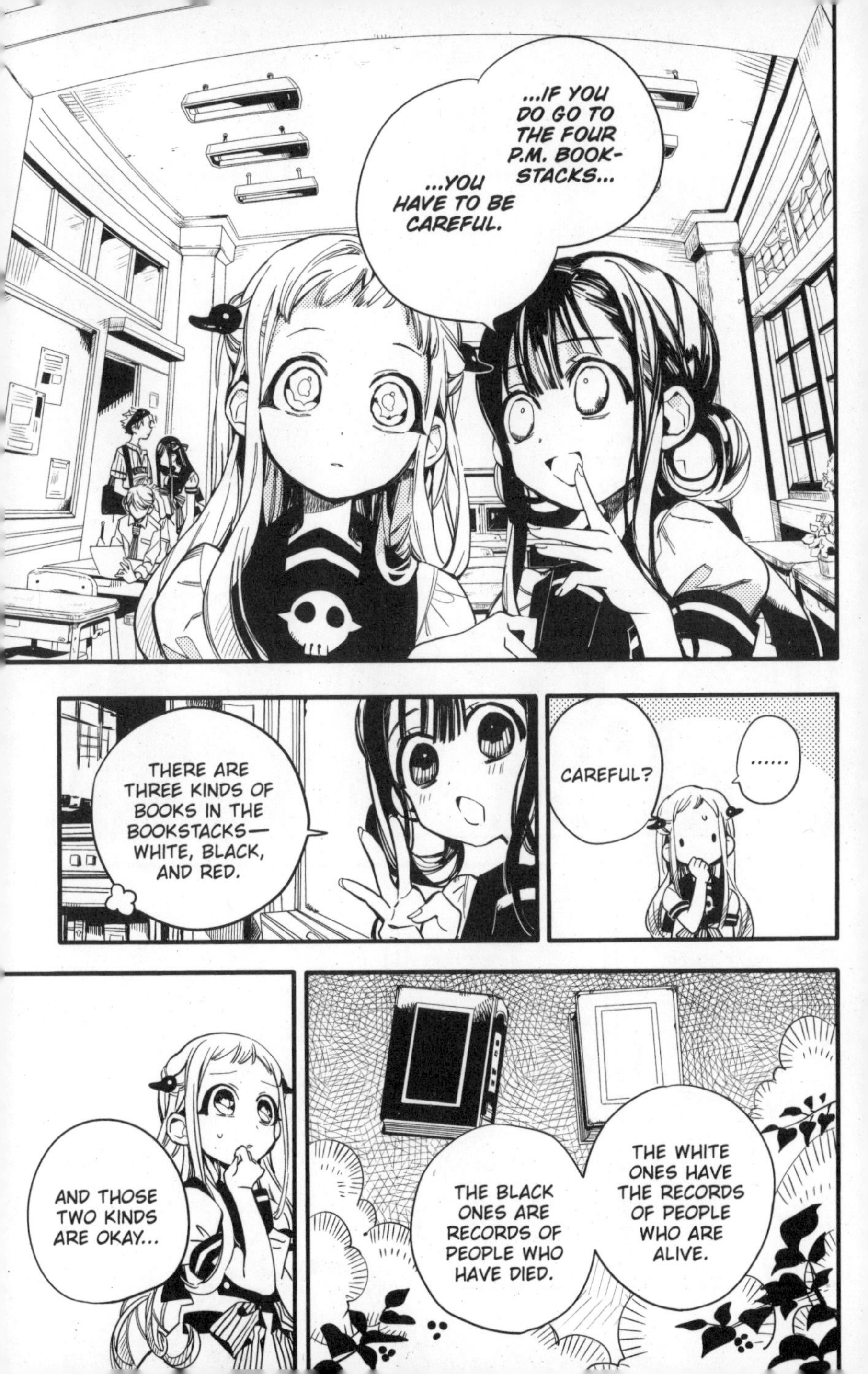
...IF YOU DO GO TO THE FOUR P.M. BOOK-STACKS...
...YOU HAVE TO BE CAREFUL.
......
CAREFUL?
THERE ARE THREE KINDS OF BOOKS IN THE BOOKSTACKS—WHITE, BLACK, AND RED.
THE WHITE ONES HAVE THE RECORDS OF PEOPLE WHO ARE ALIVE.
THE BLACK ONES ARE RECORDS OF PEOPLE WHO HAVE DIED.
AND THOSE TWO KINDS ARE OKAY...

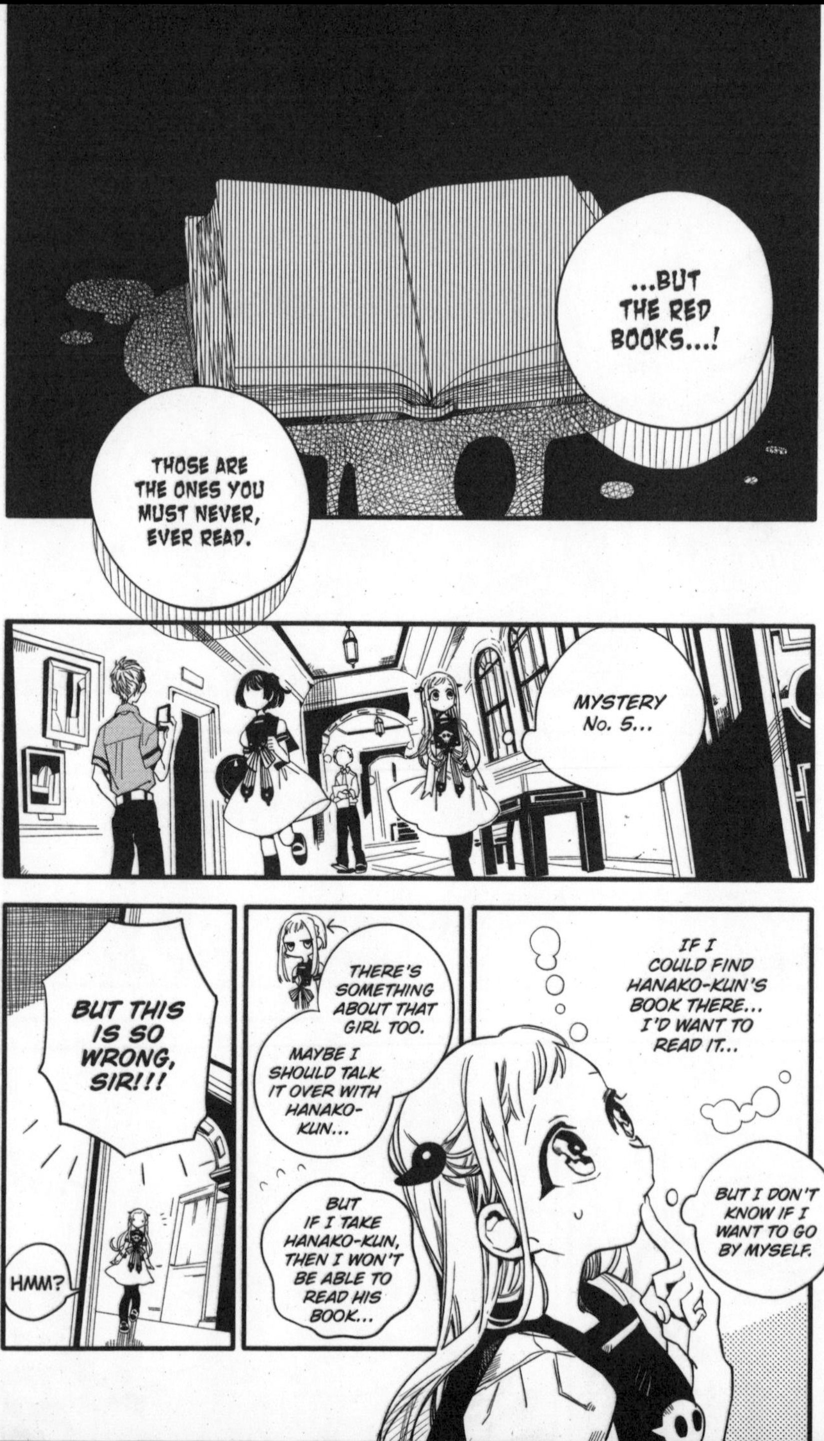
...BUT THE RED BOOKS...!
THOSE ARE THE ONES YOU MUST NEVER, EVER READ.
MYSTERY No. 5...
IF I COULD FIND HANAKO-KUN'S BOOK THERE... I'D WANT TO READ IT...
BUT I DON'T KNOW IF I WANT TO GO BY MYSELF.
THERE'S SOMETHING ABOUT THAT GIRL TOO.
MAYBE I SHOULD TALK IT OVER WITH HANAKO-KUN...
BUT IF I TAKE HANAKO-KUN, THEN I WON'T BE ABLE TO READ HIS BOOK...
BUT THIS IS SO WRONG, SIR!!!
HMM?

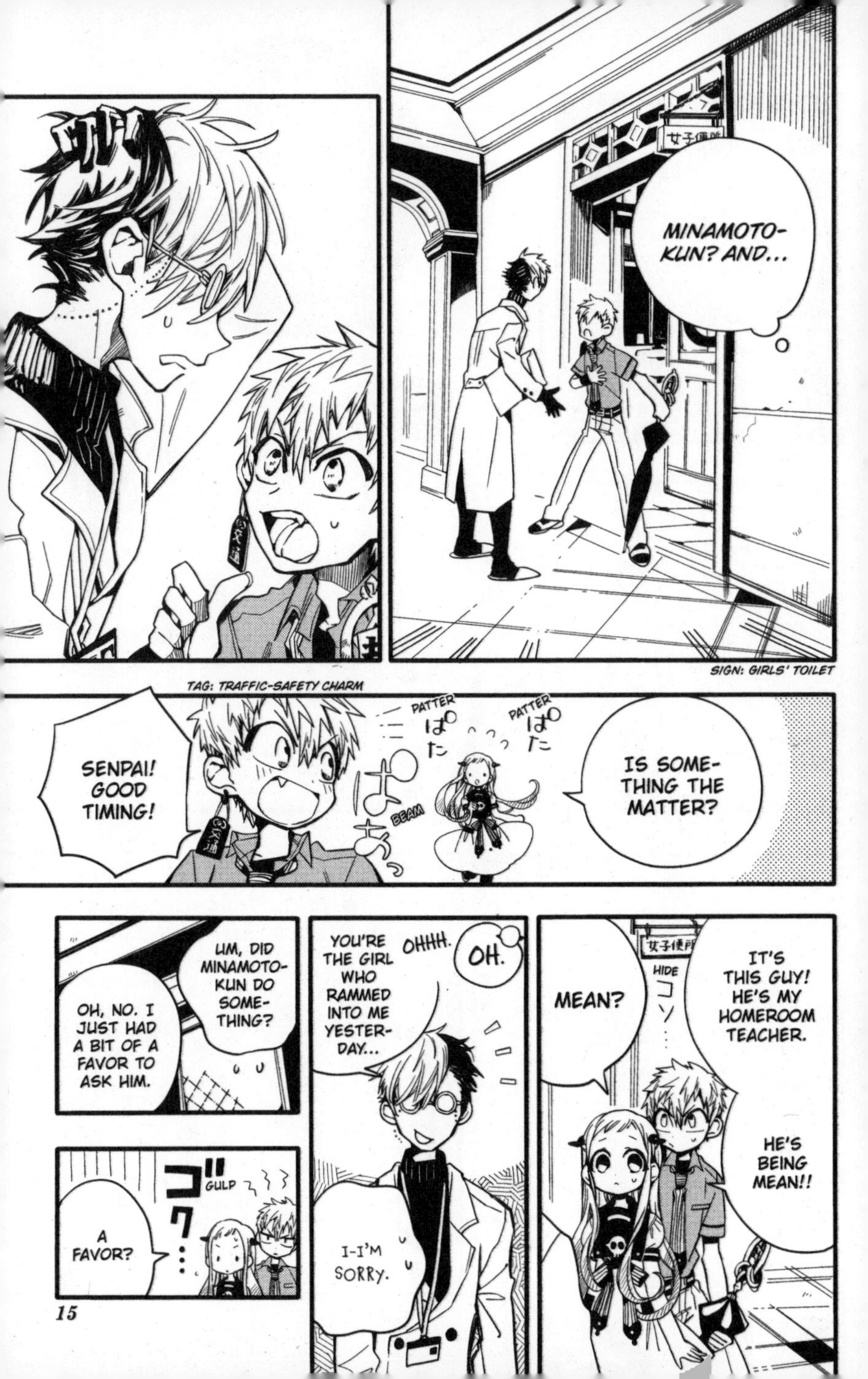
MINAMOTO-KUN? AND...
SIGN: GIRLS' TOILET
TAG: TRAFFIC-SAFETY CHARM
IS SOME-THING THE MATTER?
PATTER
PATTER
BEAM
SENPAI! GOOD TIMING!
IT'S THIS GUY! HE'S MY HOMEROOM TEACHER.
HIDE
MEAN?
HE'S BEING MEAN!!
OH.
OHHH.
YOU'RE THE GIRL WHO RAMMED INTO ME YESTER-DAY...
I-I'M SORRY.
UM, DID MINAMOTO-KUN DO SOME-THING?
OH, NO. I JUST HAD A BIT OF A FAVOR TO ASK HIM.
GULP
A FAVOR?

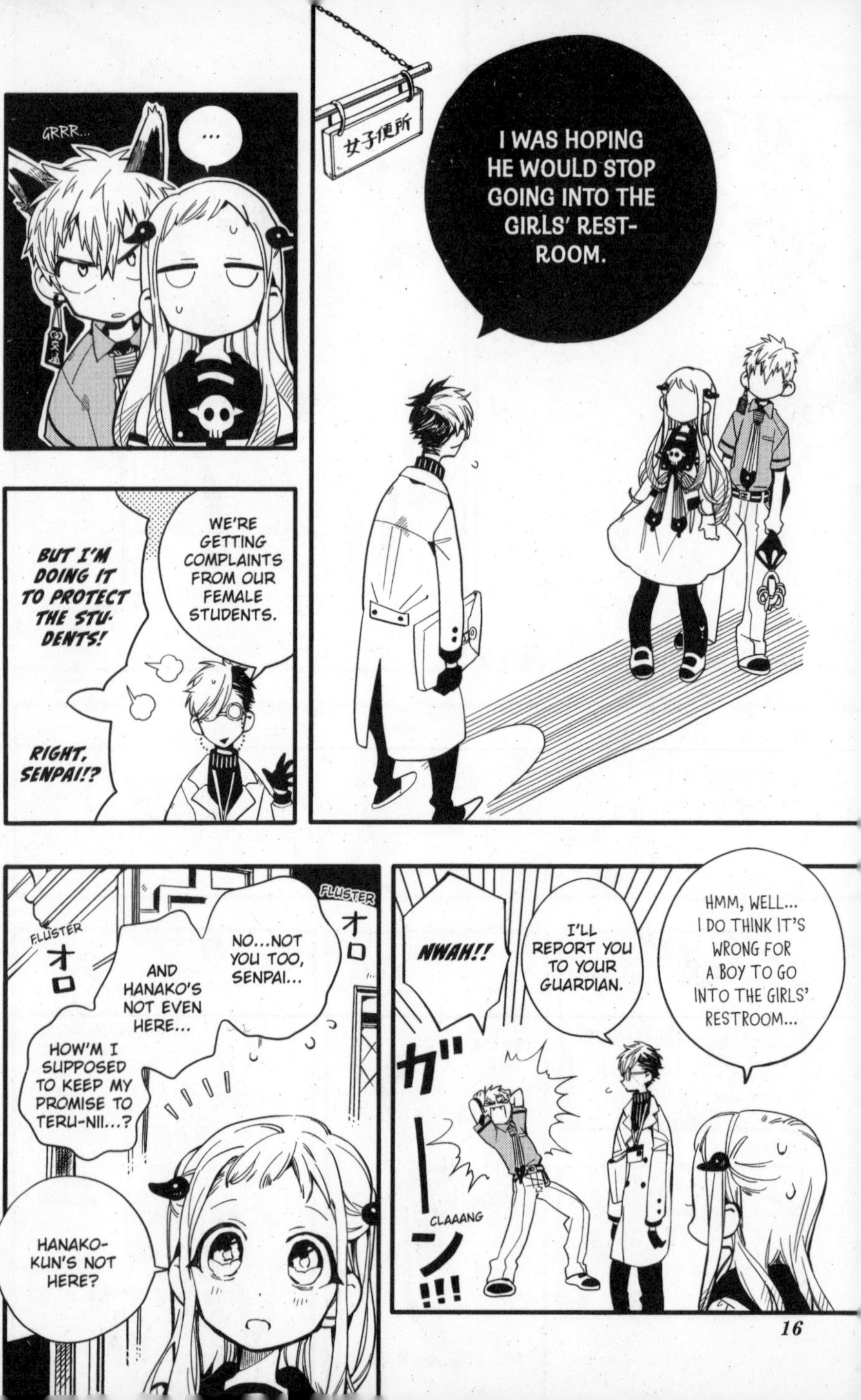
女子便所
I WAS HOPING HE WOULD STOP GOING INTO THE GIRLS' REST-ROOM.
GRRR...
...
WE'RE GETTING COMPLAINTS FROM OUR FEMALE STUDENTS.
BUT I'M DOING IT TO PROTECT THE STU-DENTS!
RIGHT, SENPAI!?
HMM, WELL... I DO THINK IT'S WRONG FOR A BOY TO GO INTO THE GIRLS' RESTROOM...
I'LL REPORT YOU TO YOUR GUARDIAN.
NWAH!!
ガーン!!!
CLAAANG
FLUSTER
オロ
NO...NOT YOU TOO, SENPAI...
FLUSTER
オロ
AND HANAKO'S NOT EVEN HERE...
HOW'M I SUPPOSED TO KEEP MY PROMISE TO TERU-NII...?
HANAKO-KUN'S NOT HERE?

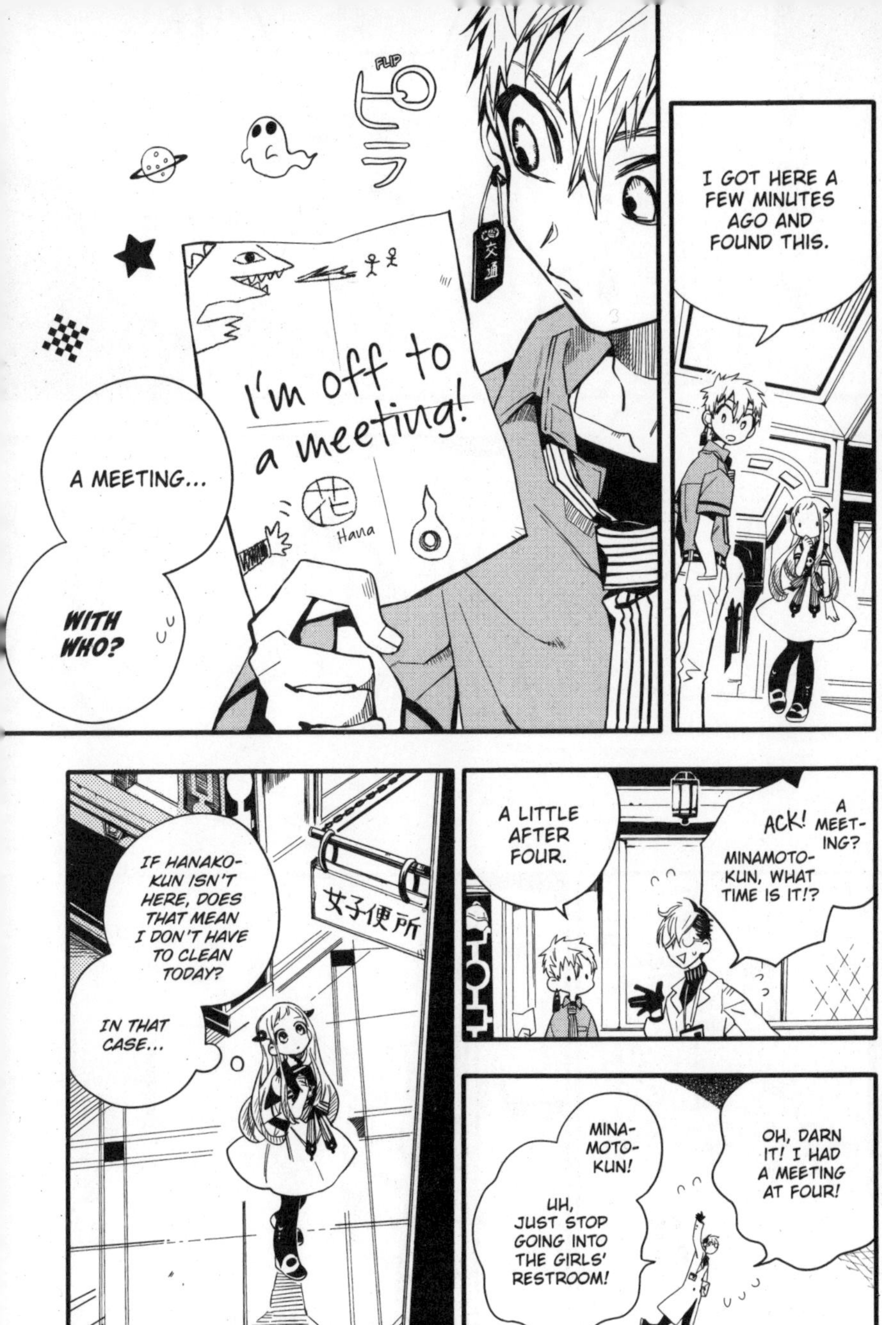
I GOT HERE A FEW MINUTES AGO AND FOUND THIS.
FLIP
I'm off to a meeting!
花
Hana
A MEETING...
WITH WHO?
ACK!
A MEET-ING?
MINAMOTO-KUN, WHAT TIME IS IT!?
A LITTLE AFTER FOUR.
OH, DARN IT! I HAD A MEETING AT FOUR!
MINA-MOTO-KUN!
UH, JUST STOP GOING INTO THE GIRLS' RESTROOM!
女子便所
IF HANAKO-KUN ISN'T HERE, DOES THAT MEAN I DON'T HAVE TO CLEAN TODAY?
IN THAT CASE...

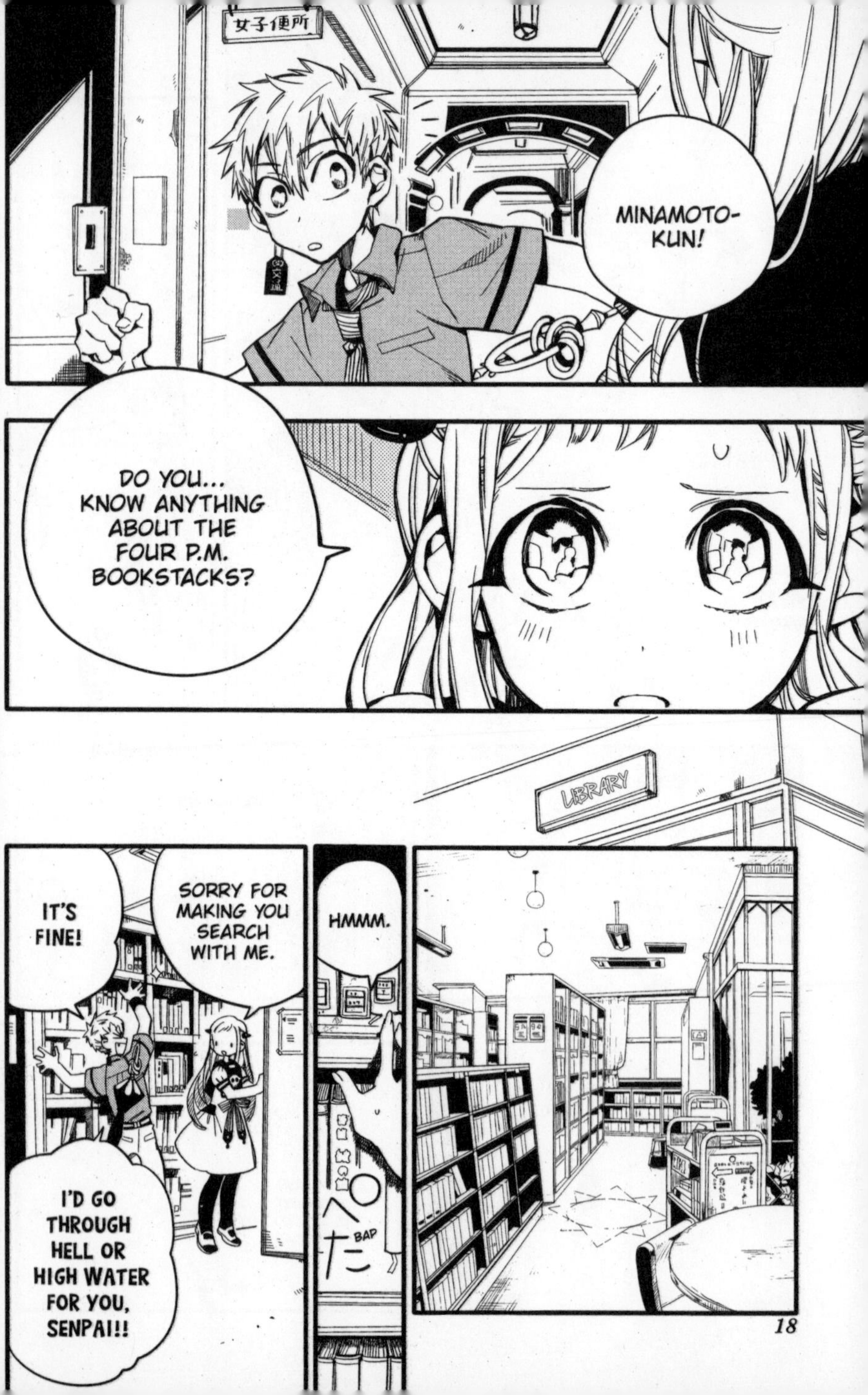
女子便所
MINAMOTO-KUN!
DO YOU... KNOW ANYTHING ABOUT THE FOUR P.M. BOOKSTACKS?
LIBRARY
HMMM.
BAP
SORRY FOR MAKING YOU SEARCH WITH ME.
IT'S FINE!
I'D GO THROUGH HELL OR HIGH WATER FOR YOU, SENPAI!!

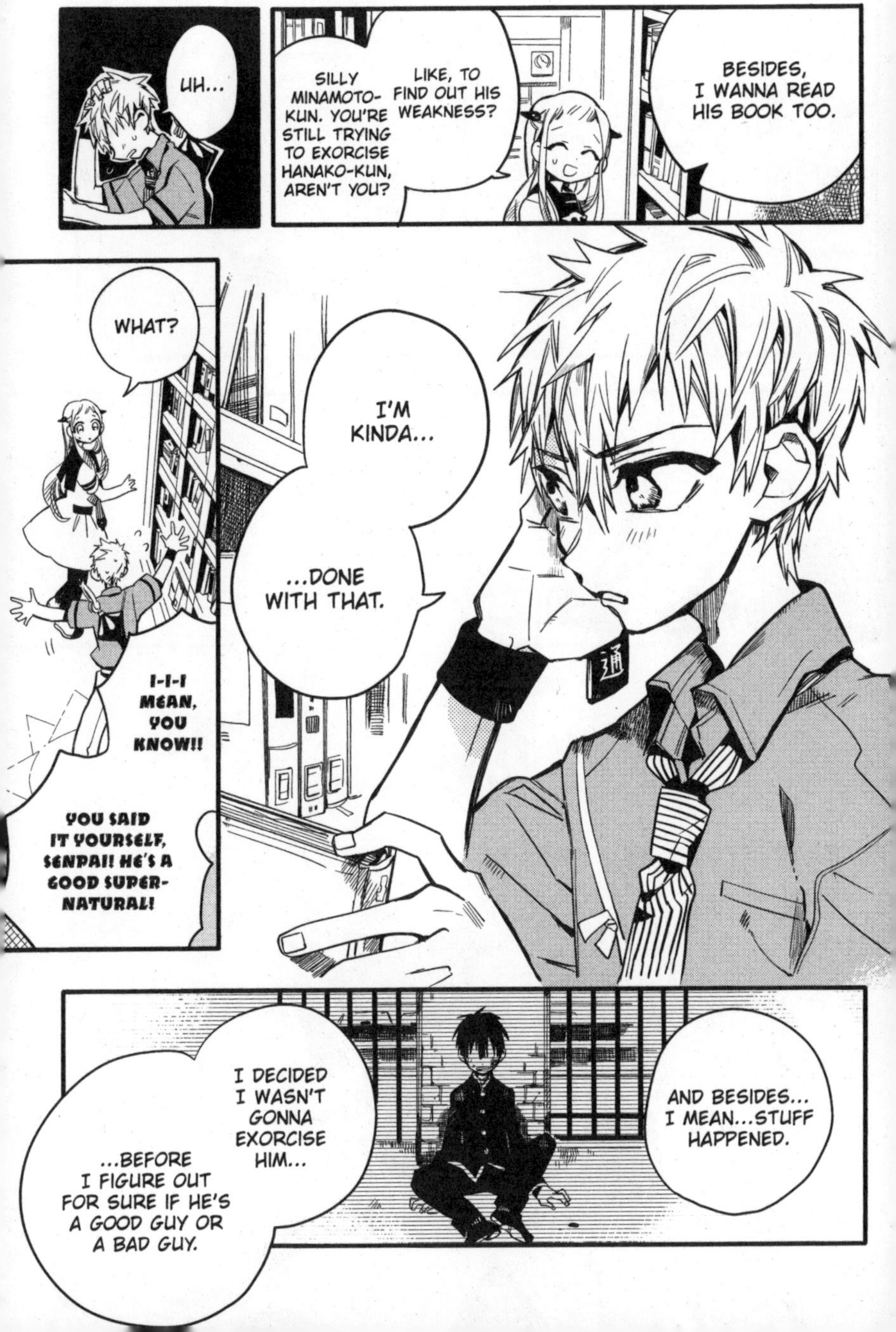
BESIDES, I WANNA READ HIS BOOK TOO.
LIKE, TO FIND OUT HIS WEAKNESS?
SILLY MINAMOTO-KUN. YOU'RE STILL TRYING TO EXORCISE HANAKO-KUN, AREN'T YOU?
UH...
I'M KINDA...
...DONE WITH THAT.
WHAT?
I-I-I MEAN, YOU KNOW!!
YOU SAID IT YOURSELF, SENPAI! HE'S A GOOD SUPER-NATURAL!
AND BESIDES... I MEAN...STUFF HAPPENED.
I DECIDED I WASN'T GONNA EXORCISE HIM...
...BEFORE I FIGURE OUT FOR SURE IF HE'S A GOOD GUY OR A BAD GUY.

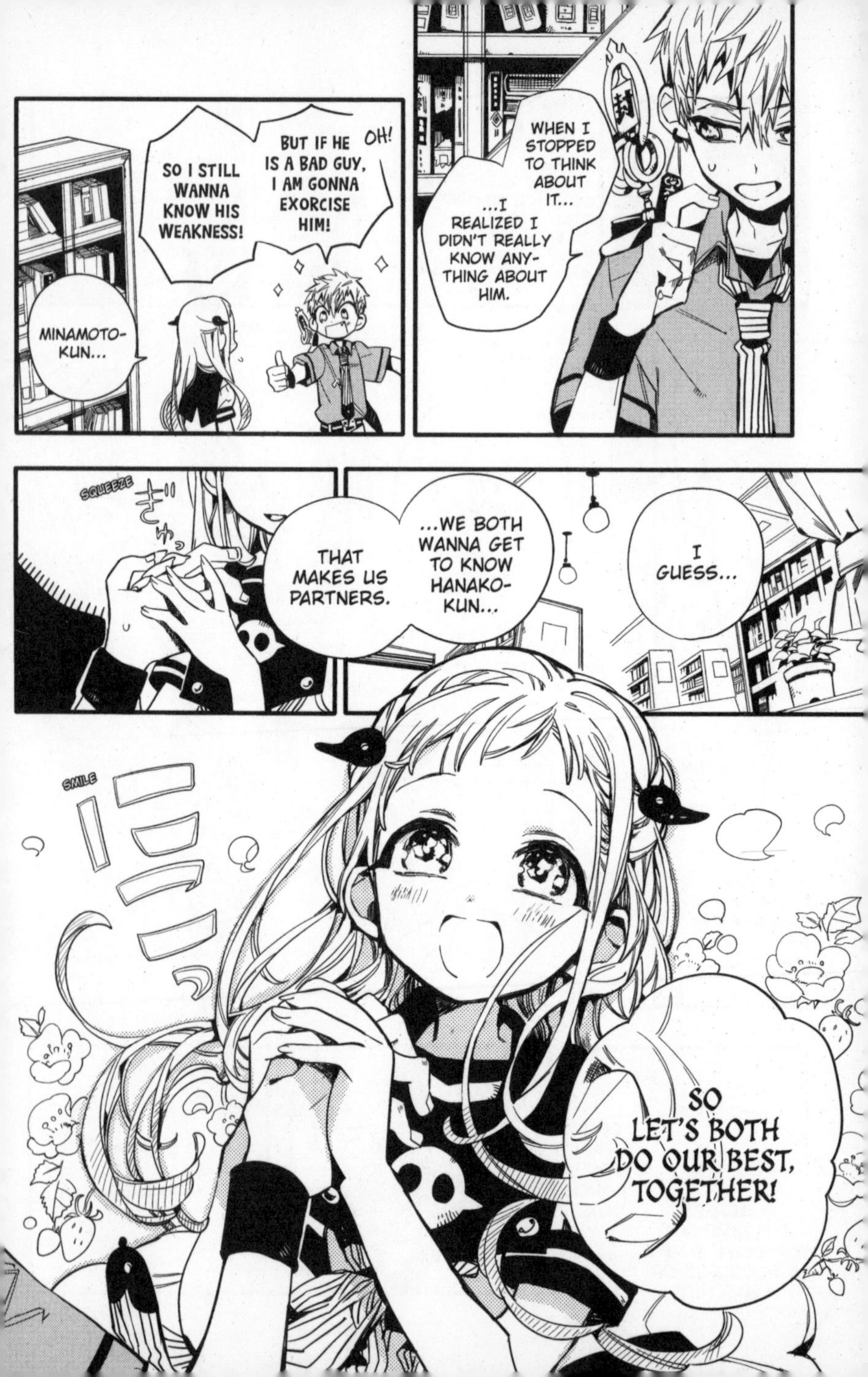
WHEN I STOPPED TO THINK ABOUT IT...
...I REALIZED I DIDN'T REALLY KNOW ANY-THING ABOUT HIM.
OH!
BUT IF HE IS A BAD GUY, I AM GONNA EXORCISE HIM!
SO I STILL WANNA KNOW HIS WEAKNESS!
MINAMOTO-KUN...
I GUESS...
...WE BOTH WANNA GET TO KNOW HANAKO-KUN...
THAT MAKES US PARTNERS.
SQUEEZE
SMILE
SO LET'S BOTH DO OUR BEST, TOGETHER!

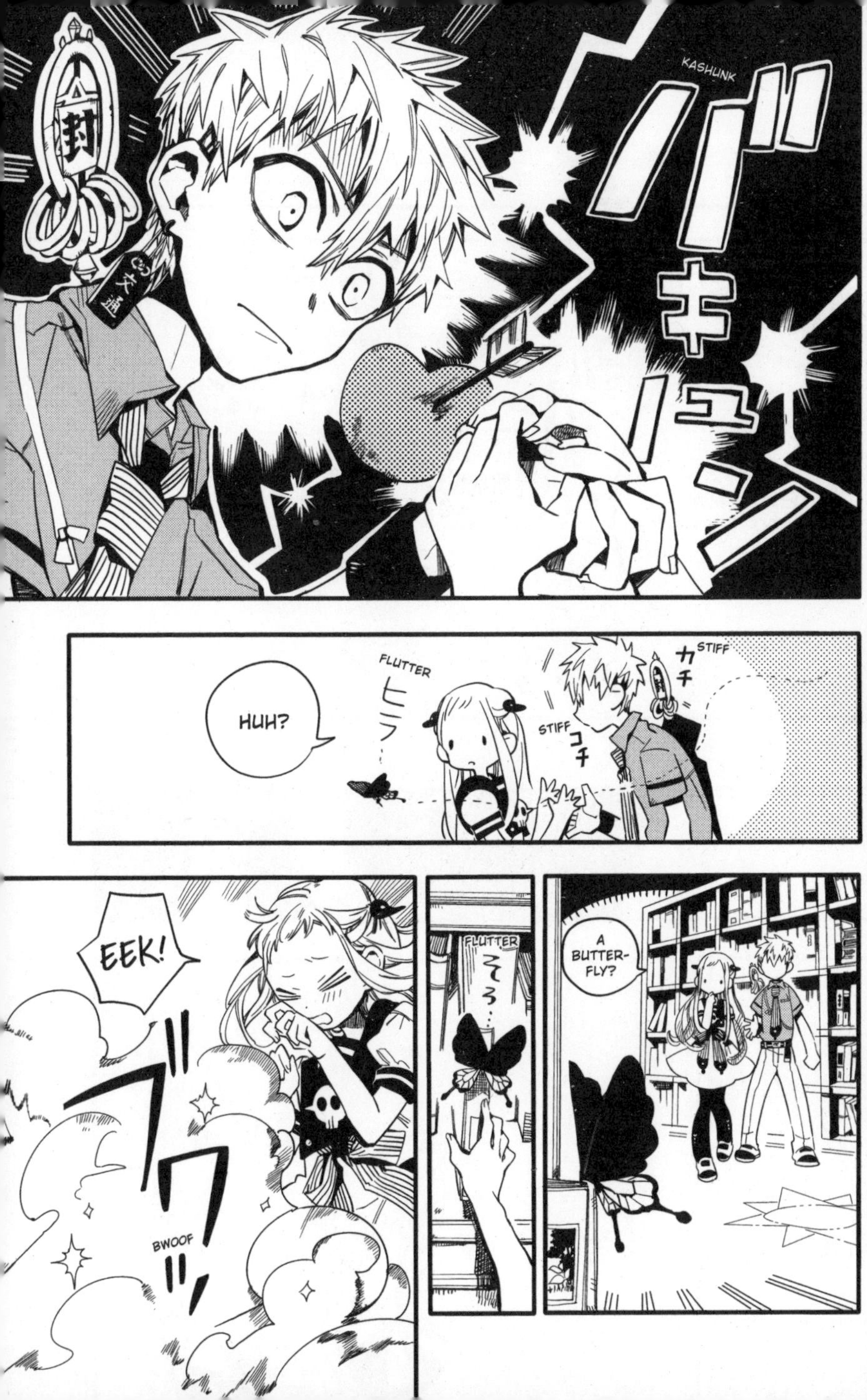
KASHUNK
バキューン
STIFF
カチ
STIFF
コチ
FLUTTER
ヒラ
HUH?
A BUTTER-FLY?
FLUTTER
そろ…
EEK!
BWOOF

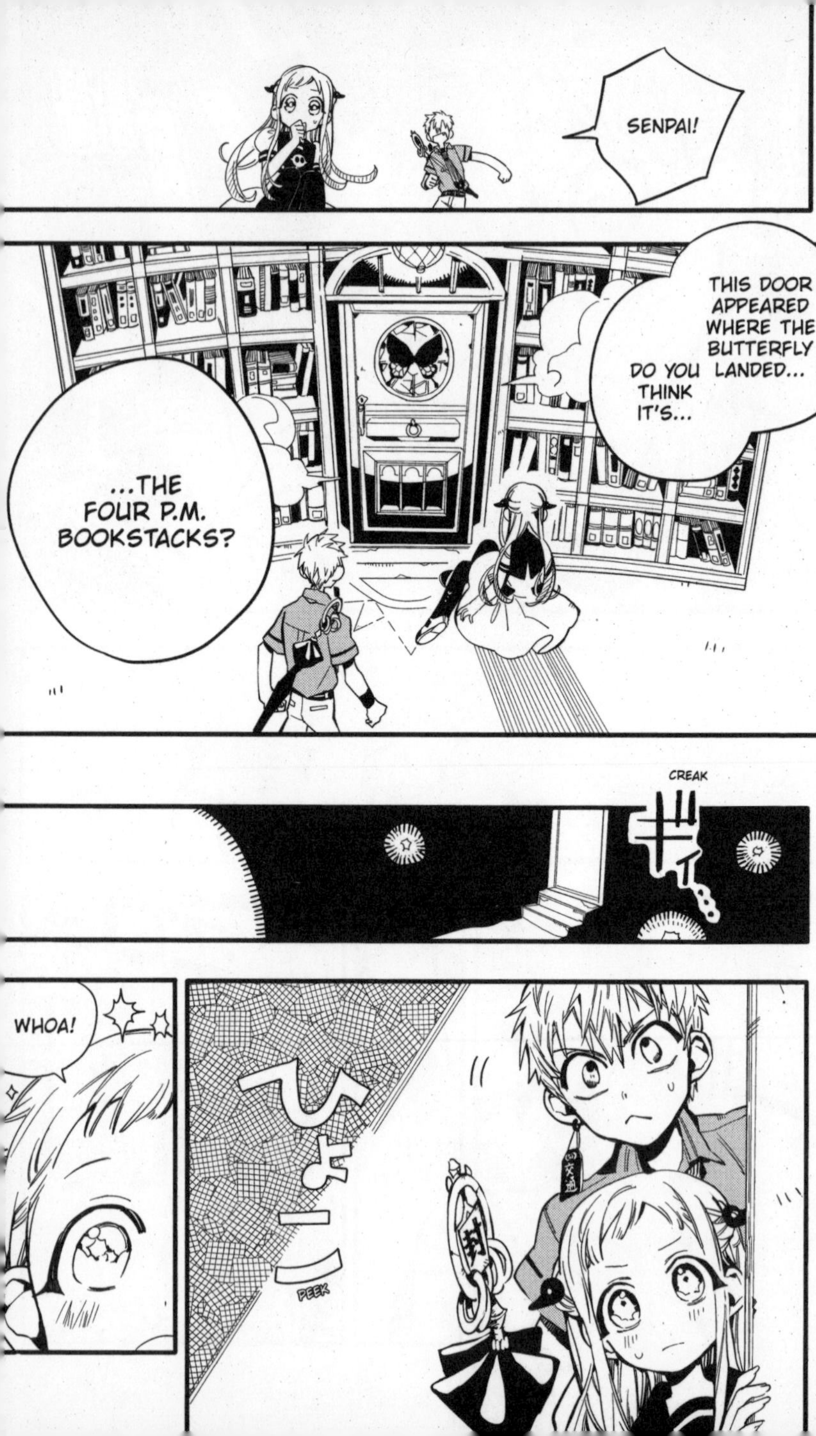
SENPAI!
THIS DOOR APPEARED WHERE THE BUTTERFLY LANDED... DO YOU THINK IT'S...
...THE FOUR P.M. BOOKSTACKS?
CREAK
PEEK
WHOA!

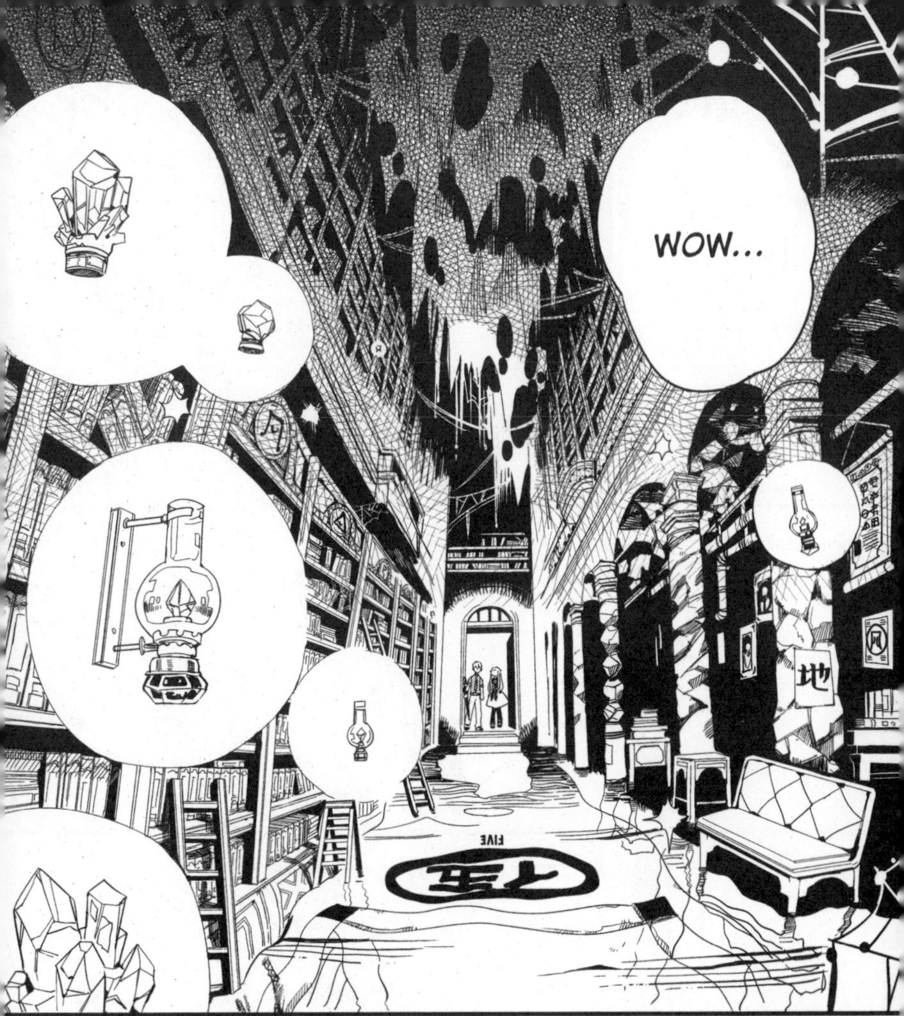
WOW...
FIVE

PATCHES: BELOW, INNER

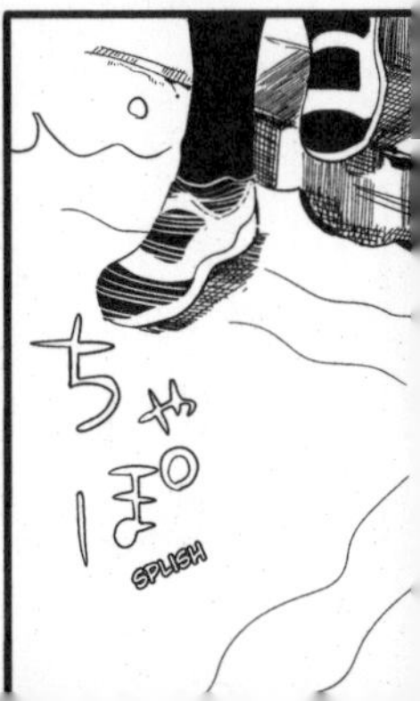
ちゃぽ
SPLISH

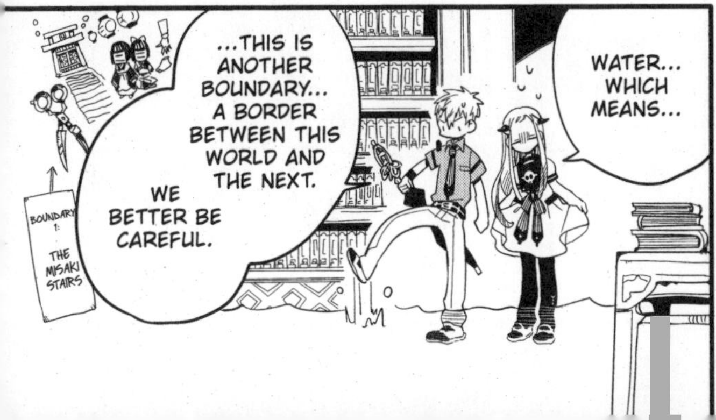
WATER... WHICH MEANS...
...THIS IS ANOTHER BOUNDARY... A BORDER BETWEEN THIS WORLD AND THE NEXT.
WE BETTER BE CAREFUL.
BOUNDARY 1: THE MISAKI STAIRS

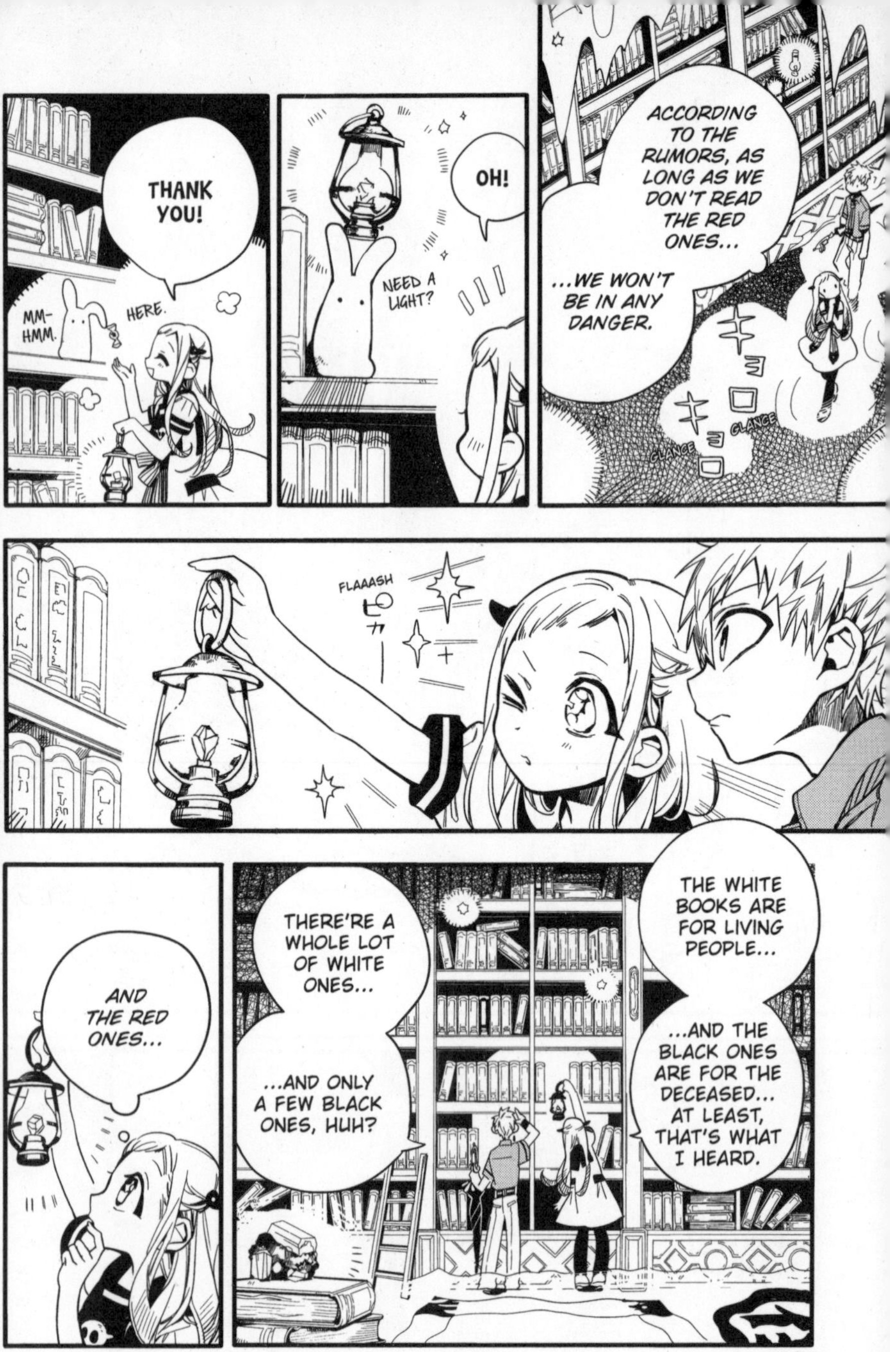
ACCORDING TO THE RUMORS, AS LONG AS WE DON'T READ THE RED ONES...
...WE WON'T BE IN ANY DANGER.
キョロキョロ
GLANCE GLANCE
OH!
NEED A LIGHT?
THANK YOU!
HERE.
MM-HMM.
FLAAASH
ピカー
THE WHITE BOOKS ARE FOR LIVING PEOPLE...
...AND THE BLACK ONES ARE FOR THE DECEASED... AT LEAST, THAT'S WHAT I HEARD.
THERE'RE A WHOLE LOT OF WHITE ONES...
...AND ONLY A FEW BLACK ONES, HUH?
AND THE RED ONES...

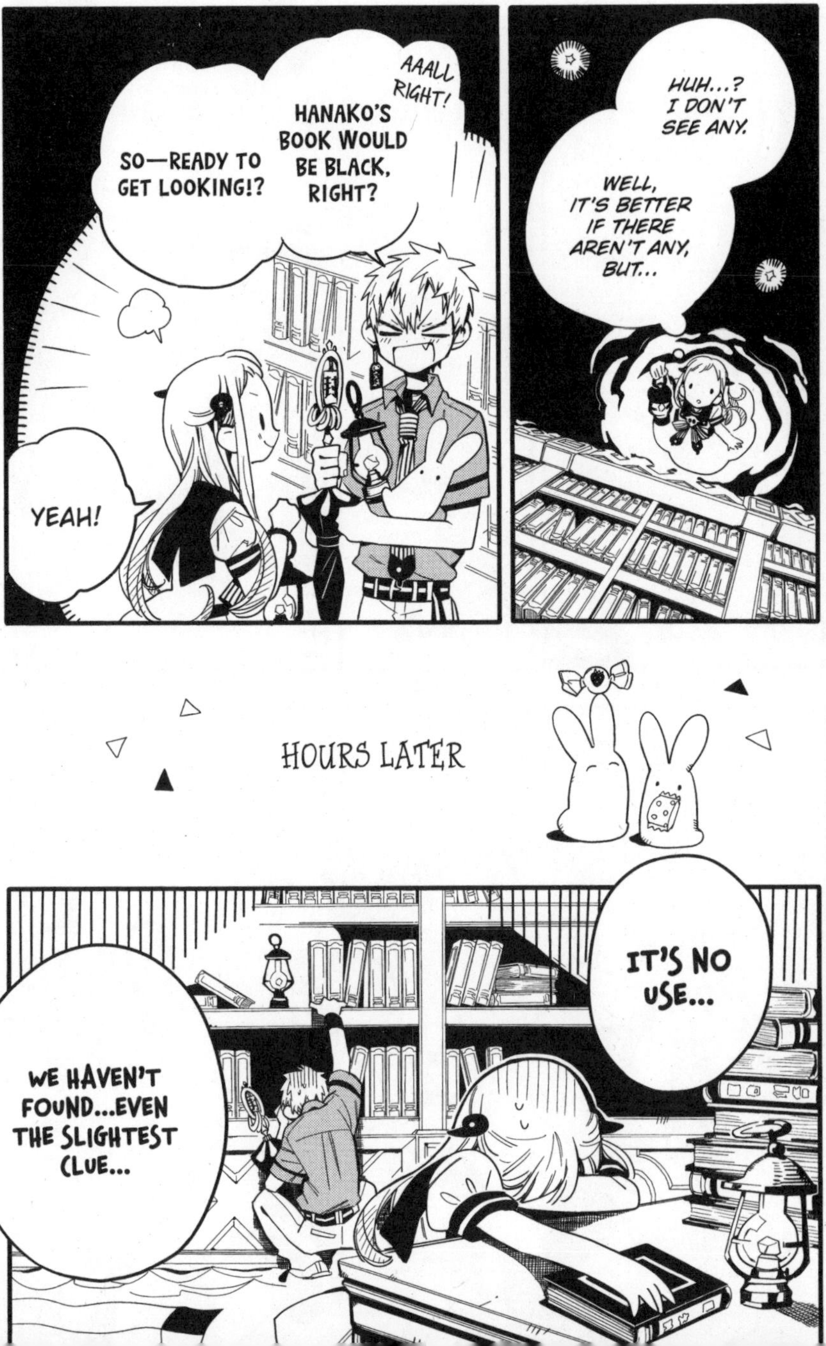
HUH...? I DON'T SEE ANY.
WELL, IT'S BETTER IF THERE AREN'T ANY, BUT...
SO—READY TO GET LOOKING!?
AAALL RIGHT!
HANAKO'S BOOK WOULD BE BLACK, RIGHT?
YEAH!
HOURS LATER
IT'S NO USE...
WE HAVEN'T FOUND...EVEN THE SLIGHTEST CLUE...

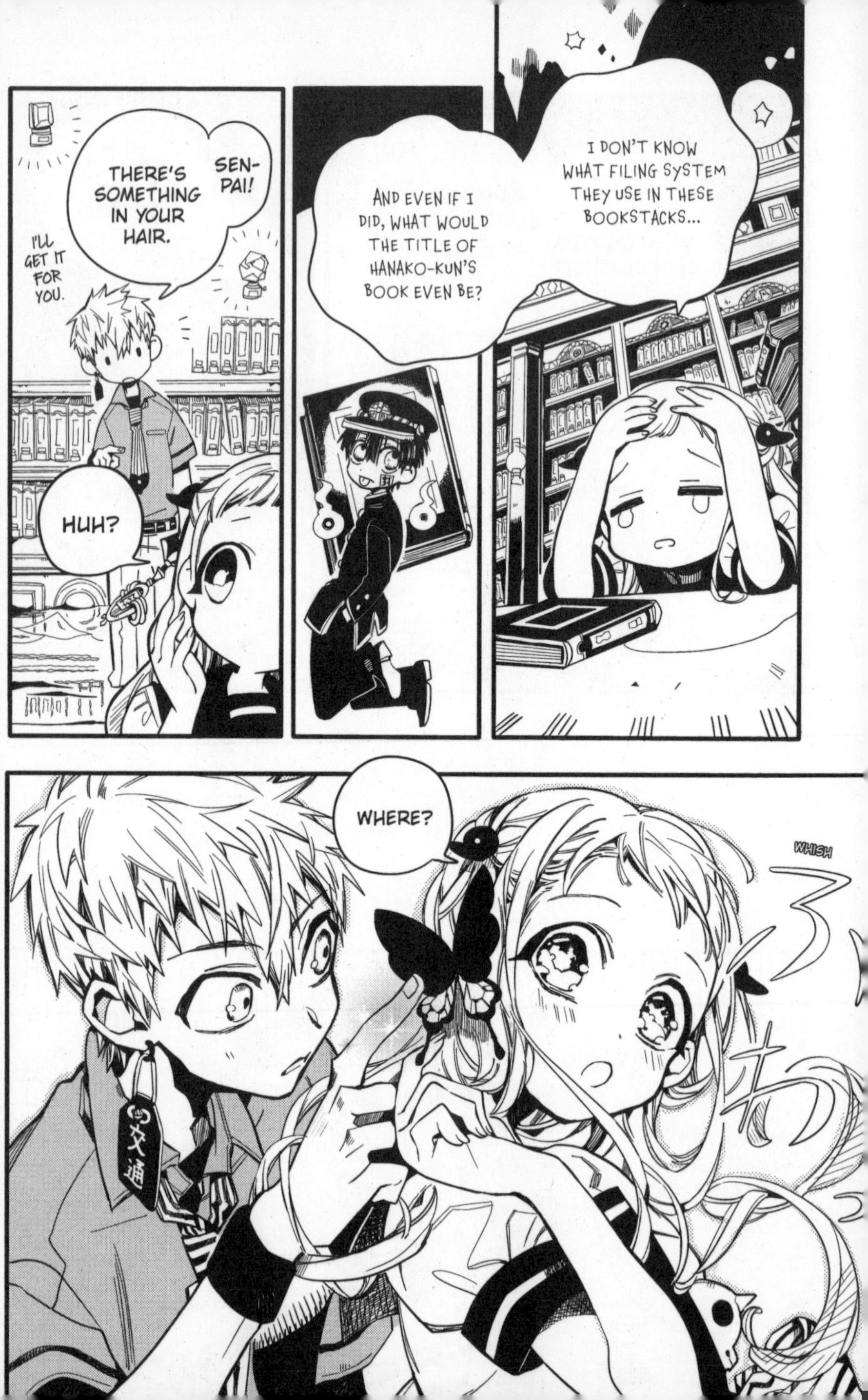
I DON'T KNOW WHAT FILING SYSTEM THEY USE IN THESE BOOKSTACKS...
AND EVEN IF I DID, WHAT WOULD THE TITLE OF HANAKO-KUN'S BOOK EVEN BE?
SEN-PAI!
THERE'S SOMETHING IN YOUR HAIR.
I'LL GET IT FOR YOU.
HUH?
WHERE?
WHISH

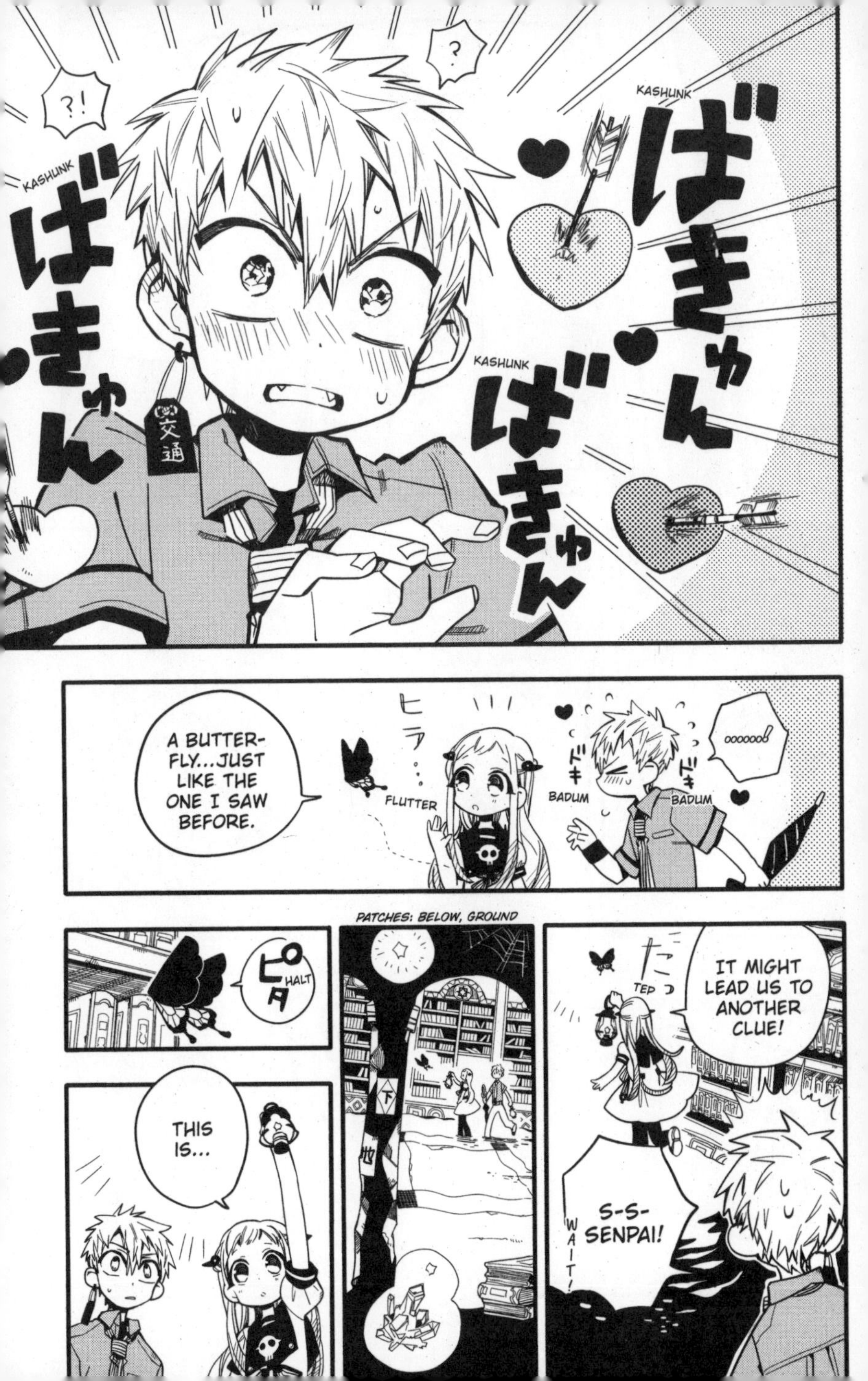
?
KASHUNK
ばきゅん
KASHUNK
ばきゅん
?!
KASHUNK
ばきゅん
交通
OOOOOO!
ドキ BADUM
ドキ BADUM
ヒラ FLUTTER
A BUTTER-FLY...JUST LIKE THE ONE I SAW BEFORE.
PATCHES: BELOW, GROUND
たっ TED
IT MIGHT LEAD US TO ANOTHER CLUE!
S-S-SENPAI!
WAIT!
下
地
ピタ HALT
THIS IS...

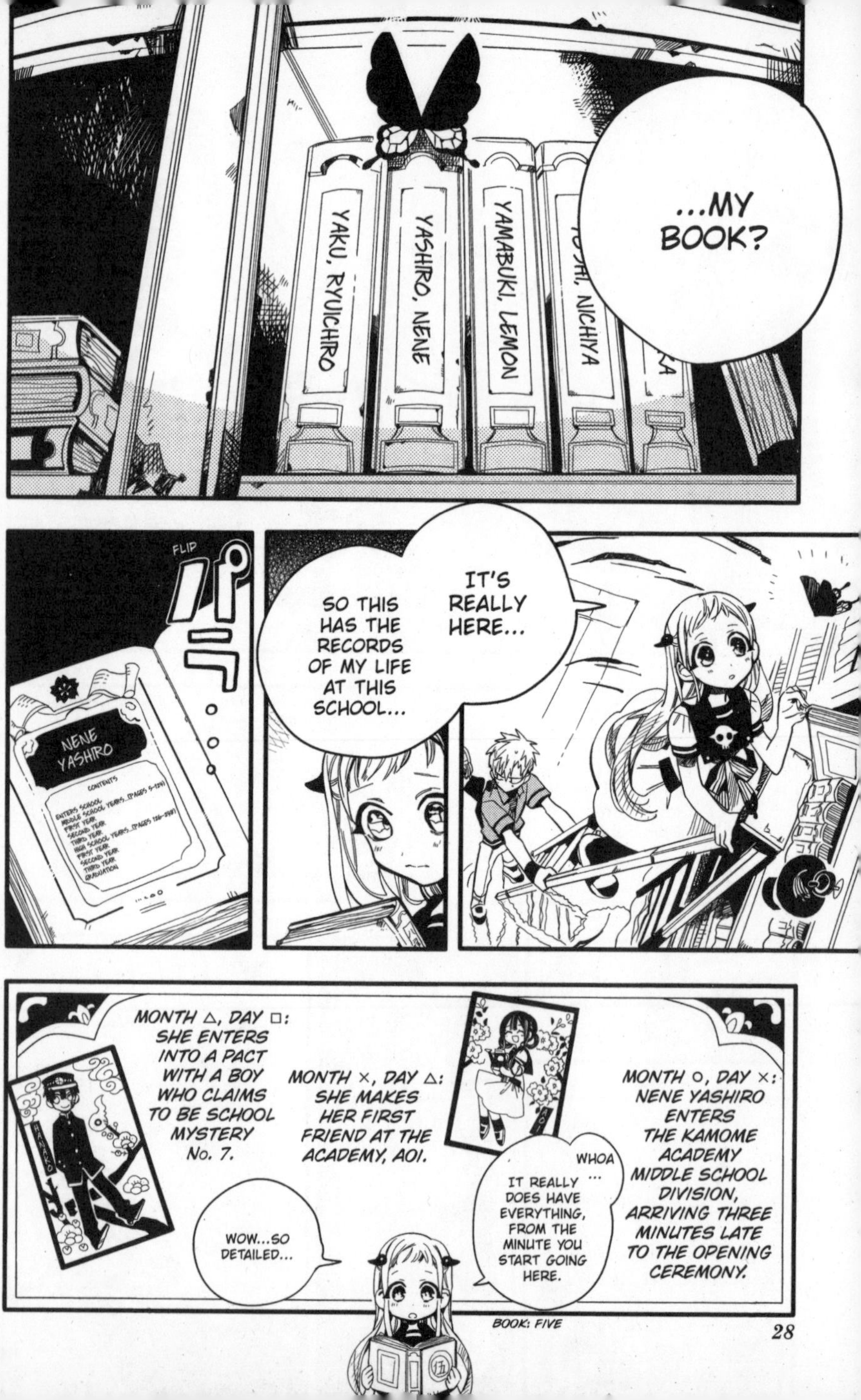
...MY BOOK?
YAMABUKI, LEMON
YASHIRO, NENE
YAKU, RYUICHIRO
IT'S REALLY HERE...
SO THIS HAS THE RECORDS OF MY LIFE AT THIS SCHOOL...
FLIP
NENE YASHIRO
CONTENTS
ENTERS SCHOOL
MIDDLE SCHOOL YEARS...(PAGES 5-124)
FIRST YEAR
SECOND YEAR
THIRD YEAR
HIGH SCHOOL YEARS...(PAGES 126-240)
FIRST YEAR
SECOND YEAR
THIRD YEAR
GRADUATION
MONTH ○, DAY ×: NENE YASHIRO ENTERS THE KAMOME ACADEMY MIDDLE SCHOOL DIVISION, ARRIVING THREE MINUTES LATE TO THE OPENING CEREMONY.
WHOA...
IT REALLY DOES HAVE EVERYTHING, FROM THE MINUTE YOU START GOING HERE.
MONTH ×, DAY △: SHE MAKES HER FIRST FRIEND AT THE ACADEMY, AOI.
WOW...SO DETAILED...
MONTH △, DAY □: SHE ENTERS INTO A PACT WITH A BOY WHO CLAIMS TO BE SCHOOL MYSTERY No. 7.
HANAKO

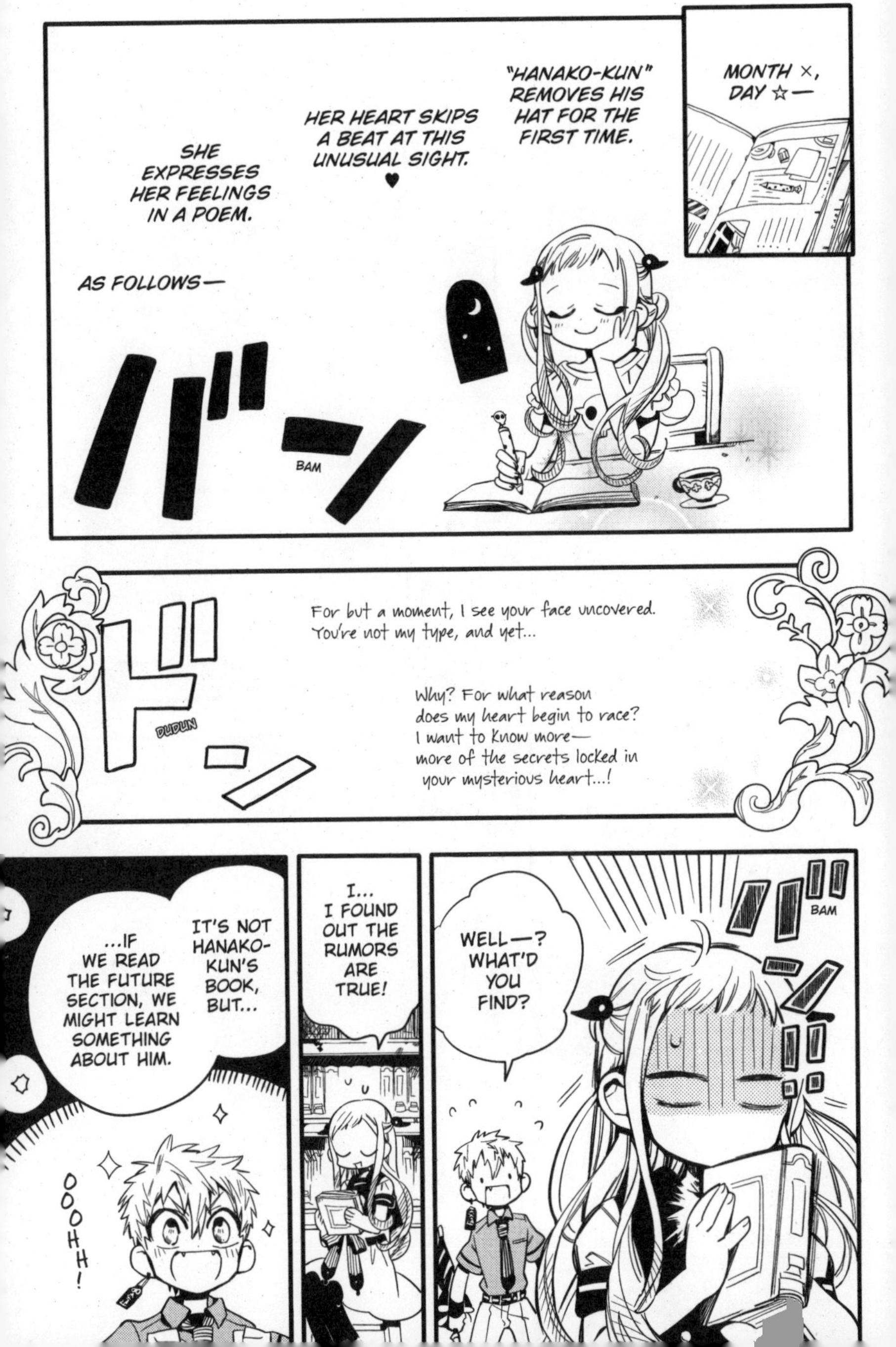
MONTH ×, DAY ☆—
"HANAKO-KUN" REMOVES HIS HAT FOR THE FIRST TIME.
HER HEART SKIPS A BEAT AT THIS UNUSUAL SIGHT. ♥
SHE EXPRESSES HER FEELINGS IN A POEM.
AS FOLLOWS—
BAM
For but a moment, I see your face uncovered.
You're not my type, and yet...
Why? For what reason
does my heart begin to race?
I want to know more—
more of the secrets locked in
your mysterious heart...!
DUDUN
BAM
WELL—? WHAT'D YOU FIND?
I... I FOUND OUT THE RUMORS ARE TRUE!
IT'S NOT HANAKO-KUN'S BOOK, BUT...
...IF WE READ THE FUTURE SECTION, WE MIGHT LEARN SOMETHING ABOUT HIM.
OOOHH!

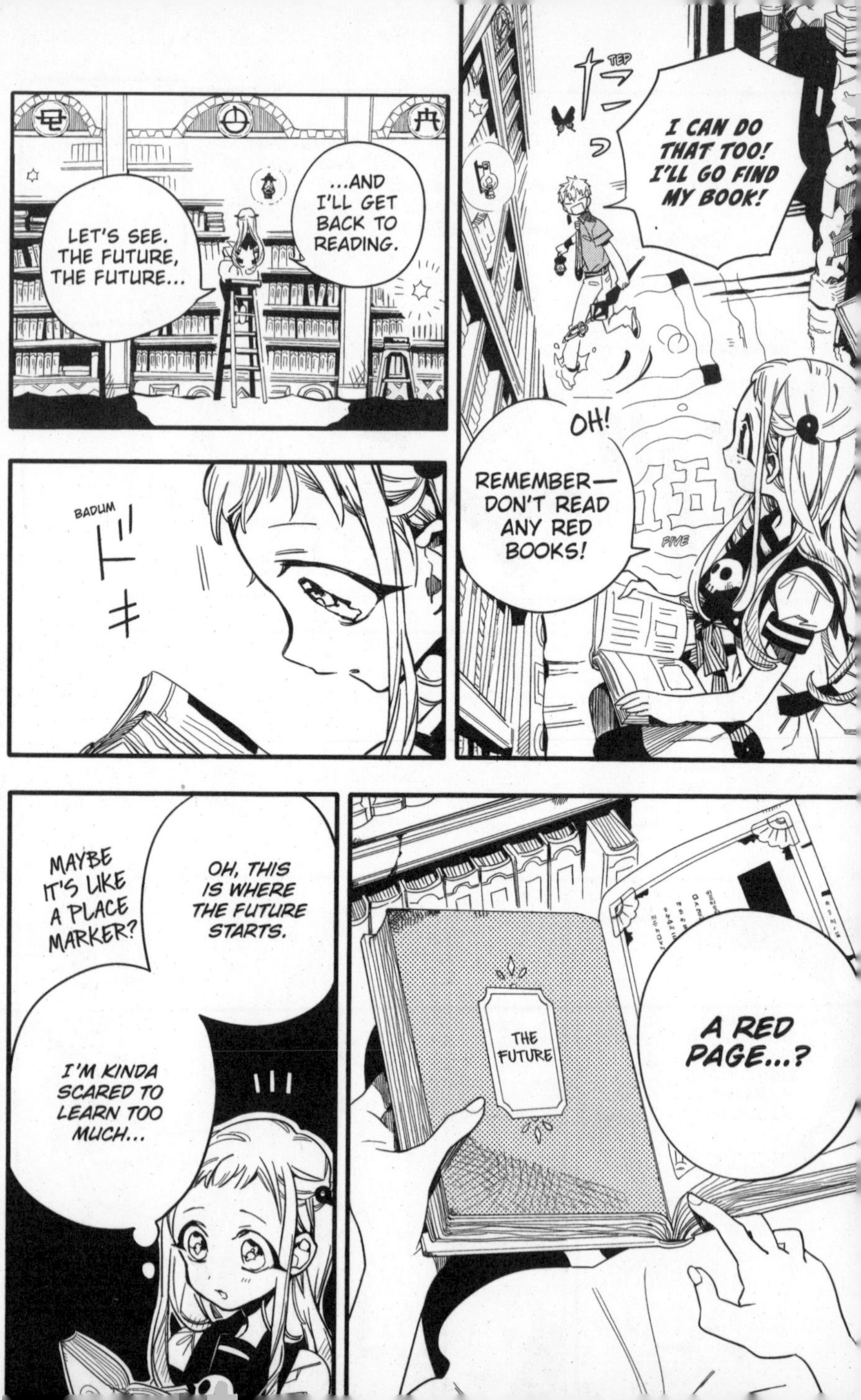
TEP
I CAN DO THAT TOO! I'LL GO FIND MY BOOK!
OH!
REMEMBER— DON'T READ ANY RED BOOKS!
FIVE
...AND I'LL GET BACK TO READING.
LET'S SEE. THE FUTURE, THE FUTURE...
BADUM
A RED PAGE...?
THE FUTURE
OH, THIS IS WHERE THE FUTURE STARTS.
MAYBE IT'S LIKE A PLACE MARKER?
I'M KINDA SCARED TO LEARN TOO MUCH...

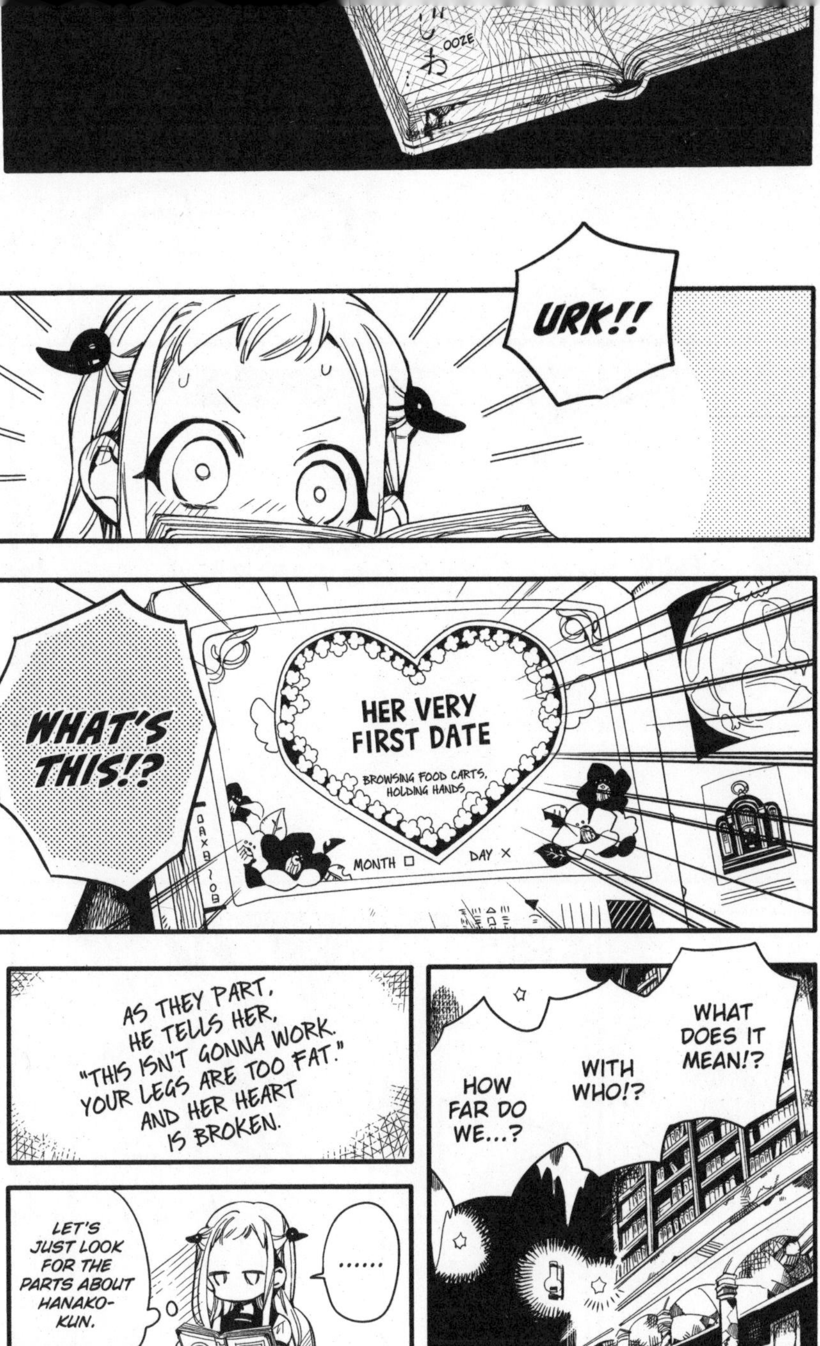
OOZE
URK!!
WHAT'S THIS!?
HER VERY FIRST DATE
BROWSING FOOD CARTS, HOLDING HANDS
MONTH □ DAY ×
WHAT DOES IT MEAN!?
WITH WHO!?
HOW FAR DO WE...?
AS THEY PART, HE TELLS HER, "THIS ISN'T GONNA WORK. YOUR LEGS ARE TOO FAT." AND HER HEART IS BROKEN.
......
LET'S JUST LOOK FOR THE PARTS ABOUT HANAKO-KUN.

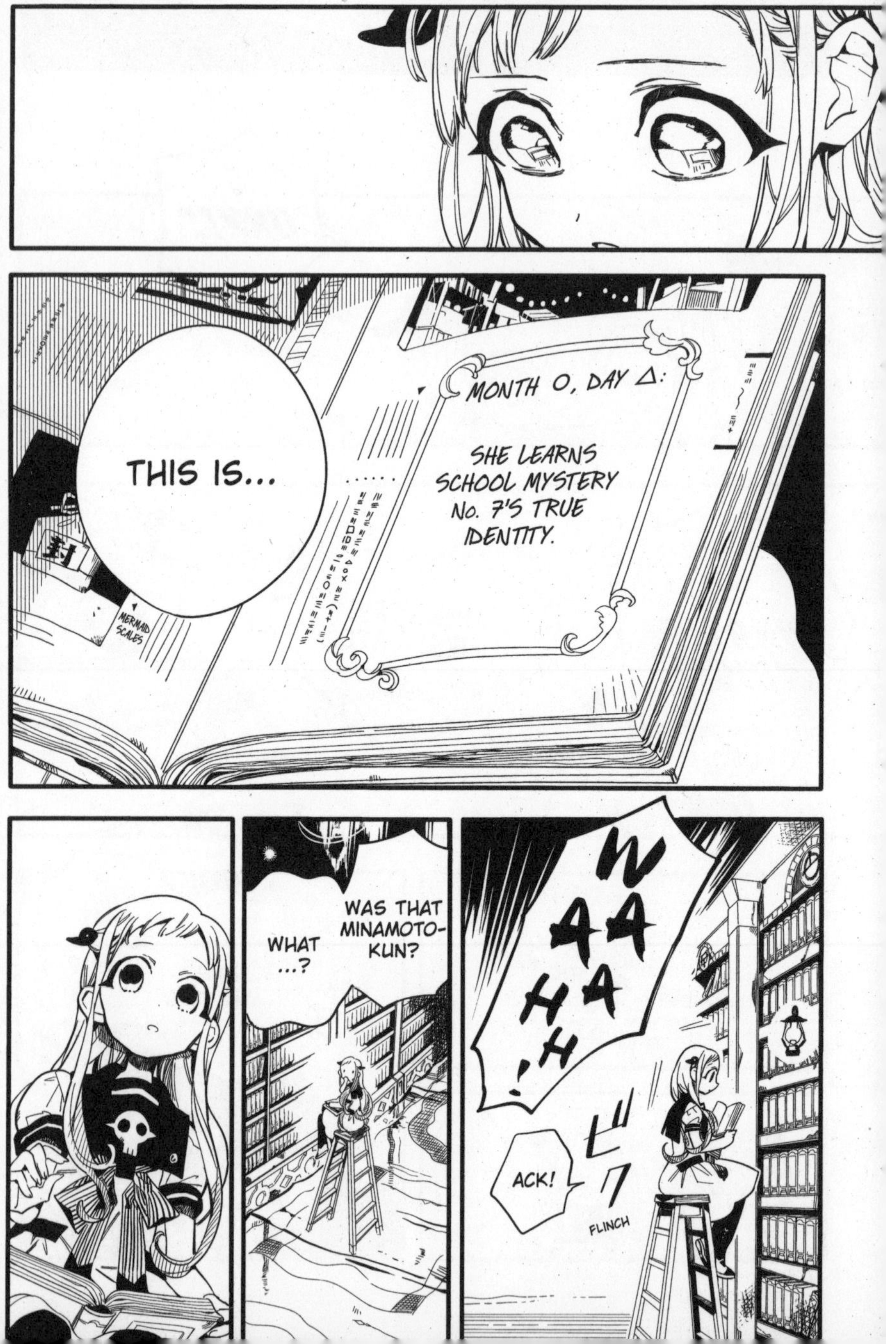
MONTH ○, DAY △:
SHE LEARNS SCHOOL MYSTERY No. 7'S TRUE IDENTITY.
THIS IS...
MERMAID SCALES
WAAAHHH!
ACK!
FLINCH
WAS THAT MINAMOTO-KUN?
WHAT ...?

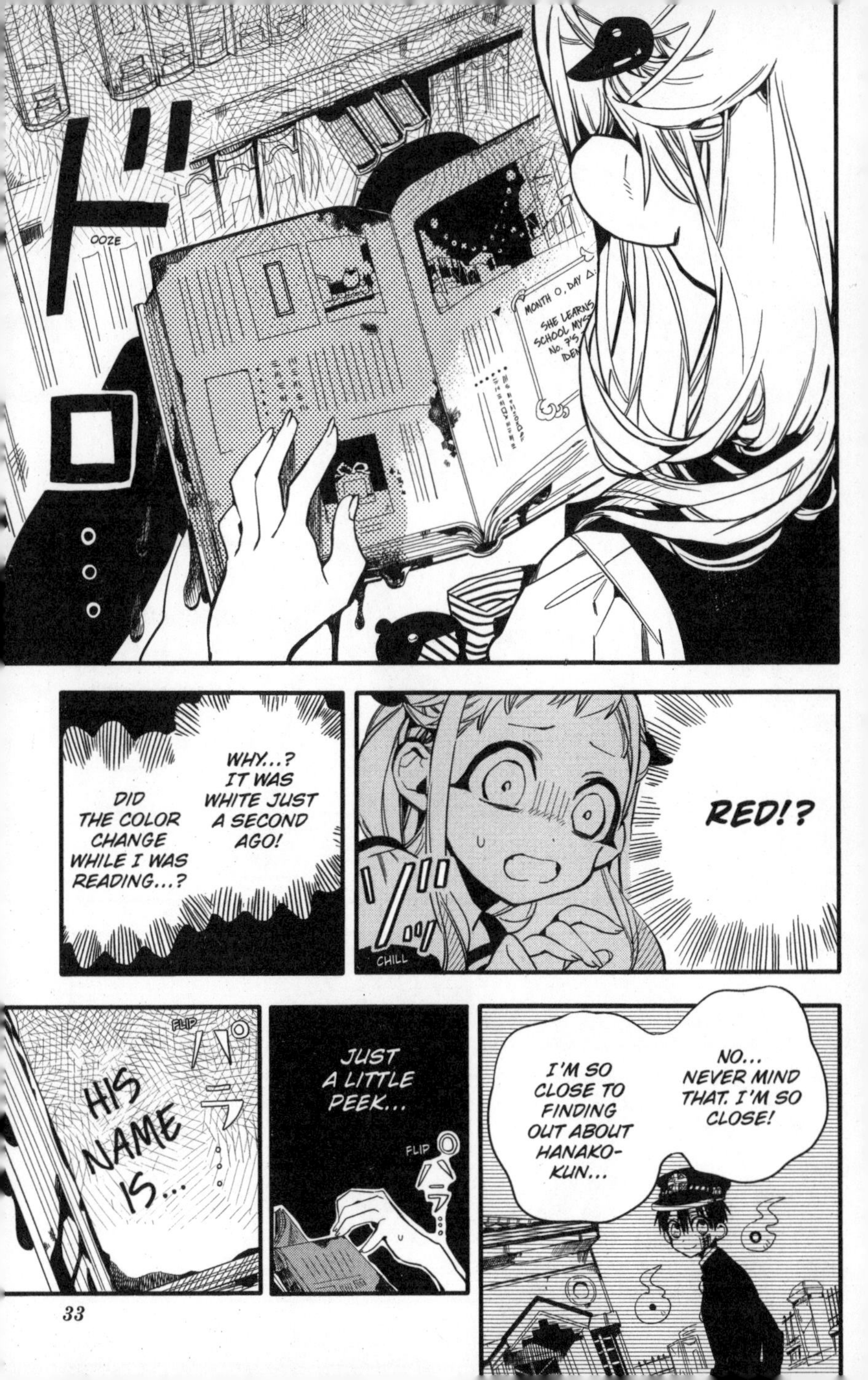
OOZE
MONTH ○, DAY △:
SHE LEARNS
RED!?
CHILL
WHY...? IT WAS WHITE JUST A SECOND AGO!
DID THE COLOR CHANGE WHILE I WAS READING...?
NO... NEVER MIND THAT. I'M SO CLOSE!
I'M SO CLOSE TO FINDING OUT ABOUT HANAKO-KUN...
JUST A LITTLE PEEK...
FLIP
FLIP
HIS NAME IS...

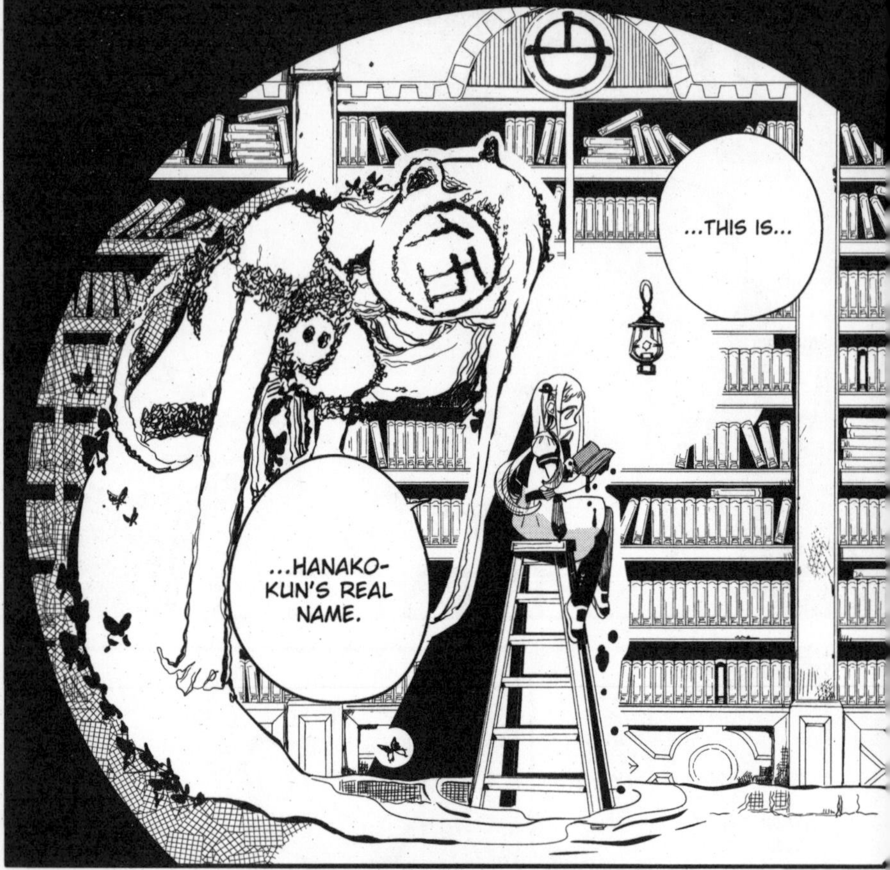
...THIS IS...
...HANAKO-KUN'S REAL NAME.

FACE: FIVE

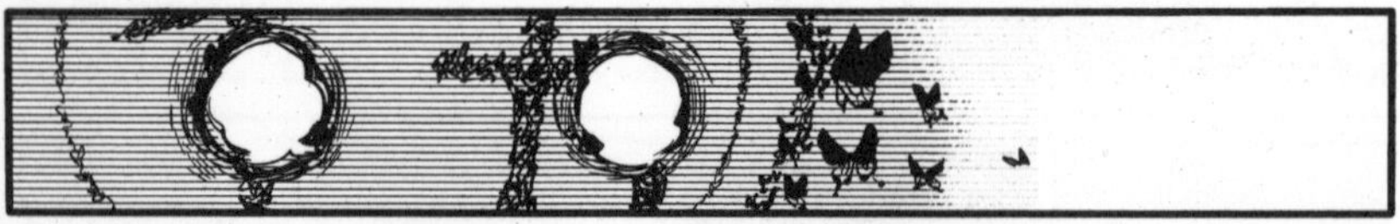

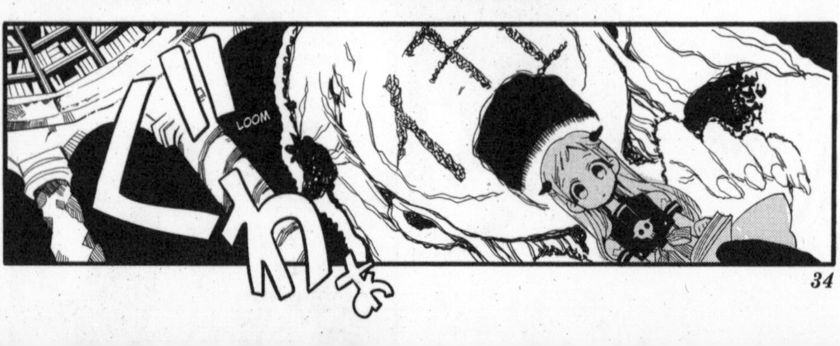
LOOM

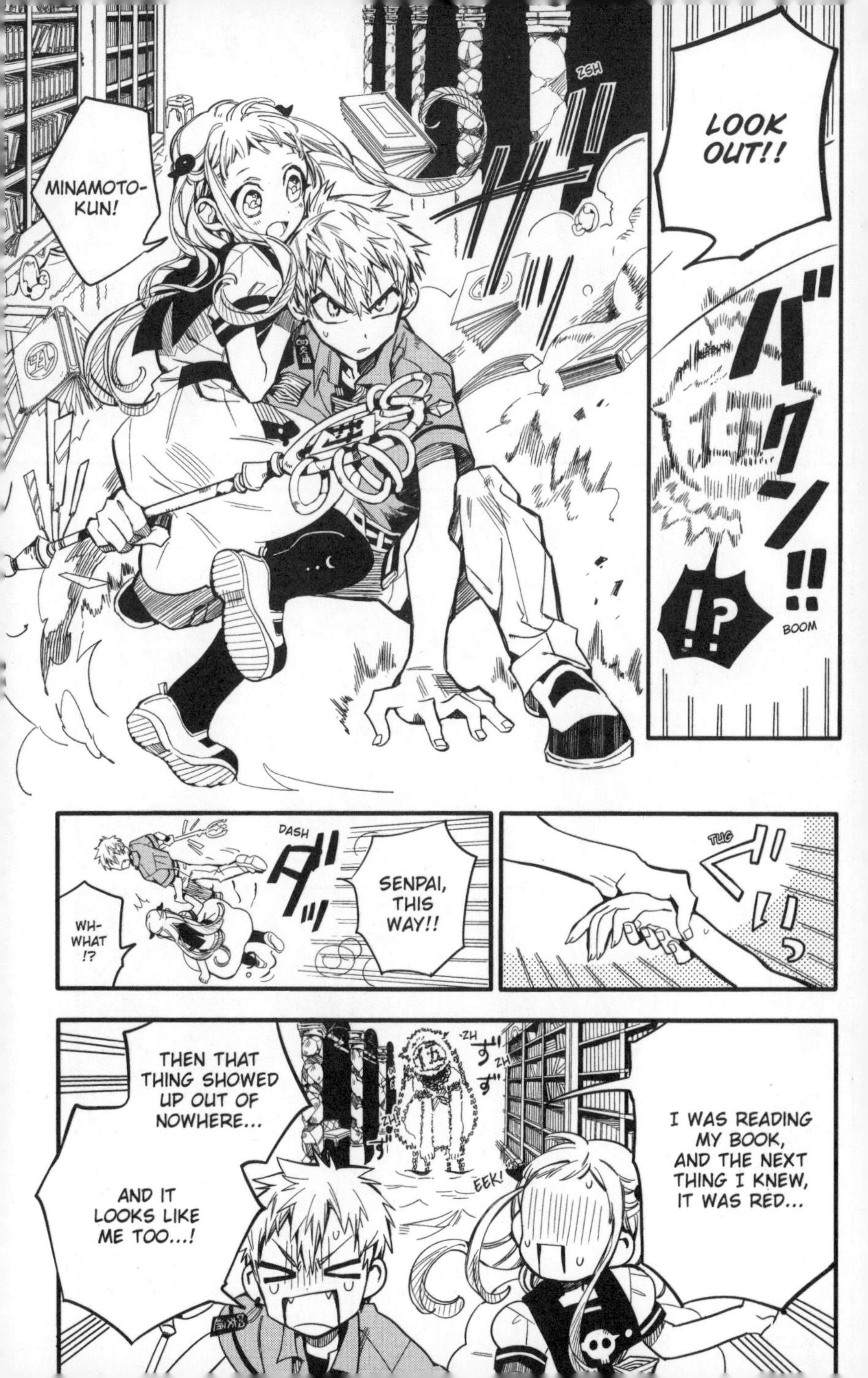
LOOK OUT!!
BOOM
!?
ZSH
MINAMOTO-KUN!
TUG
DASH
SENPAI, THIS WAY!!
WH-WHAT !?
I WAS READING MY BOOK, AND THE NEXT THING I KNEW, IT WAS RED...
EEK!
ZH
ZH
ZH
THEN THAT THING SHOWED UP OUT OF NOWHERE...
AND IT LOOKS LIKE ME TOO...!

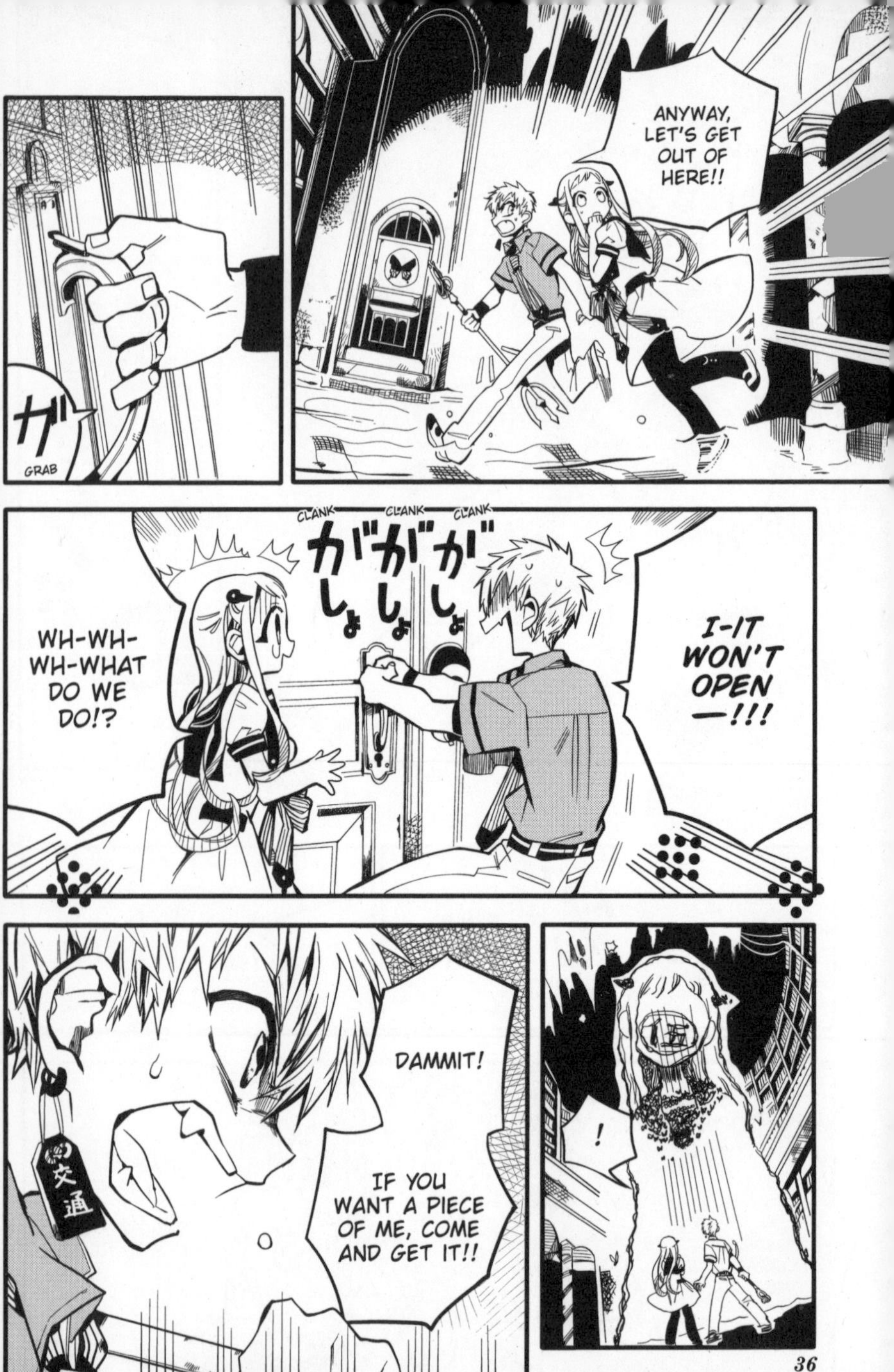

ANYWAY, LET'S GET OUT OF HERE!!
ガ
GRAB
I-IT WON'T OPEN—!!!
CLANK CLANK CLANK
がしょがしょがしょ
WH-WH-WH-WHAT DO WE DO!?
!
DAMMIT!
IF YOU WANT A PIECE OF ME, COME AND GET IT!!

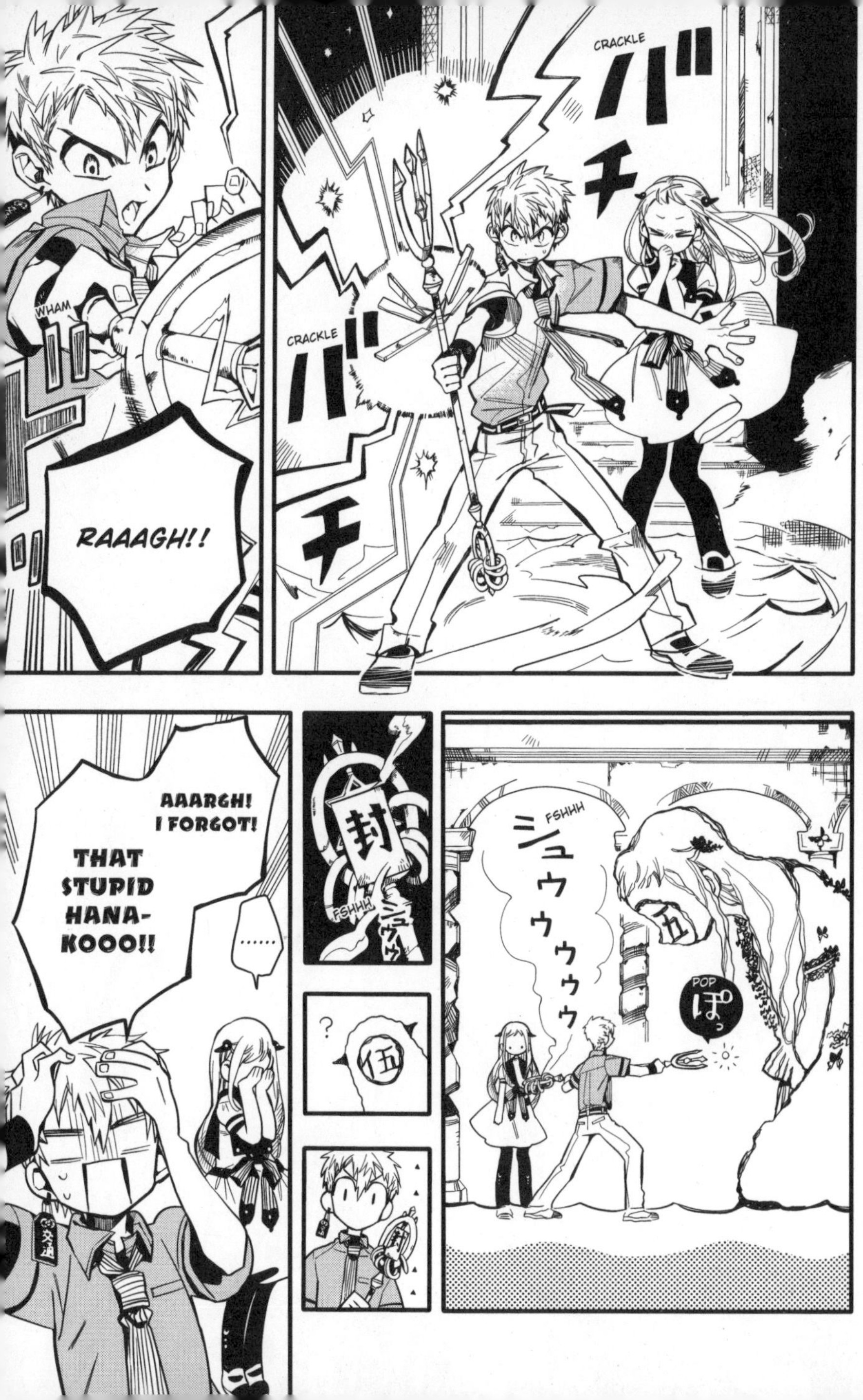
CRACKLE
バチ
CRACKLE
バチ
WHAM
RAAAGH!!
FSHHH
シュウウウウウウ
POP
ぱっ
封
FSHHH
シュウウ
?
伍
AAARGH! I FORGOT!
THAT STUPID HANA-KOOO!!
......

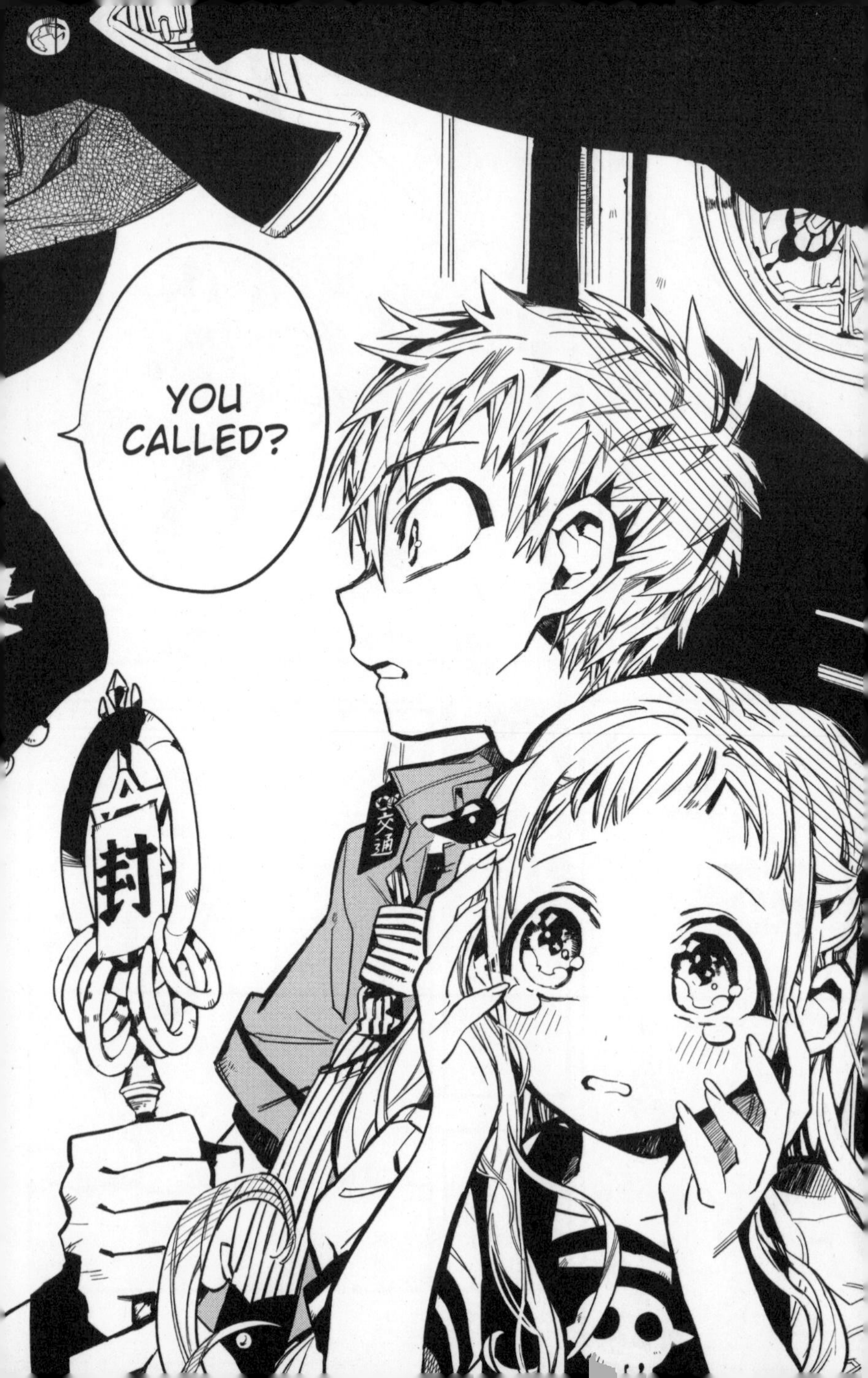
YOU CALLED?
封
交通

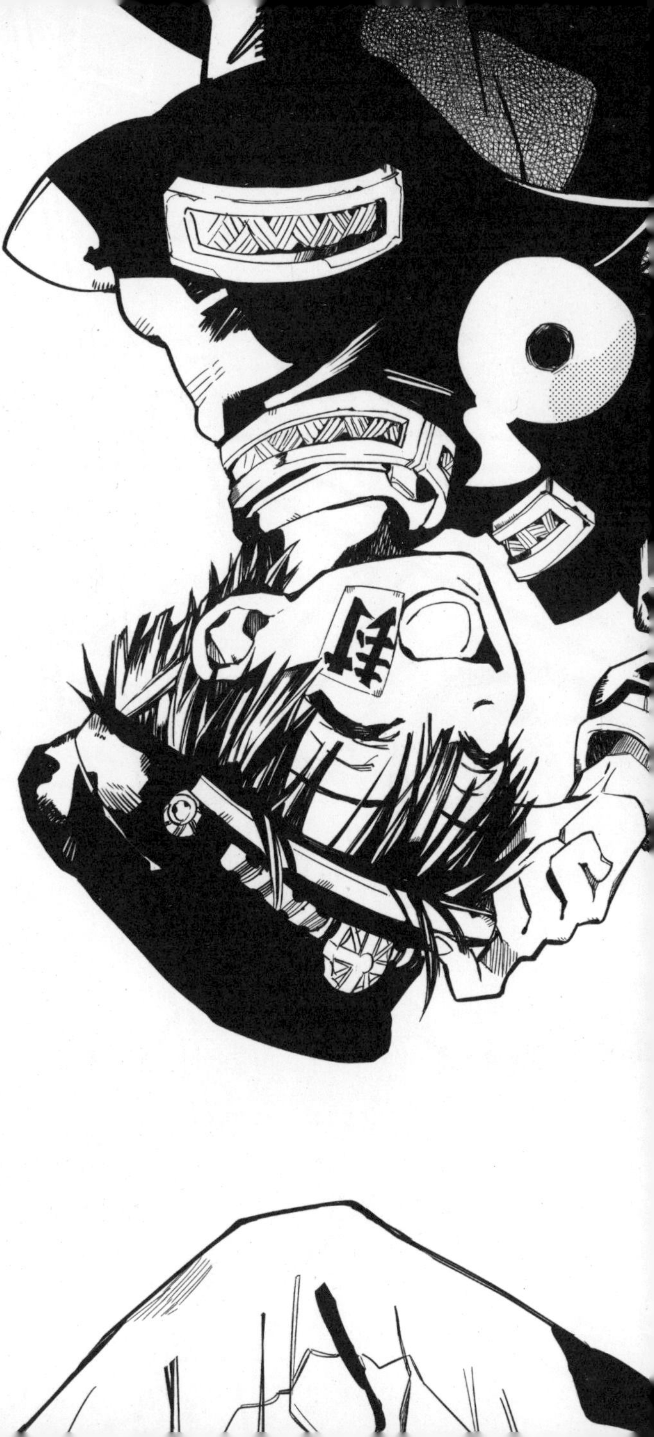

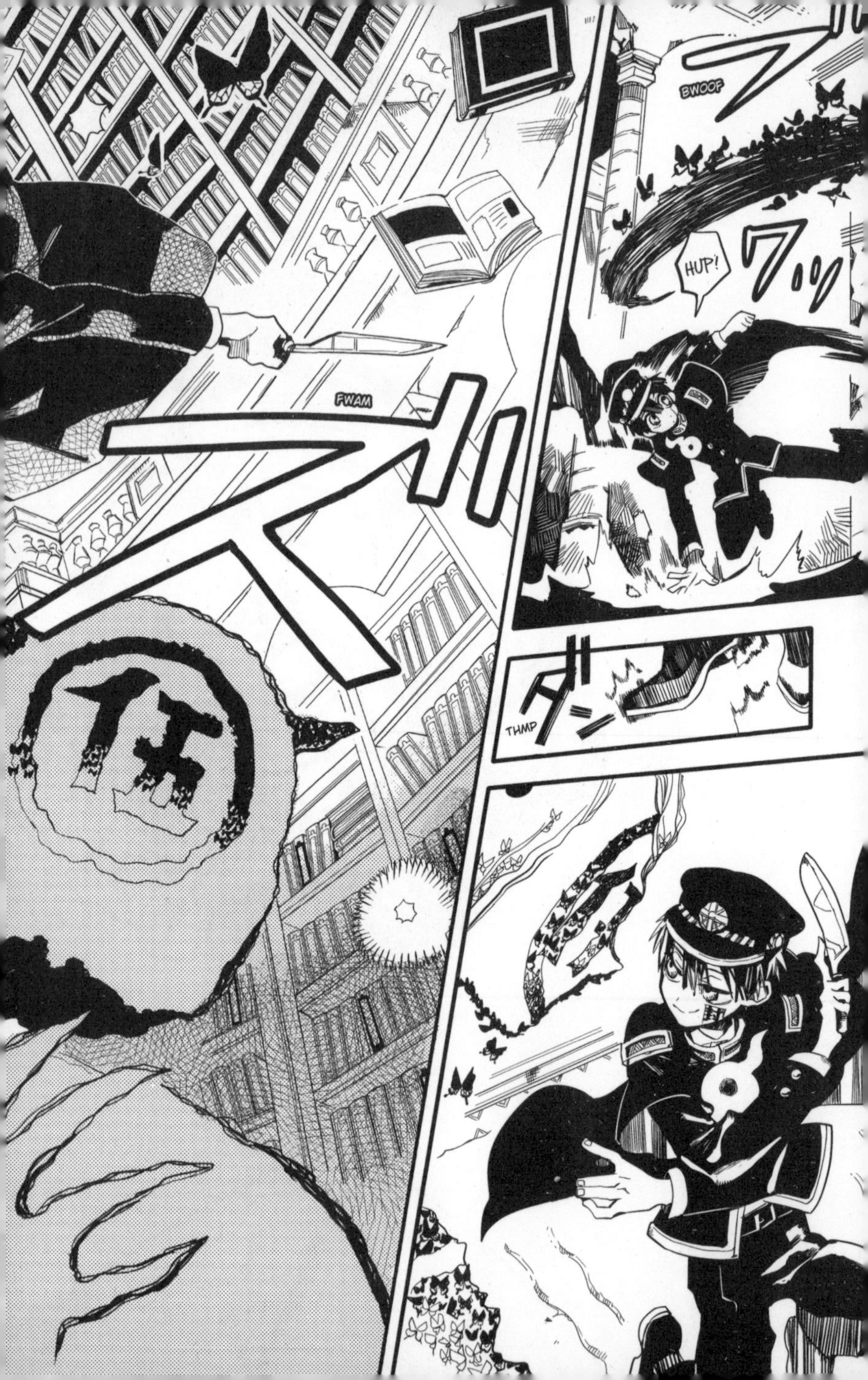
BWOOF
HUP!
THMP
FWAM

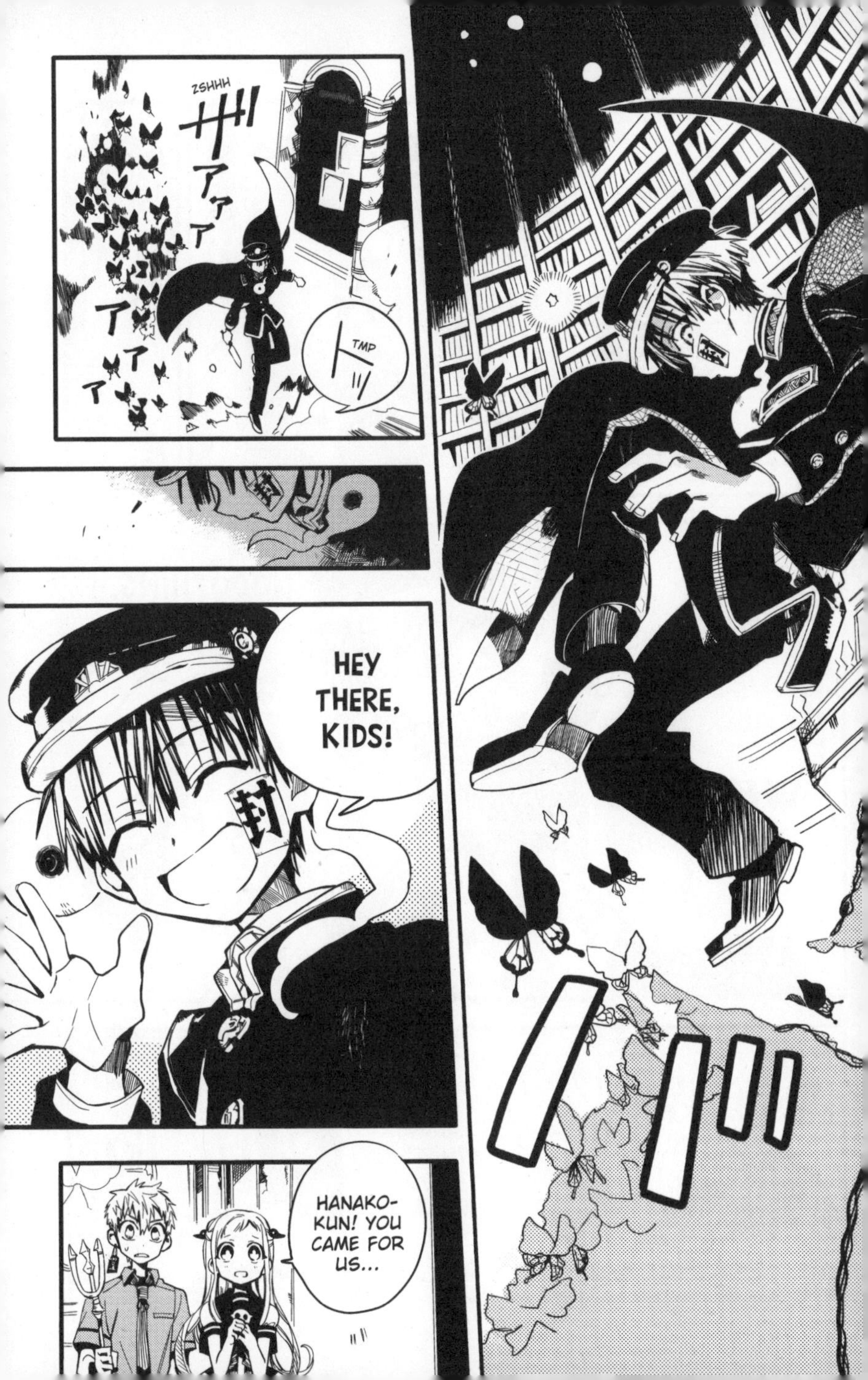
ZSHHH
ザァァァアアアア
TMP
トッ
HEY THERE, KIDS!
HANAKO-KUN! YOU CAME FOR US...

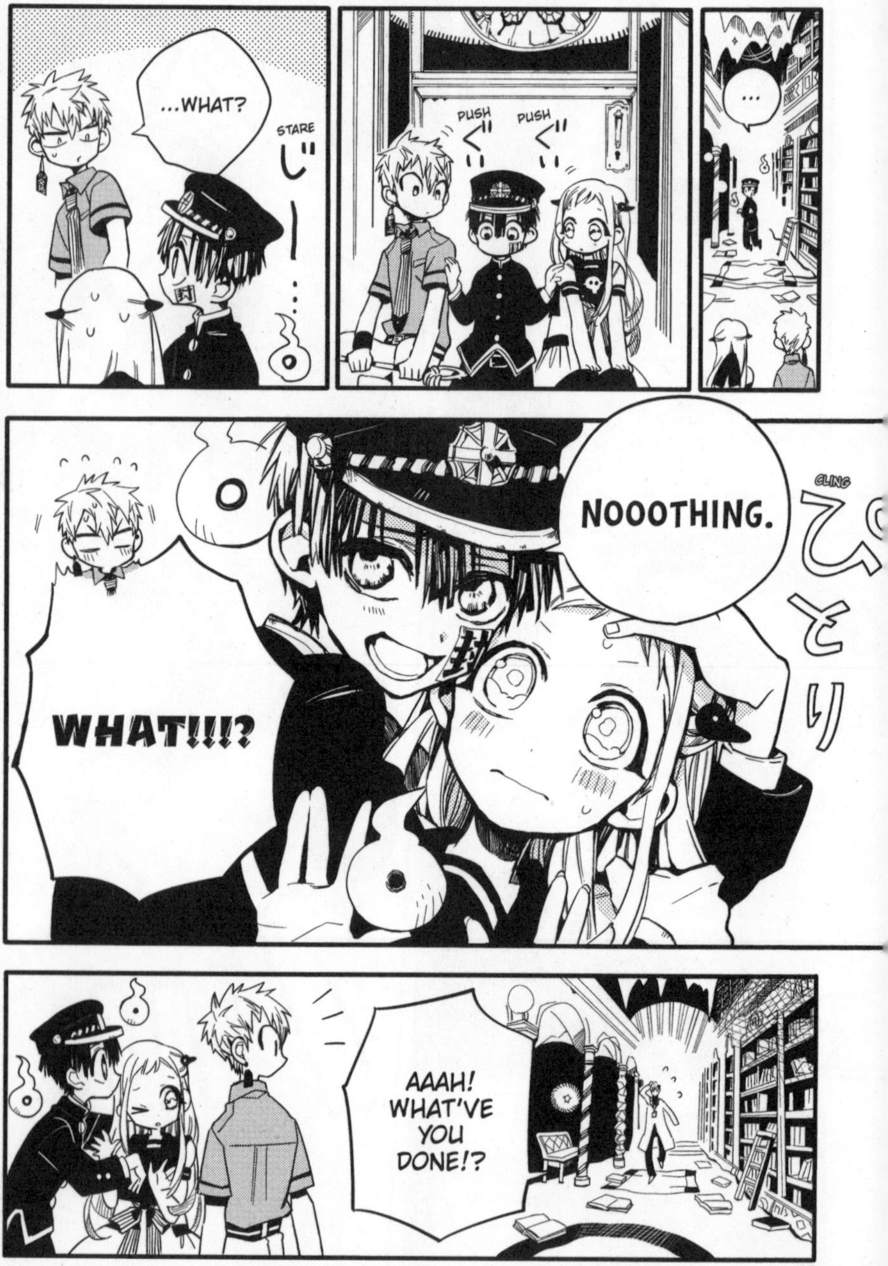
...
PUSH ぐい
PUSH ぐい
...WHAT?
STARE じー…
CLING ぴとり
NOOOTHING.
WHAT!!!?
AAAH! WHAT'VE YOU DONE!?

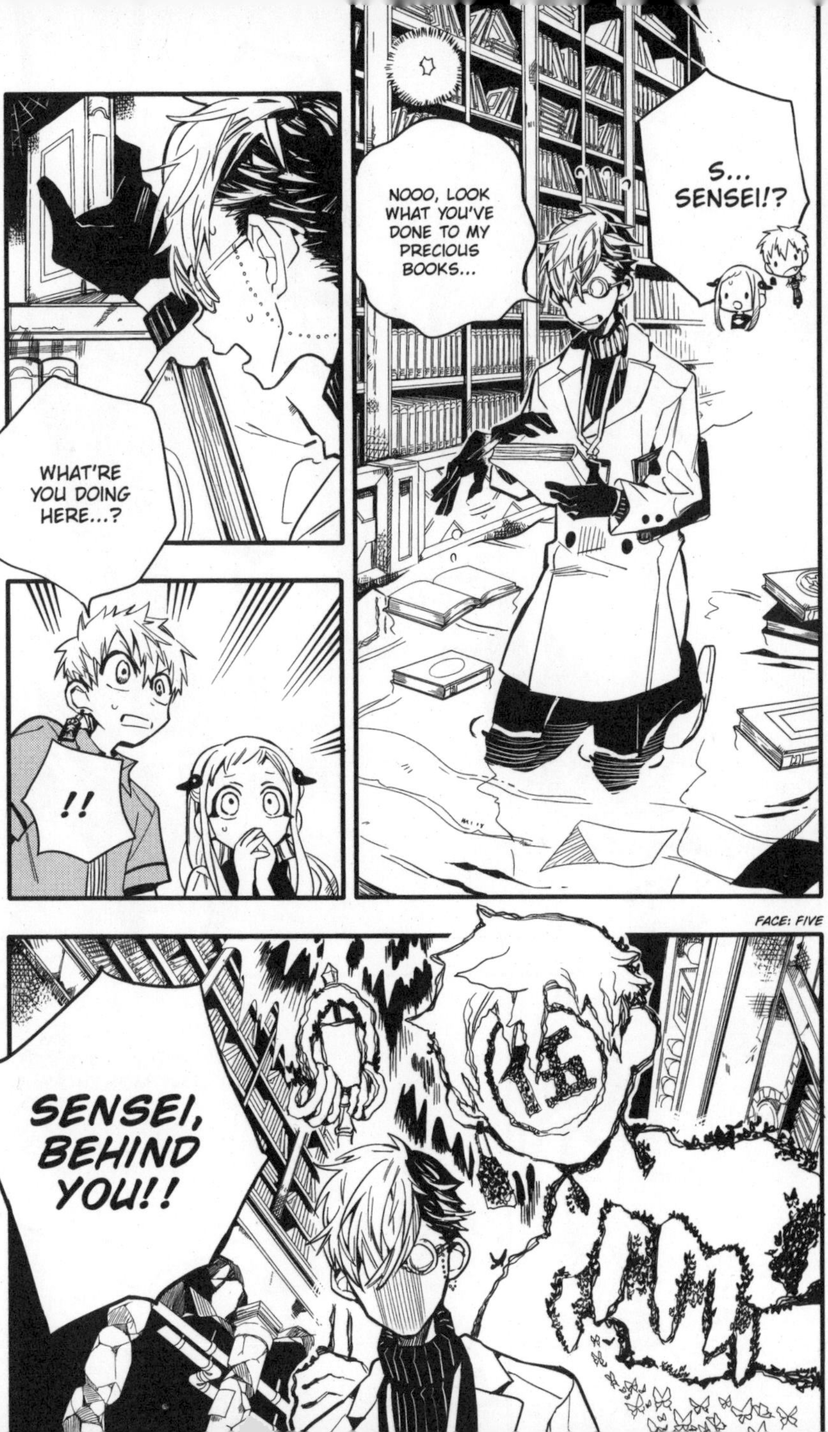
S... SENSEI!?
NOOO, LOOK WHAT YOU'VE DONE TO MY PRECIOUS BOOKS...
WHAT'RE YOU DOING HERE...?
!!
FACE: FIVE
SENSEI, BEHIND YOU!!

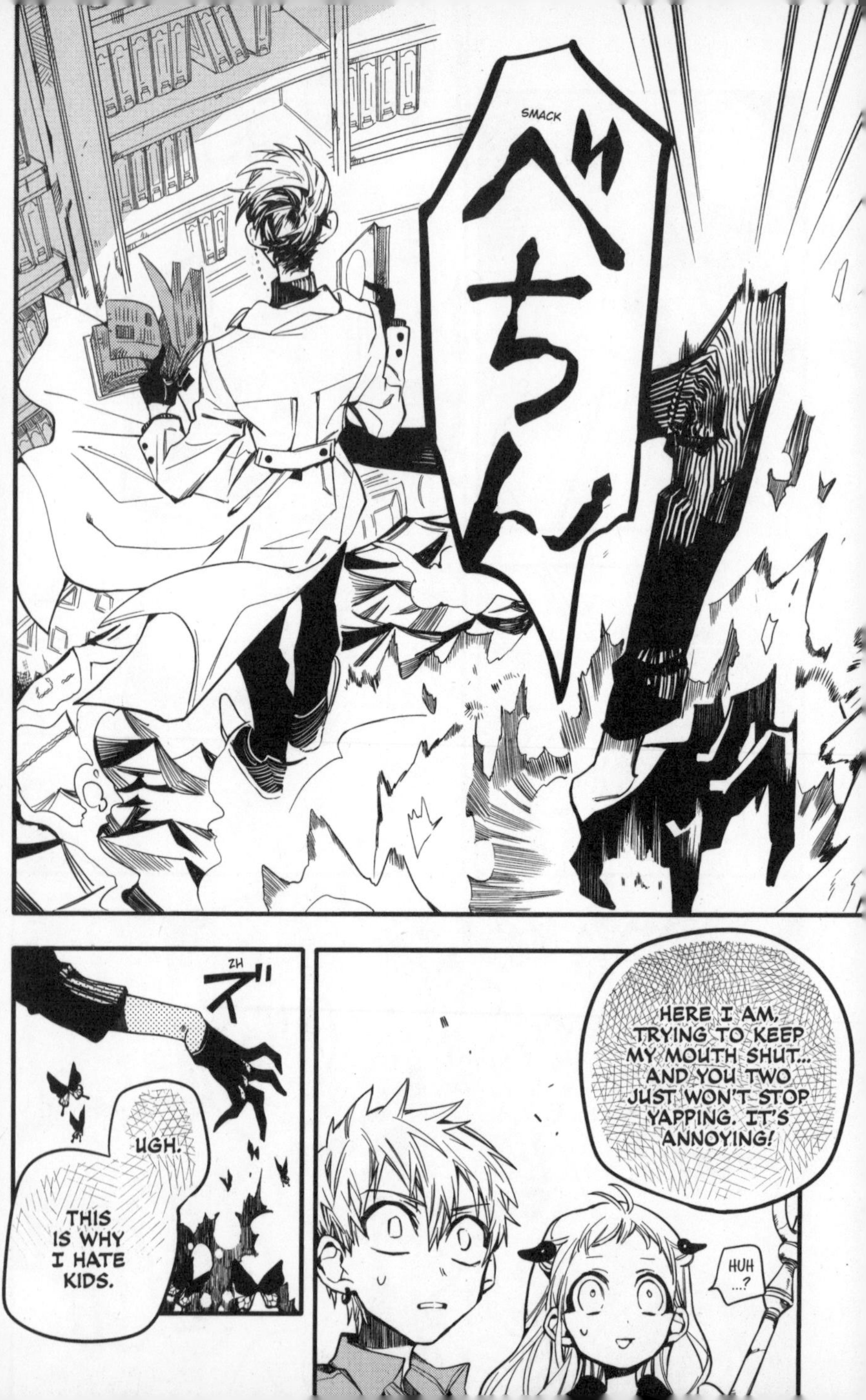
SMACK
べちん
HERE I AM, TRYING TO KEEP MY MOUTH SHUT... AND YOU TWO JUST WON'T STOP YAPPING. IT'S ANNOYING!
HUH ...?
ZH
ズ
UGH.
THIS IS WHY I HATE KIDS.

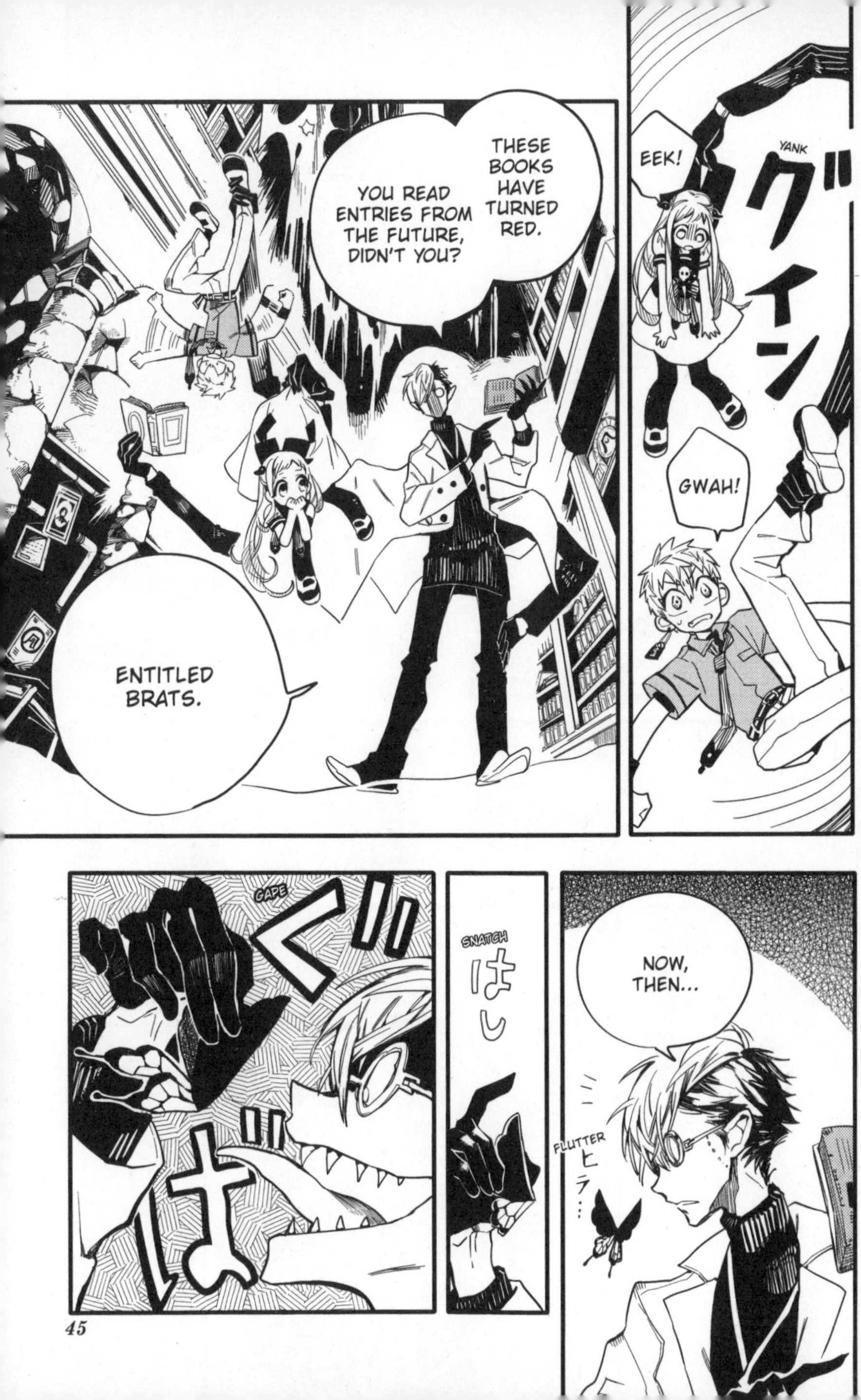
EEK!
YANK
グイン
GWAH!
THESE BOOKS HAVE TURNED RED.
YOU READ ENTRIES FROM THE FUTURE, DIDN'T YOU?
ENTITLED BRATS.
NOW, THEN...
FLUTTER
ヒラ…
SNATCH
はし
GAPE

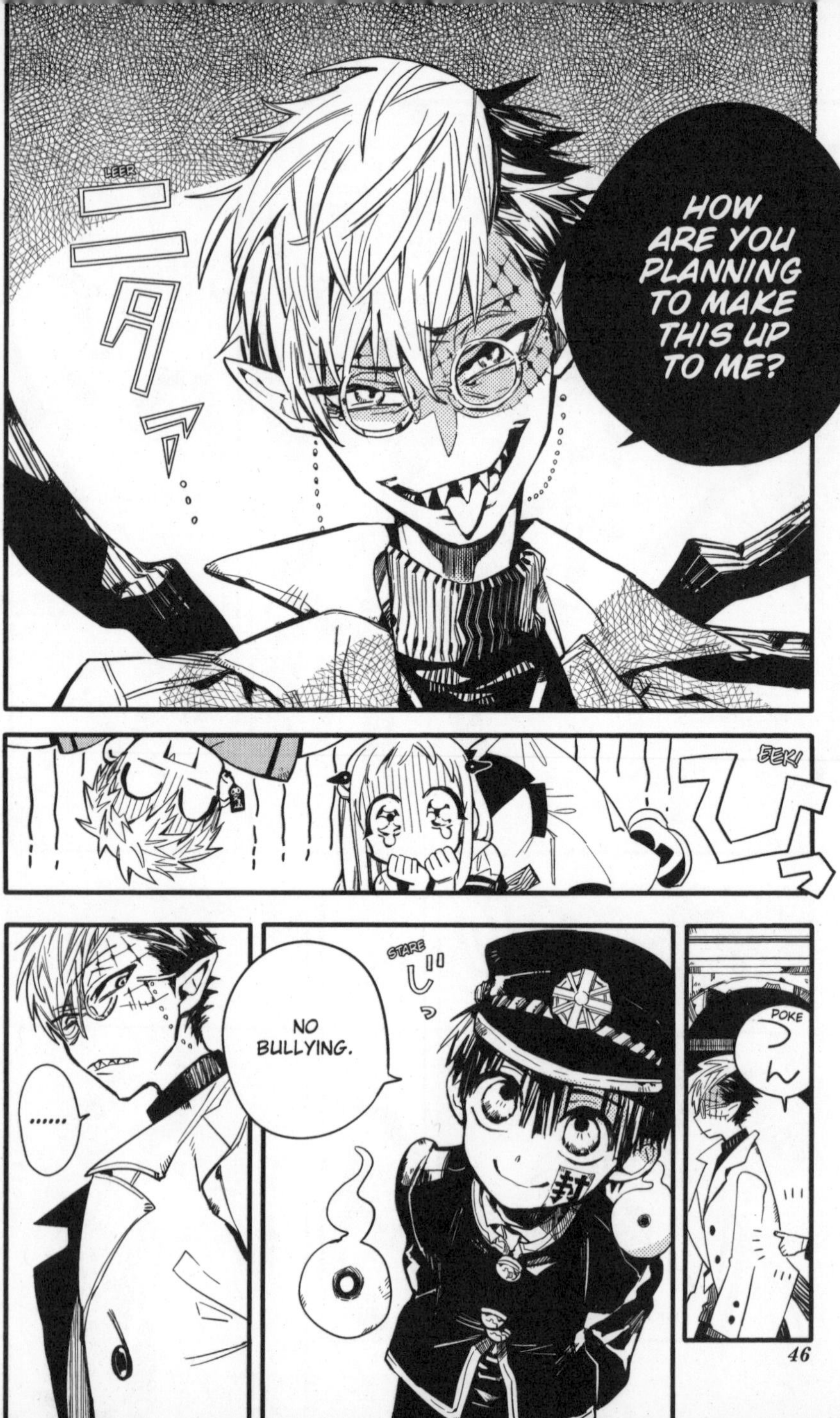
HOW ARE YOU PLANNING TO MAKE THIS UP TO ME?
LEER
EEK!
POKE
STARE
NO BULLYING.
......

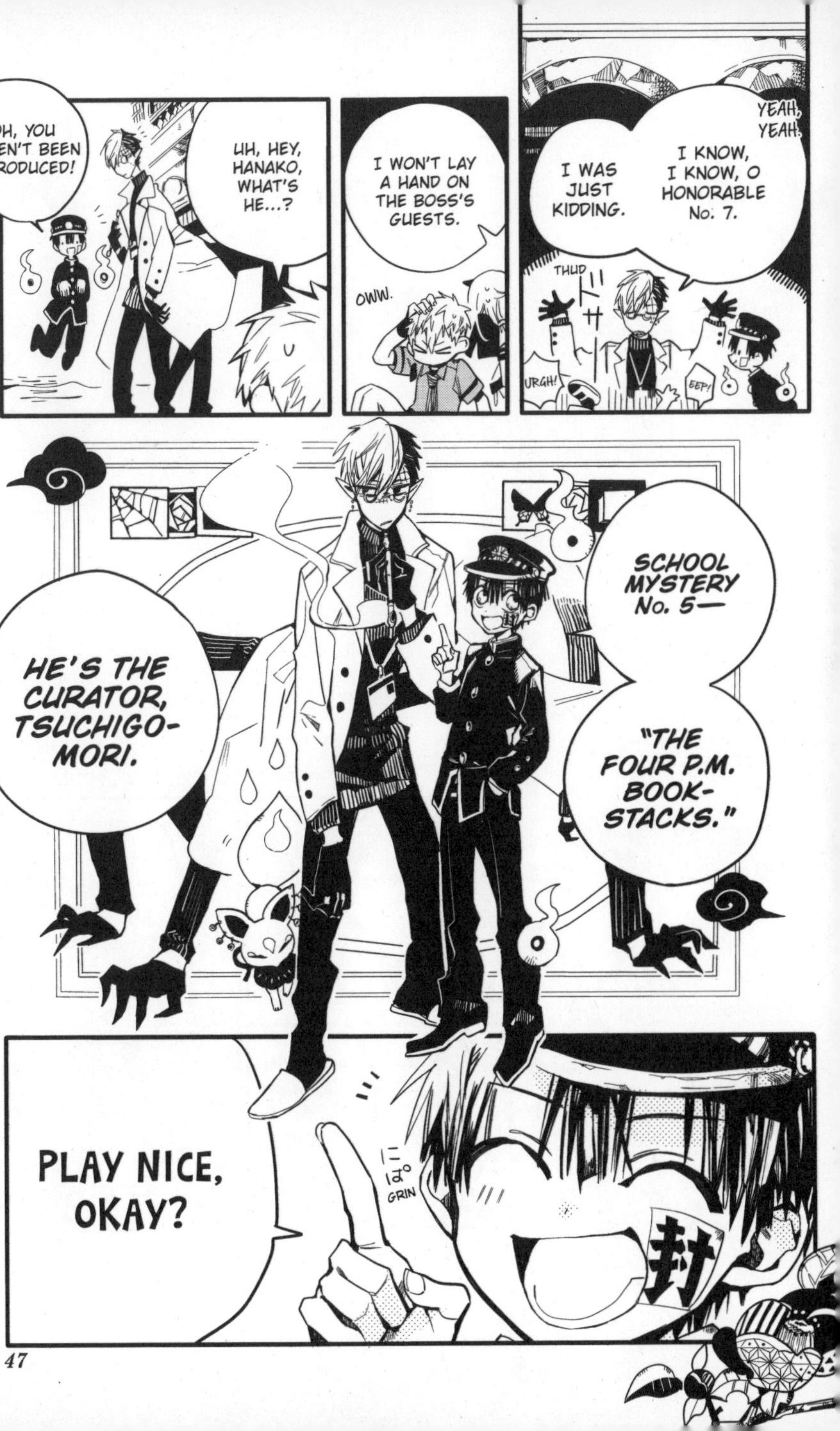
YEAH, YEAH.
I KNOW, I KNOW, O HONORABLE No. 7.
I WAS JUST KIDDING.
THUD
URGH!
EEP!
I WON'T LAY A HAND ON THE BOSS'S GUESTS.
OWW.
UH, HEY, HANAKO, WHAT'S HE...?
OH, YOU HAVEN'T BEEN INTRODUCED!
SCHOOL MYSTERY No. 5—
"THE FOUR P.M. BOOK-STACKS."
HE'S THE CURATOR, TSUCHIGOMORI.
にぱ
GRIN
PLAY NICE, OKAY?

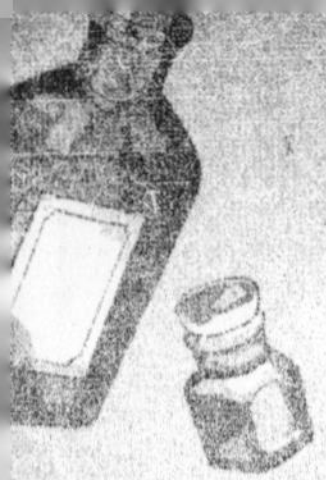

TEACH ME, TSUCHIGOMORI: -FOOD-

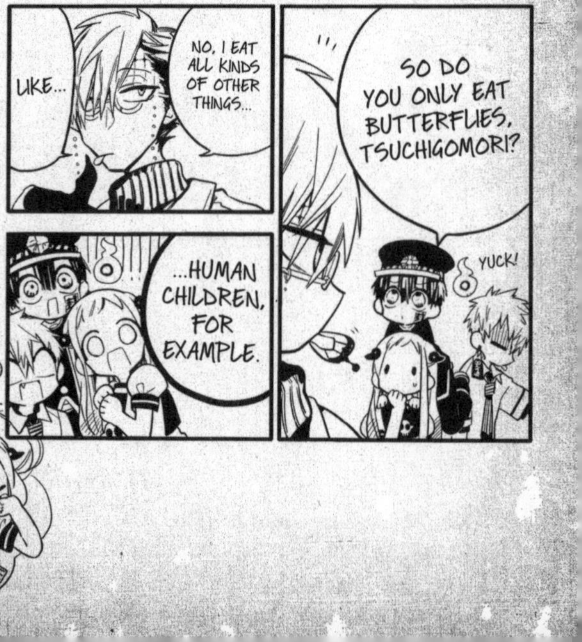
SO DO YOU ONLY EAT BUTTERFLIES, TSUCHIGOMORI?
YUCK!
NO, I EAT ALL KINDS OF OTHER THINGS...
LIKE...
...HUMAN CHILDREN, FOR EXAMPLE.

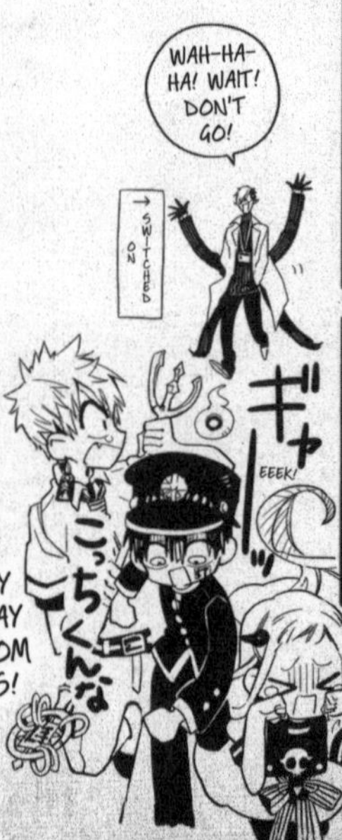
WAH-HA-HA! WAIT! DON'T GO!
→ SWITCHED ON
ギャ
EEEK!
こっちくんな
STAY AWAY FROM US!

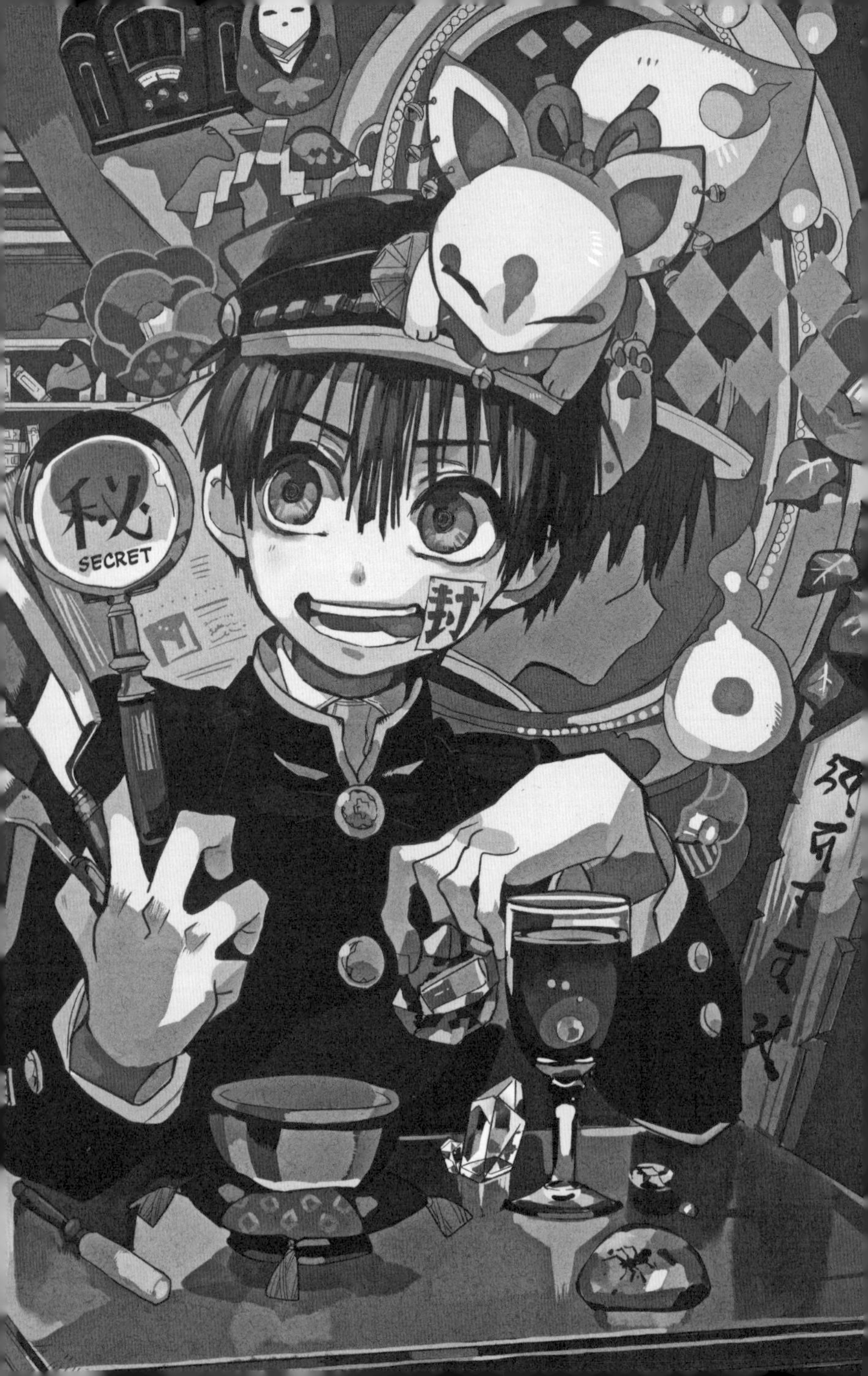
秘
SECRET
封

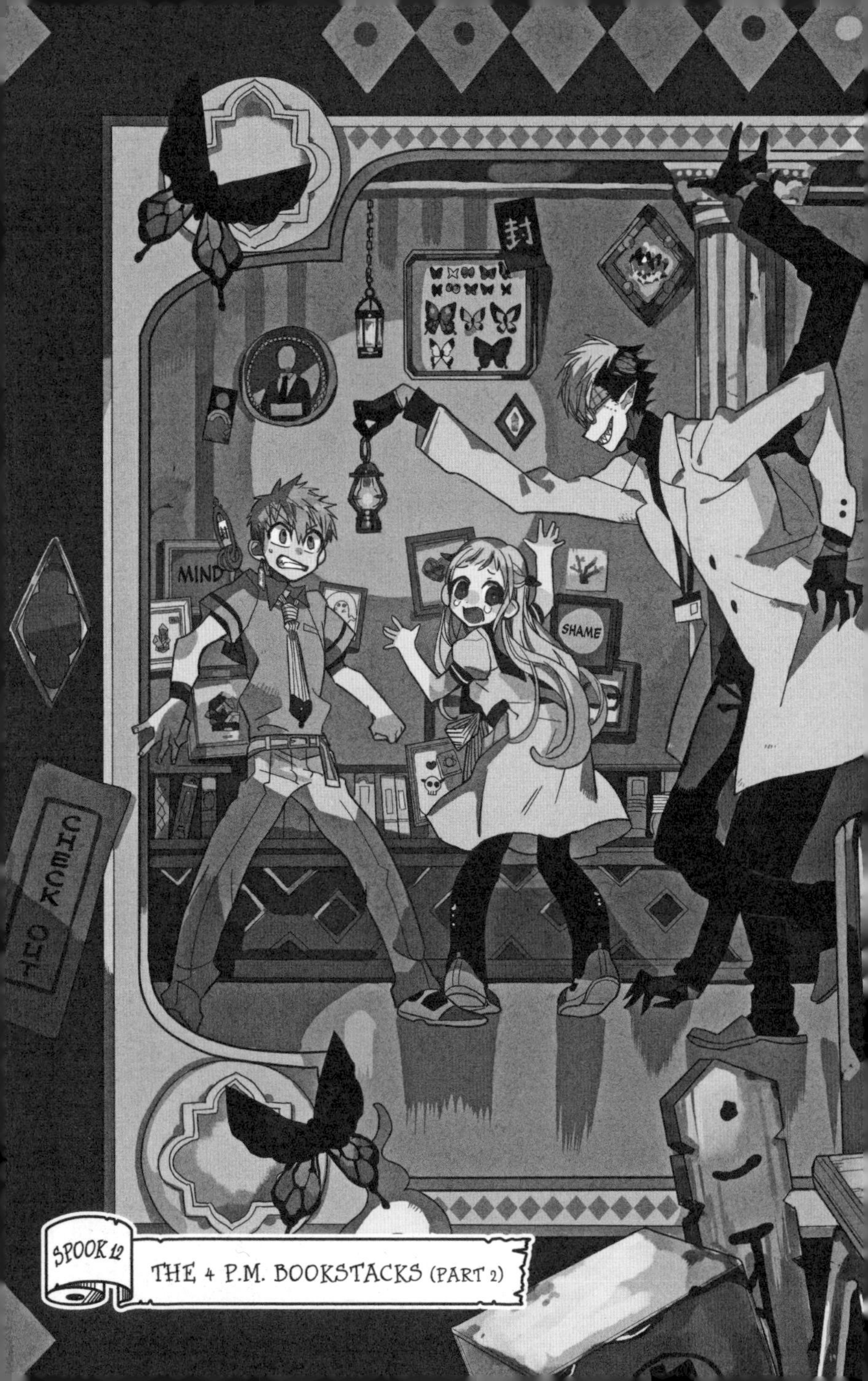
封
MIND
SHAME
CHECK OUT
SPOOK 12
THE 4 P.M. BOOKSTACKS (PART 2)

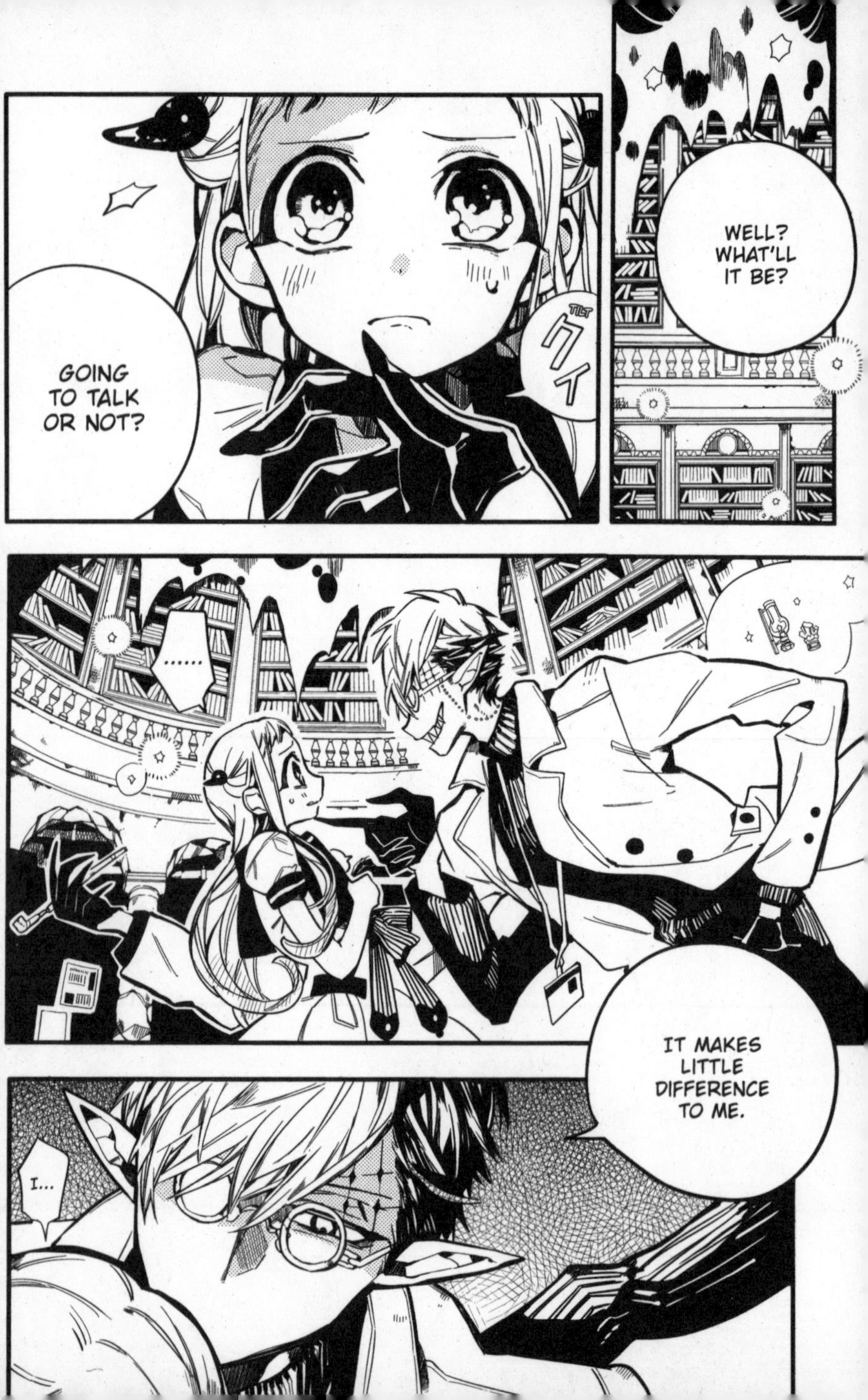
WELL? WHAT'LL IT BE?
クイ TILT
GOING TO TALK OR NOT?
......
IT MAKES LITTLE DIFFERENCE TO ME.
I...

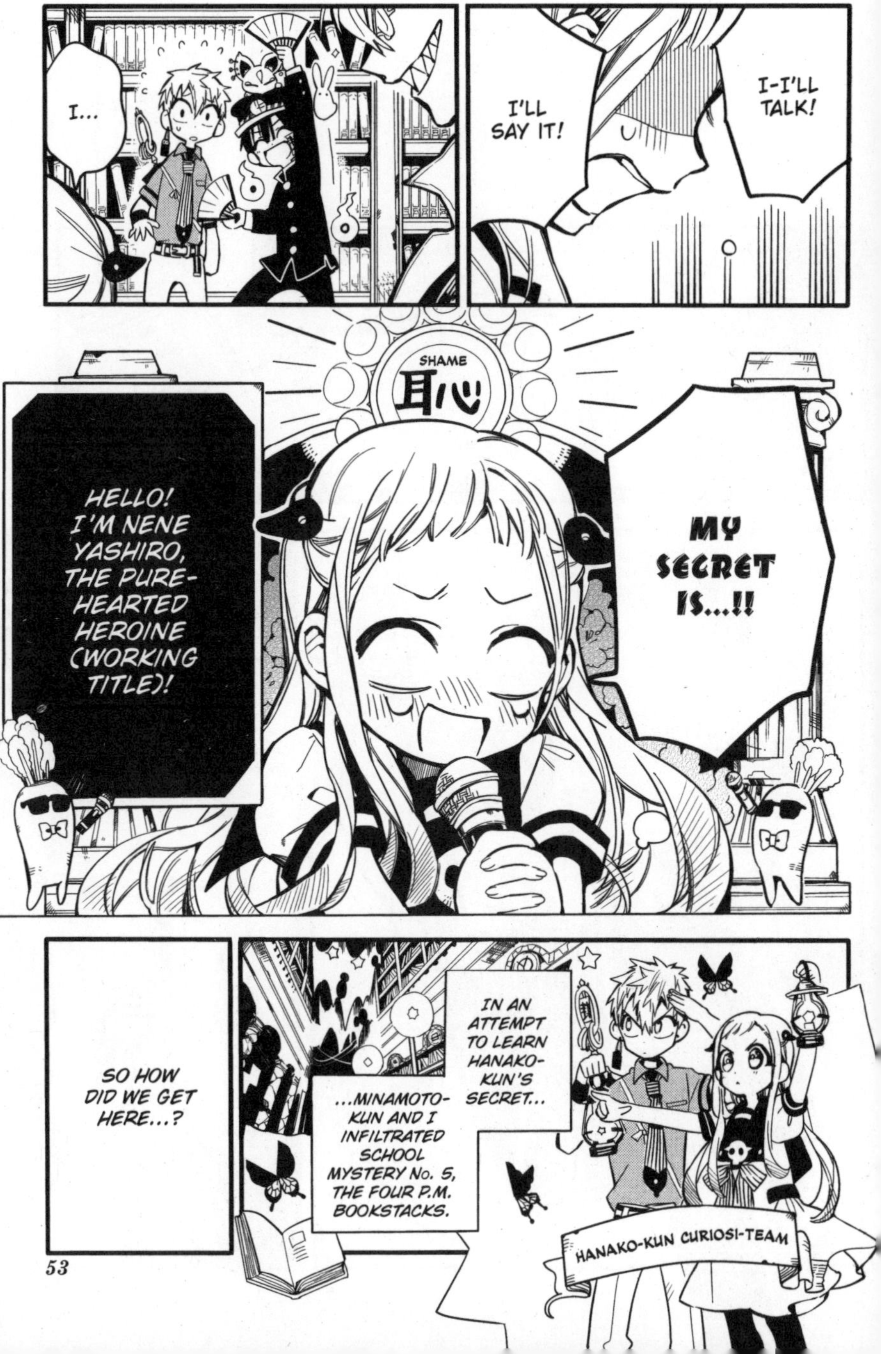
I-I'LL TALK!
I'LL SAY IT!
I...
SHAME
MY SECRET IS...!!
HELLO! I'M NENE YASHIRO, THE PURE-HEARTED HEROINE (WORKING TITLE)!
IN AN ATTEMPT TO LEARN HANAKO-KUN'S SECRET...
...MINAMOTO-KUN AND I INFILTRATED SCHOOL MYSTERY No. 5, THE FOUR P.M. BOOKSTACKS.
HANAKO-KUN CURIOSI-TEAM
SO HOW DID WE GET HERE...?

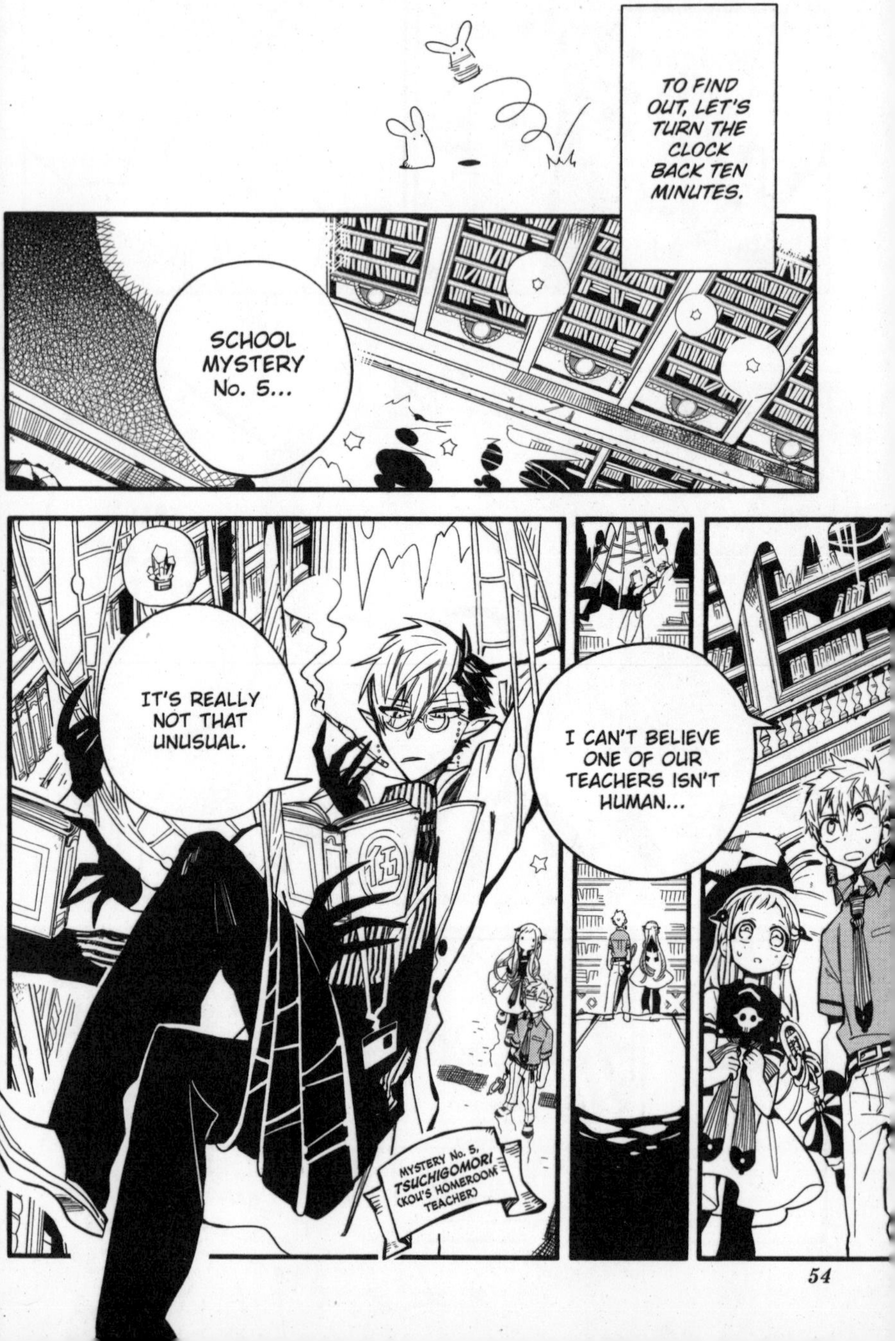
TO FIND OUT, LET'S TURN THE CLOCK BACK TEN MINUTES.
SCHOOL MYSTERY No. 5...
I CAN'T BELIEVE ONE OF OUR TEACHERS ISN'T HUMAN...
IT'S REALLY NOT THAT UNUSUAL.
MYSTERY No. 5, TSUCHIGOMORI (KOU'S HOMEROOM TEACHER)

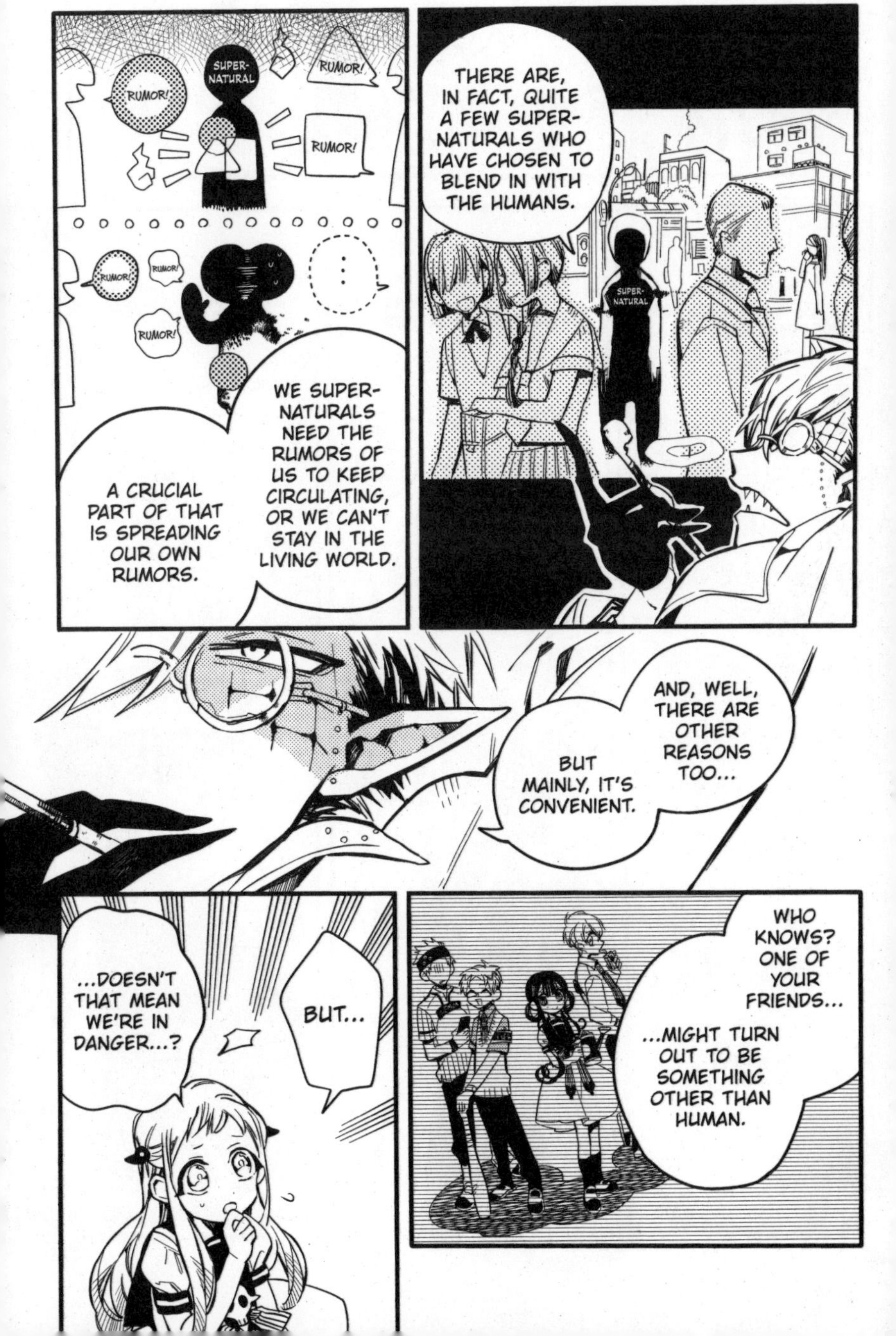
THERE ARE, IN FACT, QUITE A FEW SUPER-NATURALS WHO HAVE CHOSEN TO BLEND IN WITH THE HUMANS.
SUPER-NATURAL
RUMOR!
SUPER-NATURAL
RUMOR!
RUMOR!
...
RUMOR!
RUMOR!
RUMOR!
WE SUPER-NATURALS NEED THE RUMORS OF US TO KEEP CIRCULATING, OR WE CAN'T STAY IN THE LIVING WORLD.
A CRUCIAL PART OF THAT IS SPREADING OUR OWN RUMORS.
AND, WELL, THERE ARE OTHER REASONS TOO...
BUT MAINLY, IT'S CONVENIENT.
WHO KNOWS? ONE OF YOUR FRIENDS...
...MIGHT TURN OUT TO BE SOMETHING OTHER THAN HUMAN.
BUT...
...DOESN'T THAT MEAN WE'RE IN DANGER...?

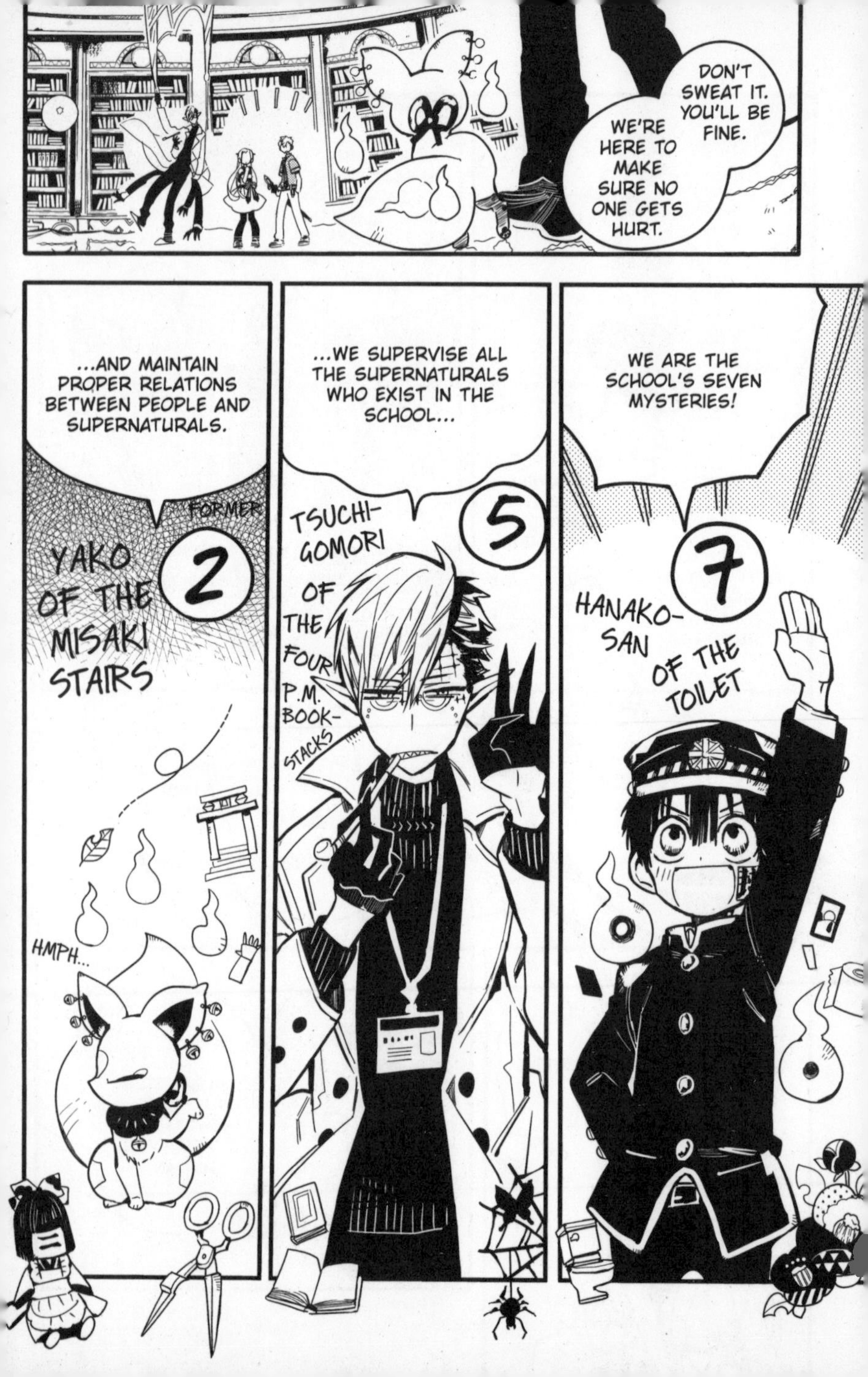
DON'T SWEAT IT. YOU'LL BE FINE.
WE'RE HERE TO MAKE SURE NO ONE GETS HURT.
WE ARE THE SCHOOL'S SEVEN MYSTERIES!
7
HANAKO-SAN OF THE TOILET
...WE SUPERVISE ALL THE SUPERNATURALS WHO EXIST IN THE SCHOOL...
5
TSUCHIGOMORI OF THE FOUR P.M. BOOKSTACKS
...AND MAINTAIN PROPER RELATIONS BETWEEN PEOPLE AND SUPERNATURALS.
FORMER
2
YAKO OF THE MISAKI STAIRS
HMPH...

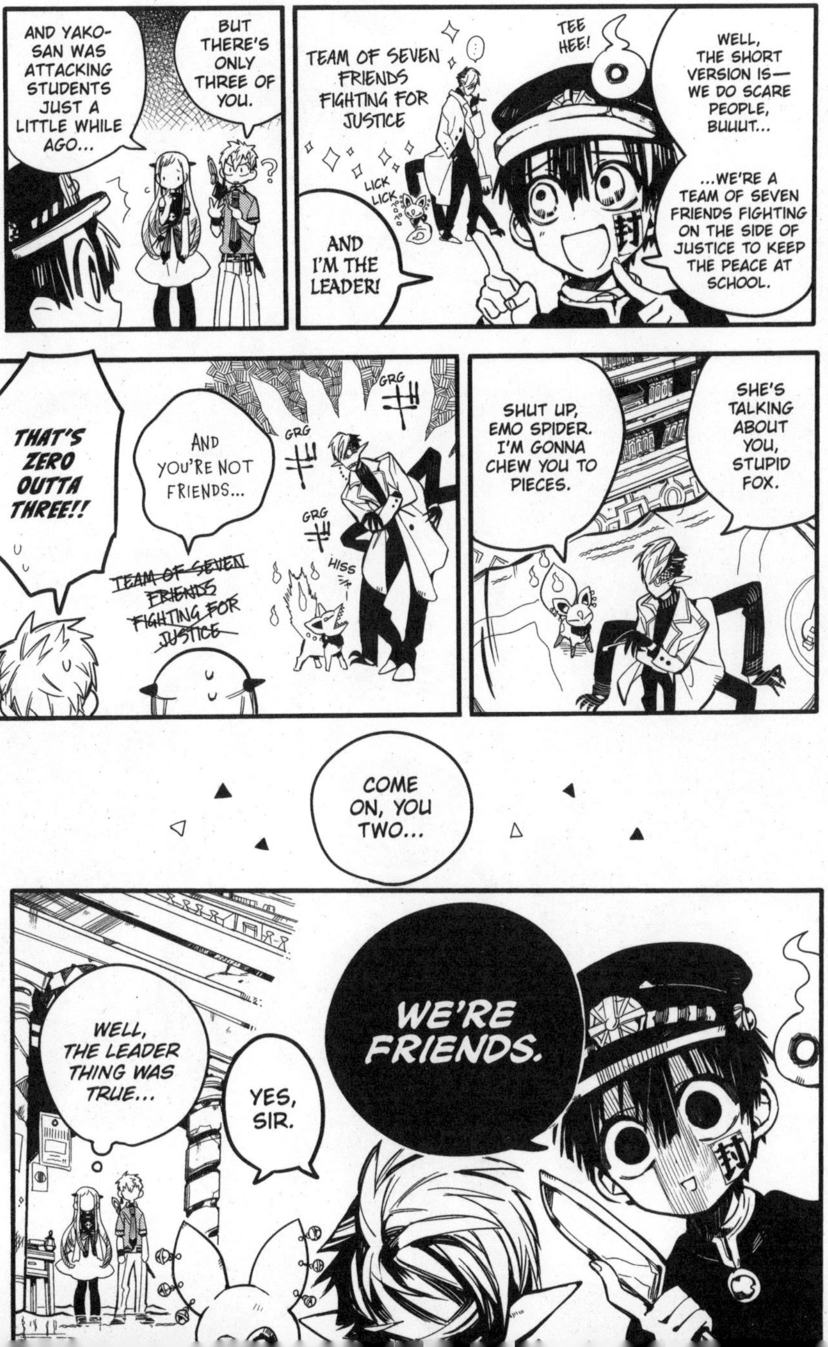
WELL, THE SHORT VERSION IS— WE DO SCARE PEOPLE, BUUUT...
TEE HEE!
...WE'RE A TEAM OF SEVEN FRIENDS FIGHTING ON THE SIDE OF JUSTICE TO KEEP THE PEACE AT SCHOOL.
TEAM OF SEVEN FRIENDS FIGHTING FOR JUSTICE
LICK LICK
AND I'M THE LEADER!
BUT THERE'S ONLY THREE OF YOU.
AND YAKO-SAN WAS ATTACKING STUDENTS JUST A LITTLE WHILE AGO...
SHE'S TALKING ABOUT YOU, STUPID FOX.
SHUT UP, EMO SPIDER. I'M GONNA CHEW YOU TO PIECES.
GRG
GRG
GRG
AND YOU'RE NOT FRIENDS...
HISS
~~TEAM OF SEVEN FRIENDS FIGHTING FOR JUSTICE~~
THAT'S ZERO OUTTA THREE!!
COME ON, YOU TWO...
WE'RE FRIENDS.
YES, SIR.
WELL, THE LEADER THING WAS TRUE...

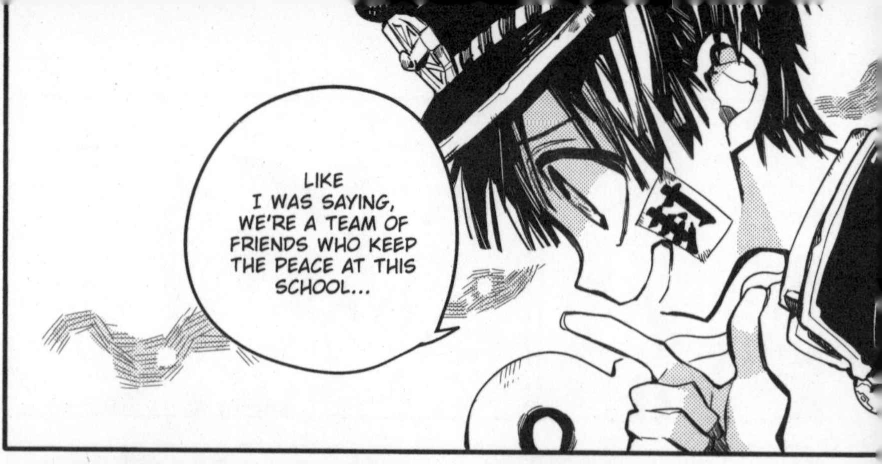
LIKE I WAS SAYING, WE'RE A TEAM OF FRIENDS WHO KEEP THE PEACE AT THIS SCHOOL...

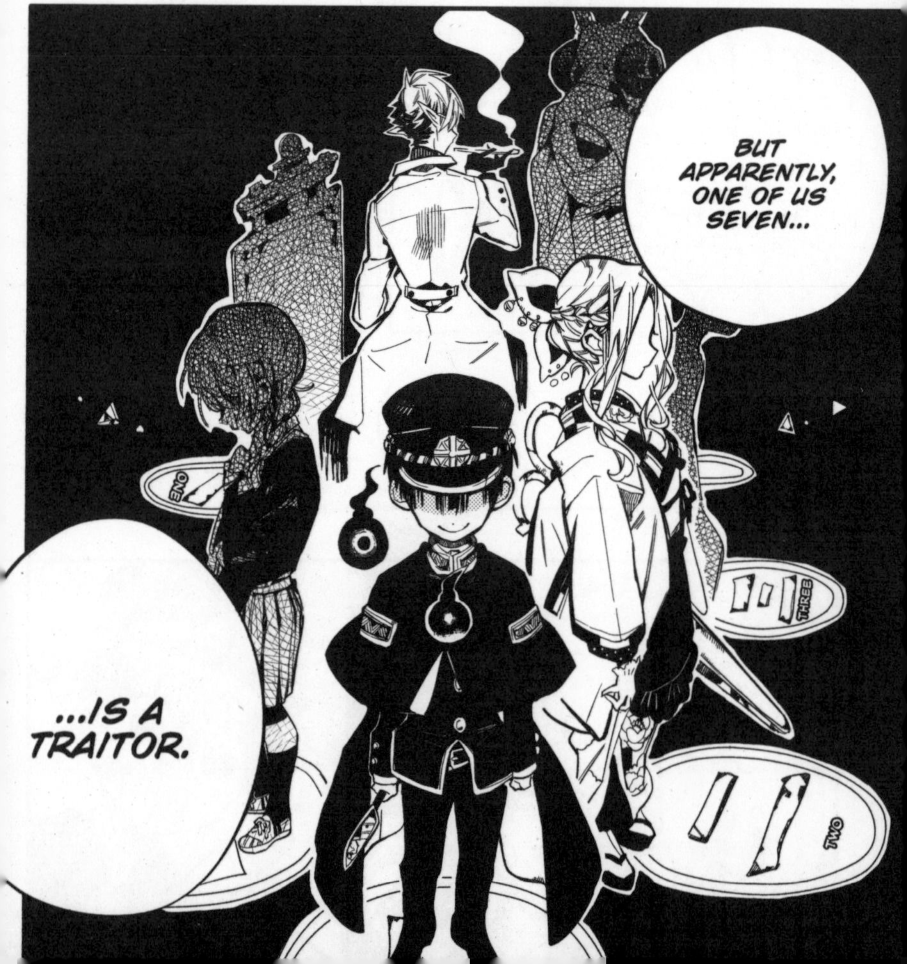
BUT APPARENTLY, ONE OF US SEVEN...
ONE
THREE
TWO
...IS A TRAITOR.

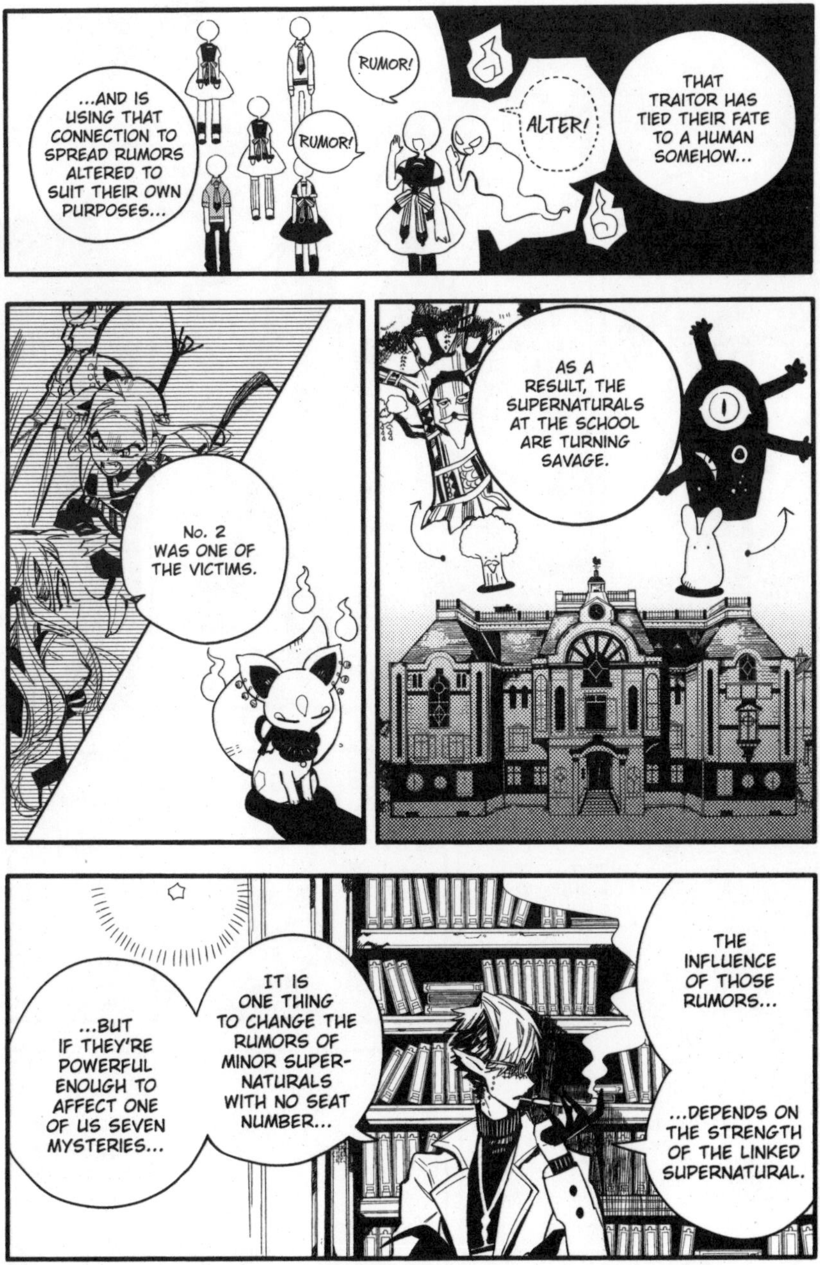
THAT TRAITOR HAS TIED THEIR FATE TO A HUMAN SOMEHOW...
ALTER!
RUMOR!
RUMOR!
...AND IS USING THAT CONNECTION TO SPREAD RUMORS ALTERED TO SUIT THEIR OWN PURPOSES...
AS A RESULT, THE SUPERNATURALS AT THE SCHOOL ARE TURNING SAVAGE.
No. 2 WAS ONE OF THE VICTIMS.
THE INFLUENCE OF THOSE RUMORS...
...DEPENDS ON THE STRENGTH OF THE LINKED SUPERNATURAL.
IT IS ONE THING TO CHANGE THE RUMORS OF MINOR SUPER-NATURALS WITH NO SEAT NUMBER...
...BUT IF THEY'RE POWERFUL ENOUGH TO AFFECT ONE OF US SEVEN MYSTERIES...

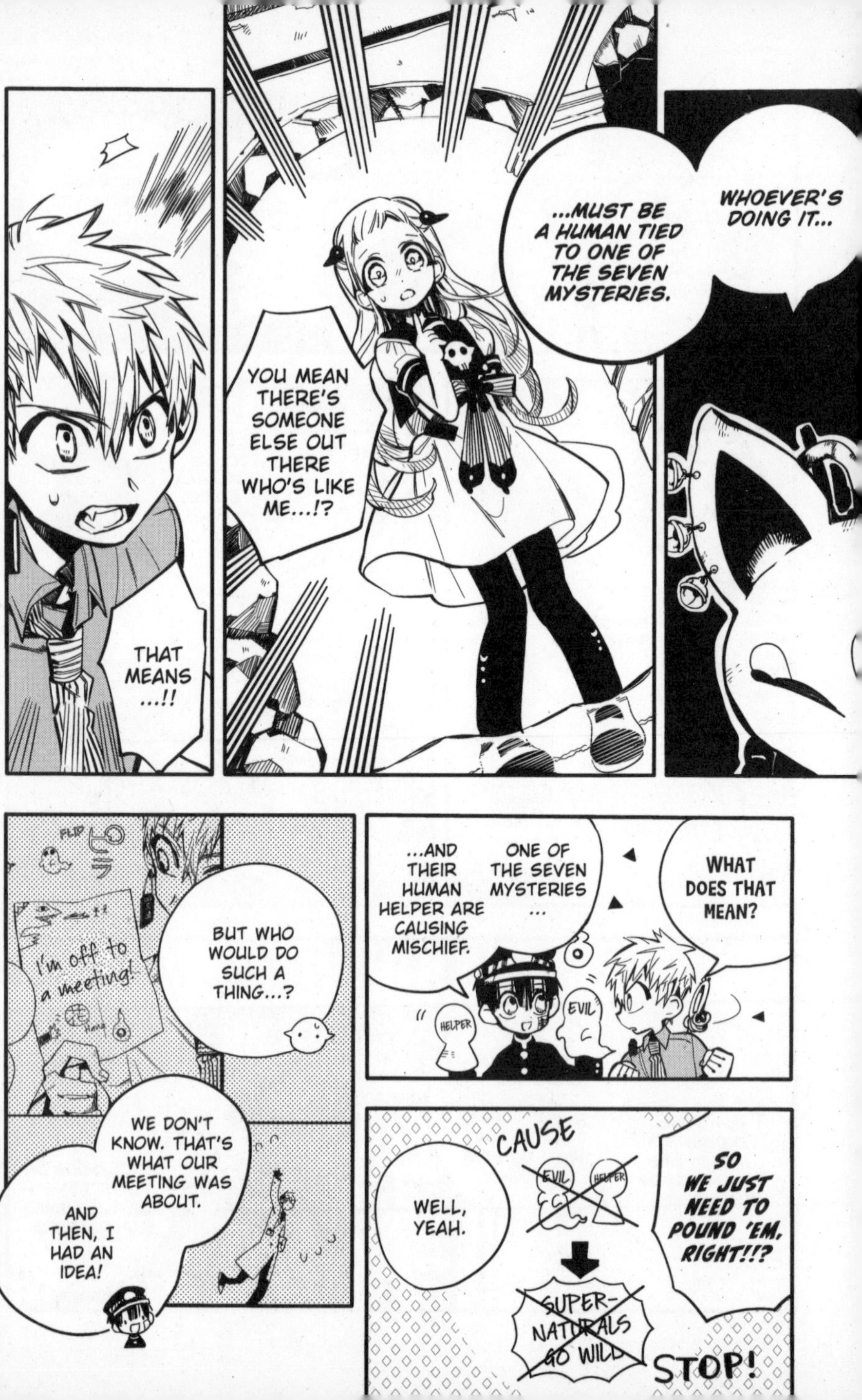
WHOEVER'S DOING IT...
...MUST BE A HUMAN TIED TO ONE OF THE SEVEN MYSTERIES.
YOU MEAN THERE'S SOMEONE ELSE OUT THERE WHO'S LIKE ME...!?
THAT MEANS ...!!
WHAT DOES THAT MEAN?
ONE OF THE SEVEN MYSTERIES ...
...AND THEIR HUMAN HELPER ARE CAUSING MISCHIEF.
EVIL
HELPER
FLIP
I'm off to a meeting!
BUT WHO WOULD DO SUCH A THING...?
SO WE JUST NEED TO POUND 'EM, RIGHT!!?
CAUSE
EVIL
HELPER
SUPER-NATURALS GO WILD
STOP!
WELL, YEAH.
WE DON'T KNOW. THAT'S WHAT OUR MEETING WAS ABOUT.
AND THEN, I HAD AN IDEA!

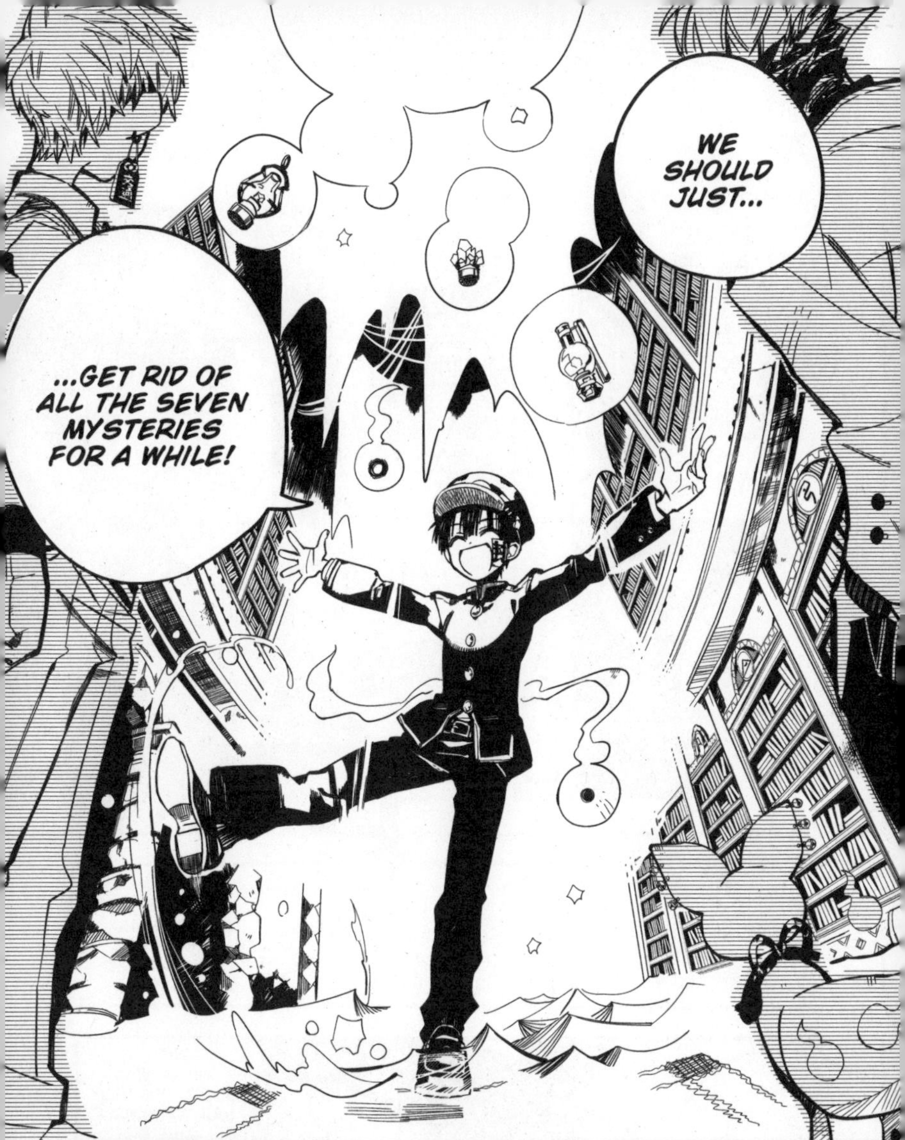
WE SHOULD JUST...
...GET RID OF ALL THE SEVEN MYSTERIES FOR A WHILE!

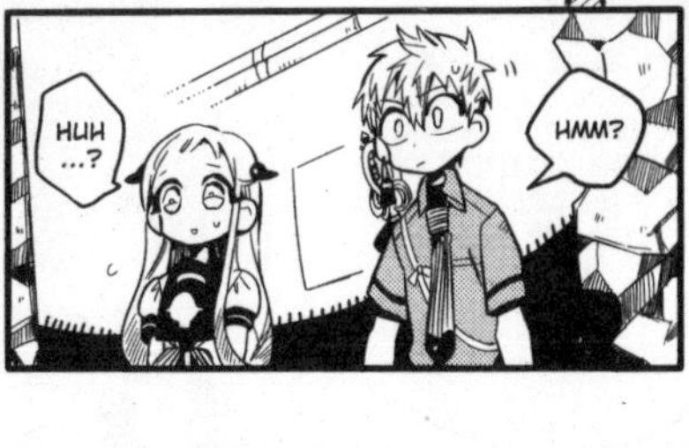
HMM?
HUH ...?

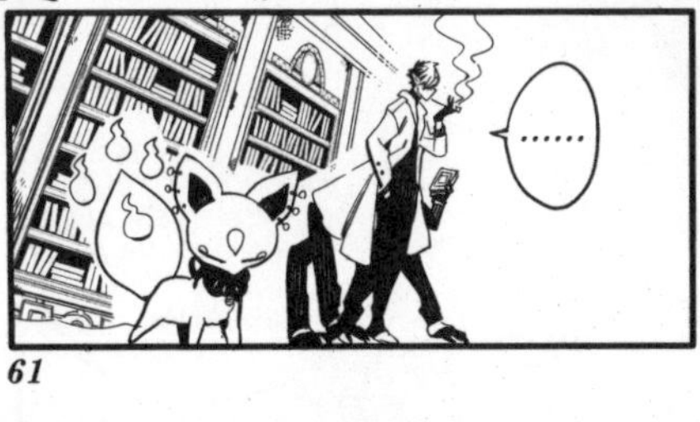
......

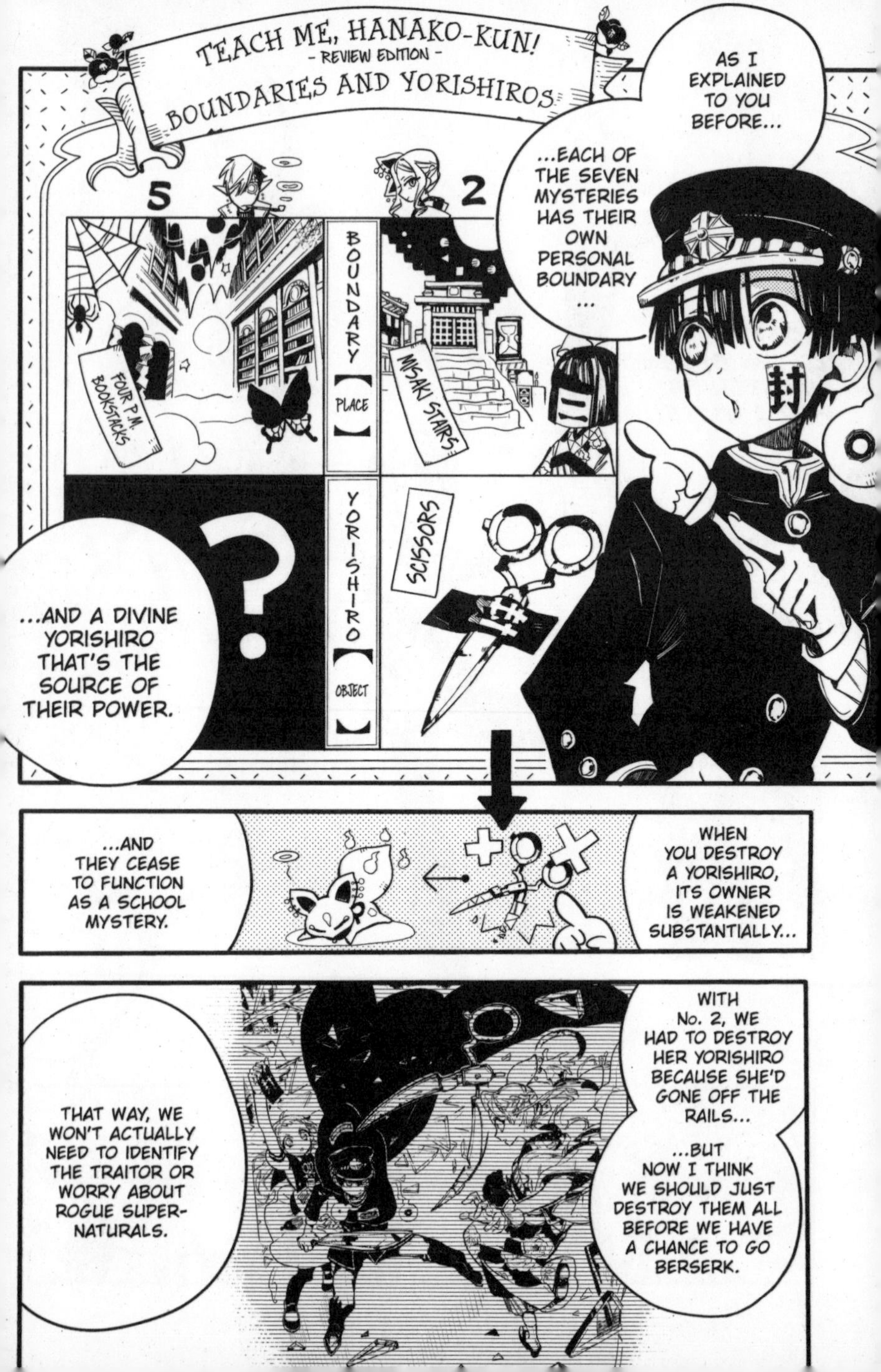
TEACH ME, HANAKO-KUN!
- REVIEW EDITION -
BOUNDARIES AND YORISHIROS
AS I EXPLAINED TO YOU BEFORE...
...EACH OF THE SEVEN MYSTERIES HAS THEIR OWN PERSONAL BOUNDARY...
2
5
BOUNDARY
PLACE
MISAKI STAIRS
FOUR P.M. BOOKSTACKS
YORISHIRO
OBJECT
SCISSORS
?
...AND A DIVINE YORISHIRO THAT'S THE SOURCE OF THEIR POWER.
WHEN YOU DESTROY A YORISHIRO, ITS OWNER IS WEAKENED SUBSTANTIALLY...
...AND THEY CEASE TO FUNCTION AS A SCHOOL MYSTERY.
WITH No. 2, WE HAD TO DESTROY HER YORISHIRO BECAUSE SHE'D GONE OFF THE RAILS...
...BUT NOW I THINK WE SHOULD JUST DESTROY THEM ALL BEFORE WE HAVE A CHANCE TO GO BERSERK.
THAT WAY, WE WON'T ACTUALLY NEED TO IDENTIFY THE TRAITOR OR WORRY ABOUT ROGUE SUPER-NATURALS.

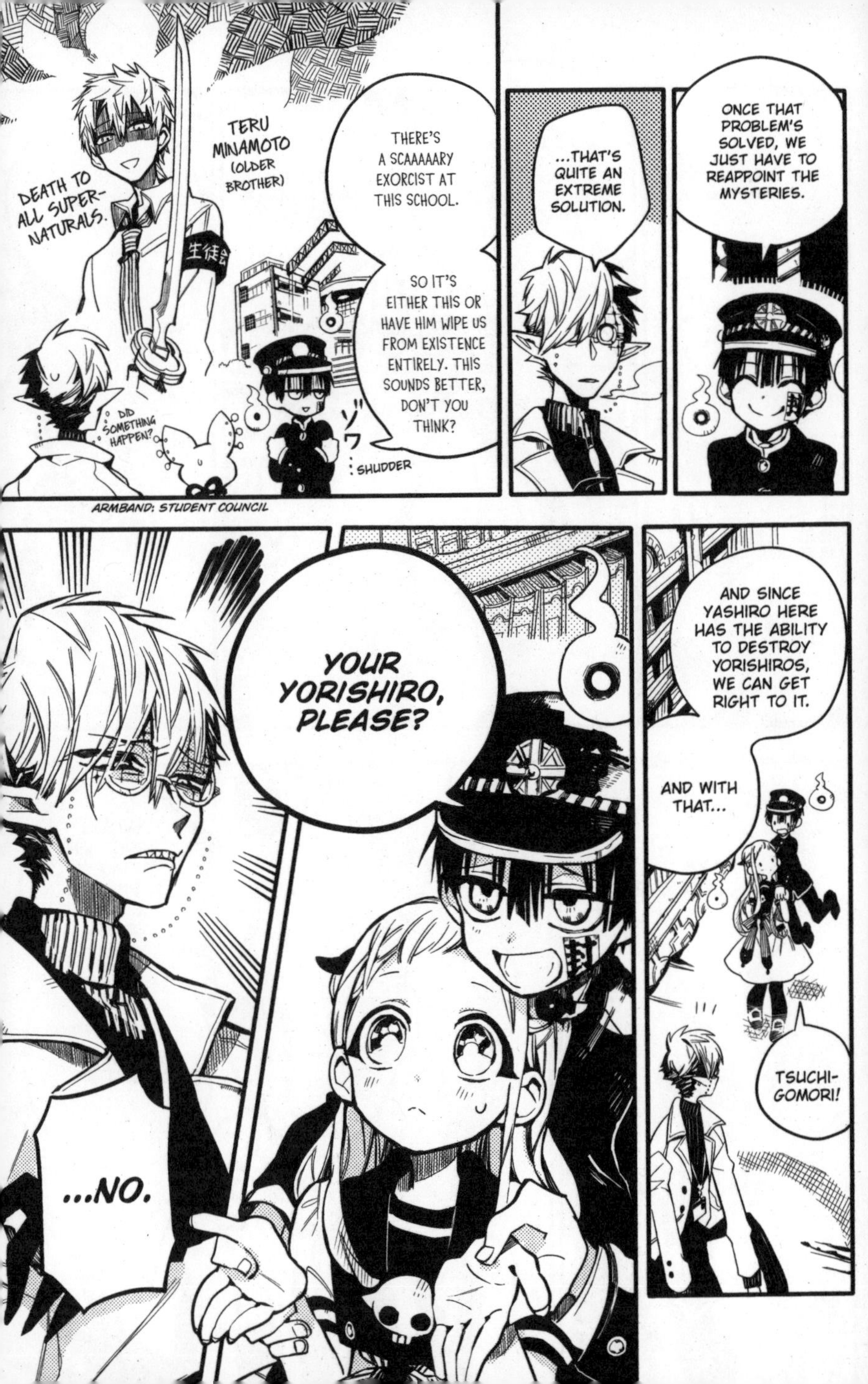
ONCE THAT PROBLEM'S SOLVED, WE JUST HAVE TO REAPPOINT THE MYSTERIES.
...THAT'S QUITE AN EXTREME SOLUTION.
THERE'S A SCAAAAARY EXORCIST AT THIS SCHOOL.
SO IT'S EITHER THIS OR HAVE HIM WIPE US FROM EXISTENCE ENTIRELY. THIS SOUNDS BETTER, DON'T YOU THINK?
TERU MINAMOTO (OLDER BROTHER)
DEATH TO ALL SUPER-NATURALS.
生徒会
ゾワ
SHUDDER
DID SOMETHING HAPPEN?
AND SINCE YASHIRO HERE HAS THE ABILITY TO DESTROY YORISHIROS, WE CAN GET RIGHT TO IT.
AND WITH THAT...
TSUCHI-GOMORI!
YOUR YORISHIRO, PLEASE?
...NO.
ARMBAND: STUDENT COUNCIL

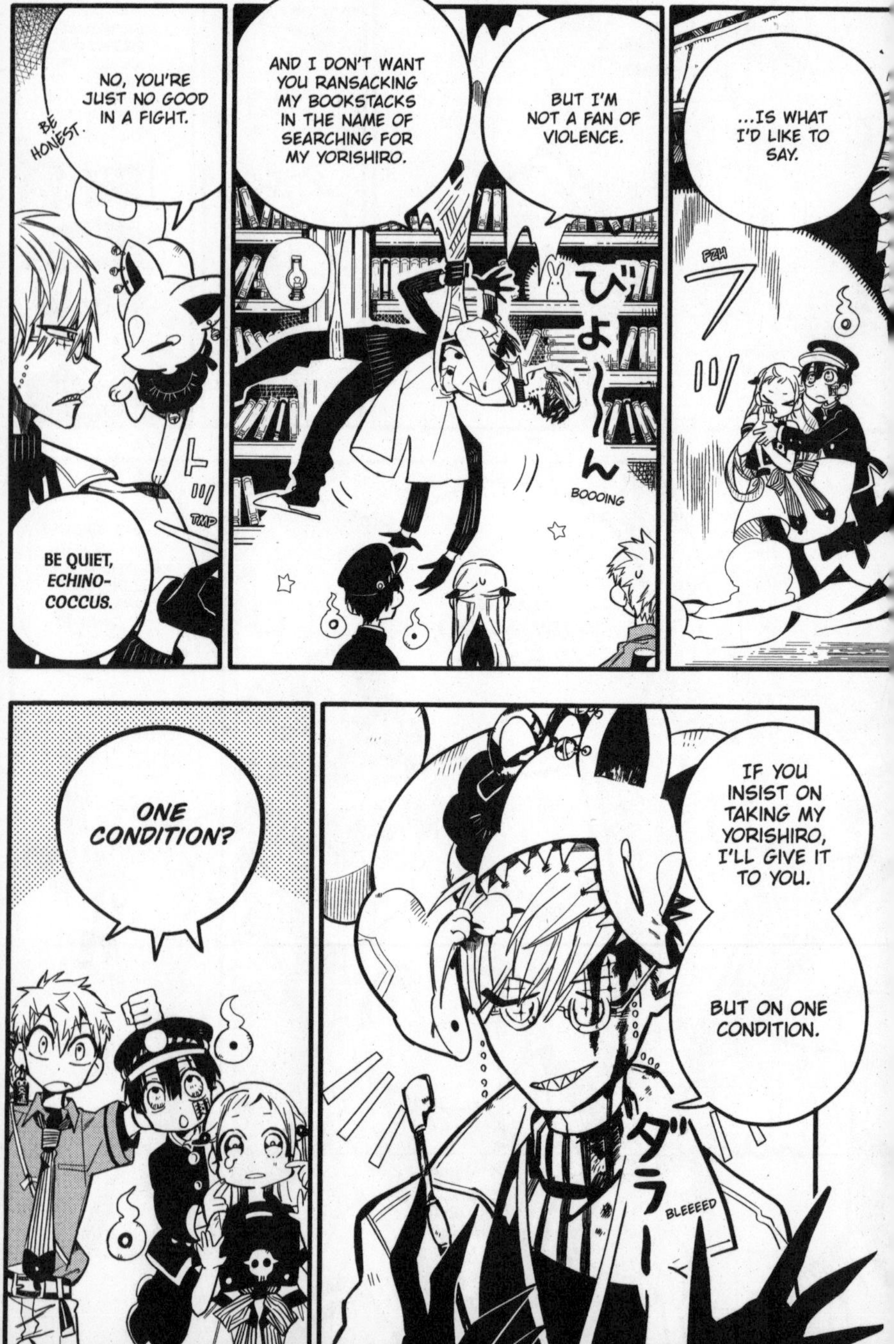
...IS WHAT I'D LIKE TO SAY.
FZH
BUT I'M NOT A FAN OF VIOLENCE.
AND I DON'T WANT YOU RANSACKING MY BOOKSTACKS IN THE NAME OF SEARCHING FOR MY YORISHIRO.
びよ～ん
BOOOING
NO, YOU'RE JUST NO GOOD IN A FIGHT.
BE HONEST.
TMP
BE QUIET, *ECHINOCOCCUS*.
IF YOU INSIST ON TAKING MY YORISHIRO, I'LL GIVE IT TO YOU.
BUT ON ONE CONDITION.
ダラー
BLEEEED
ONE CONDITION?

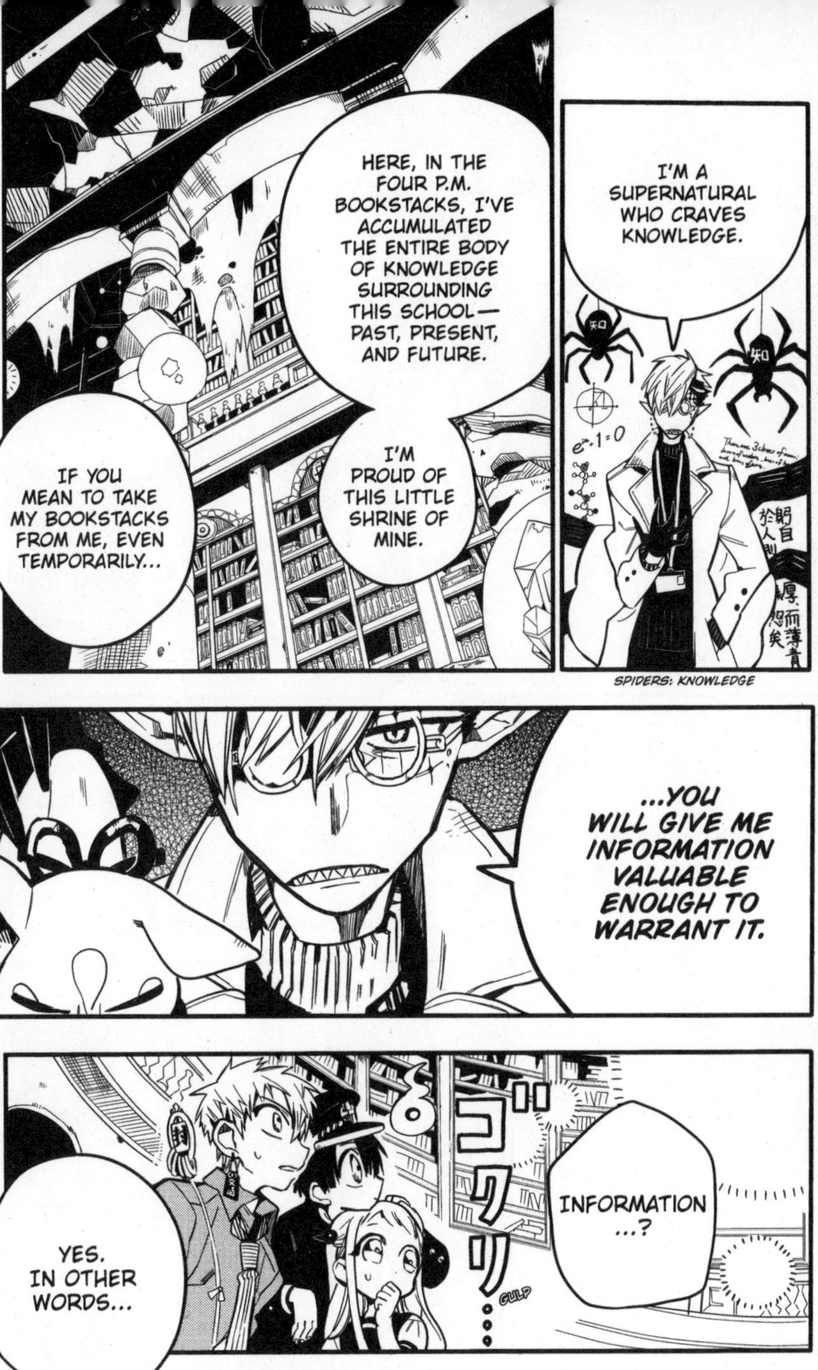
I'M A SUPERNATURAL WHO CRAVES KNOWLEDGE.
知
知
HERE, IN THE FOUR P.M. BOOKSTACKS, I'VE ACCUMULATED THE ENTIRE BODY OF KNOWLEDGE SURROUNDING THIS SCHOOL—PAST, PRESENT, AND FUTURE.
I'M PROUD OF THIS LITTLE SHRINE OF MINE.
IF YOU MEAN TO TAKE MY BOOKSTACKS FROM ME, EVEN TEMPORARILY...
...YOU WILL GIVE ME INFORMATION VALUABLE ENOUGH TO WARRANT IT.
INFORMATION ...?
ゴクリ
GULP
YES. IN OTHER WORDS...
SPIDERS: KNOWLEDGE

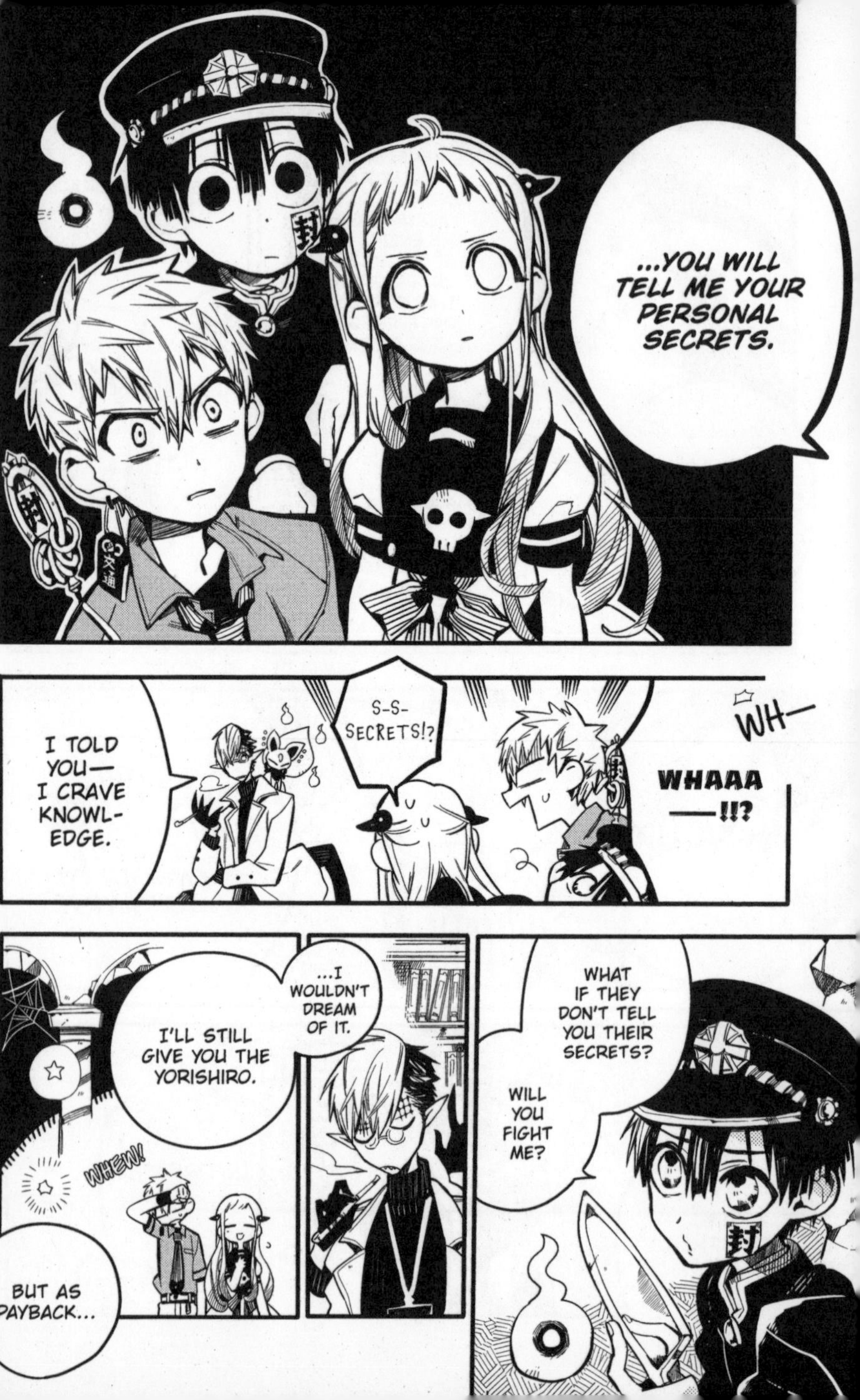
...YOU WILL TELL ME YOUR PERSONAL SECRETS.
WH—
WHAAA—!!?
S-S-SECRETS!?
I TOLD YOU— I CRAVE KNOWL-EDGE.
WHAT IF THEY DON'T TELL YOU THEIR SECRETS?
WILL YOU FIGHT ME?
...I WOULDN'T DREAM OF IT.
I'LL STILL GIVE YOU THE YORISHIRO.
WHEW!
BUT AS PAYBACK...

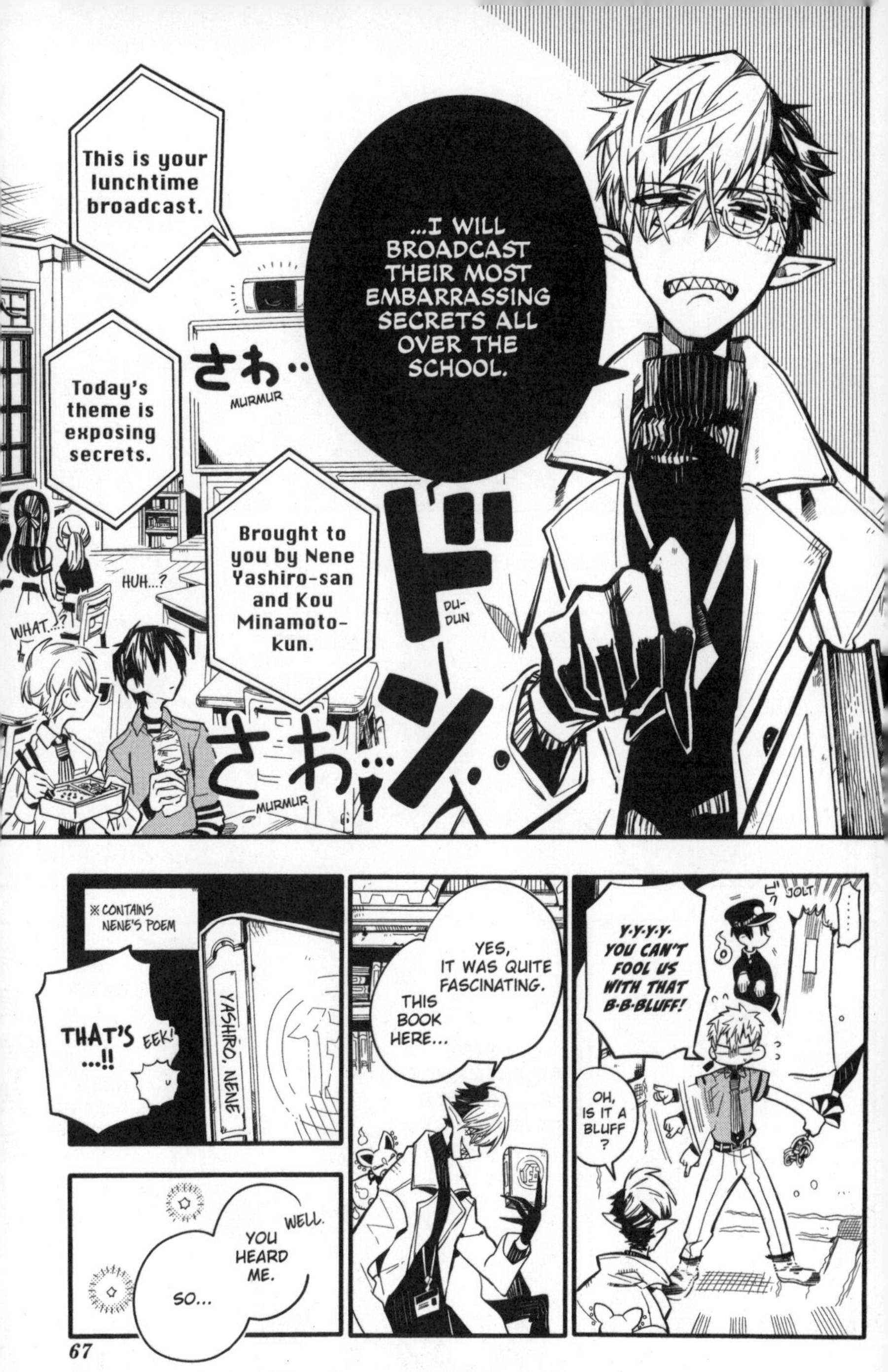
...I WILL BROADCAST THEIR MOST EMBARRASSING SECRETS ALL OVER THE SCHOOL.
ドーン
DU-DUN
This is your lunchtime broadcast.
さわ‥
MURMUR
Today's theme is exposing secrets.
Brought to you by Nene Yashiro-san and Kou Minamoto-kun.
HUH...?
WHAT...?
さわ‥
MURMUR
JOLT
......
Y-Y-Y-Y. YOU CAN'T FOOL US WITH THAT B-B-BLUFF!
OH, IS IT A BLUFF?
YES, IT WAS QUITE FASCINATING.
THIS BOOK HERE...
※CONTAINS NENE'S POEM
YASHIRO, NENE
THAT'S ...!!
EEK!
WELL.
YOU HEARD ME.
SO...

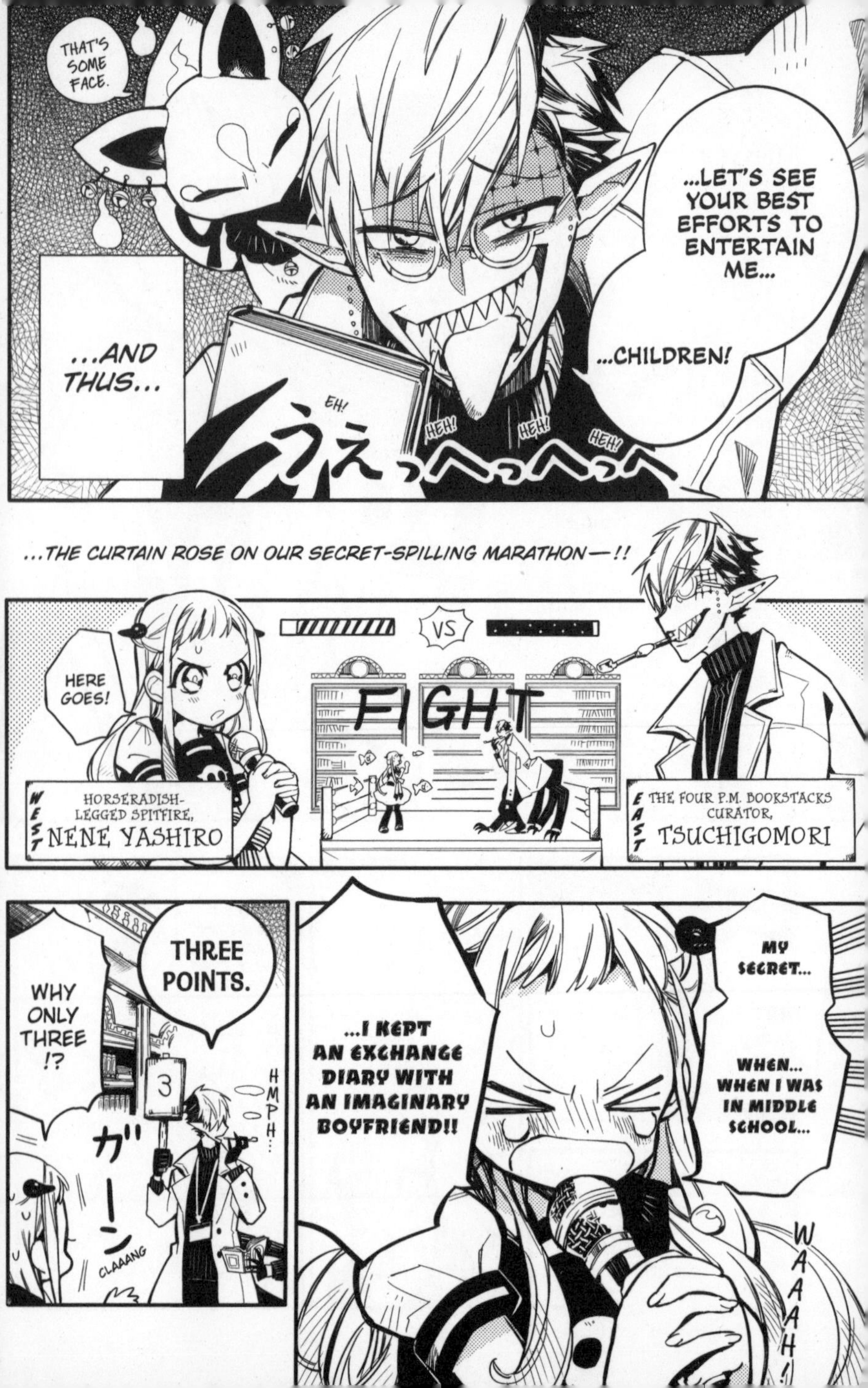
...LET'S SEE YOUR BEST EFFORTS TO ENTERTAIN ME...
...CHILDREN!
THAT'S SOME FACE.
...AND THUS...
うえっへっへっへ
EH!
HEH!
HEH!
HEH!
...THE CURTAIN ROSE ON OUR SECRET-SPILLING MARATHON—!!
EAST THE FOUR P.M. BOOKSTACKS CURATOR, TSUCHIGOMORI
FIGHT
VS
HERE GOES!
WEST HORSERADISH-LEGGED SPITFIRE, NENE YASHIRO
MY SECRET...
WHEN... WHEN I WAS IN MIDDLE SCHOOL...
...I KEPT AN EXCHANGE DIARY WITH AN IMAGINARY BOYFRIEND!!
WAAAAH!
THREE POINTS.
WHY ONLY THREE !?
HMPH...
3
ガーン
CLAAANG

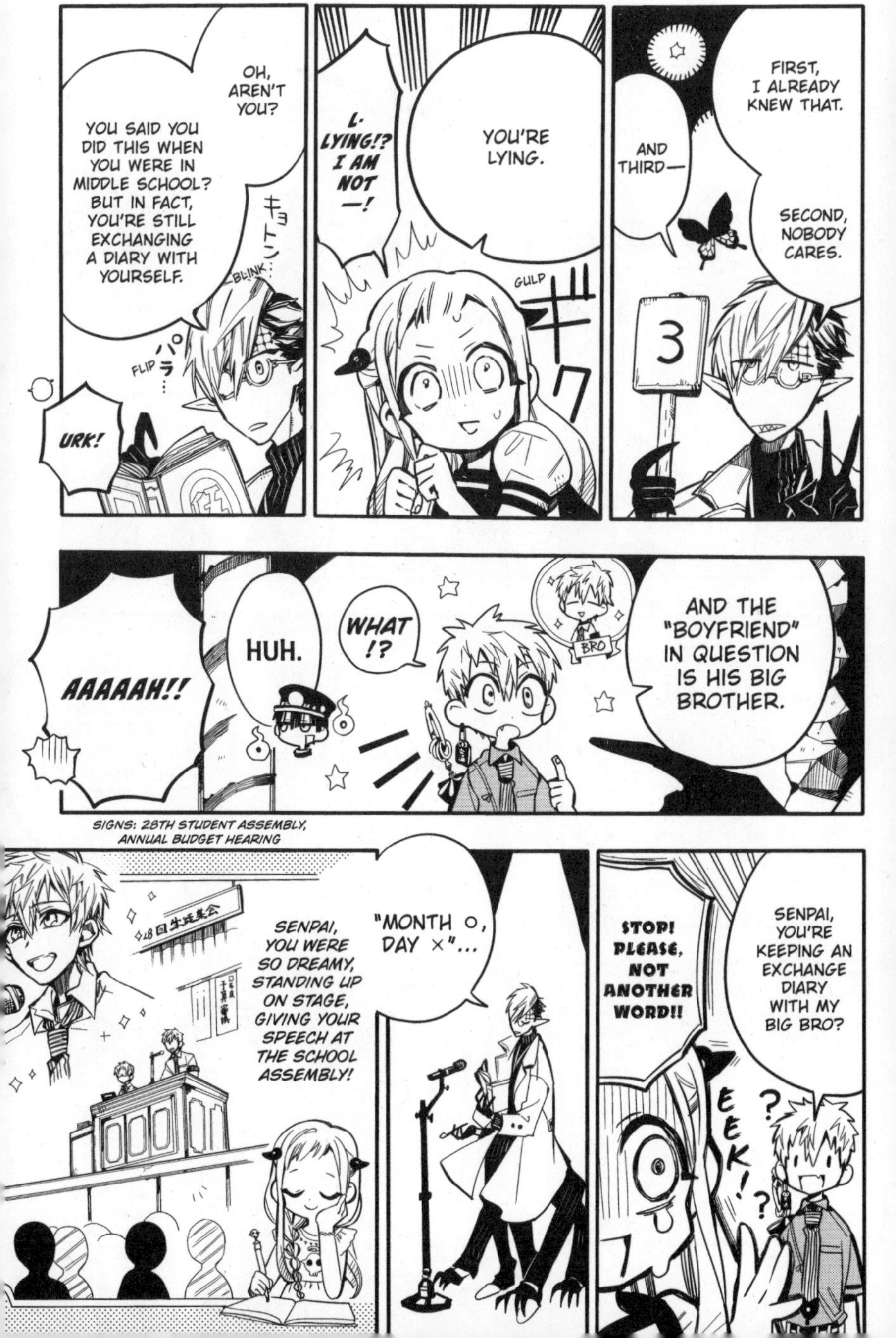

FIRST, I ALREADY KNEW THAT.
SECOND, NOBODY CARES.
AND THIRD—
3
YOU'RE LYING.
L-LYING!? I AM NOT—!
ギク
GULP
OH, AREN'T YOU?
YOU SAID YOU DID THIS WHEN YOU WERE IN MIDDLE SCHOOL? BUT IN FACT, YOU'RE STILL EXCHANGING A DIARY WITH YOURSELF.
キョトン…
BLINK
パラ…
FLIP
URK!
AND THE "BOYFRIEND" IN QUESTION IS HIS BIG BROTHER.
BRO
WHAT!?
HUH.
AAAAAH!!
SIGNS: 28TH STUDENT ASSEMBLY, ANNUAL BUDGET HEARING
SENPAI, YOU'RE KEEPING AN EXCHANGE DIARY WITH MY BIG BRO?
STOP! PLEASE, NOT ANOTHER WORD!!
EEK!
"MONTH ○, DAY ×"...
SENPAI, YOU WERE SO DREAMY, STANDING UP ON STAGE, GIVING YOUR SPEECH AT THE SCHOOL ASSEMBLY!

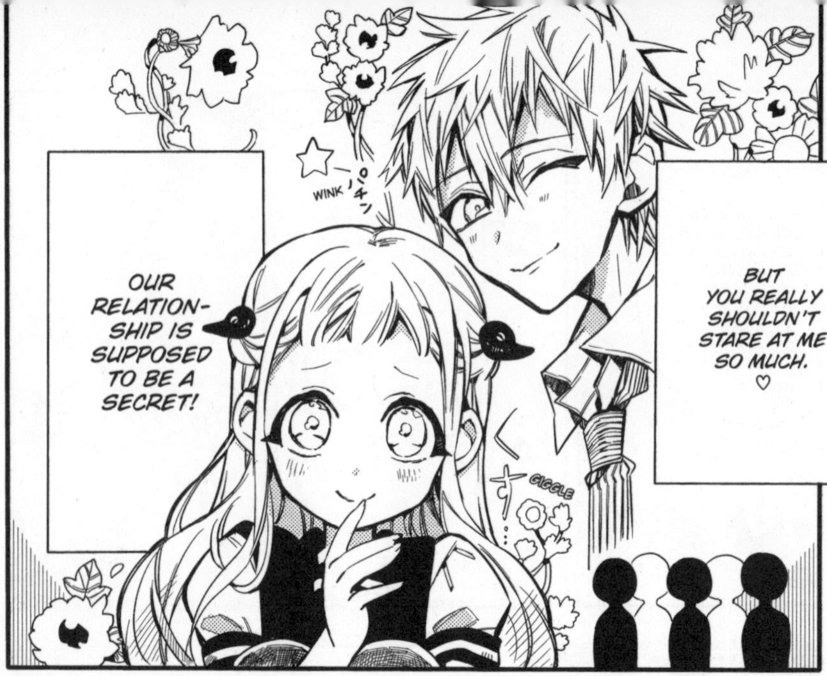
BUT YOU REALLY SHOULDN'T STARE AT ME SO MUCH. ♡
WINK
OUR RELATIONSHIP IS SUPPOSED TO BE A SECRET!
GIGGLE

DYING MESSAGE: PUBLIC DIARY READING

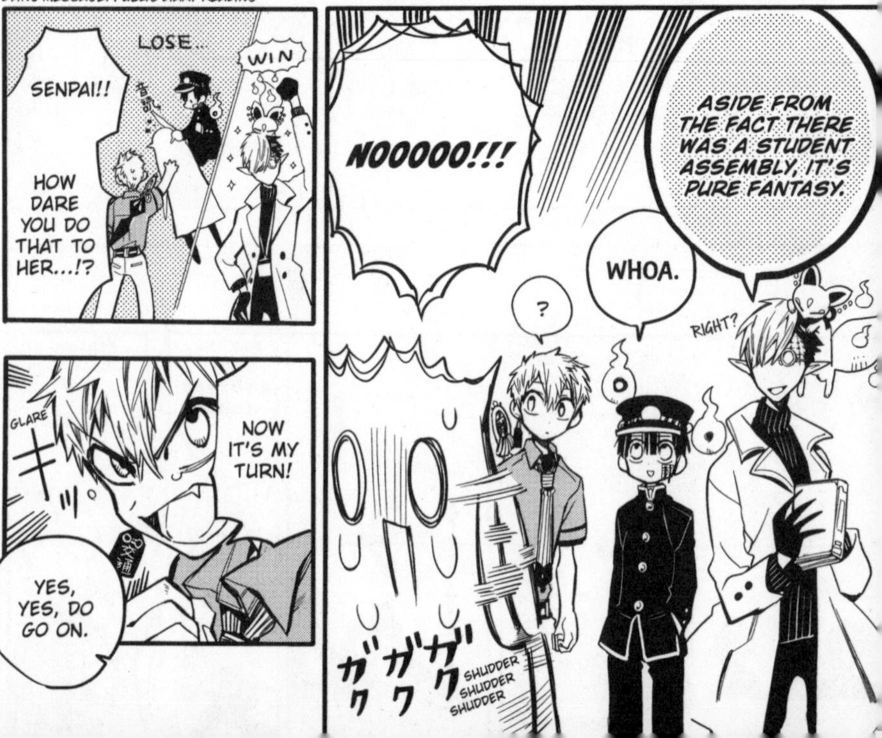
LOSE...
WIN
SENPAI!!
HOW DARE YOU DO THAT TO HER...!?
GLARE
NOW IT'S MY TURN!
YES, YES, DO GO ON.
ASIDE FROM THE FACT THERE WAS A STUDENT ASSEMBLY, IT'S PURE FANTASY.
NOOOOO!!!
RIGHT?
WHOA.
?
SHUDDER SHUDDER SHUDDER

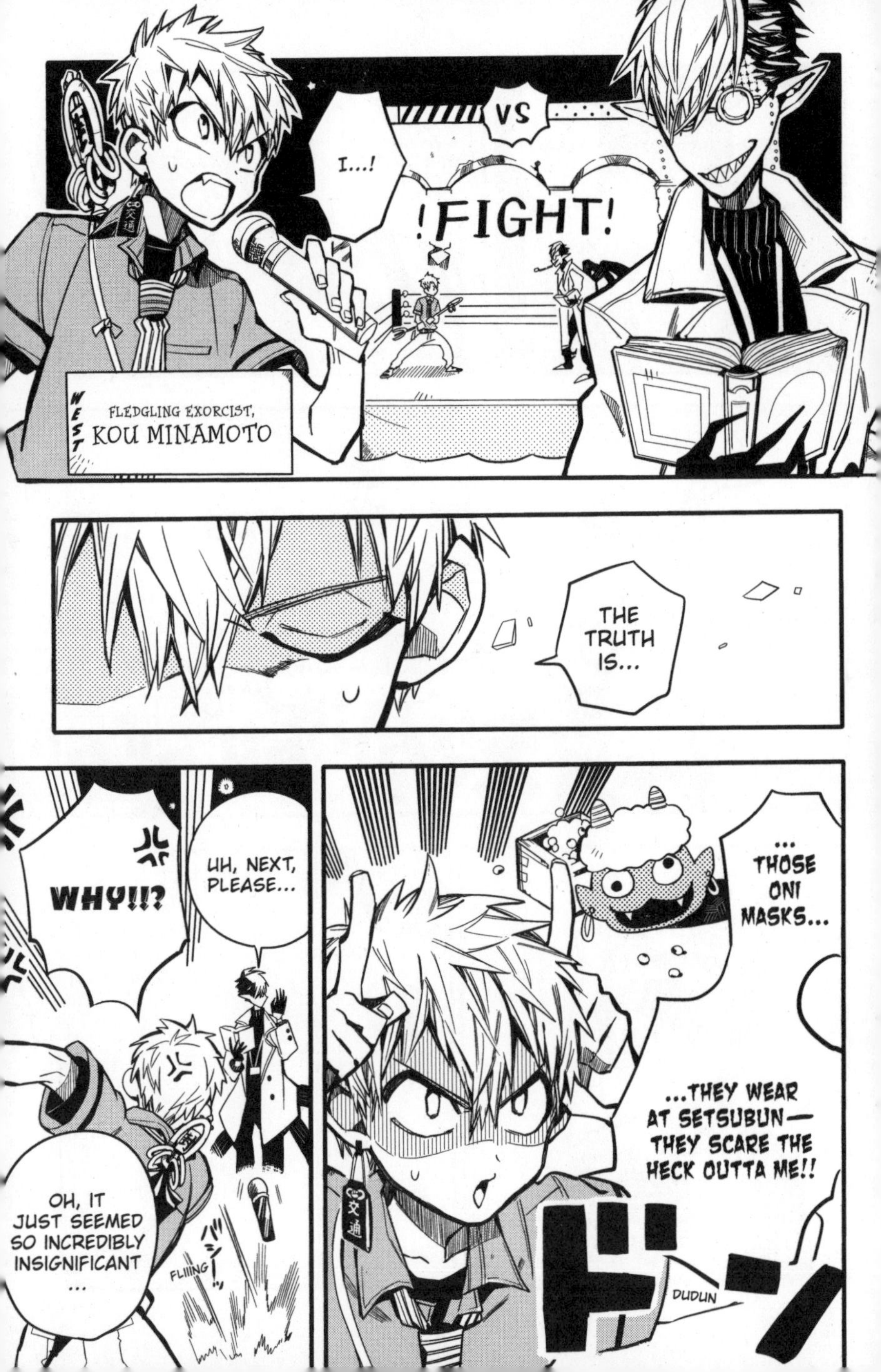
VS
I...!
!FIGHT!
WEST
FLEDGLING EXORCIST, KOU MINAMOTO
THE TRUTH IS...
... THOSE ONI MASKS...
...THEY WEAR AT SETSUBUN—THEY SCARE THE HECK OUTTA ME!!
DUDUN
UH, NEXT, PLEASE...
WHY!!?
OH, IT JUST SEEMED SO INCREDIBLY INSIGNIFICANT ...
FLIIING

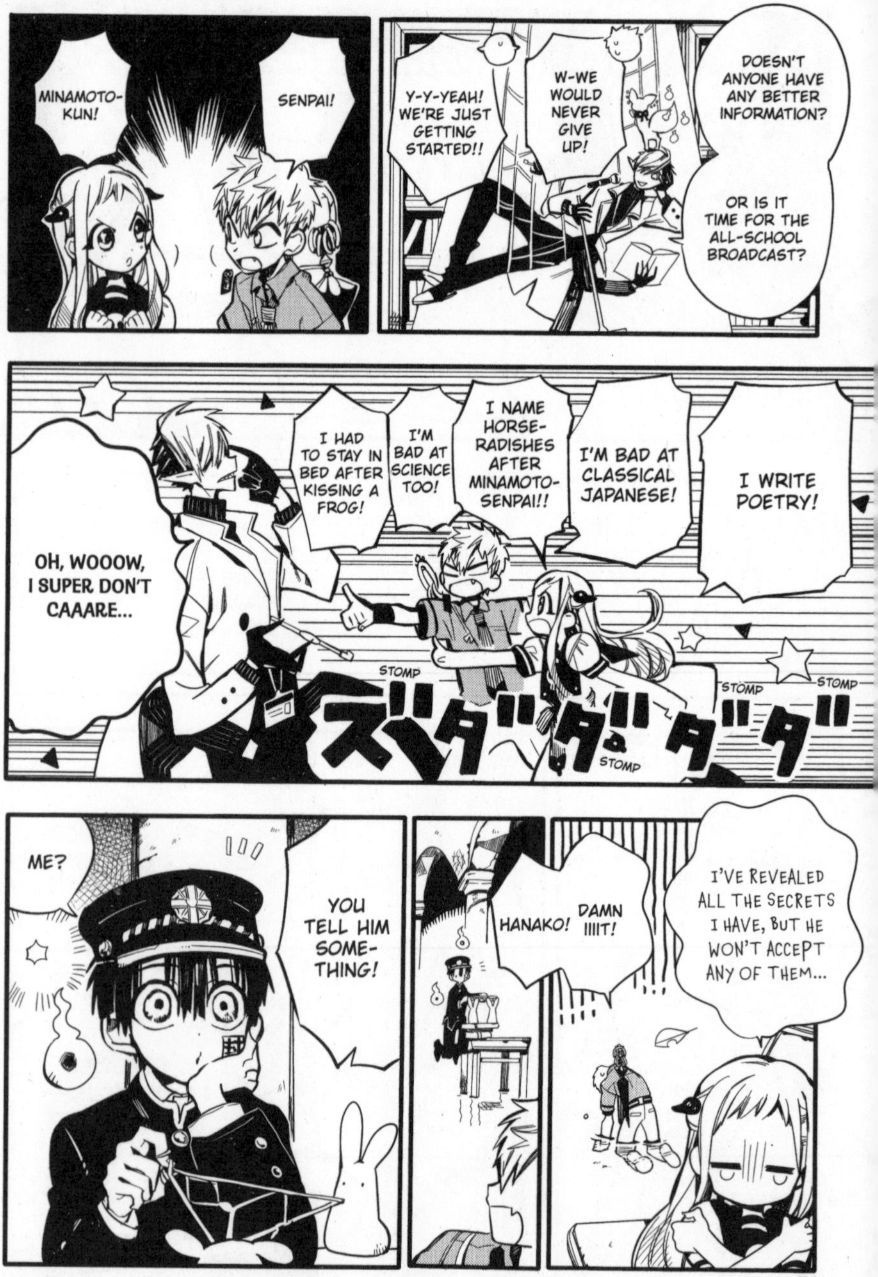
DOESN'T ANYONE HAVE ANY BETTER INFORMATION?
OR IS IT TIME FOR THE ALL-SCHOOL BROADCAST?
W-WE WOULD NEVER GIVE UP!
Y-Y-YEAH! WE'RE JUST GETTING STARTED!!
SENPAI!
MINAMOTO-KUN!
I WRITE POETRY!
I'M BAD AT CLASSICAL JAPANESE!
I NAME HORSE-RADISHES AFTER MINAMOTO-SENPAI!!
I'M BAD AT SCIENCE TOO!
I HAD TO STAY IN BED AFTER KISSING A FROG!
OH, WOOOW, I SUPER DON'T CAAARE...
STOMP
STOMP
STOMP
STOMP
ズダダ!!ダダ
I'VE REVEALED ALL THE SECRETS I HAVE, BUT HE WON'T ACCEPT ANY OF THEM...
DAMN IIIIT!
HANAKO!
YOU TELL HIM SOME-THING!
ME?

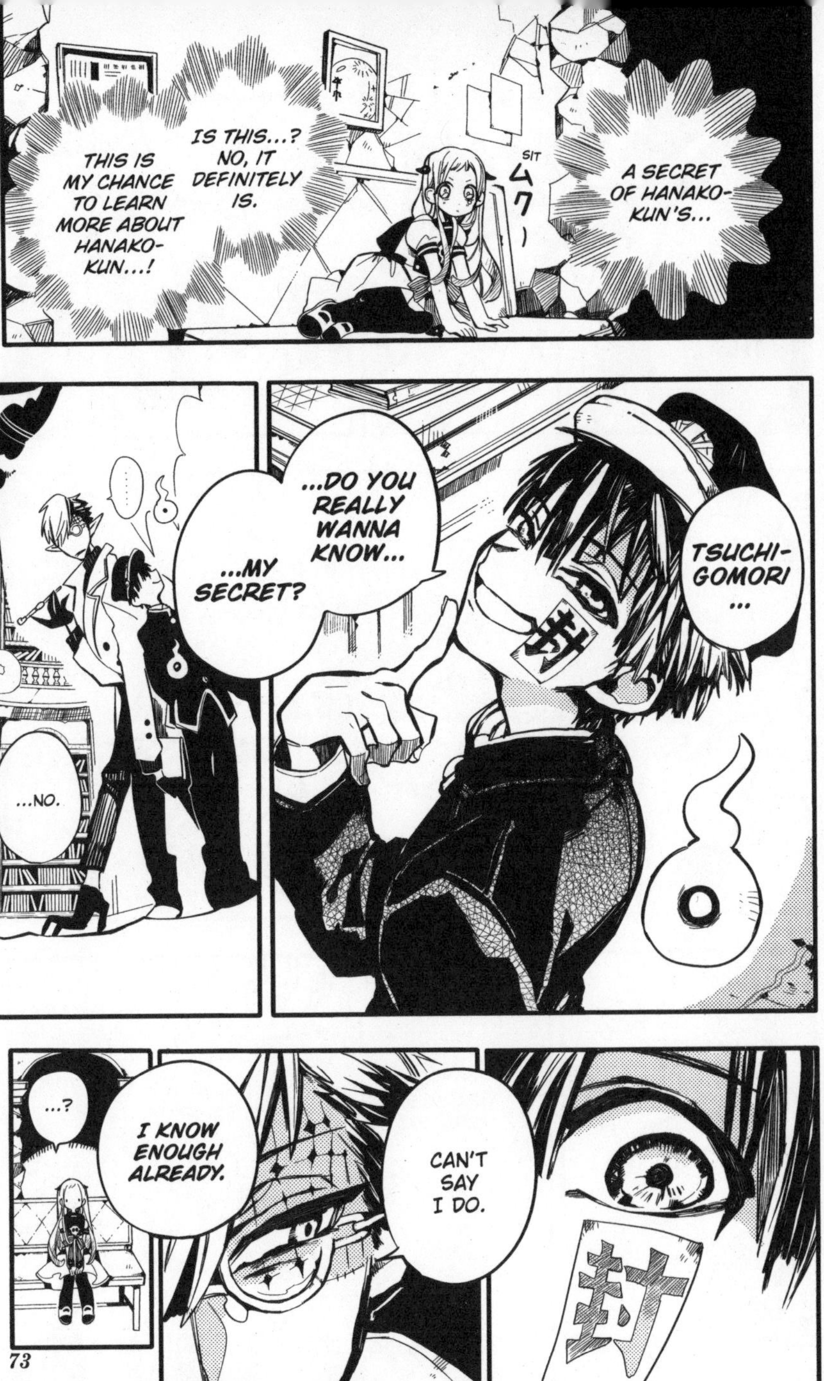
A SECRET OF HANAKO-KUN'S...
SIT
IS THIS...? NO, IT DEFINITELY IS.
THIS IS MY CHANCE TO LEARN MORE ABOUT HANAKO-KUN...!
TSUCHIGOMORI...
...DO YOU REALLY WANNA KNOW...
...MY SECRET?
......
...NO.
CAN'T SAY I DO.
I KNOW ENOUGH ALREADY.
...?

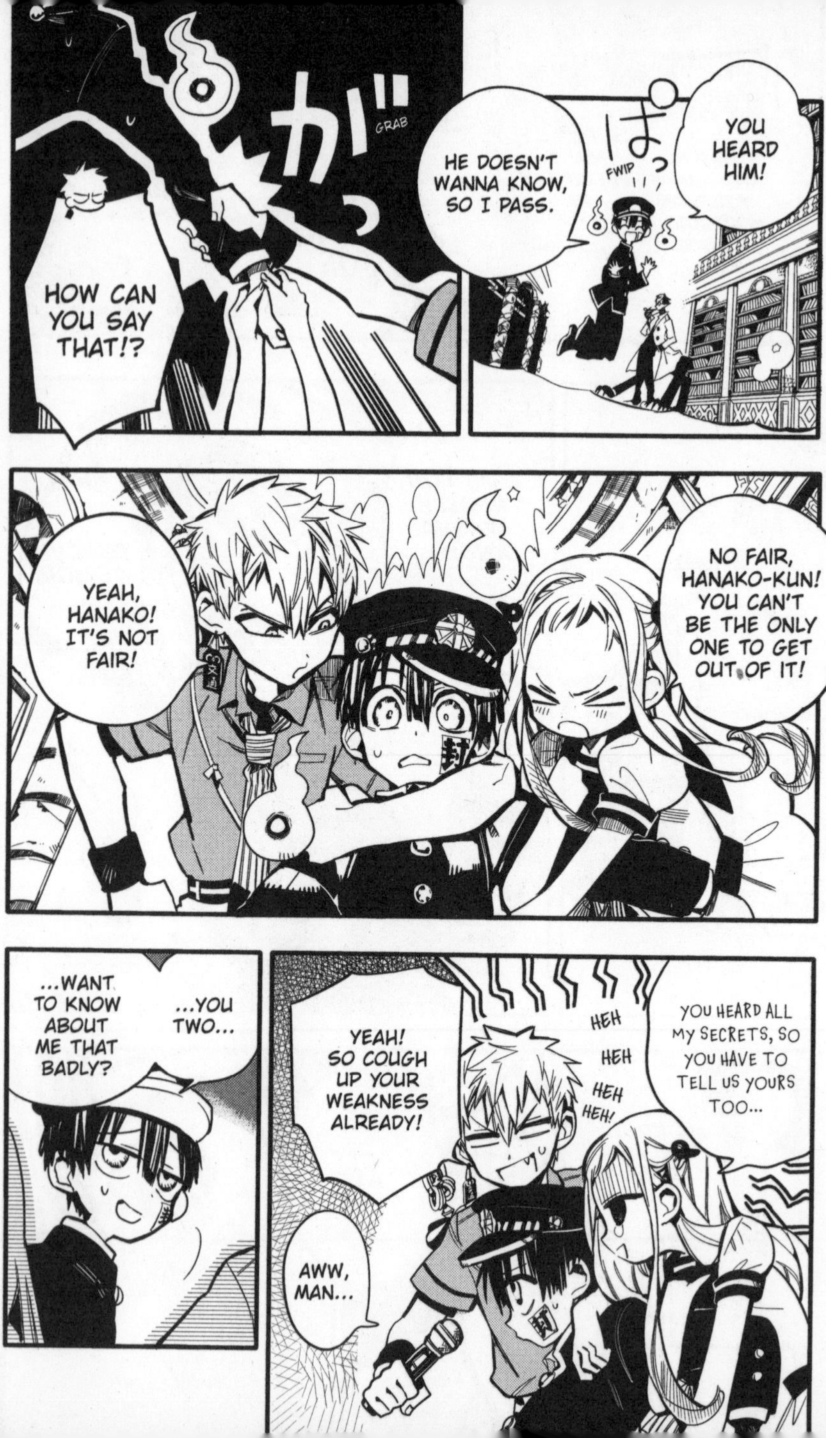
ぱっ
FWIP
YOU HEARD HIM!
HE DOESN'T WANNA KNOW, SO I PASS.
かっ
GRAB
HOW CAN YOU SAY THAT!?
NO FAIR, HANAKO-KUN! YOU CAN'T BE THE ONLY ONE TO GET OUT OF IT!
YEAH, HANAKO! IT'S NOT FAIR!
YOU HEARD ALL MY SECRETS, SO YOU HAVE TO TELL US YOURS TOO...
HEH HEH HEH HEH!
YEAH! SO COUGH UP YOUR WEAKNESS ALREADY!
AWW, MAN...
...YOU TWO...
...WANT TO KNOW ABOUT ME THAT BADLY?

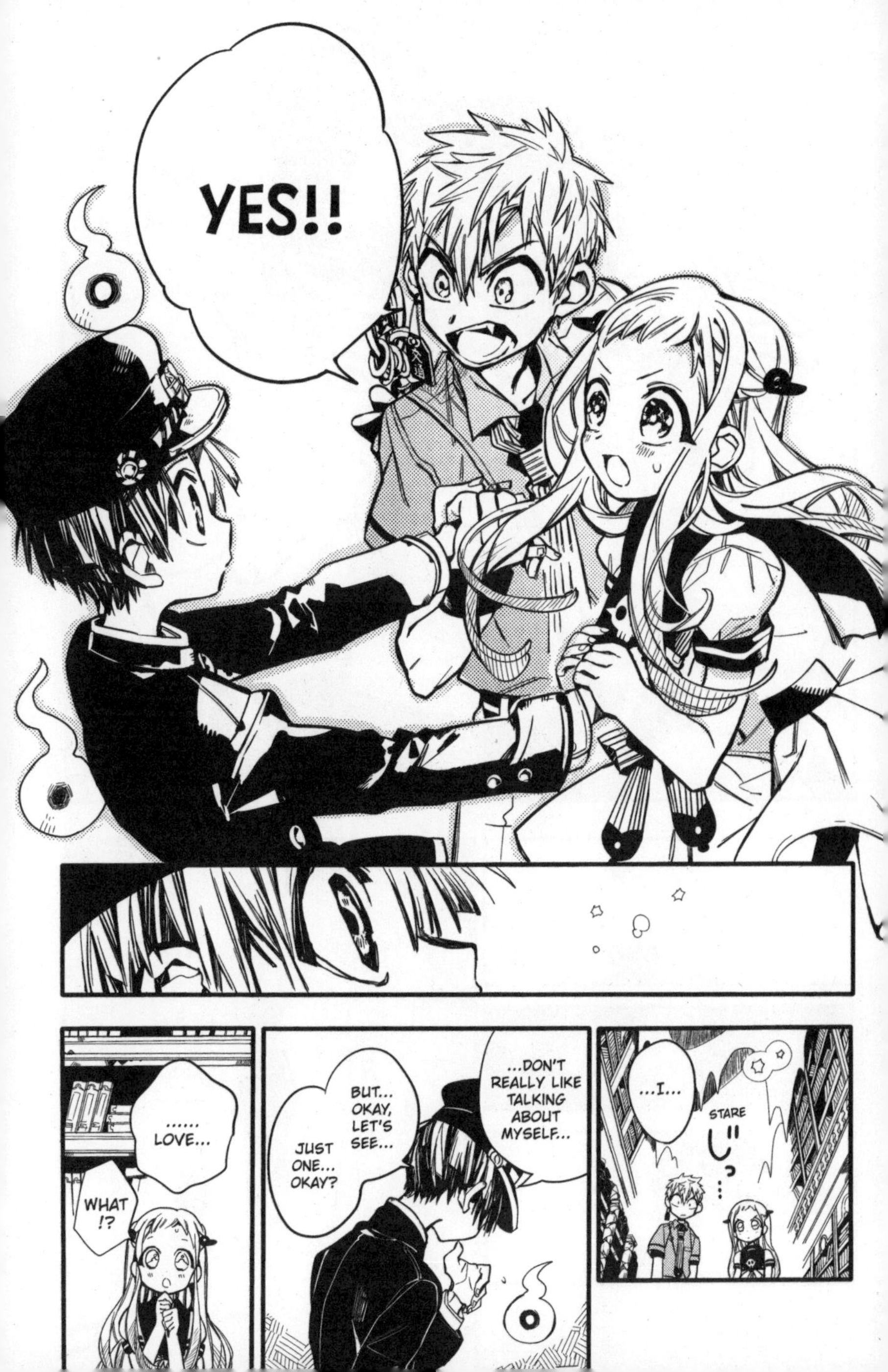
YES!!
...I...
STARE
...DON'T REALLY LIKE TALKING ABOUT MYSELF...
BUT... OKAY, LET'S SEE...
JUST ONE... OKAY?
...... LOVE...
WHAT !?

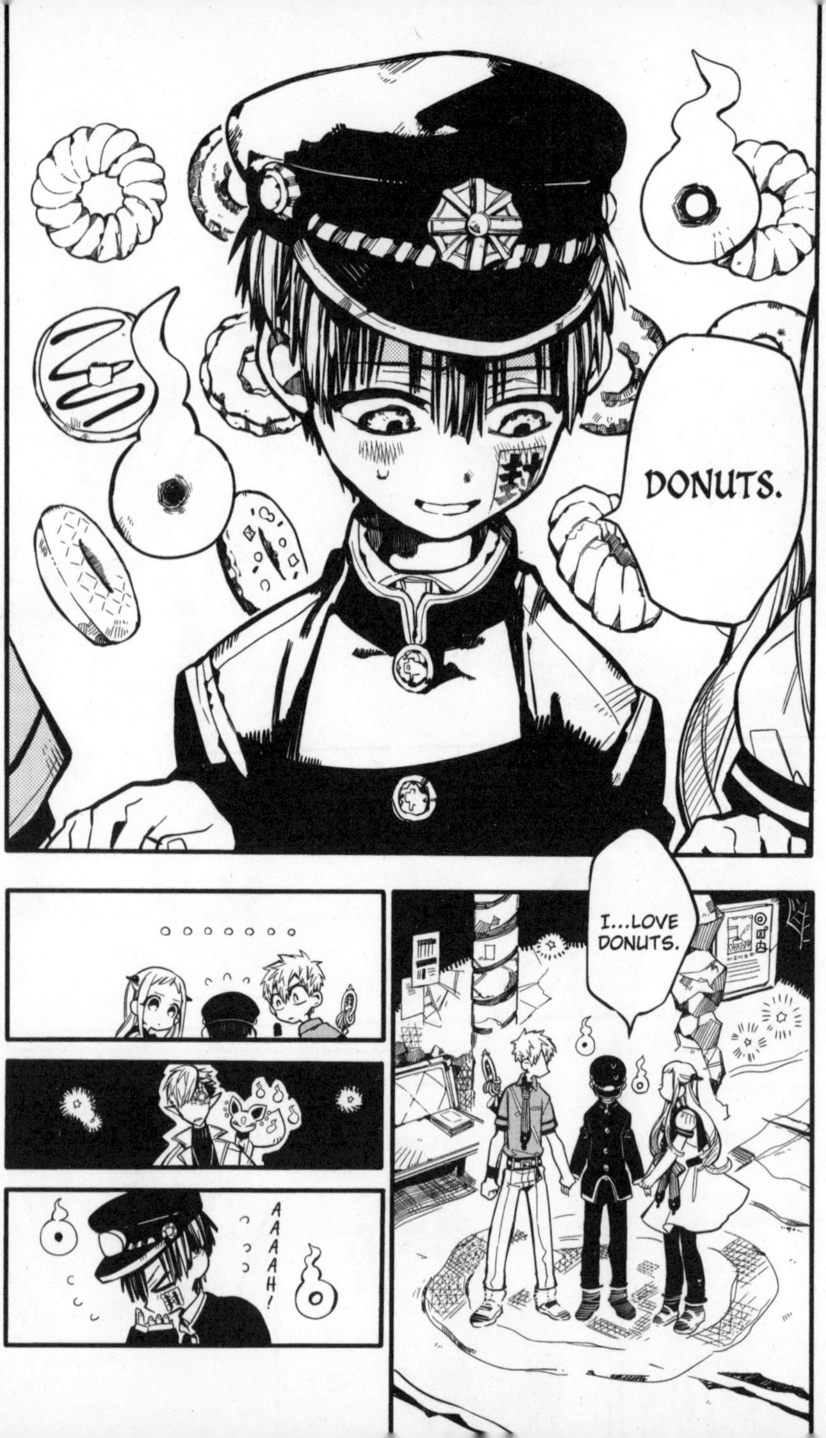
DONUTS.
I...LOVE DONUTS.
AAAAAH!

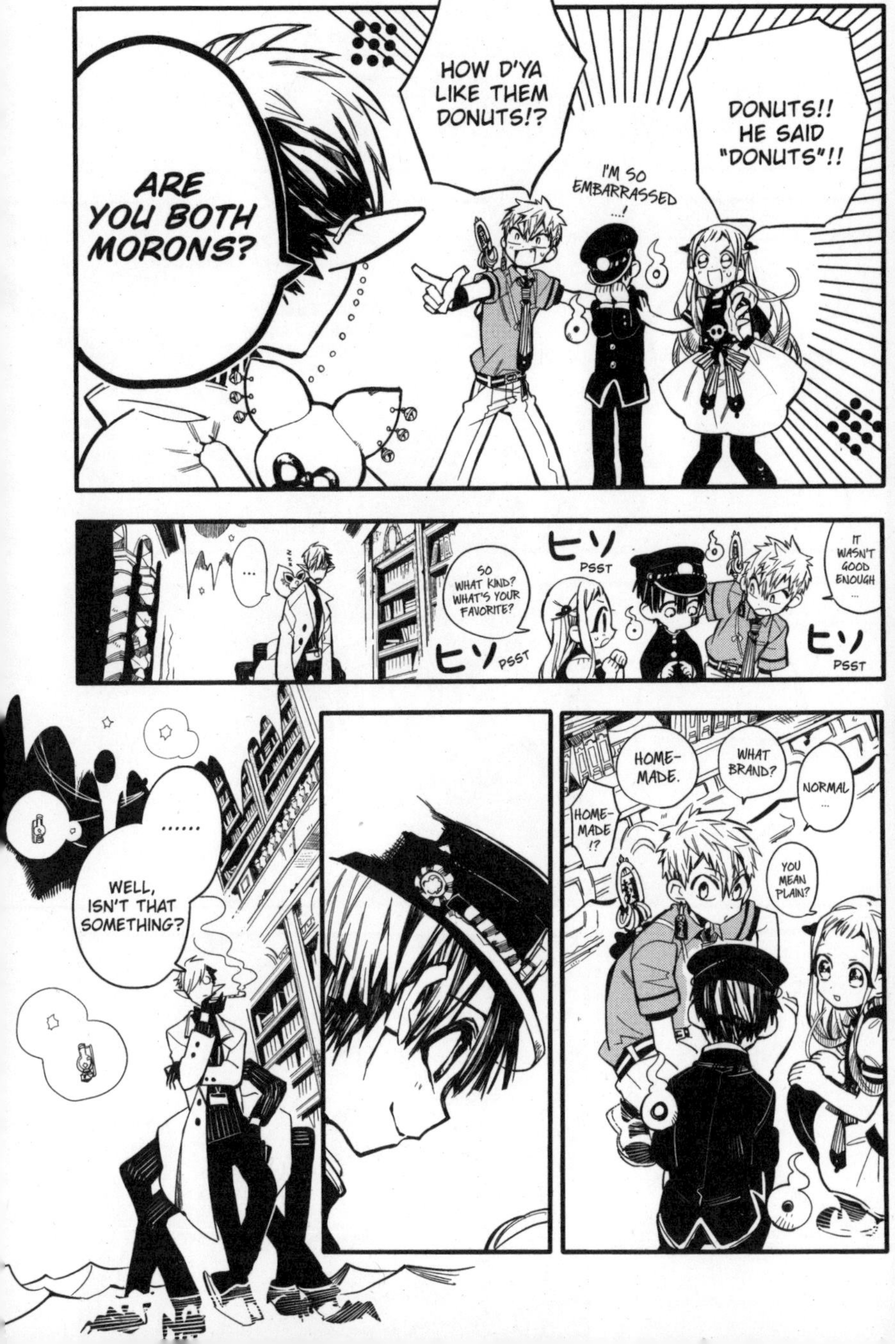
DONUTS!! HE SAID "DONUTS"!!
I'M SO EMBARRASSED ...!
HOW D'YA LIKE THEM DONUTS!?
ARE YOU BOTH MORONS?
IT WASN'T GOOD ENOUGH ...
ヒソ PSST
ヒソ PSST
SO WHAT KIND? WHAT'S YOUR FAVORITE?
ヒソ PSST
...
WHAT BRAND?
NORMAL ...
YOU MEAN PLAIN?
HOME-MADE.
HOME-MADE!?
......
WELL, ISN'T THAT SOMETHING?

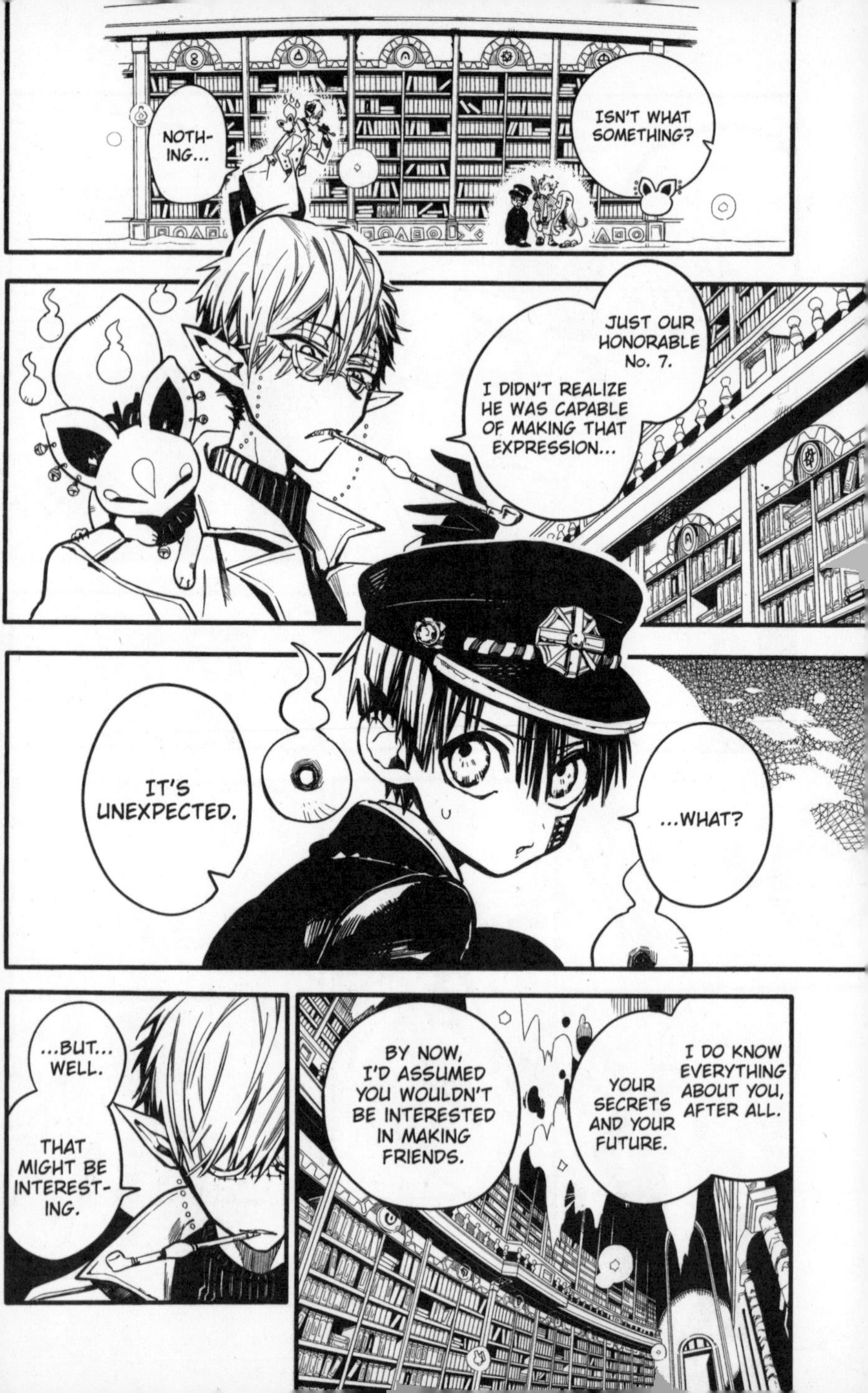
ISN'T WHAT SOMETHING?
NOTH-ING...
JUST OUR HONORABLE No. 7.
I DIDN'T REALIZE HE WAS CAPABLE OF MAKING THAT EXPRESSION...
...WHAT?
IT'S UNEXPECTED.
I DO KNOW EVERYTHING ABOUT YOU, AFTER ALL.
YOUR SECRETS AND YOUR FUTURE.
BY NOW, I'D ASSUMED YOU WOULDN'T BE INTERESTED IN MAKING FRIENDS.
...BUT... WELL.
THAT MIGHT BE INTEREST-ING.

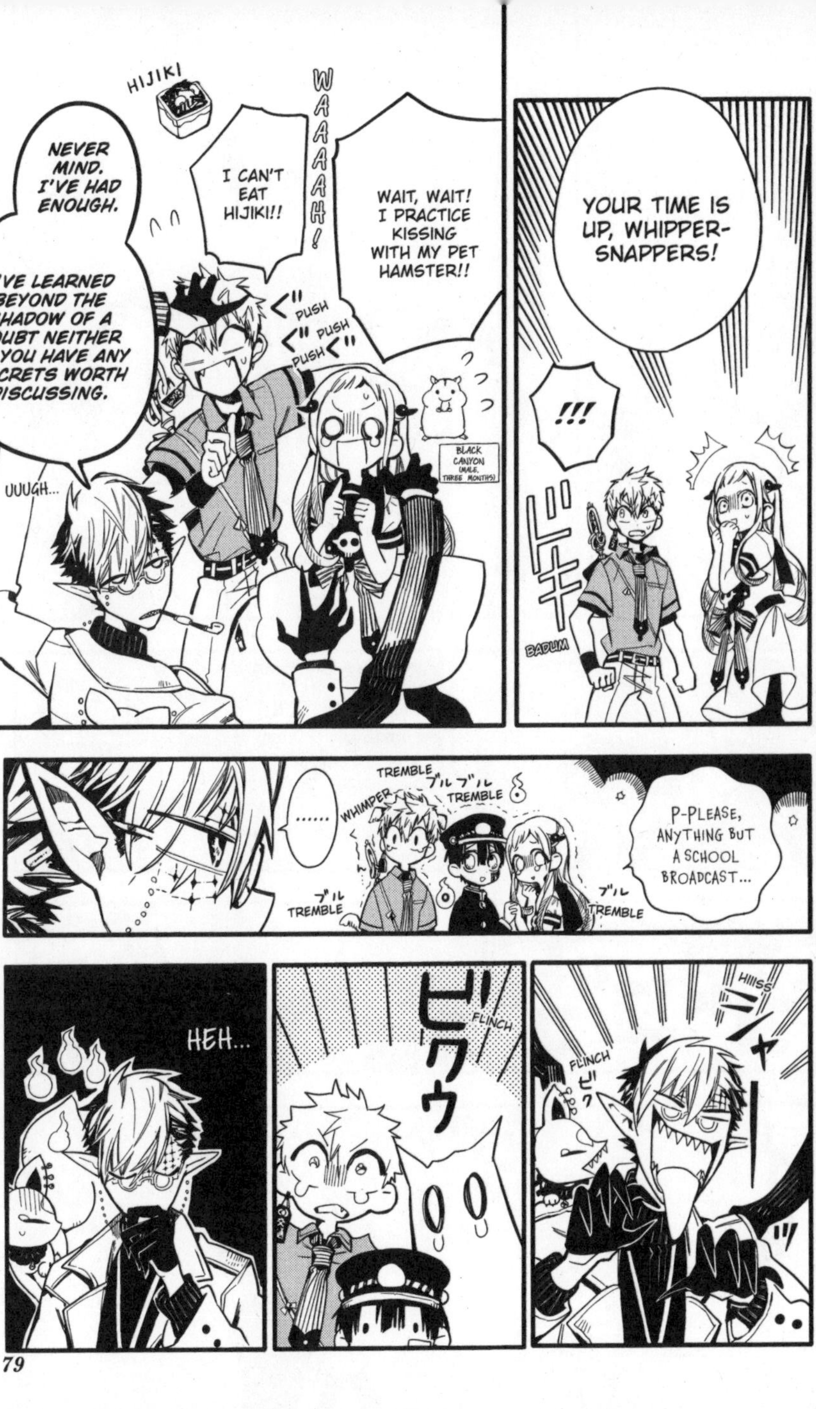
YOUR TIME IS UP, WHIPPER-SNAPPERS!
!!!
BADUM
WAAAAAAH!
WAIT, WAIT! I PRACTICE KISSING WITH MY PET HAMSTER!!
I CAN'T EAT HIJIKI!!
HIJIKI
PUSH
PUSH
PUSH
NEVER MIND. I'VE HAD ENOUGH.
I'VE LEARNED BEYOND THE SHADOW OF A DOUBT NEITHER OF YOU HAVE ANY SECRETS WORTH DISCUSSING.
BLACK CANYON (MALE, THREE MONTHS)
UUUGH...
P-PLEASE, ANYTHING BUT A SCHOOL BROADCAST...
TREMBLE
TREMBLE
WHIMPER
TREMBLE
TREMBLE
......
HIIISS
FLINCH
FLINCH
HEH...

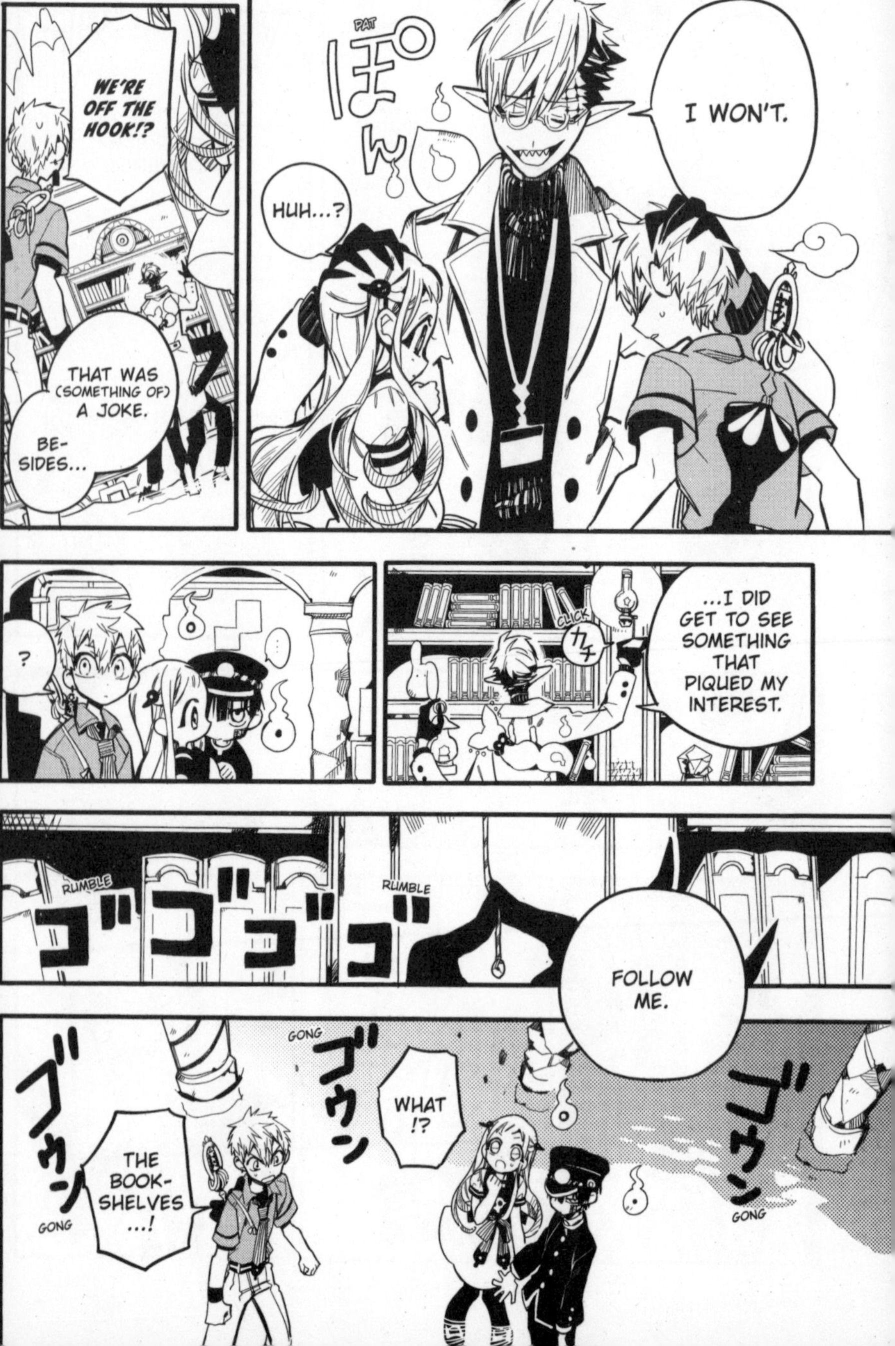
I WON'T.
PAT
ぽん
HUH...?
WE'RE OFF THE HOOK!?
THAT WAS (SOMETHING OF) A JOKE.
BE-SIDES...
...I DID GET TO SEE SOMETHING THAT PIQUED MY INTEREST.
CLICK
カチ
...
?
FOLLOW ME.
RUMBLE
ゴゴ
RUMBLE
ゴゴ
GONG
ゴウン
WHAT !?
GONG
ゴウン
THE BOOK-SHELVES ...!
GONG
ゴウン

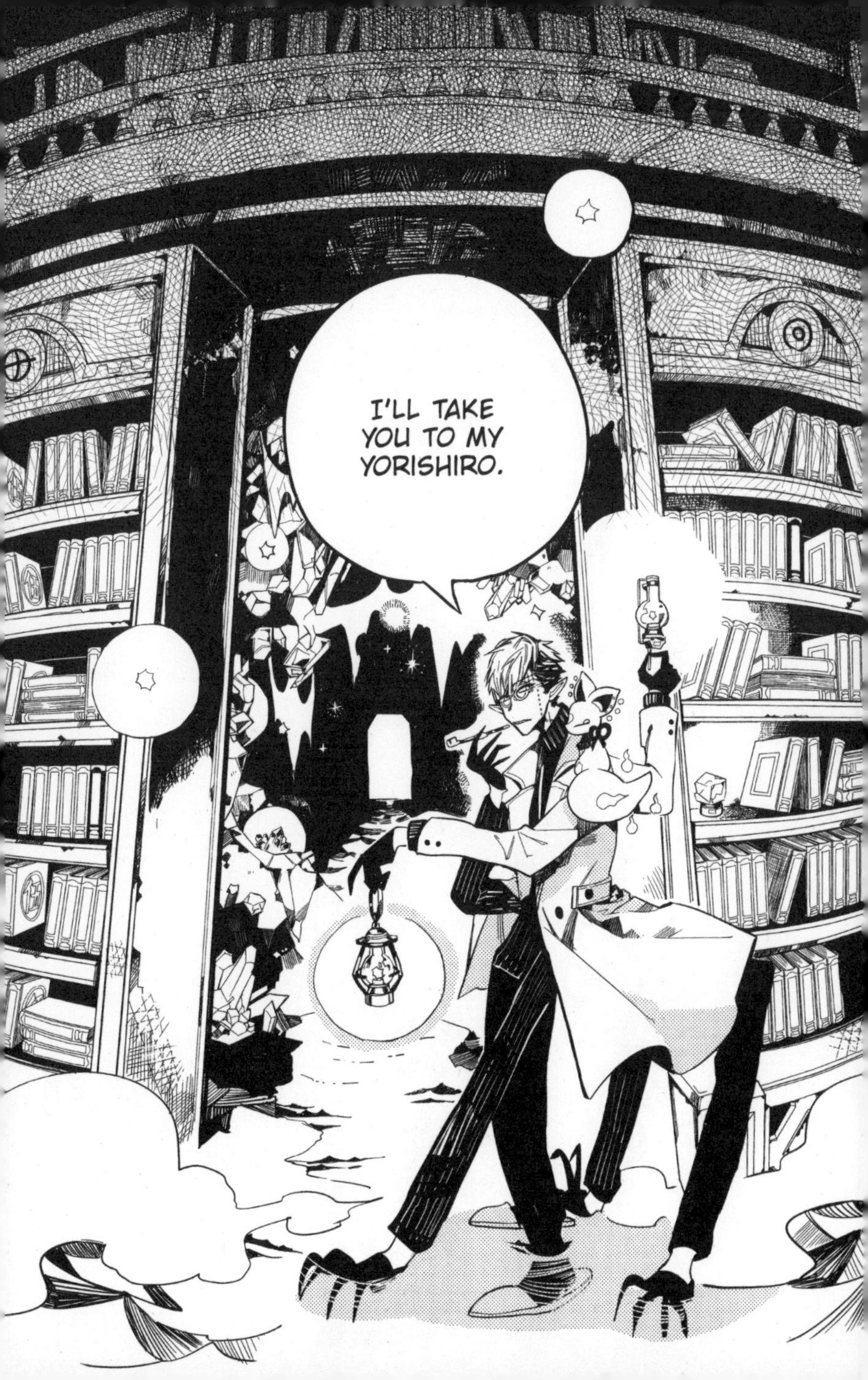
I'LL TAKE YOU TO MY YORISHIRO.

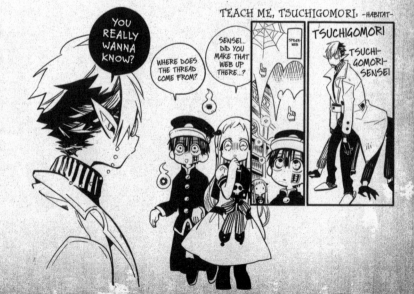

TEACH ME, TSUCHIGOMORI: -HABITAT-

TSUCHIGOMORI
TSUCHI-GOMORI-SENSEI
SPIDER-WEB
SENSEI... DID YOU MAKE THAT WEB UP THERE...?
WHERE DOES THE THREAD COME FROM?
YOU REALLY WANNA KNOW?

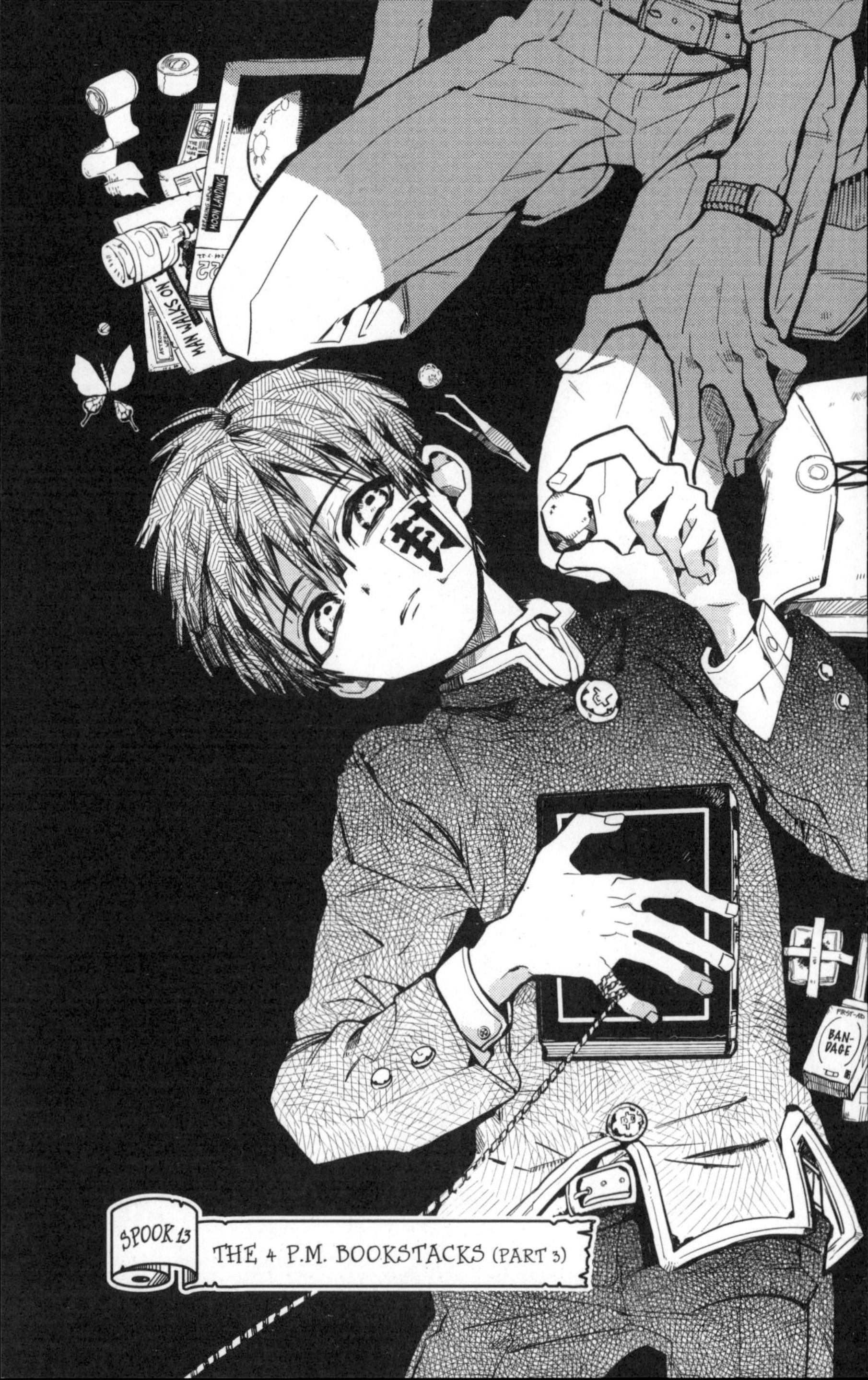
MAN WALKS ON
MOON LANDING
BAN-DAGE
SPOOK 13
THE 4 P.M. BOOKSTACKS (PART 3)

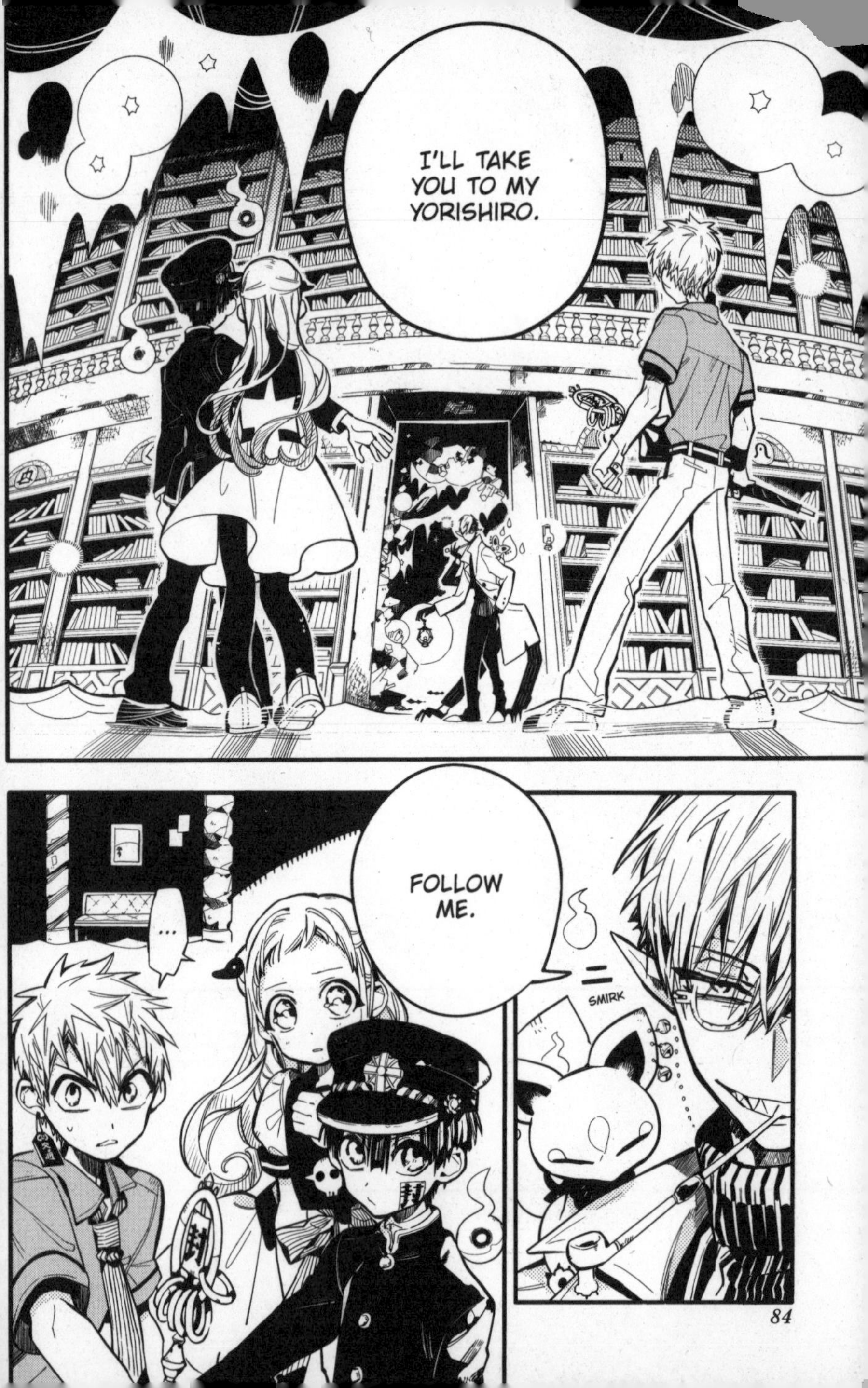
I'LL TAKE YOU TO MY YORISHIRO.
FOLLOW ME.
SMIRK
...

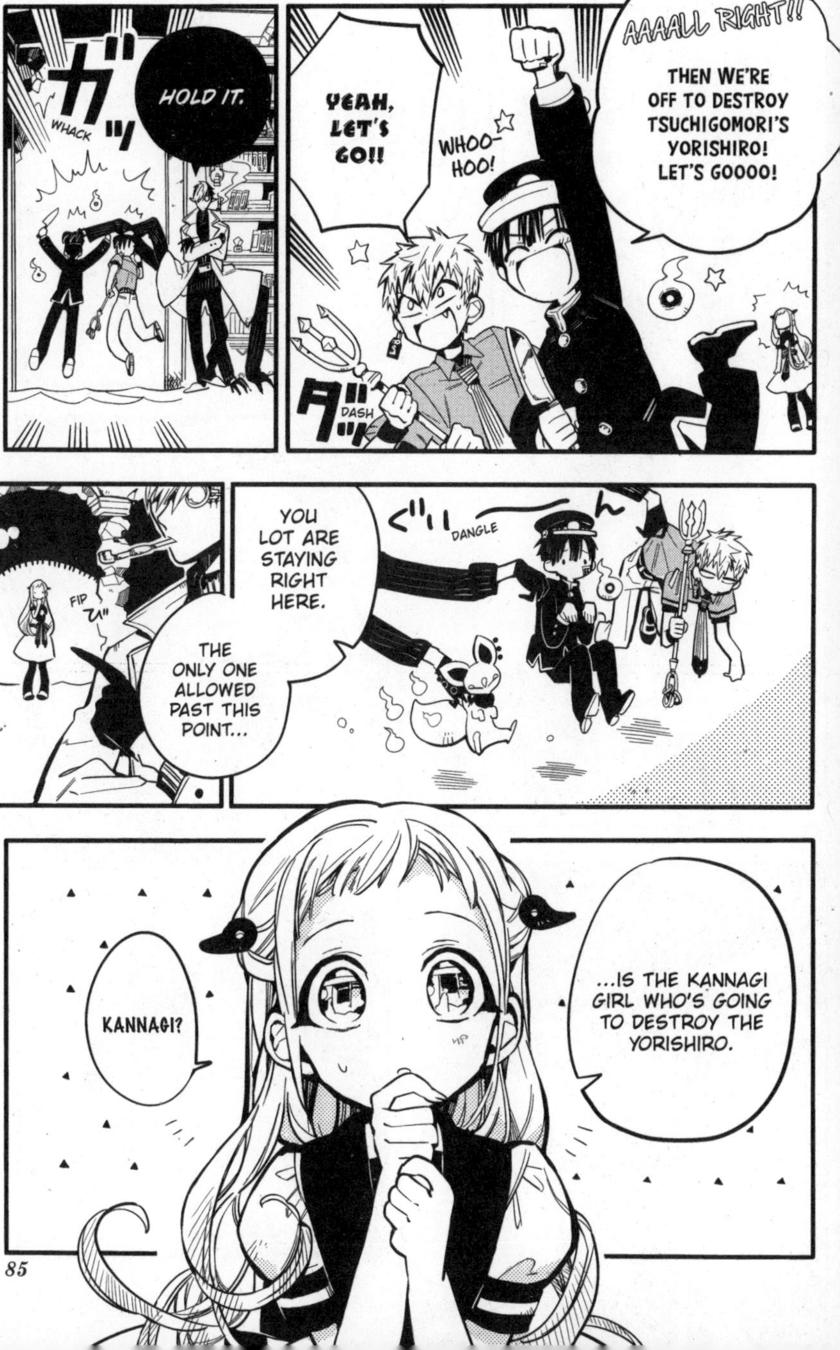
AAAALL RIGHT!!
THEN WE'RE OFF TO DESTROY TSUCHIGOMORI'S YORISHIRO! LET'S GOOOO!
WHOO-HOO!
YEAH, LET'S GO!!
DASH
HOLD IT.
WHACK
DANGLE
YOU LOT ARE STAYING RIGHT HERE.
THE ONLY ONE ALLOWED PAST THIS POINT...
FIP
...IS THE KANNAGI GIRL WHO'S GOING TO DESTROY THE YORISHIRO.
KANNAGI?

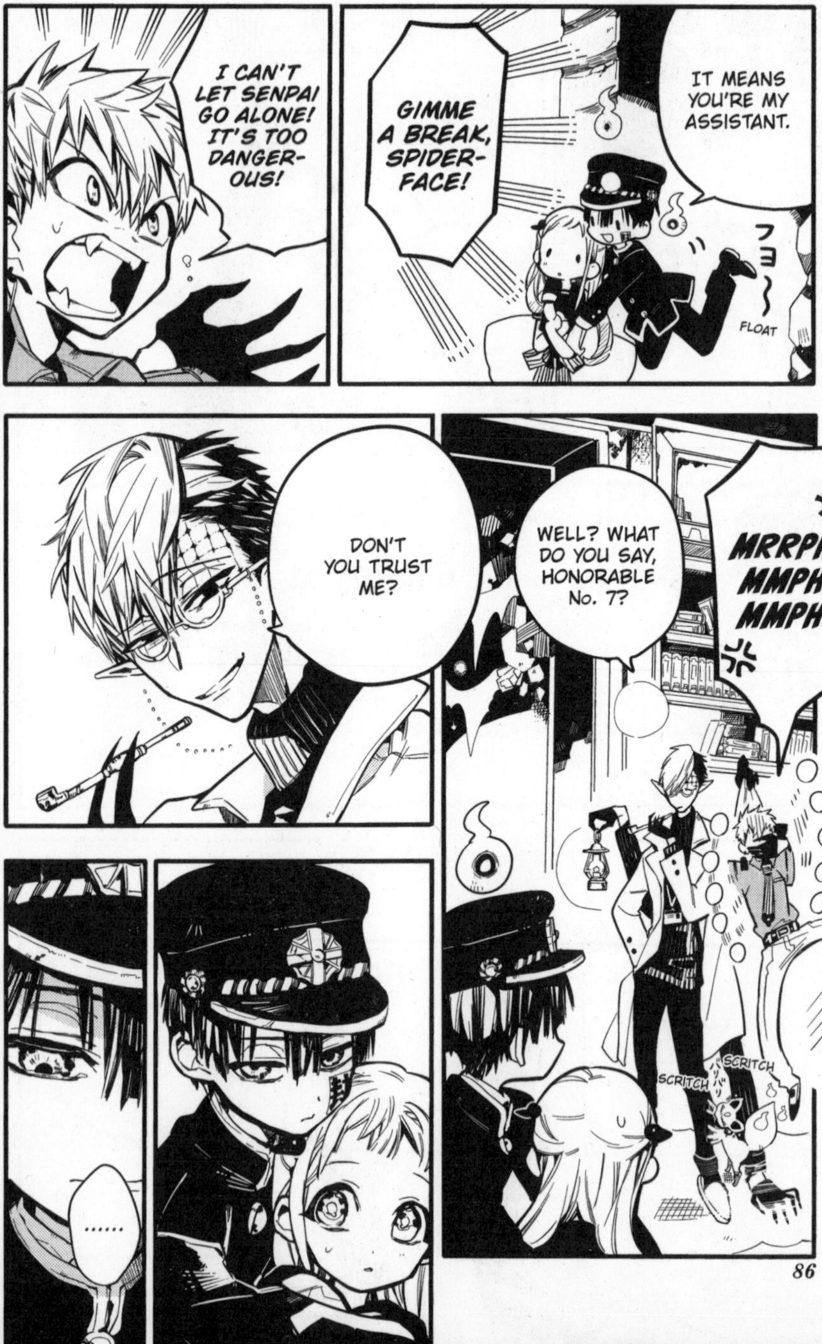
IT MEANS YOU'RE MY ASSISTANT.
フヨ~
FLOAT
GIMME A BREAK, SPIDER-FACE!
I CAN'T LET SENPAI GO ALONE! IT'S TOO DANGER-OUS!
MRRPH, MMPH, MMPH!
WELL? WHAT DO YOU SAY, HONORABLE No. 7?
SCRITCH
SCRITCH
DON'T YOU TRUST ME?
......

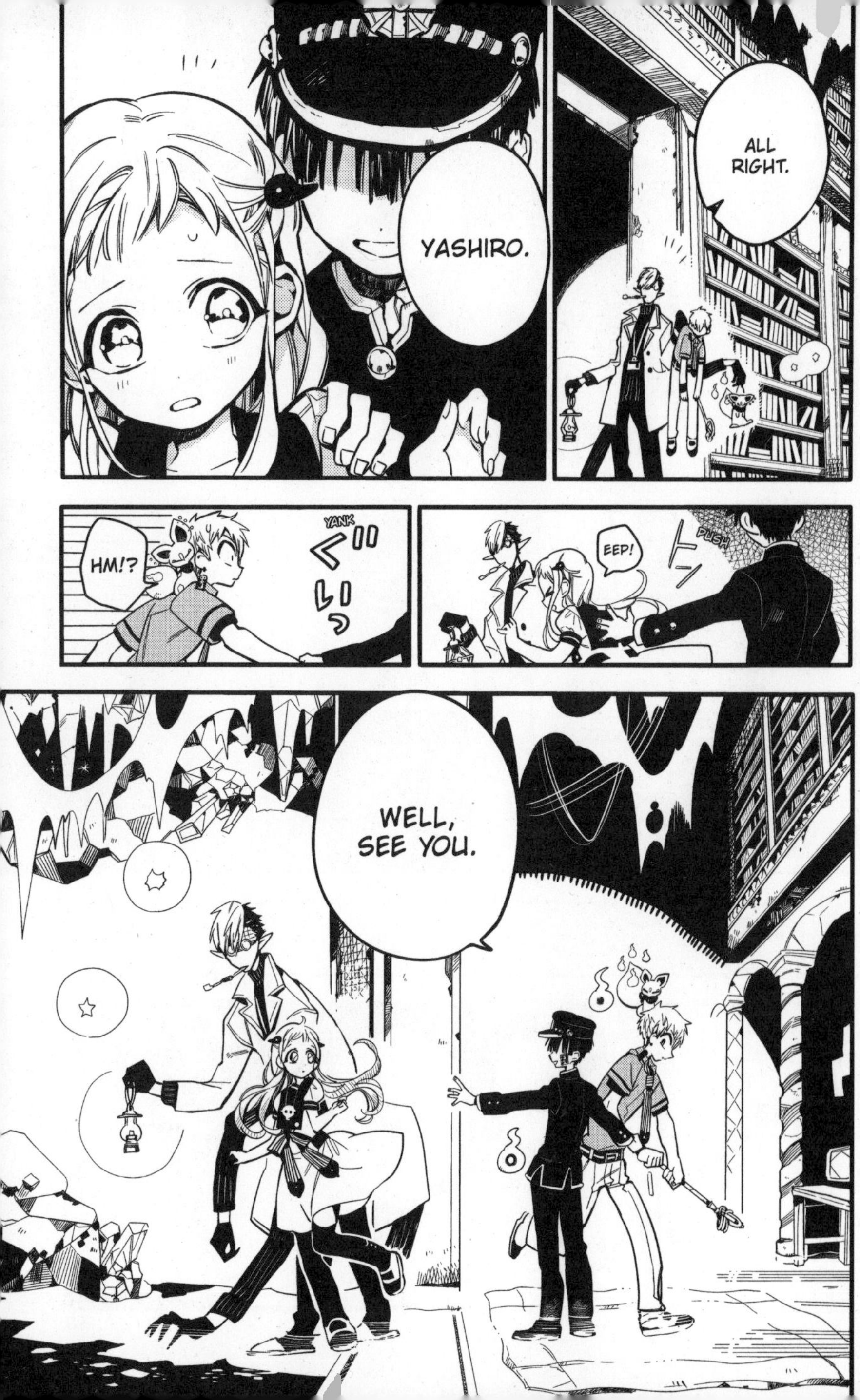
ALL RIGHT.
YASHIRO.
PUSH
EEP!
YANK
HM!?
WELL, SEE YOU.

TAKE GOOD CARE OF MY ASSISTANT...

...TSUCHI-GOMORI-SENSEI.

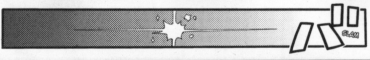

SLAM

THIS WAY.

I-I'M REALLY GOING ALONE...?

...

88

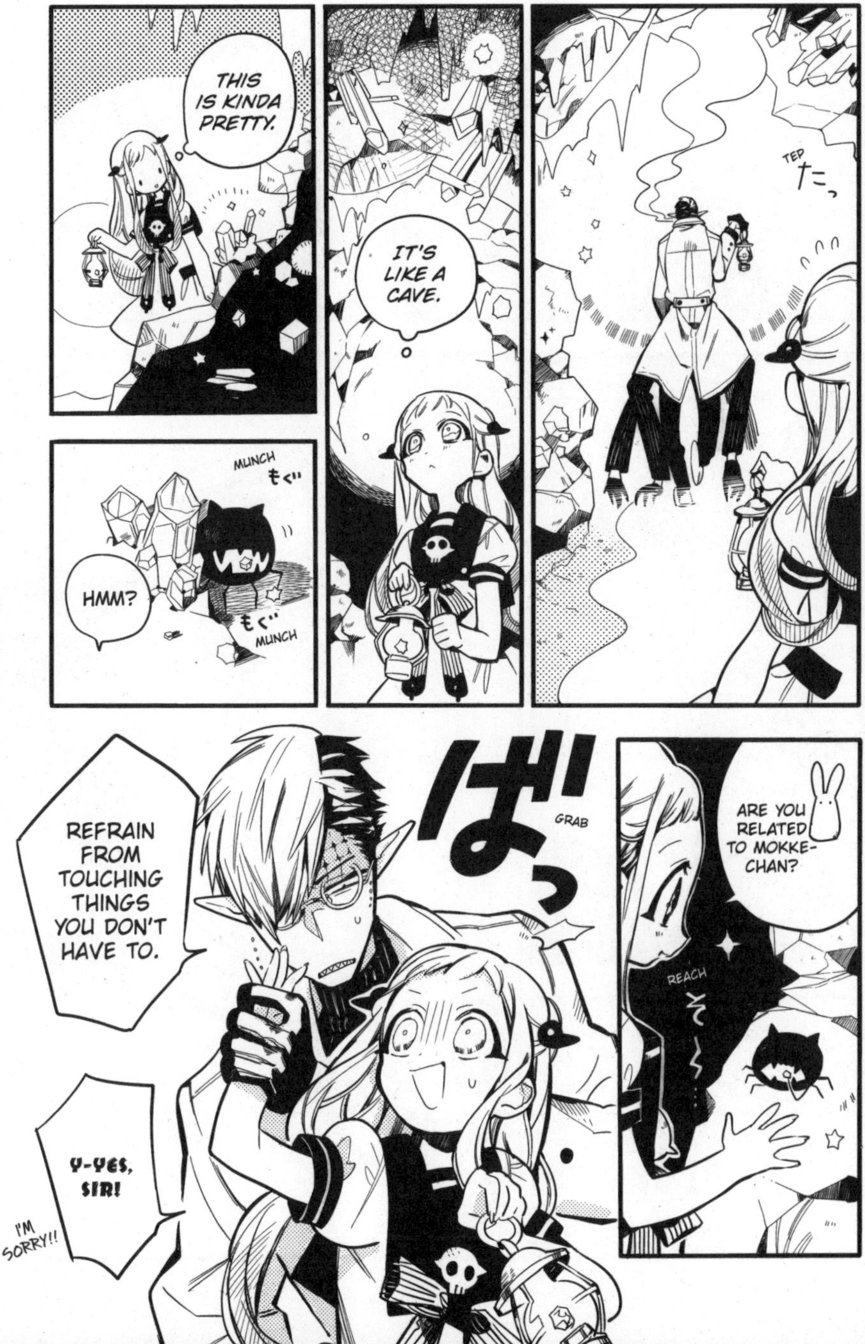
TEP
たっ
IT'S LIKE A CAVE.
THIS IS KINDA PRETTY.
MUNCH
もぐ
HMM?
もぐ
MUNCH
ARE YOU RELATED TO MOKKE-CHAN?
REACH
そ〜
ぱっ
GRAB
REFRAIN FROM TOUCHING THINGS YOU DON'T HAVE TO.
Y-YES, SIR!
I'M SORRY!!

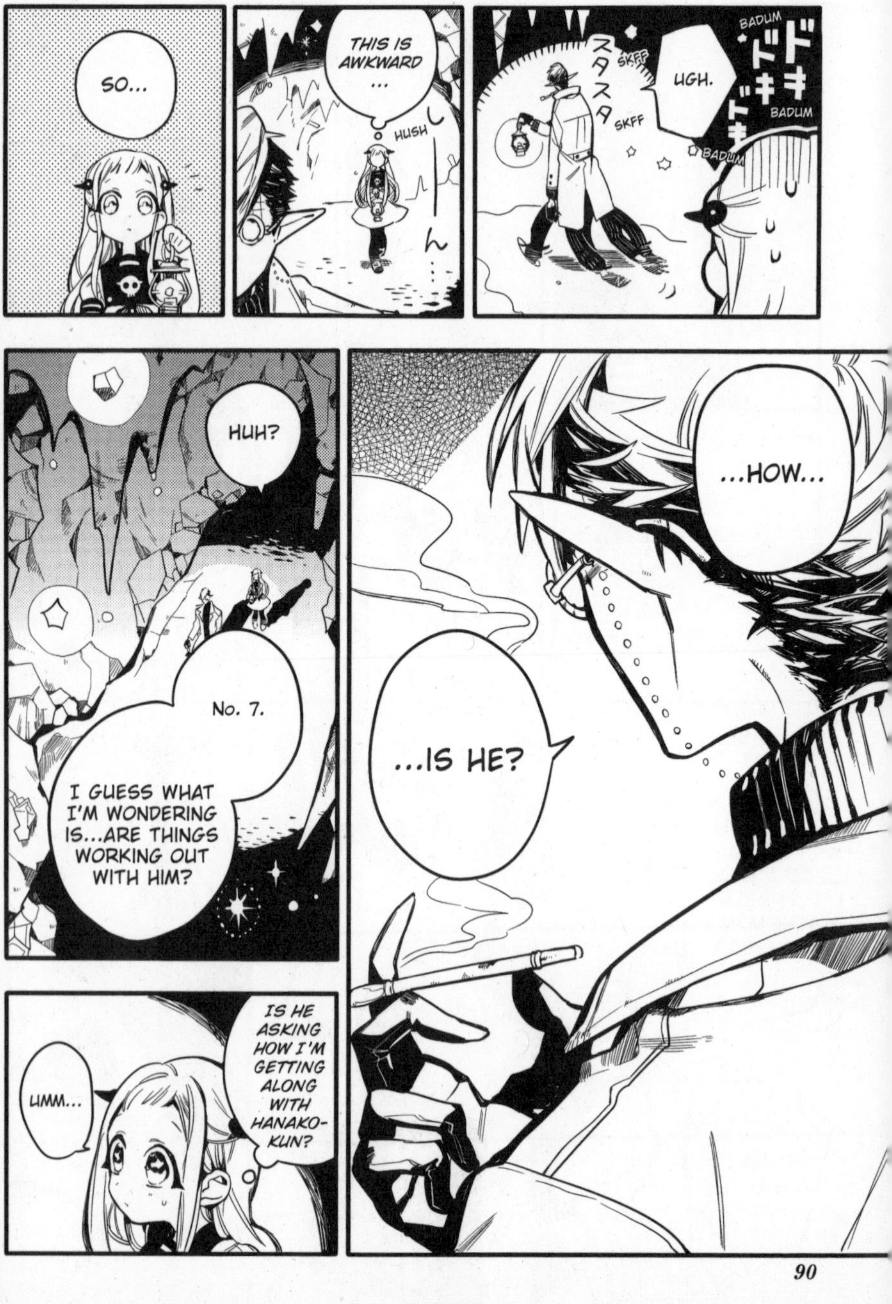
ドキドキドキ
BADUM
BADUM
BADUM
UGH.
スタスタ
SKFF
SKFF
THIS IS AWKWARD...
しーん
HUSH
SO...
...HOW...
...IS HE?
HUH?
No. 7.
I GUESS WHAT I'M WONDERING IS...ARE THINGS WORKING OUT WITH HIM?
IS HE ASKING HOW I'M GETTING ALONG WITH HANAKO-KUN?
UMM...

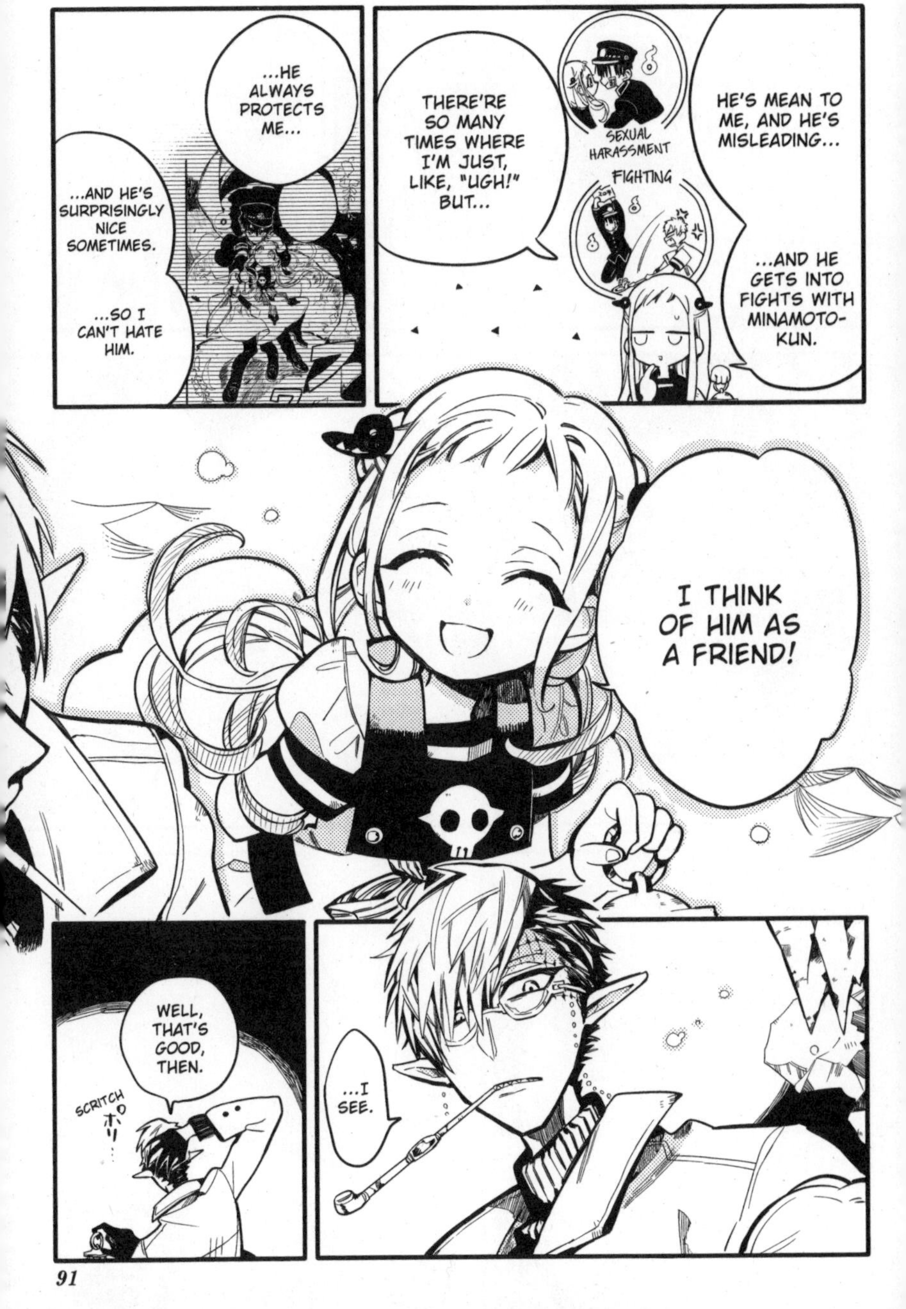
HE'S MEAN TO ME, AND HE'S MISLEADING...
SEXUAL HARASSMENT
FIGHTING
...AND HE GETS INTO FIGHTS WITH MINAMOTO-KUN.
THERE'RE SO MANY TIMES WHERE I'M JUST, LIKE, "UGH!" BUT...
...HE ALWAYS PROTECTS ME...
...AND HE'S SURPRISINGLY NICE SOMETIMES.
...SO I CAN'T HATE HIM.
I THINK OF HIM AS A FRIEND!
...I SEE.
WELL, THAT'S GOOD, THEN.
SCRITCH

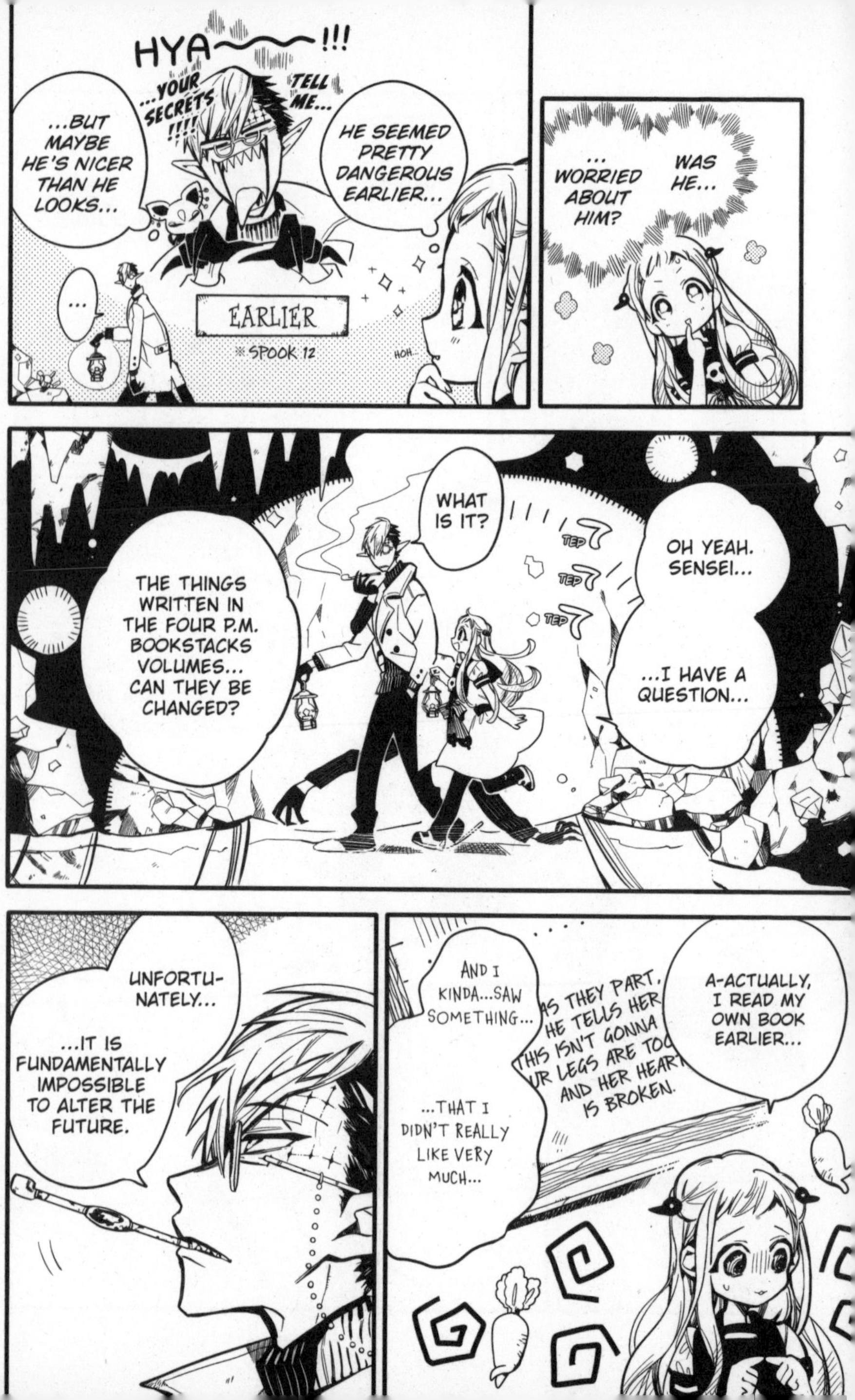
...WAS HE... WORRIED ABOUT HIM?
HE SEEMED PRETTY DANGEROUS EARLIER...
TELL ME...
...YOUR SECRETS!!!!
HYA~~~!!!
...BUT MAYBE HE'S NICER THAN HE LOOKS...
...
EARLIER
※SPOOK 12
HOH...
OH YEAH. SENSEI... ...I HAVE A QUESTION...
TEP
TEP
TEP
WHAT IS IT?
THE THINGS WRITTEN IN THE FOUR P.M. BOOKSTACKS VOLUMES... CAN THEY BE CHANGED?
A-ACTUALLY, I READ MY OWN BOOK EARLIER...
AND I KINDA...SAW SOMETHING...
AS THEY PART, HE TELLS HER THIS ISN'T GONNA UR LEGS ARE TOO AND HER HEART IS BROKEN.
...THAT I DIDN'T REALLY LIKE VERY MUCH...
UNFORTUNATELY...
...IT IS FUNDAMENTALLY IMPOSSIBLE TO ALTER THE FUTURE.

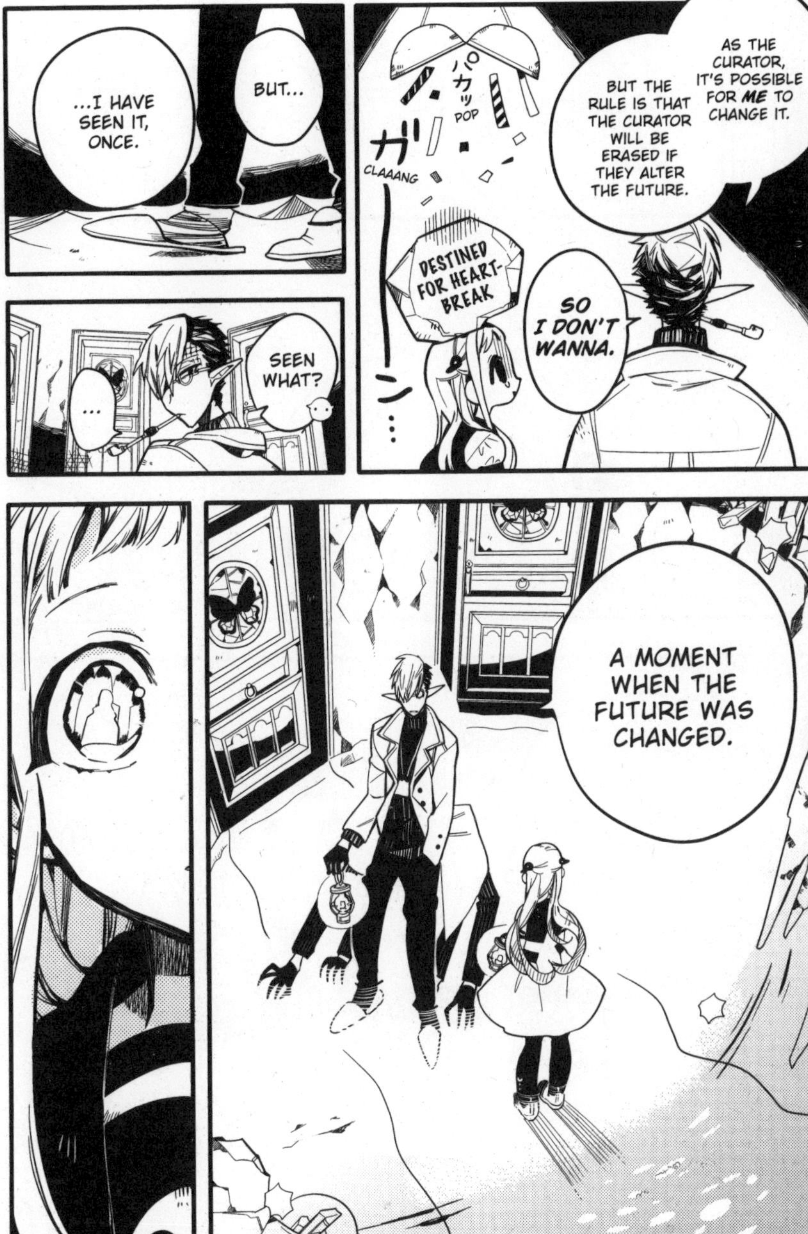
AS THE CURATOR, IT'S POSSIBLE FOR ME TO CHANGE IT.
BUT THE RULE IS THAT THE CURATOR WILL BE ERASED IF THEY ALTER THE FUTURE.
パカッ
POP
ガ
CLAAANG
DESTINED FOR HEART-BREAK
SO I DON'T WANNA.
BUT...
...I HAVE SEEN IT, ONCE.
SEEN WHAT?
...
A MOMENT WHEN THE FUTURE WAS CHANGED.

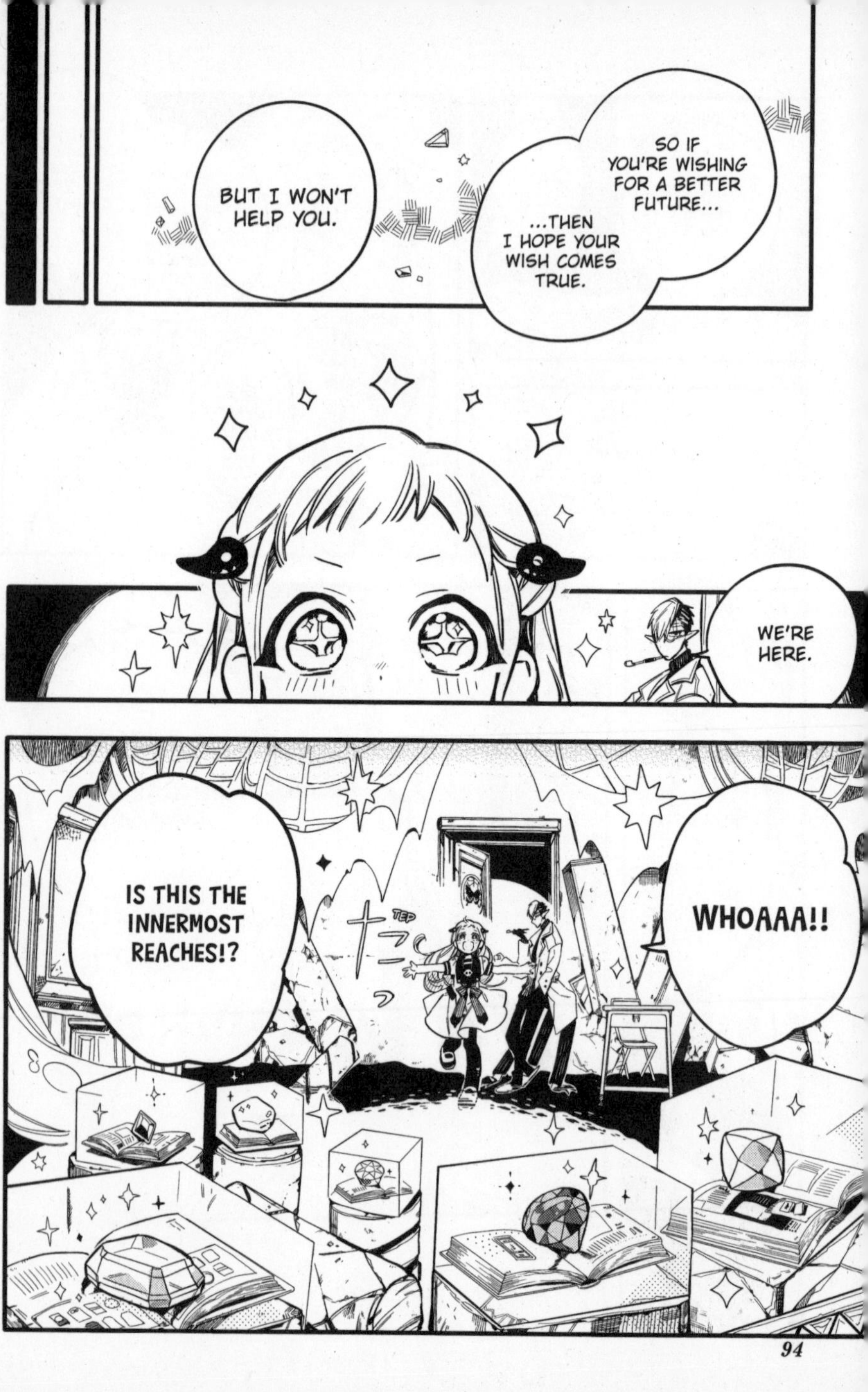
SO IF YOU'RE WISHING FOR A BETTER FUTURE...
...THEN I HOPE YOUR WISH COMES TRUE.
BUT I WON'T HELP YOU.
WE'RE HERE.
WHOAAA!!
TEP
IS THIS THE INNERMOST REACHES!?

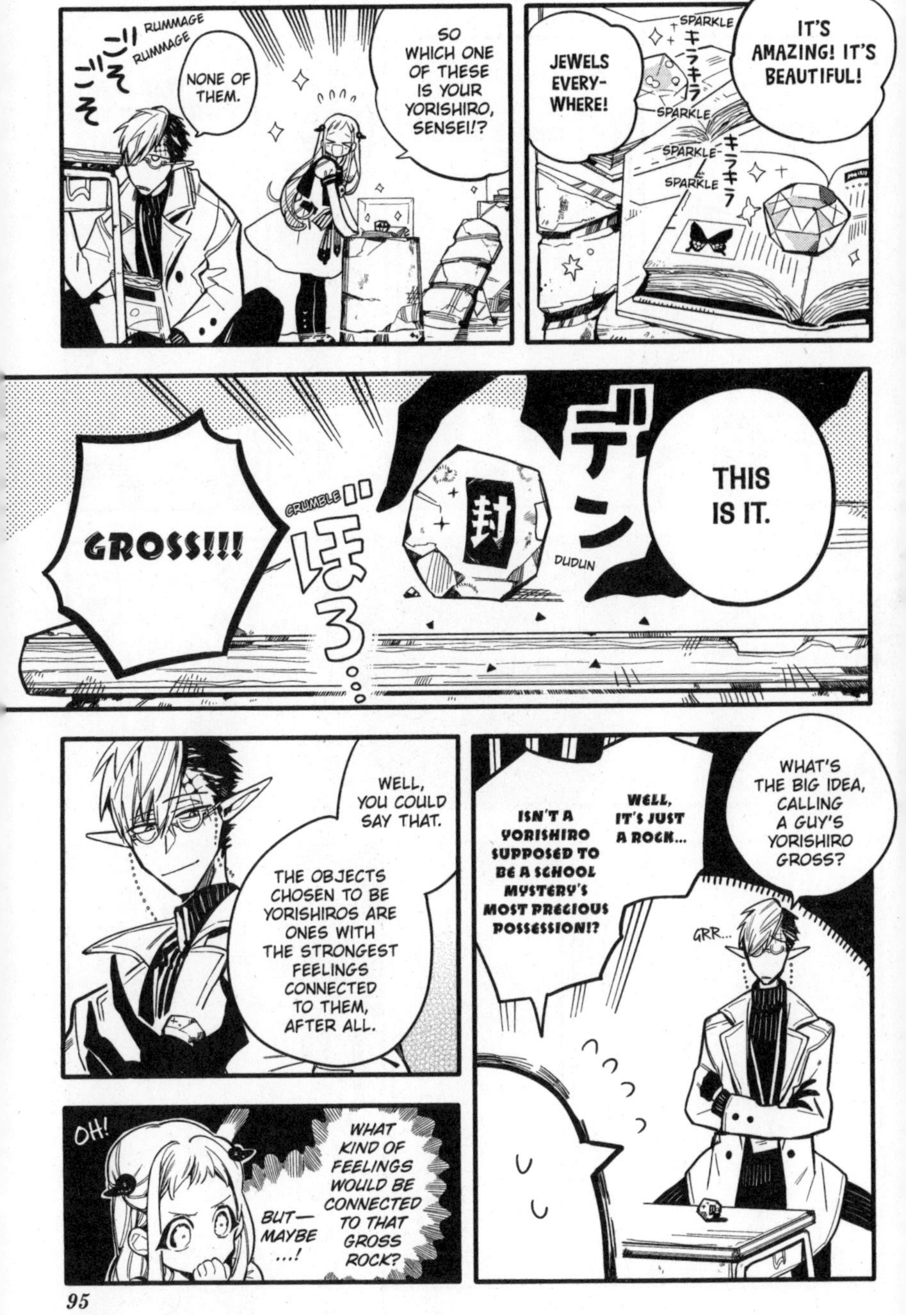
IT'S AMAZING! IT'S BEAUTIFUL!
JEWELS EVERY-WHERE!
キラキラ
SPARKLE
SPARKLE
キラキラ
SPARKLE
SPARKLE
SO WHICH ONE OF THESE IS YOUR YORISHIRO, SENSEI!?
NONE OF THEM.
ごそごそ
RUMMAGE
RUMMAGE
THIS IS IT.
デン
DUDUN
ぼろ
CRUMBLE
GROSS!!!
WHAT'S THE BIG IDEA, CALLING A GUY'S YORISHIRO GROSS?
WELL, IT'S JUST A ROCK...
ISN'T A YORISHIRO SUPPOSED TO BE A SCHOOL MYSTERY'S MOST PRECIOUS POSSESSION!?
GRR...
WELL, YOU COULD SAY THAT.
THE OBJECTS CHOSEN TO BE YORISHIROS ARE ONES WITH THE STRONGEST FEELINGS CONNECTED TO THEM, AFTER ALL.
WHAT KIND OF FEELINGS WOULD BE CONNECTED TO THAT GROSS ROCK?
BUT— MAYBE ...!
OH!

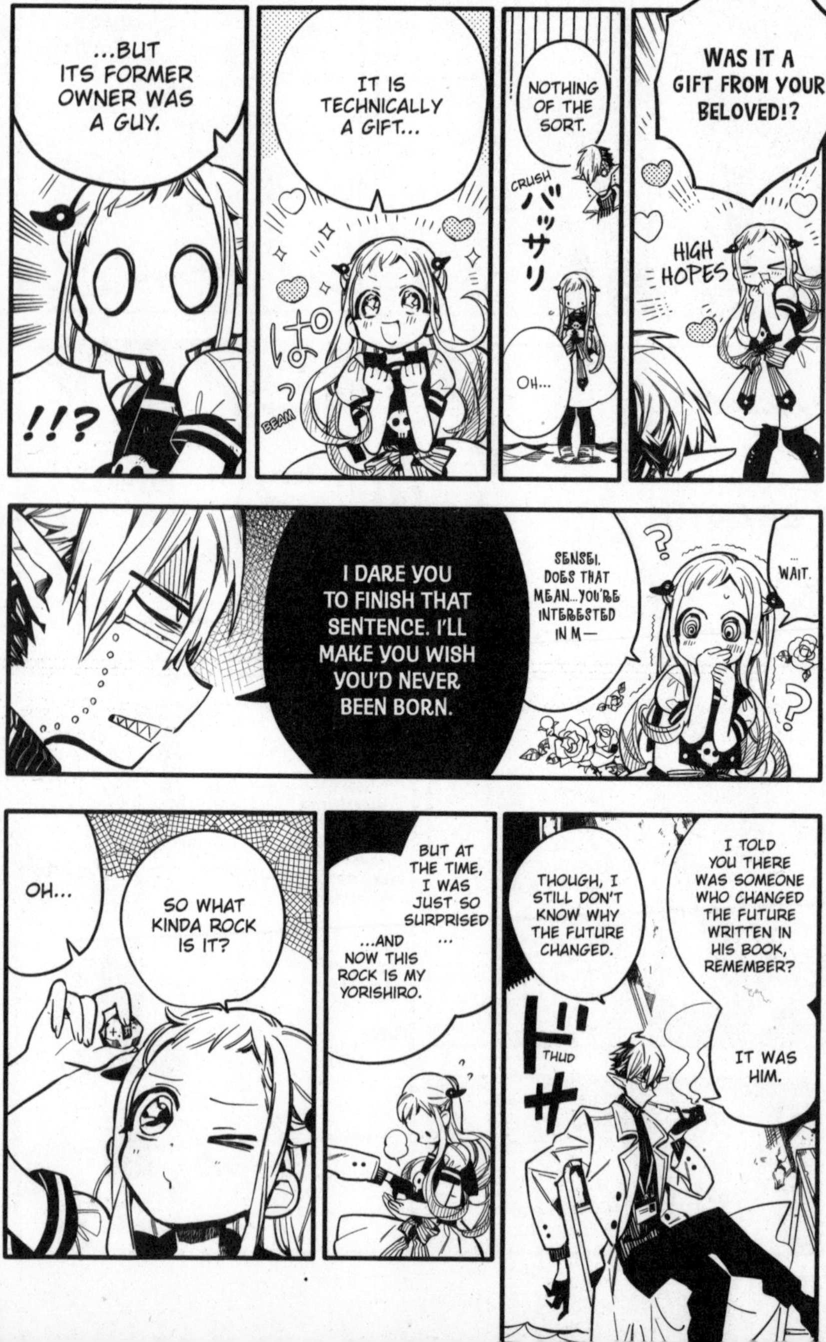
WAS IT A GIFT FROM YOUR BELOVED!?
HIGH HOPES
NOTHING OF THE SORT.
CRUSH
バッサリ
OH...
IT IS TECHNICALLY A GIFT...
ぱっ
BEAM
...BUT ITS FORMER OWNER WAS A GUY.
!!?
...WAIT.
SENSEI. DOES THAT MEAN...YOU'RE INTERESTED IN M—
I DARE YOU TO FINISH THAT SENTENCE. I'LL MAKE YOU WISH YOU'D NEVER BEEN BORN.
I TOLD YOU THERE WAS SOMEONE WHO CHANGED THE FUTURE WRITTEN IN HIS BOOK, REMEMBER?
IT WAS HIM.
THOUGH, I STILL DON'T KNOW WHY THE FUTURE CHANGED.
ドサ
THUD
BUT AT THE TIME, I WAS JUST SO SURPRISED...
...AND NOW THIS ROCK IS MY YORISHIRO.
OH...
SO WHAT KINDA ROCK IS IT?

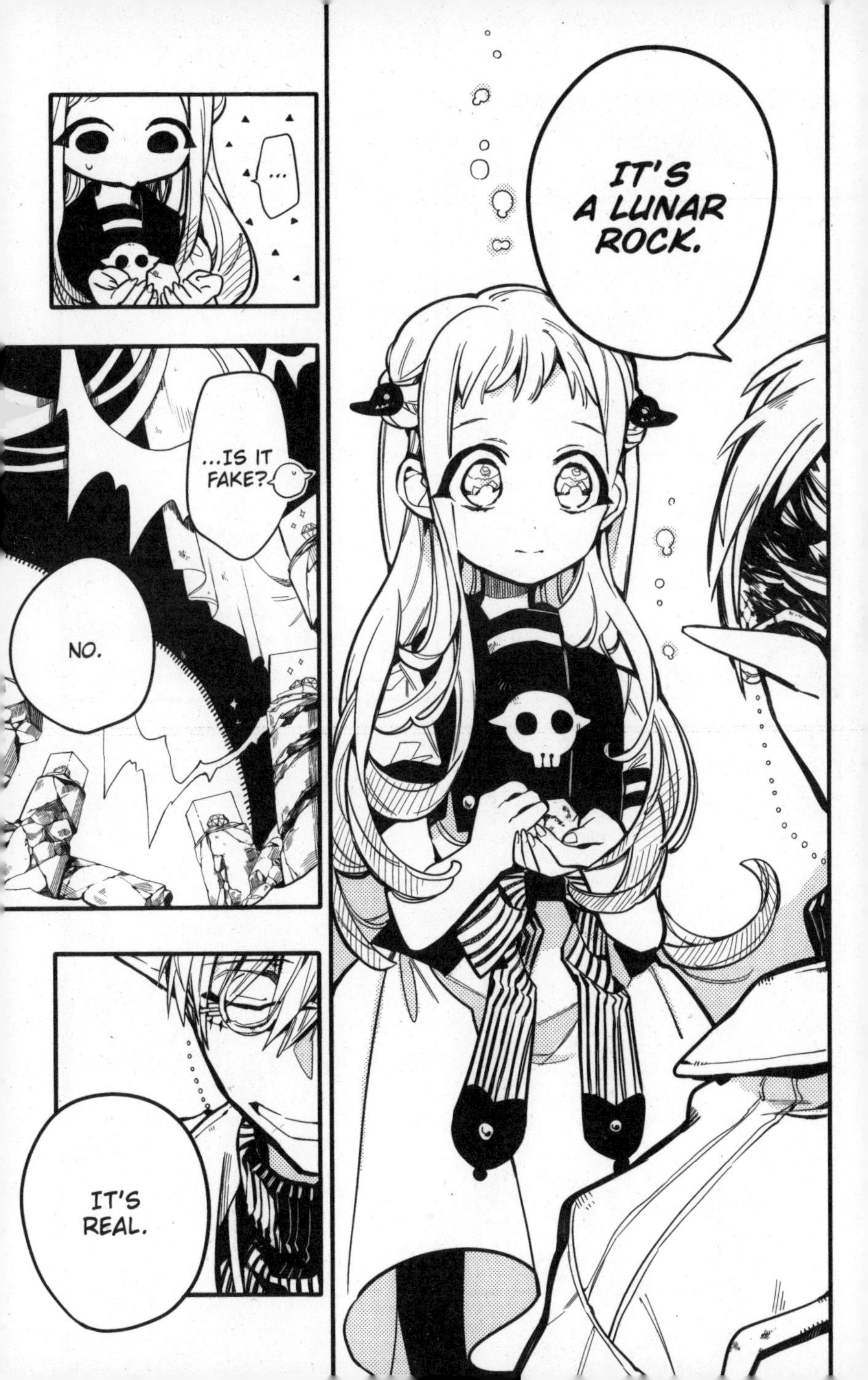
IT'S A LUNAR ROCK.
...
...IS IT FAKE?
NO.
IT'S REAL.

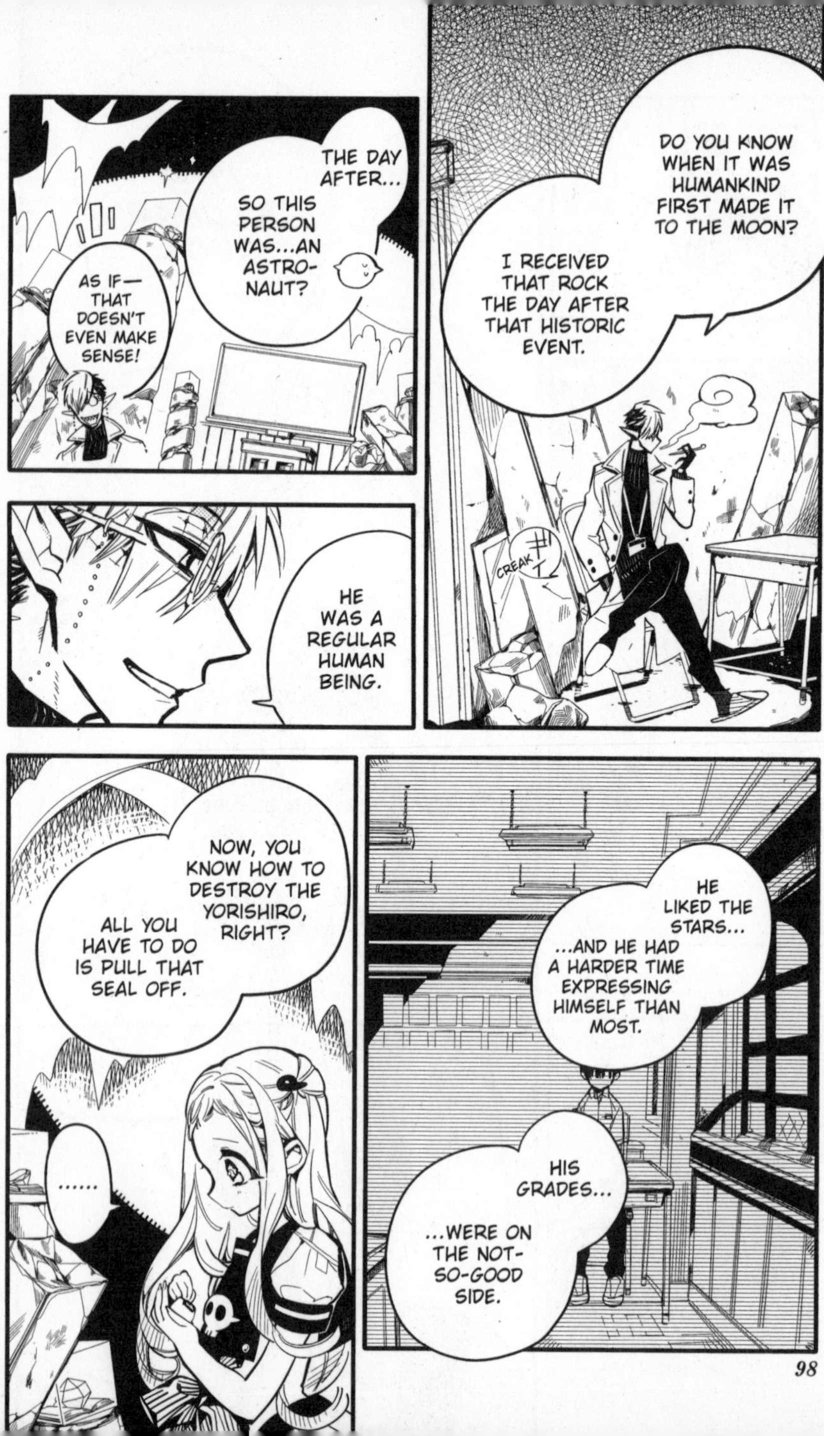

DO YOU KNOW WHEN IT WAS HUMANKIND FIRST MADE IT TO THE MOON?
I RECEIVED THAT ROCK THE DAY AFTER THAT HISTORIC EVENT.
CREAK
THE DAY AFTER...
SO THIS PERSON WAS...AN ASTRONAUT?
AS IF—THAT DOESN'T EVEN MAKE SENSE!
HE WAS A REGULAR HUMAN BEING.
HE LIKED THE STARS...
...AND HE HAD A HARDER TIME EXPRESSING HIMSELF THAN MOST.
HIS GRADES...
...WERE ON THE NOT-SO-GOOD SIDE.
NOW, YOU KNOW HOW TO DESTROY THE YORISHIRO, RIGHT?
ALL YOU HAVE TO DO IS PULL THAT SEAL OFF.
......

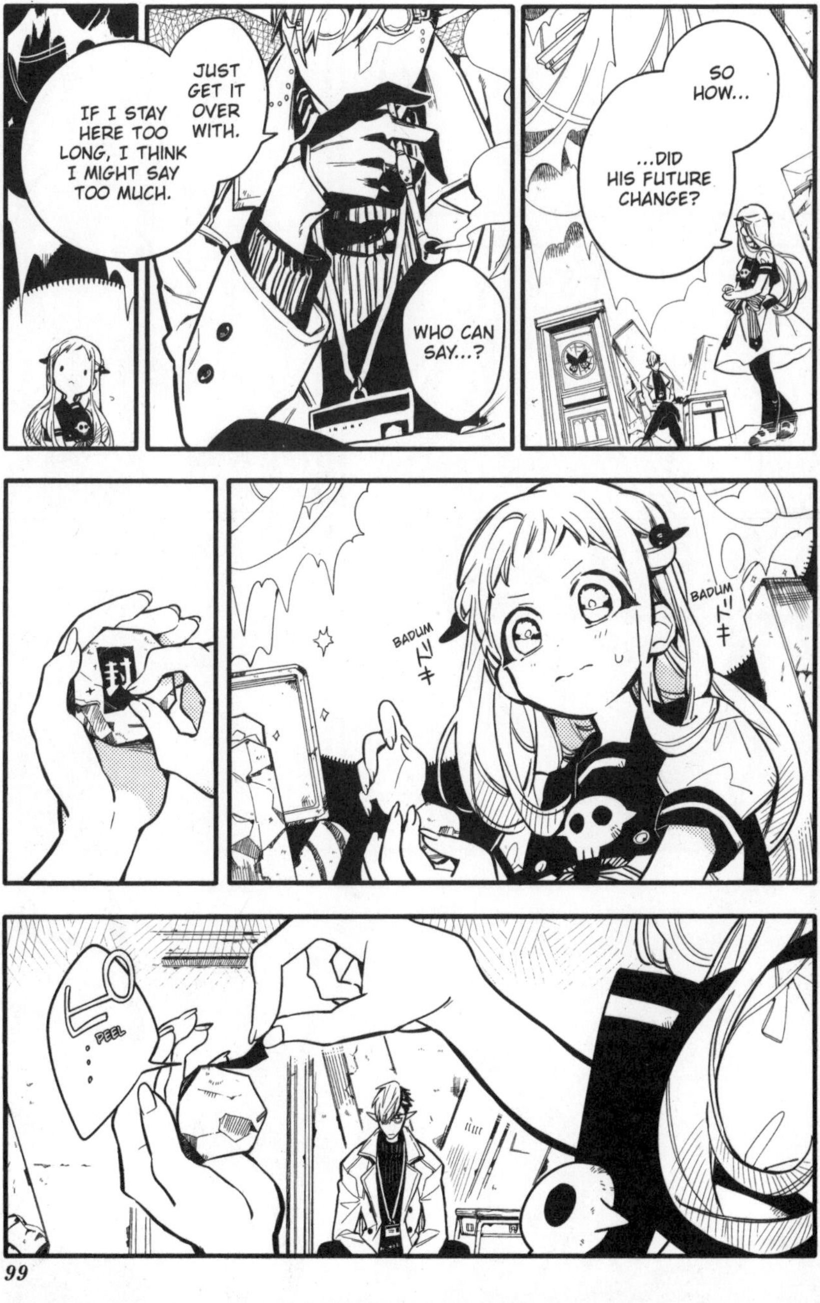
SO HOW...
...DID HIS FUTURE CHANGE?
WHO CAN SAY...?
JUST GET IT OVER WITH.
IF I STAY HERE TOO LONG, I THINK I MIGHT SAY TOO MUCH.
BADUM ドキ
BADUM ドキ
PEEL

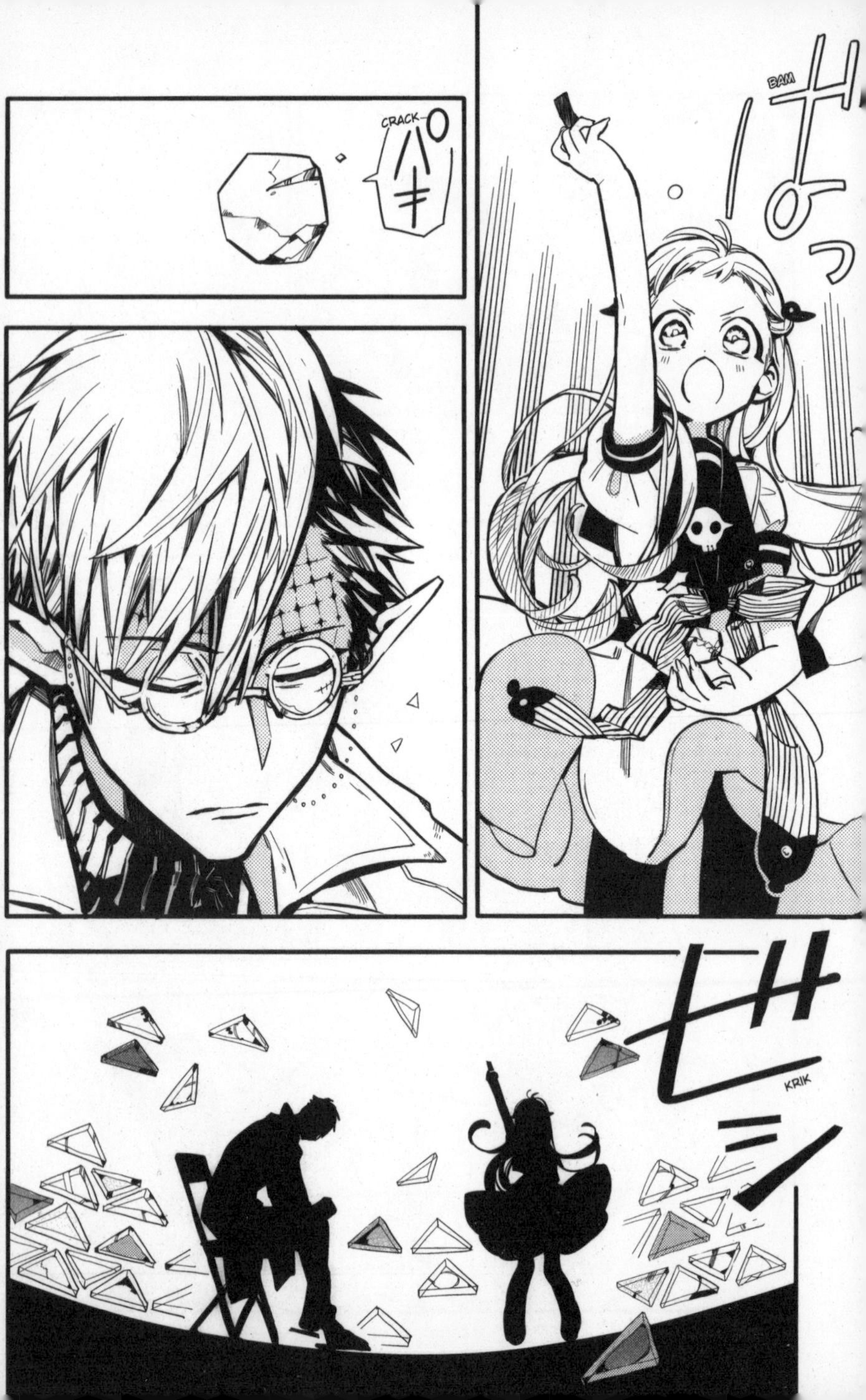

はっ
BAM
パキ
CRACK
KRIK

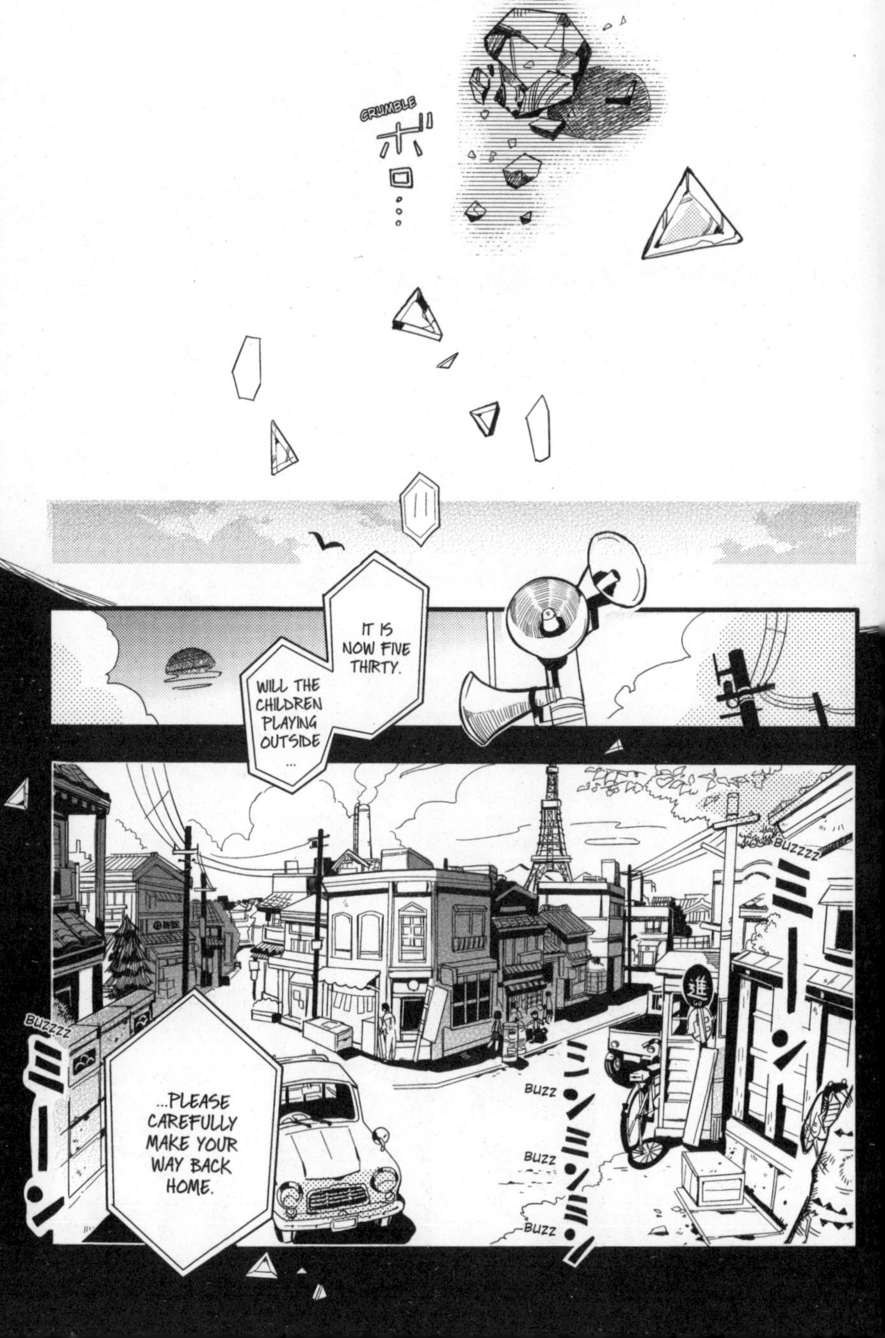
CRUMBLE
ボロ…
IT IS NOW FIVE THIRTY.
WILL THE CHILDREN PLAYING OUTSIDE …
…PLEASE CAREFULLY MAKE YOUR WAY BACK HOME.
BUZZZZ
BUZZ
BUZZ
BUZZ
BUZZZZ

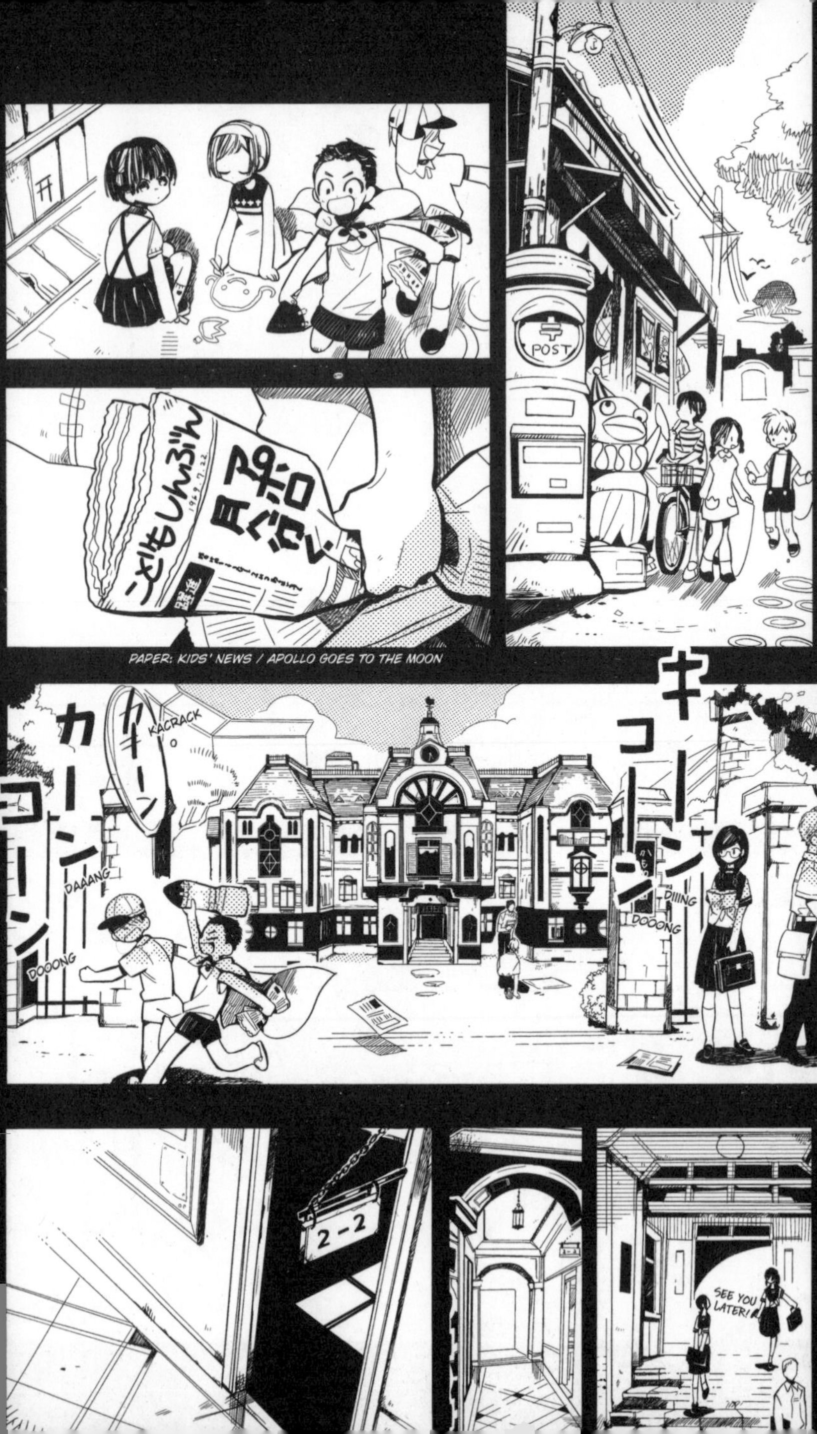
こどもしんぶん
アポロ 月へいく
PAPER: KIDS' NEWS / APOLLO GOES TO THE MOON
キーンコーン
DIIING
DOOONG
カキーン
KACRACK
カーンコーン
DAAANG
DOOONG
SEE YOU LATER!

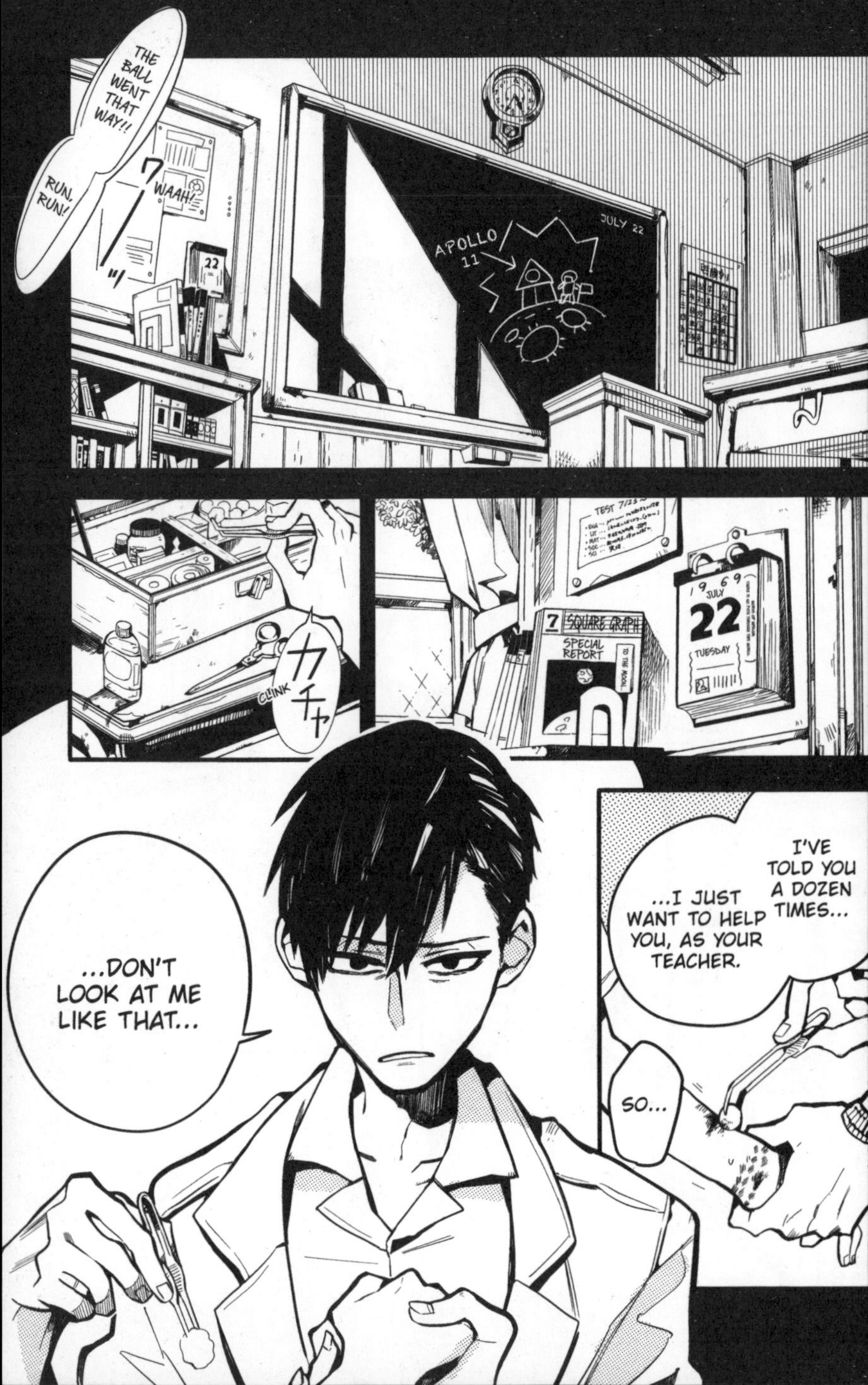
THE BALL WENT THAT WAY!!
RUN, RUN!
WAAH!
JULY 22
APOLLO 11
TEST 7/23
1969
JULY
22
TUESDAY
7 SQUARE GRAPH
SPECIAL REPORT
TO THE MOON
CLINK
I'VE TOLD YOU A DOZEN TIMES...
...I JUST WANT TO HELP YOU, AS YOUR TEACHER.
SO...
...DON'T LOOK AT ME LIKE THAT...

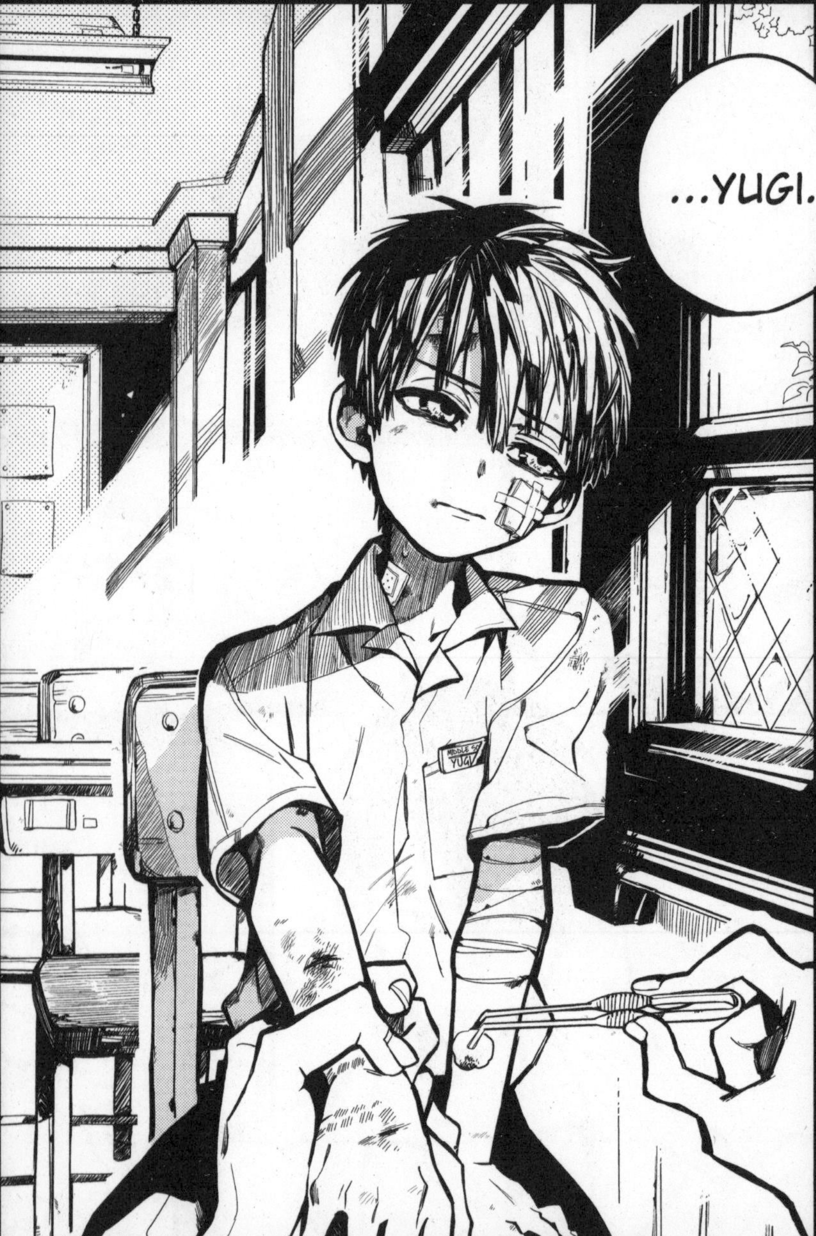
...YUGI.

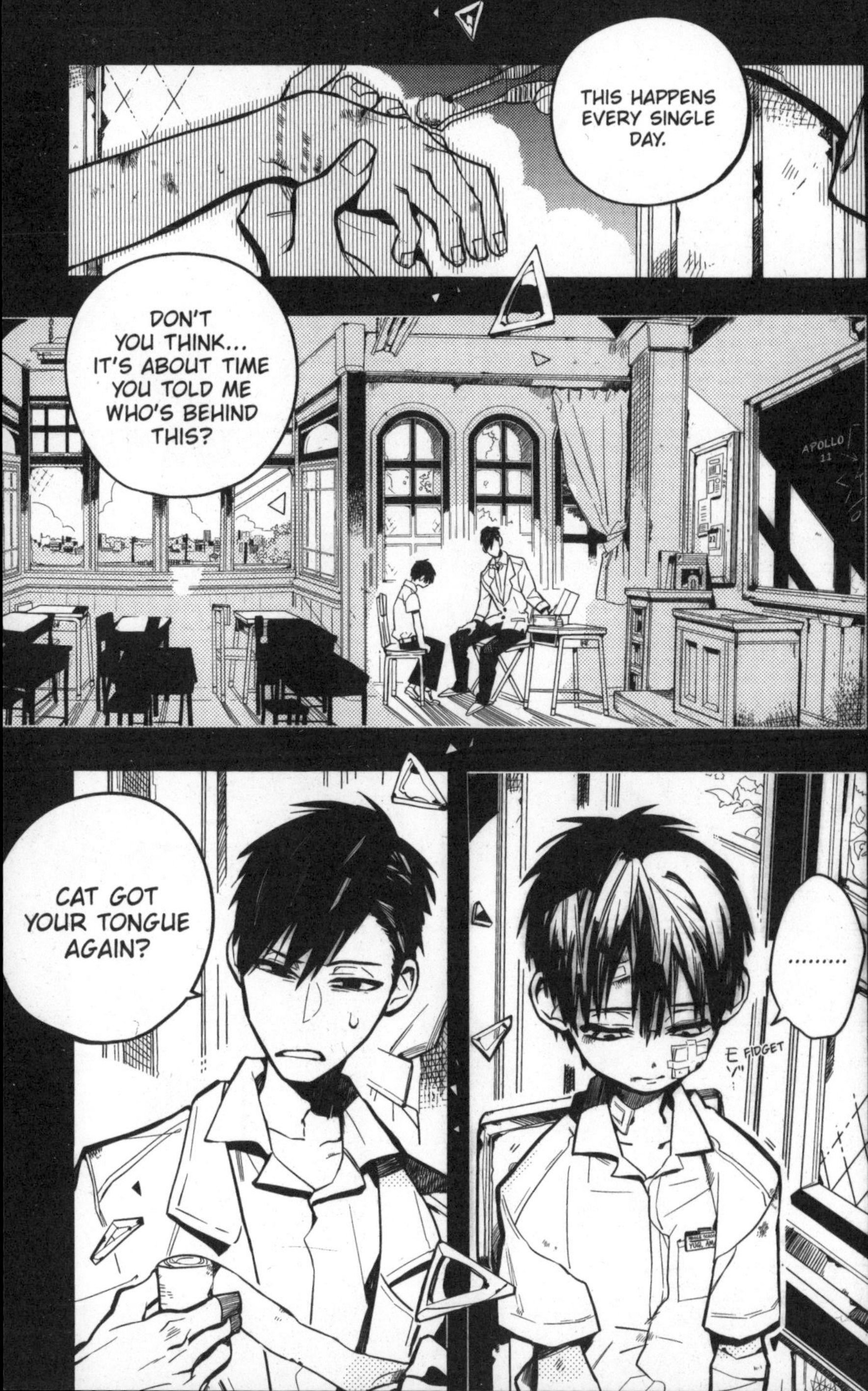
THIS HAPPENS EVERY SINGLE DAY.
DON'T YOU THINK... IT'S ABOUT TIME YOU TOLD ME WHO'S BEHIND THIS?
APOLLO 11
....
FIDGET
CAT GOT YOUR TONGUE AGAIN?

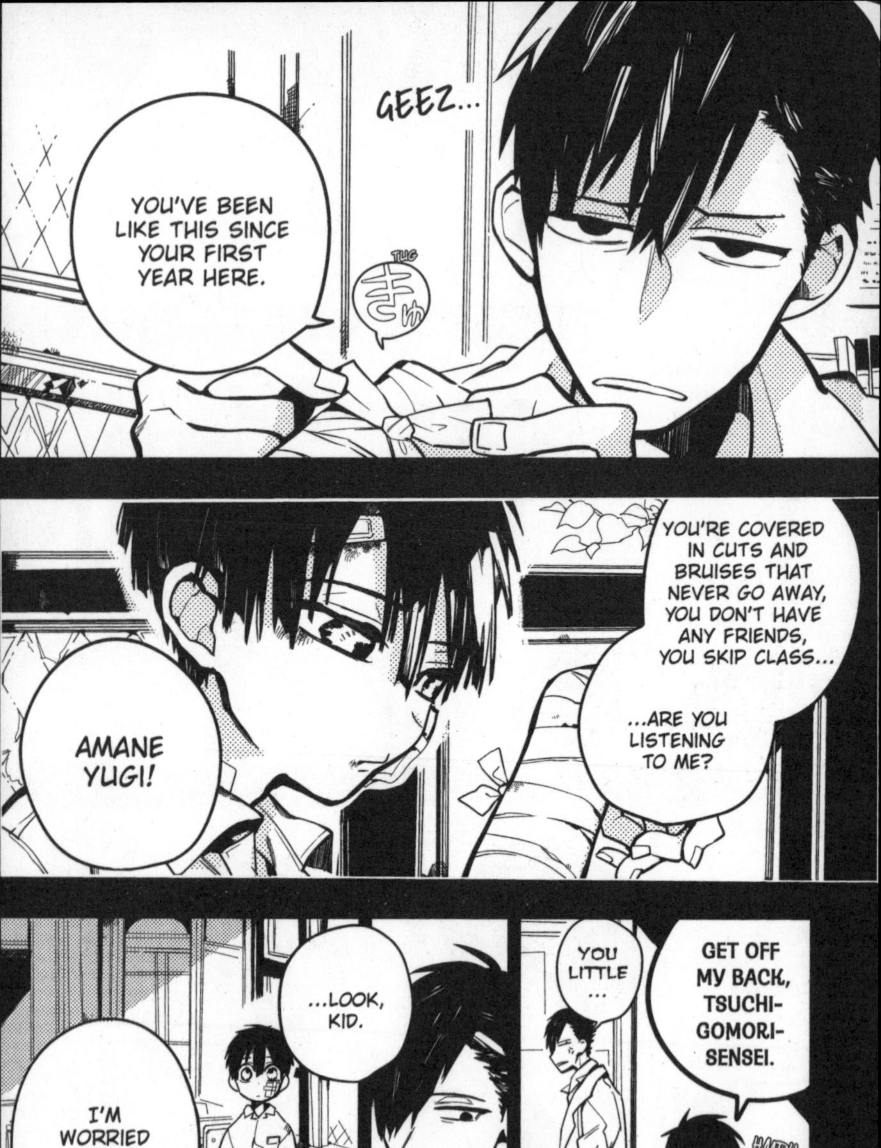
GEEZ...
TUG
きゅ
YOU'VE BEEN LIKE THIS SINCE YOUR FIRST YEAR HERE.
YOU'RE COVERED IN CUTS AND BRUISES THAT NEVER GO AWAY, YOU DON'T HAVE ANY FRIENDS, YOU SKIP CLASS...
...ARE YOU LISTENING TO ME?
AMANE YUGI!
GET OFF MY BACK, TSUCHI-GOMORI-SENSEI.
YOU LITTLE ...
HMPH.
...LOOK, KID.
I'M WORRIED ABOUT YOU.

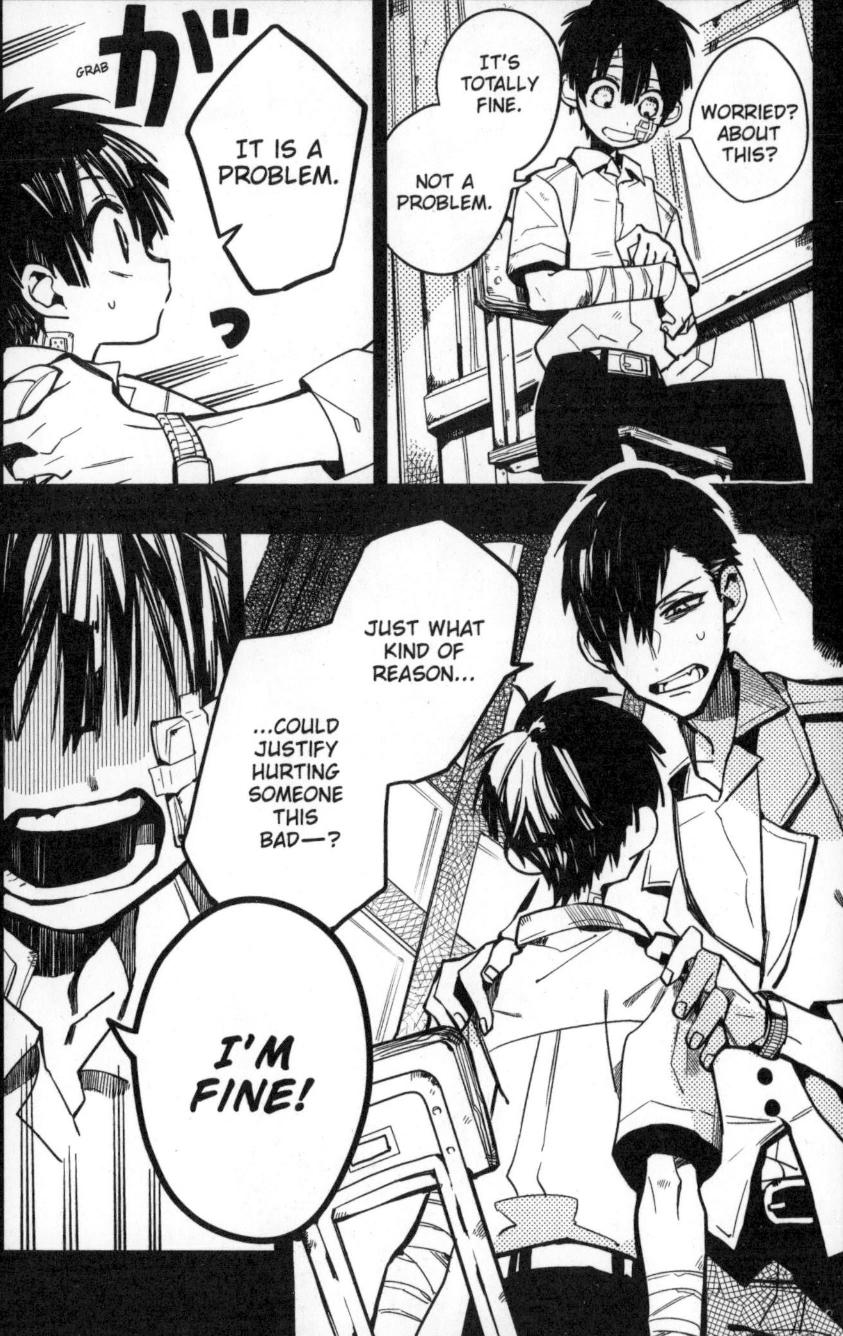
WORRIED? ABOUT THIS?
IT'S TOTALLY FINE.
NOT A PROBLEM.
ガ
GRAB
IT IS A PROBLEM.
JUST WHAT KIND OF REASON...
...COULD JUSTIFY HURTING SOMEONE THIS BAD—?
I'M FINE!

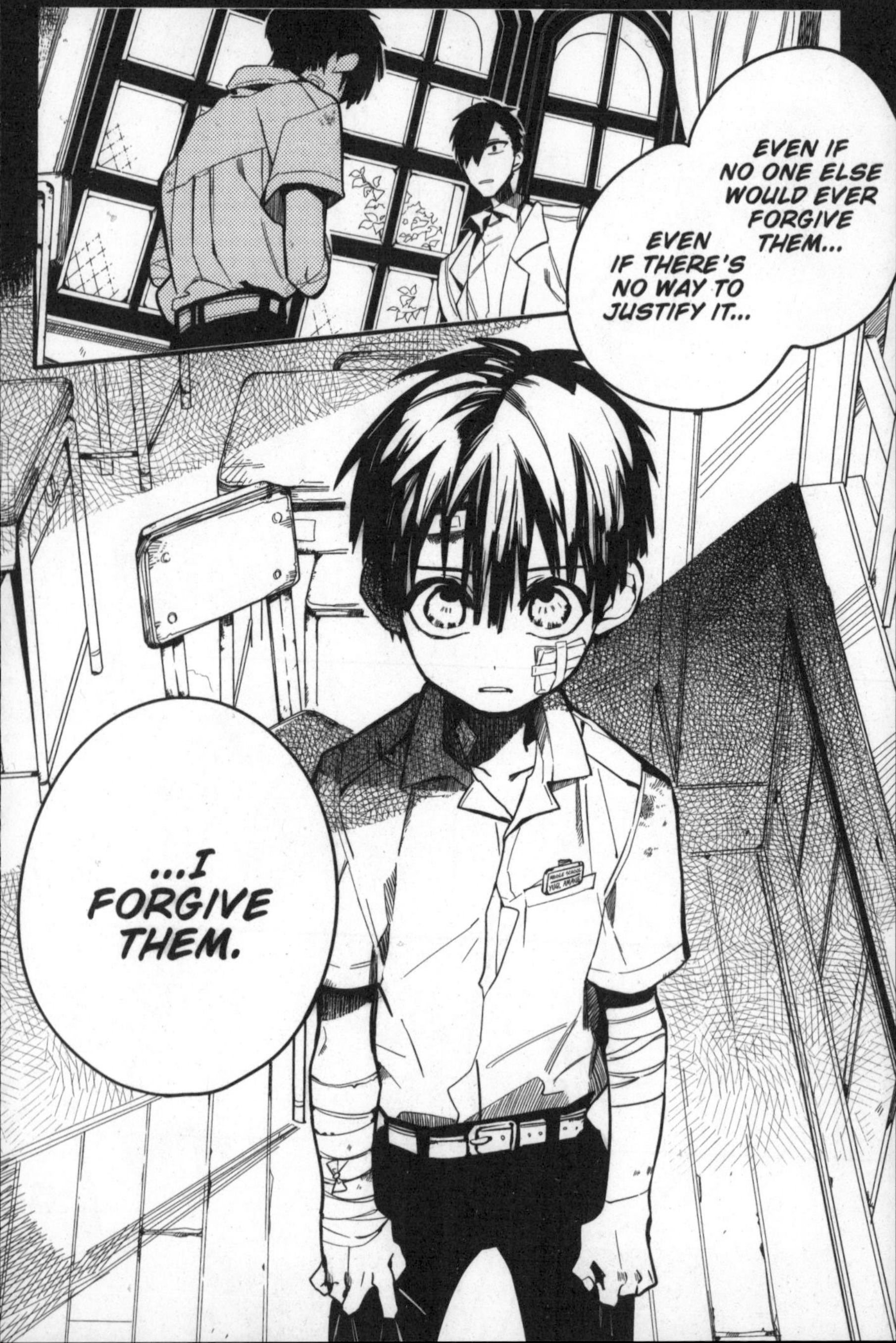
EVEN IF NO ONE ELSE WOULD EVER FORGIVE THEM... EVEN IF THERE'S NO WAY TO JUSTIFY IT...
...I FORGIVE THEM.

SPOOK 14
THE 4 P.M. BOOKSTACKS (PART 4)

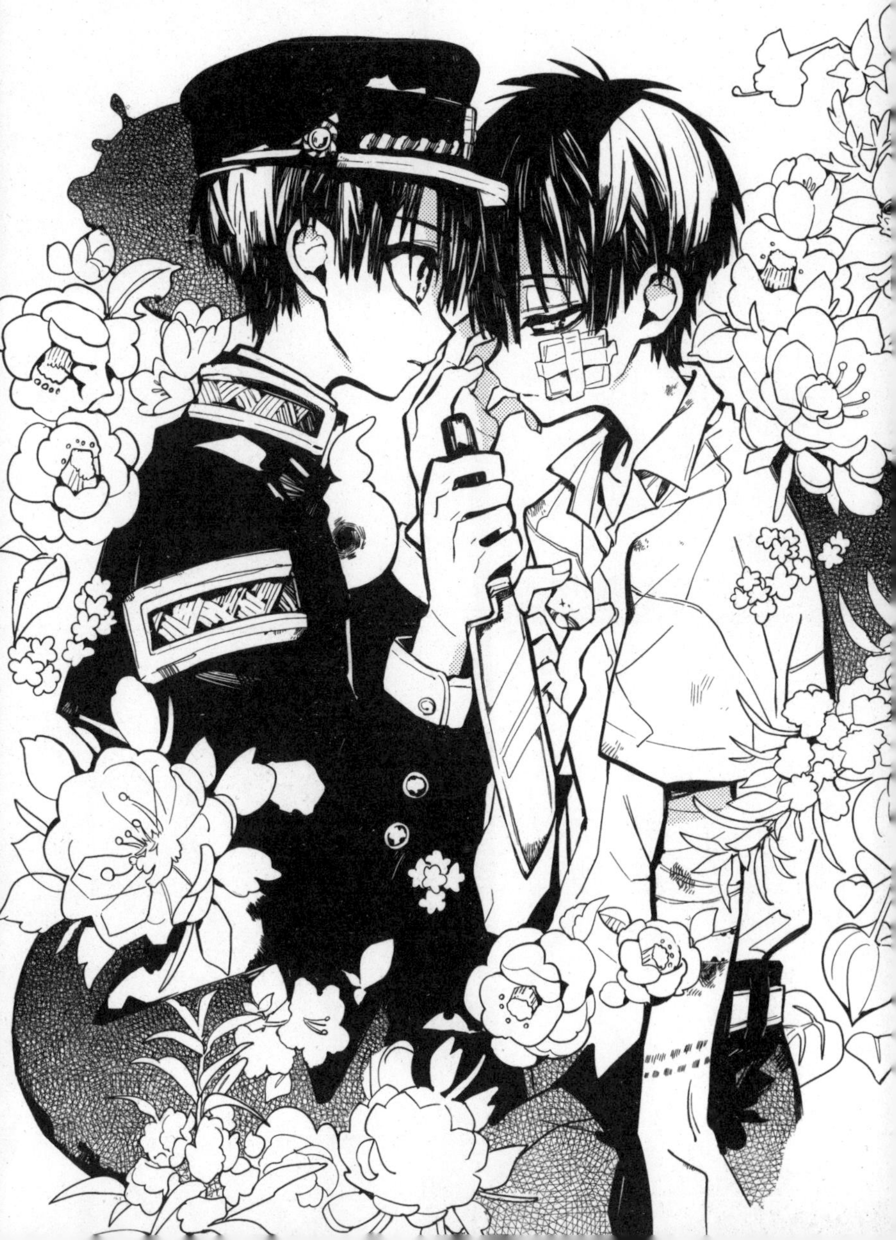

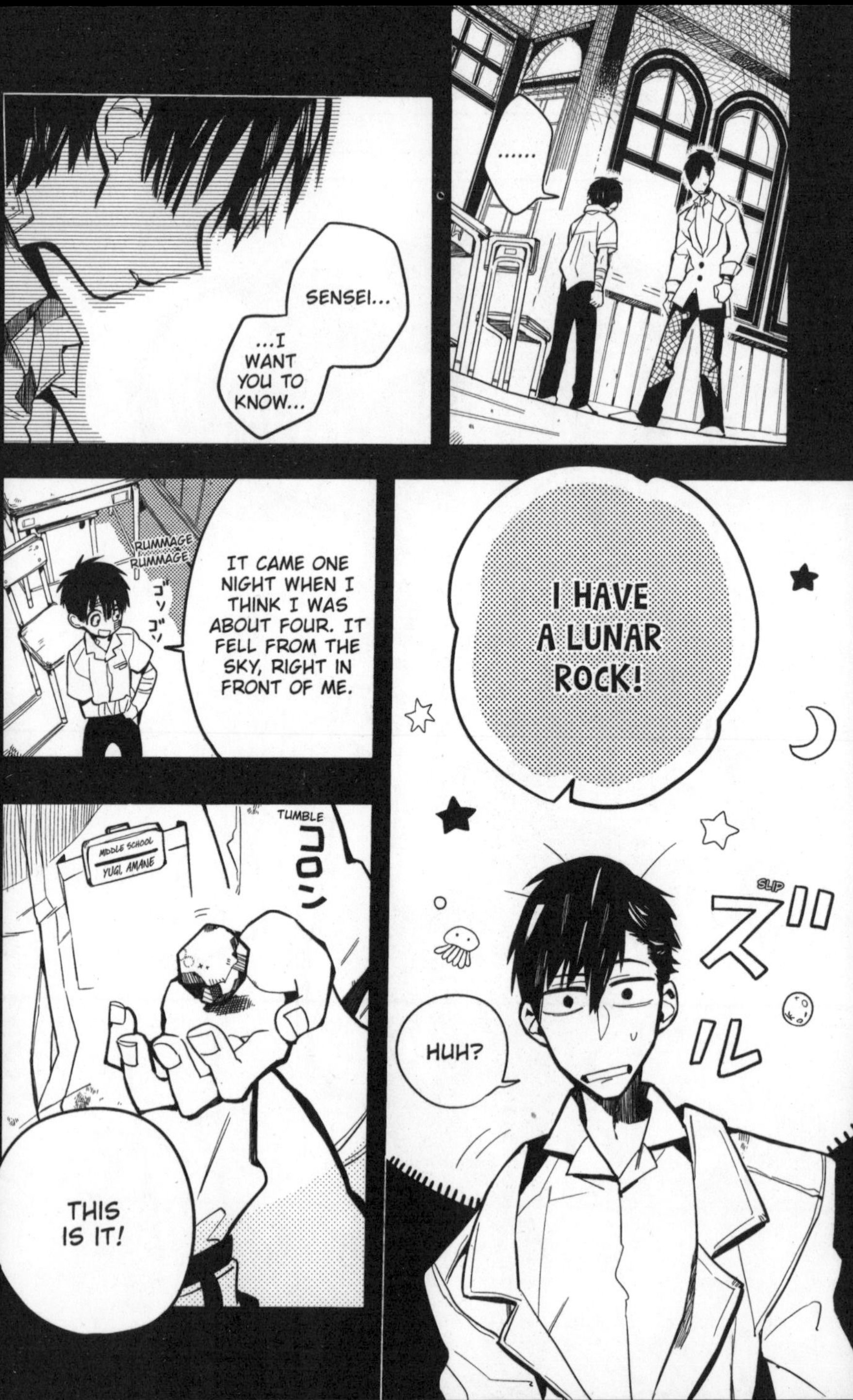

......
SENSEI...
...I WANT YOU TO KNOW...
I HAVE A LUNAR ROCK!
ズル
SLIP
HUH?
IT CAME ONE NIGHT WHEN I THINK I WAS ABOUT FOUR. IT FELL FROM THE SKY, RIGHT IN FRONT OF ME.
ゴソゴソ
RUMMAGE RUMMAGE
コロン
TUMBLE
MIDDLE SCHOOL
YUGI, AMANE
THIS IS IT!

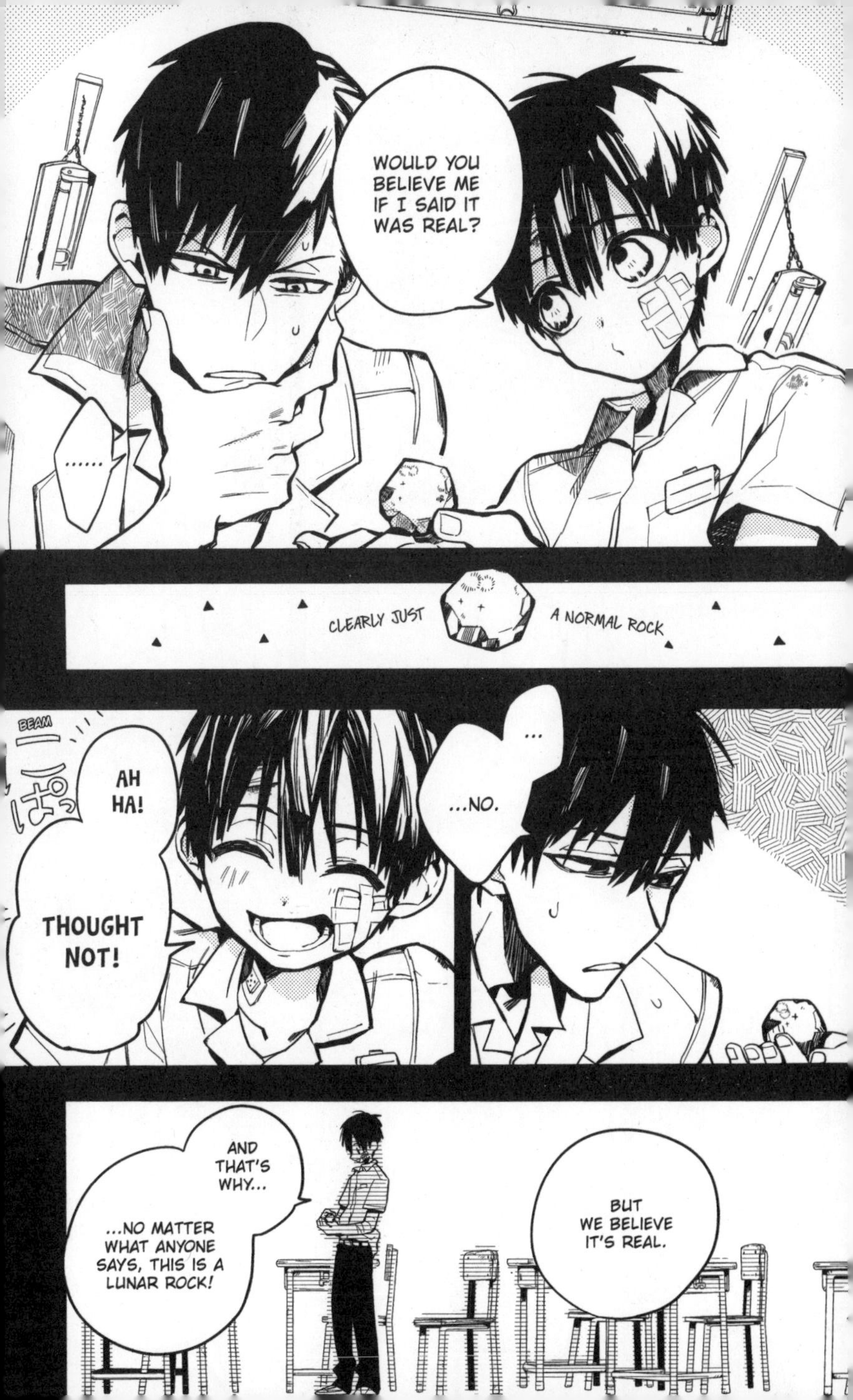

WOULD YOU BELIEVE ME IF I SAID IT WAS REAL?
......
CLEARLY JUST A NORMAL ROCK
...
...NO.
BEAM
ぱっ
AH HA!
THOUGHT NOT!
BUT WE BELIEVE IT'S REAL.
AND THAT'S WHY...
...NO MATTER WHAT ANYONE SAYS, THIS IS A LUNAR ROCK!

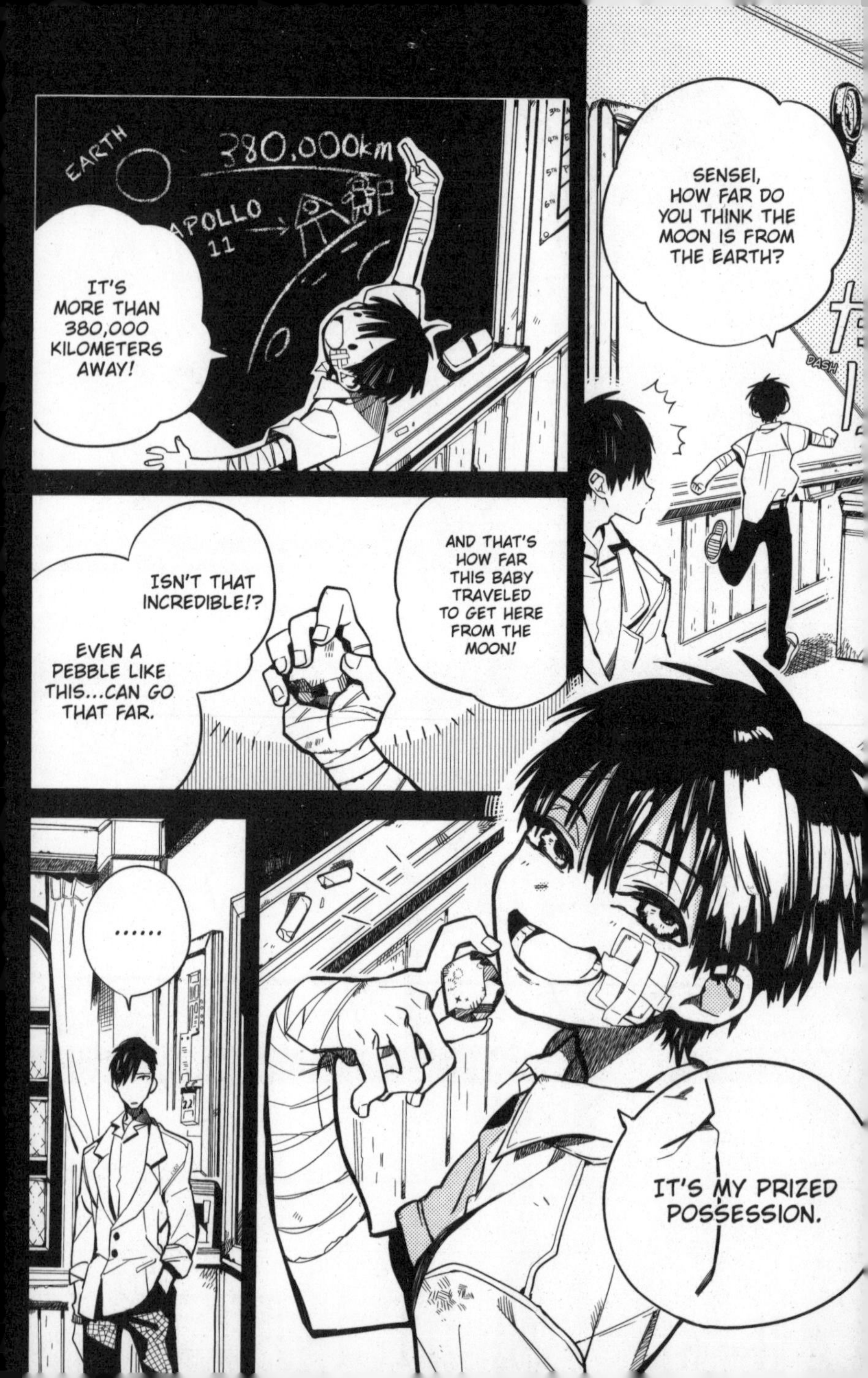
SENSEI, HOW FAR DO YOU THINK THE MOON IS FROM THE EARTH?
DASH
EARTH
380,000km
APOLLO 11
IT'S MORE THAN 380,000 KILOMETERS AWAY!
AND THAT'S HOW FAR THIS BABY TRAVELED TO GET HERE FROM THE MOON!
ISN'T THAT INCREDIBLE!?
EVEN A PEBBLE LIKE THIS...CAN GO THAT FAR.
IT'S MY PRIZED POSSESSION.
......

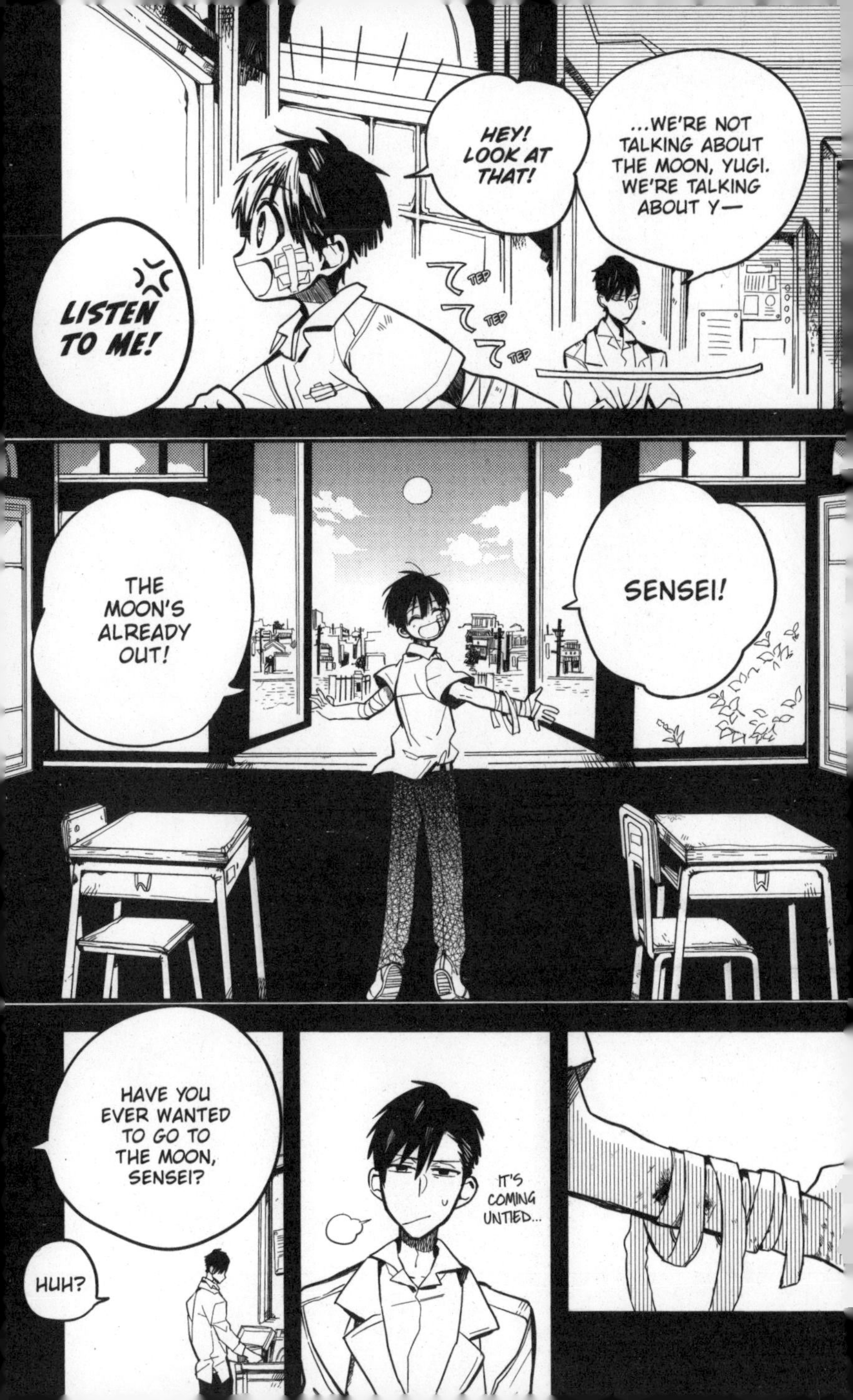
...WE'RE NOT TALKING ABOUT THE MOON, YUGI. WE'RE TALKING ABOUT Y—
HEY! LOOK AT THAT!
TEP
TEP
TEP
LISTEN TO ME!
SENSEI!
THE MOON'S ALREADY OUT!
IT'S COMING UNTIED...
HAVE YOU EVER WANTED TO GO TO THE MOON, SENSEI?
HUH?

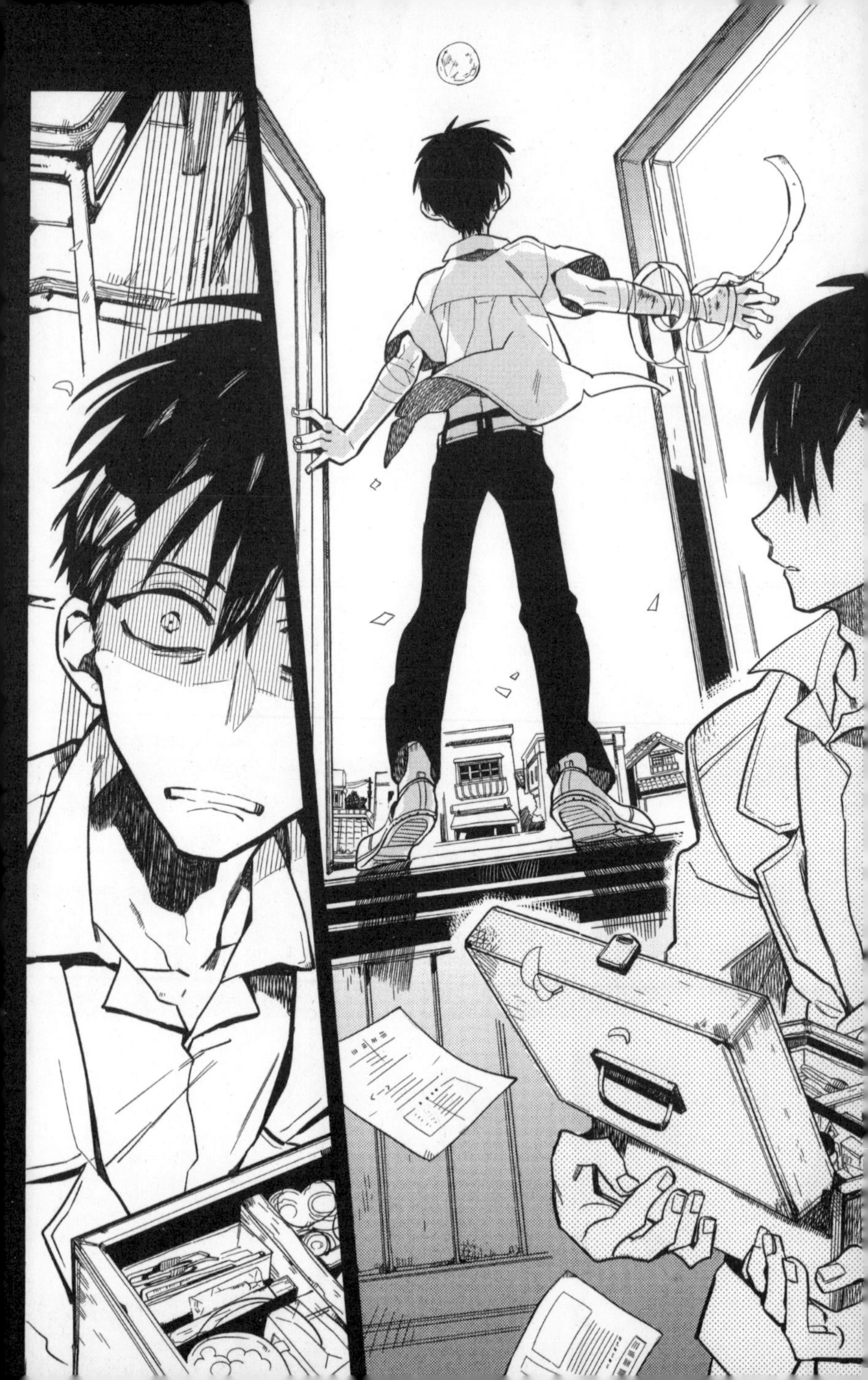

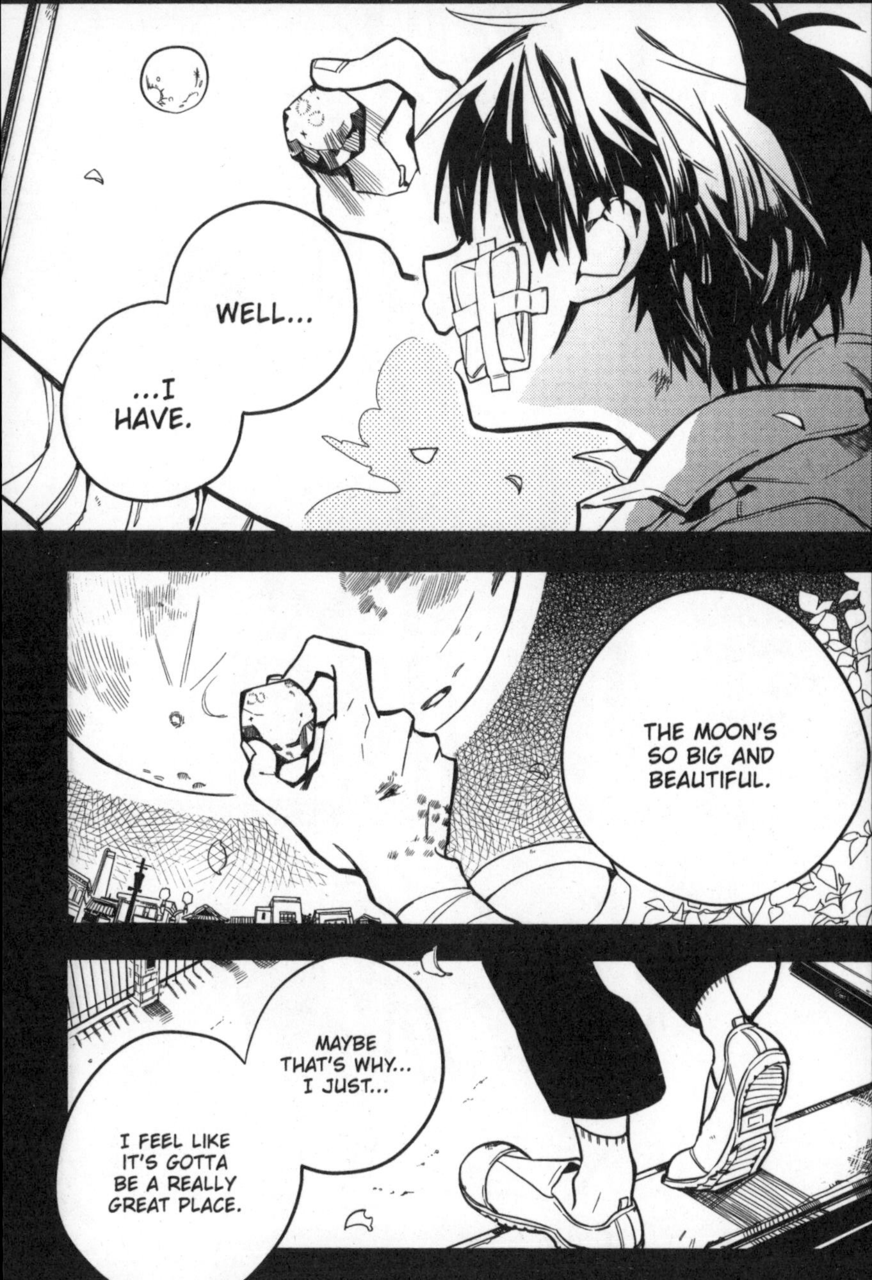
WELL...
...I HAVE.
THE MOON'S SO BIG AND BEAUTIFUL.
MAYBE THAT'S WHY... I JUST...
I FEEL LIKE IT'S GOTTA BE A REALLY GREAT PLACE.

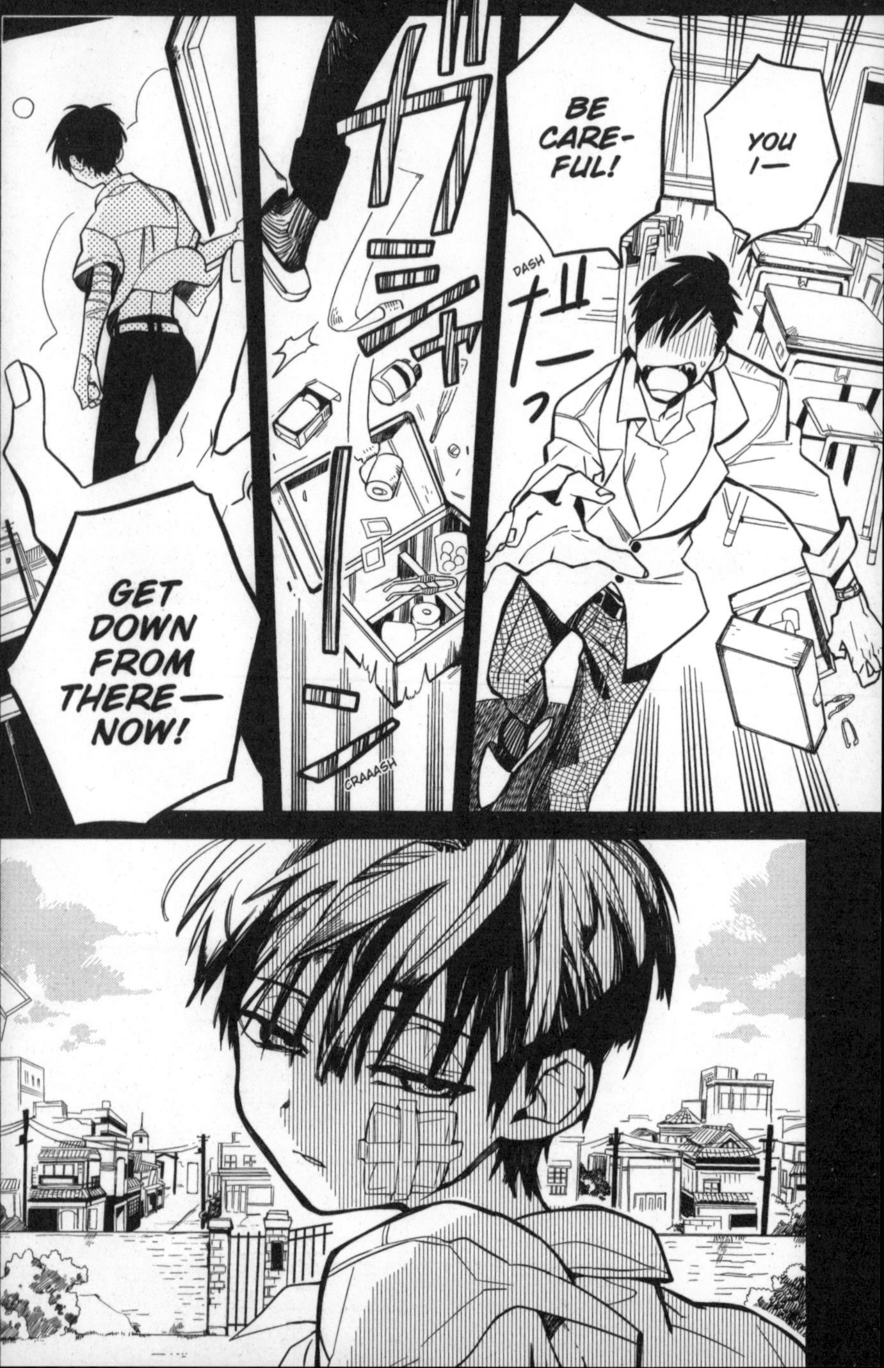
YOU I—
BE CAREFUL!
DASH
CRAAASH
GET DOWN FROM THERE—NOW!

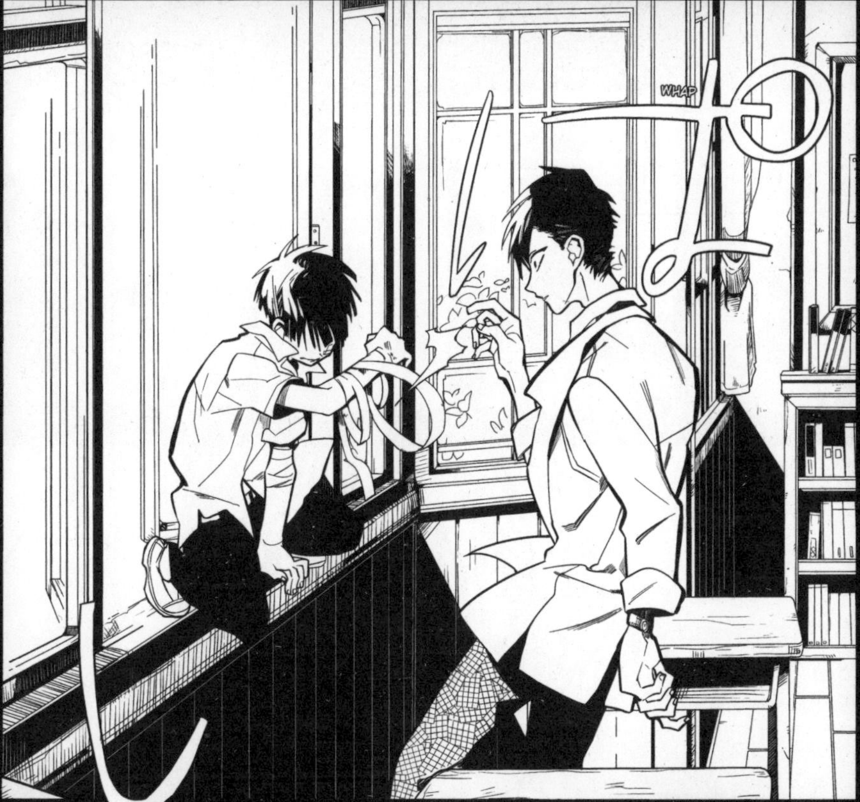
WHAP

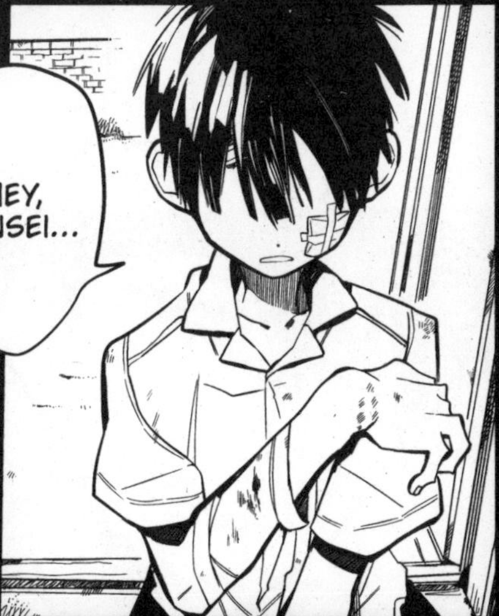

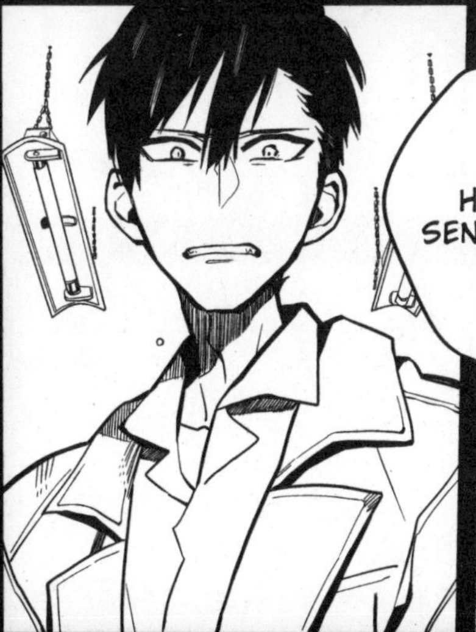
HEY, SENSEI...

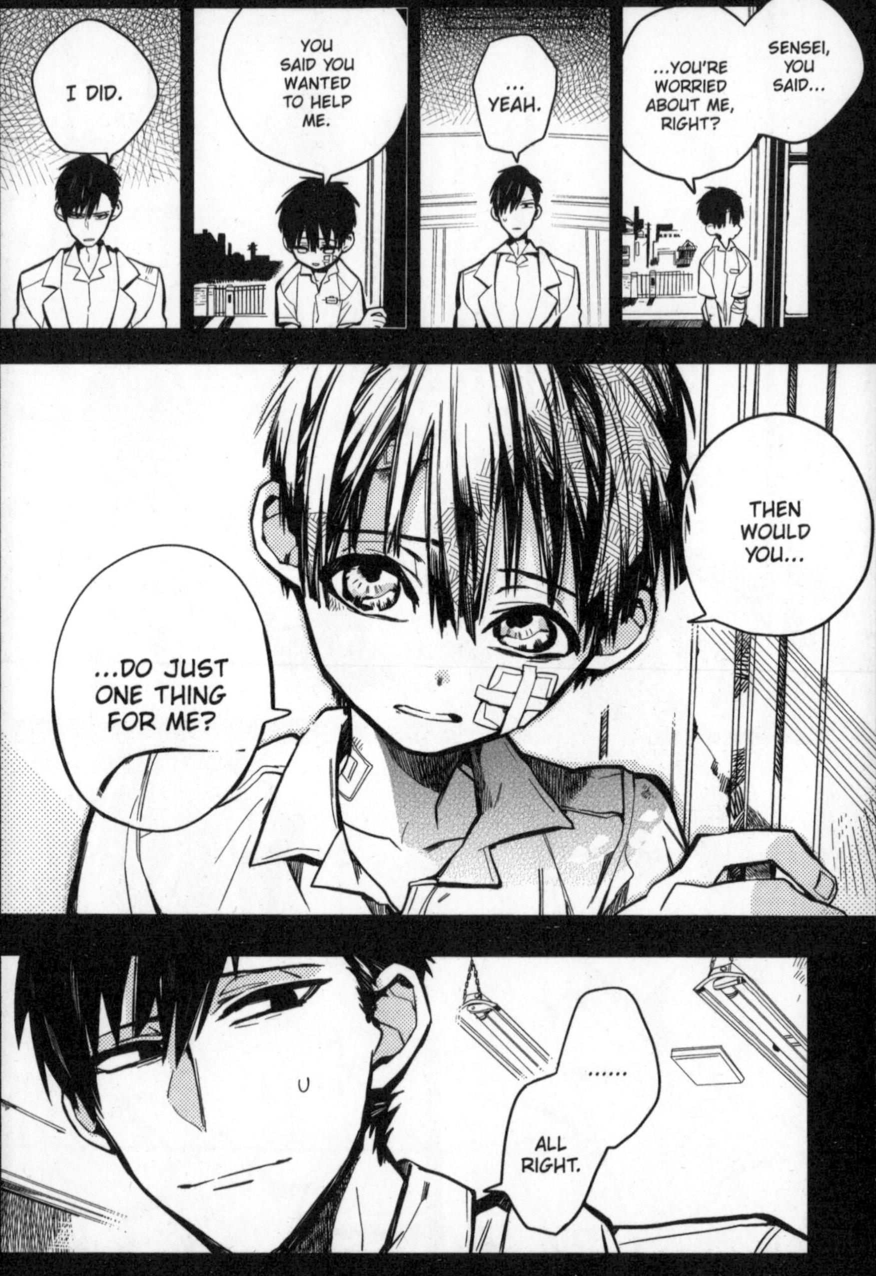
SENSEI, YOU SAID...
...YOU'RE WORRIED ABOUT ME, RIGHT?
... YEAH.
YOU SAID YOU WANTED TO HELP ME.
I DID.
THEN WOULD YOU...
...DO JUST ONE THING FOR ME?
......
ALL RIGHT.

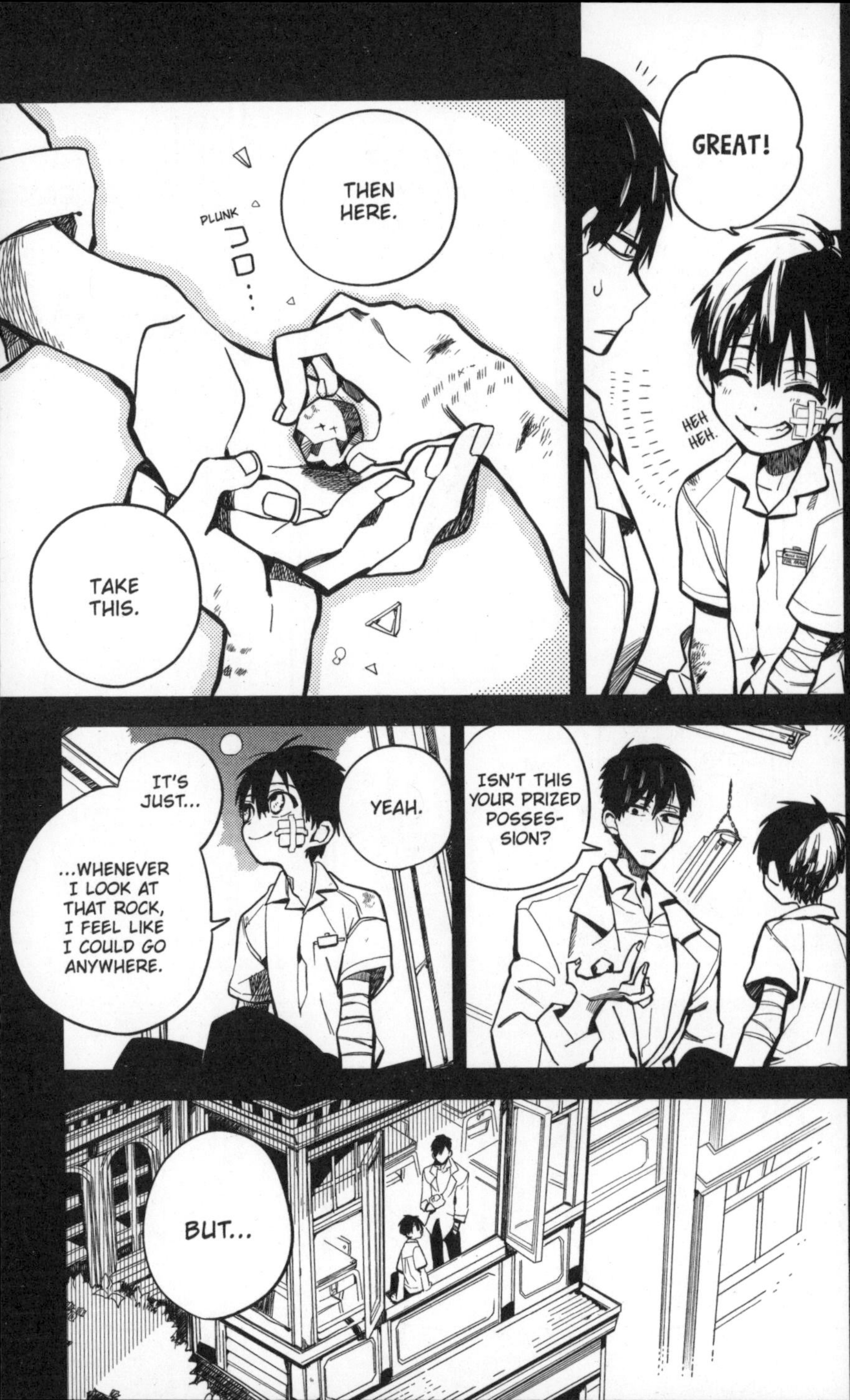
GREAT!
HEH HEH.
THEN HERE.
PLUNK
TAKE THIS.
ISN'T THIS YOUR PRIZED POSSES-SION?
YEAH.
IT'S JUST...
...WHENEVER I LOOK AT THAT ROCK, I FEEL LIKE I COULD GO ANYWHERE.
BUT...

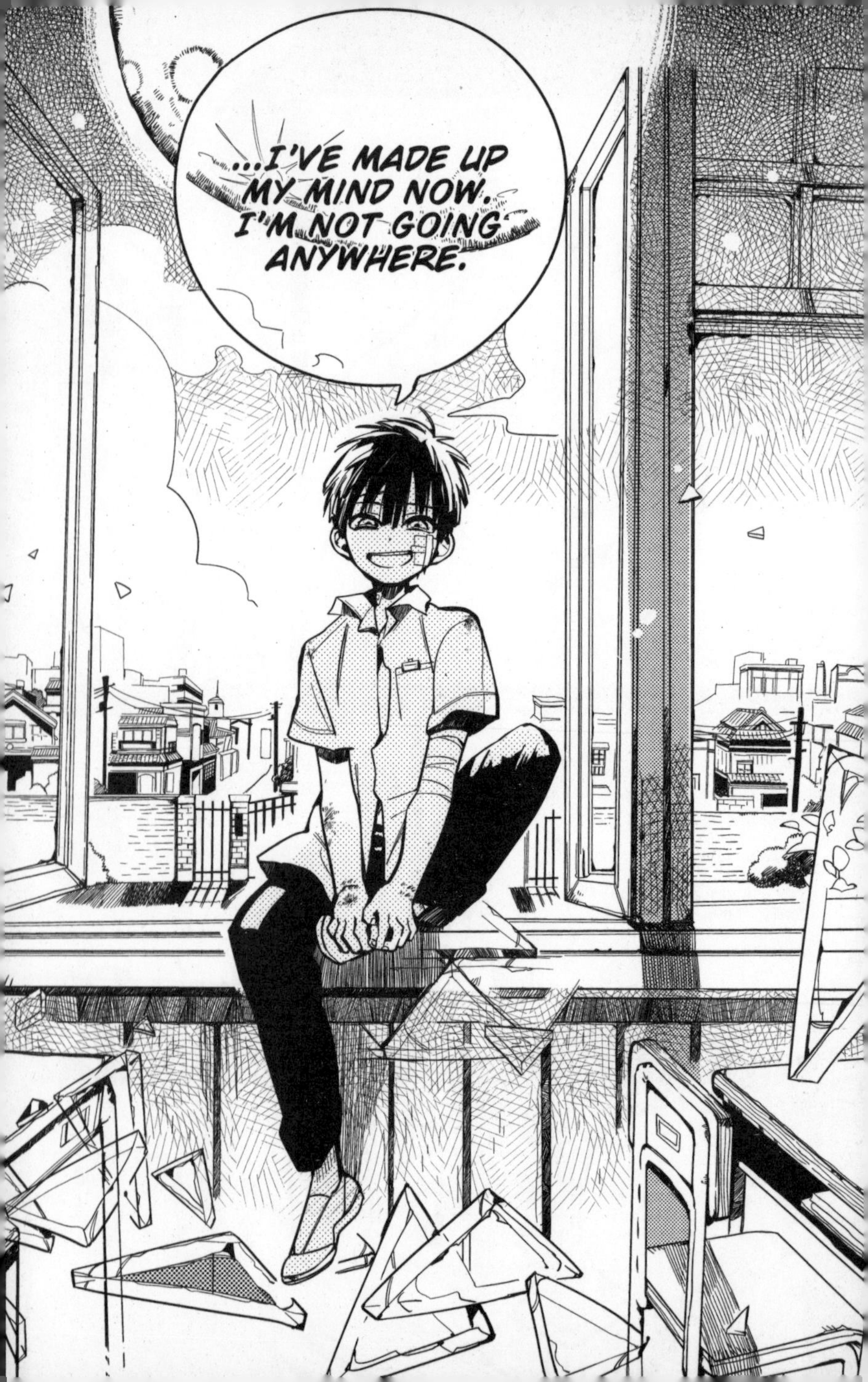
...I'VE MADE UP MY MIND NOW. I'M NOT GOING ANYWHERE.

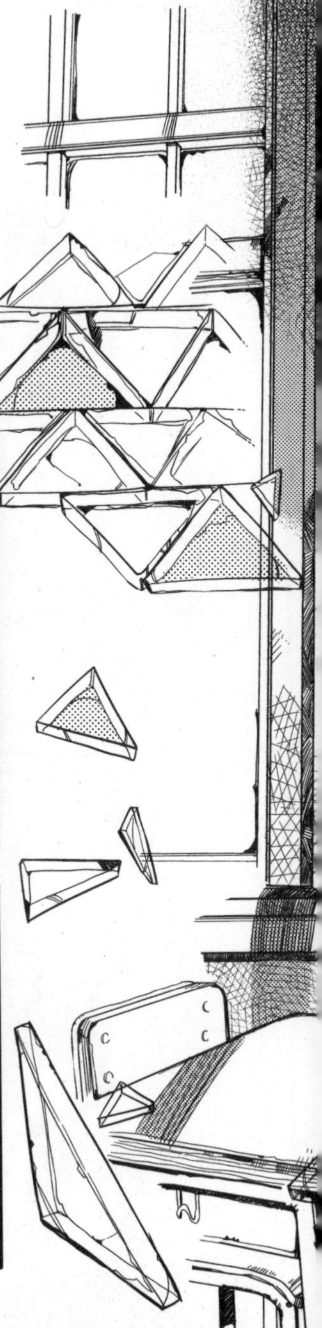

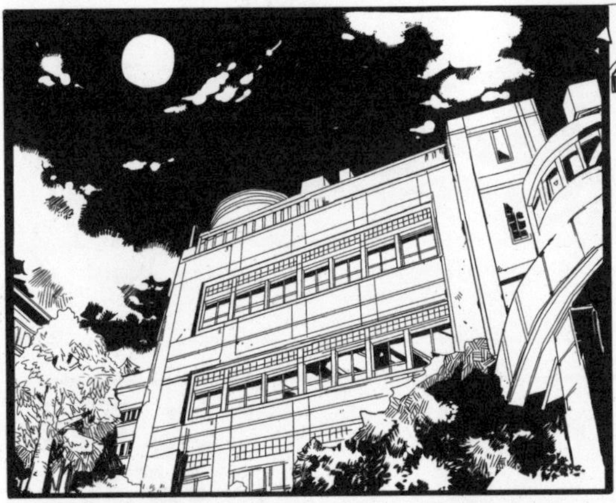

SIGN: NURSE'S OFFICE

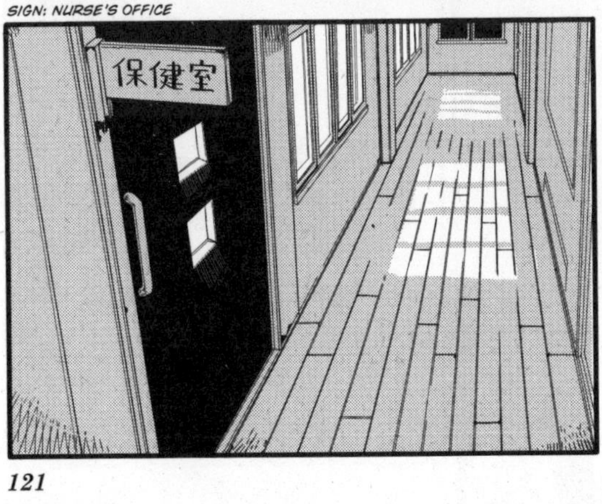
保健室

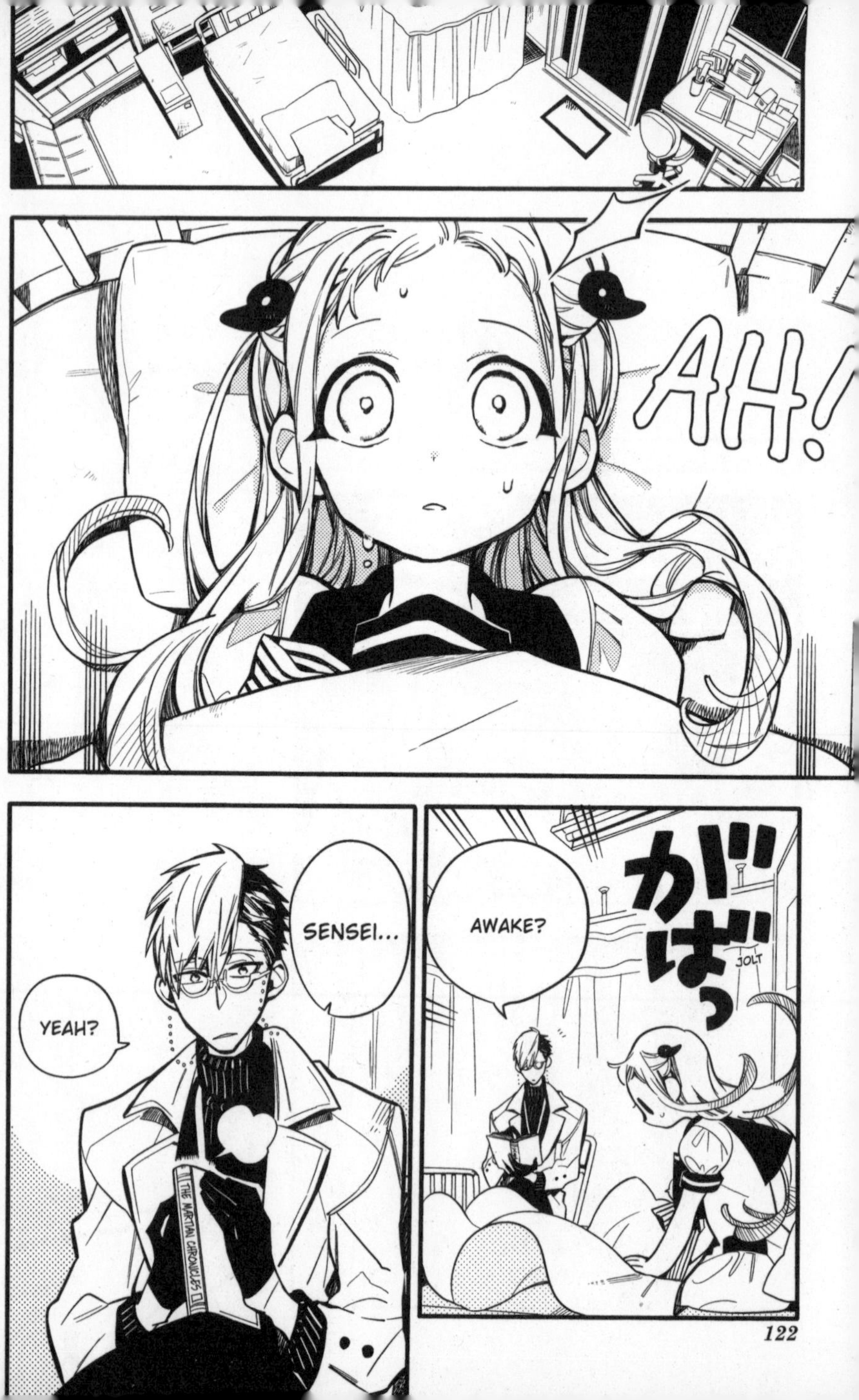
AH!
がばっ
JOLT
AWAKE?
SENSEI...
YEAH?
THE MARTIAN CHRONICLES

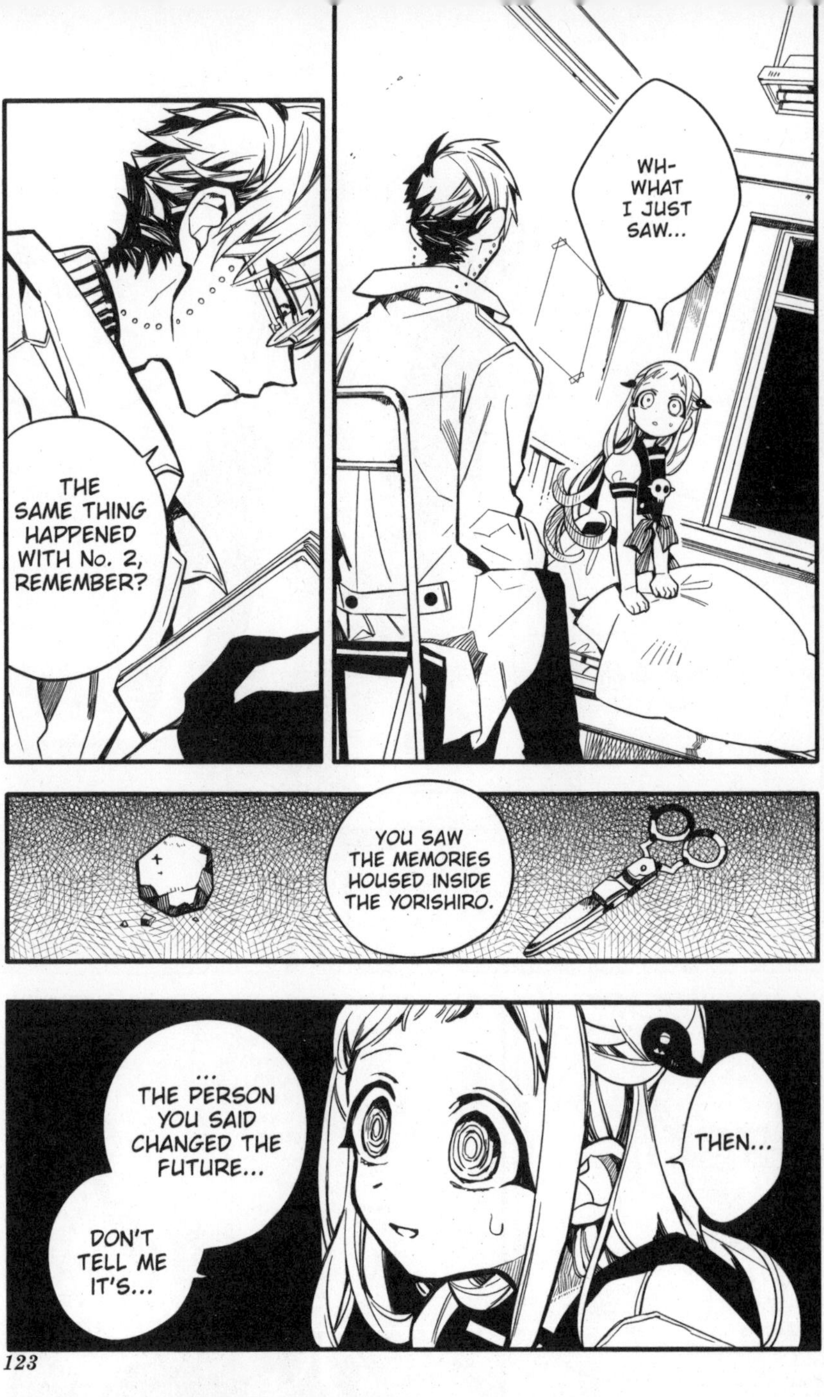
WH- WHAT I JUST SAW...
THE SAME THING HAPPENED WITH No. 2, REMEMBER?
YOU SAW THE MEMORIES HOUSED INSIDE THE YORISHIRO.
THEN...
... THE PERSON YOU SAID CHANGED THE FUTURE...
DON'T TELL ME IT'S...

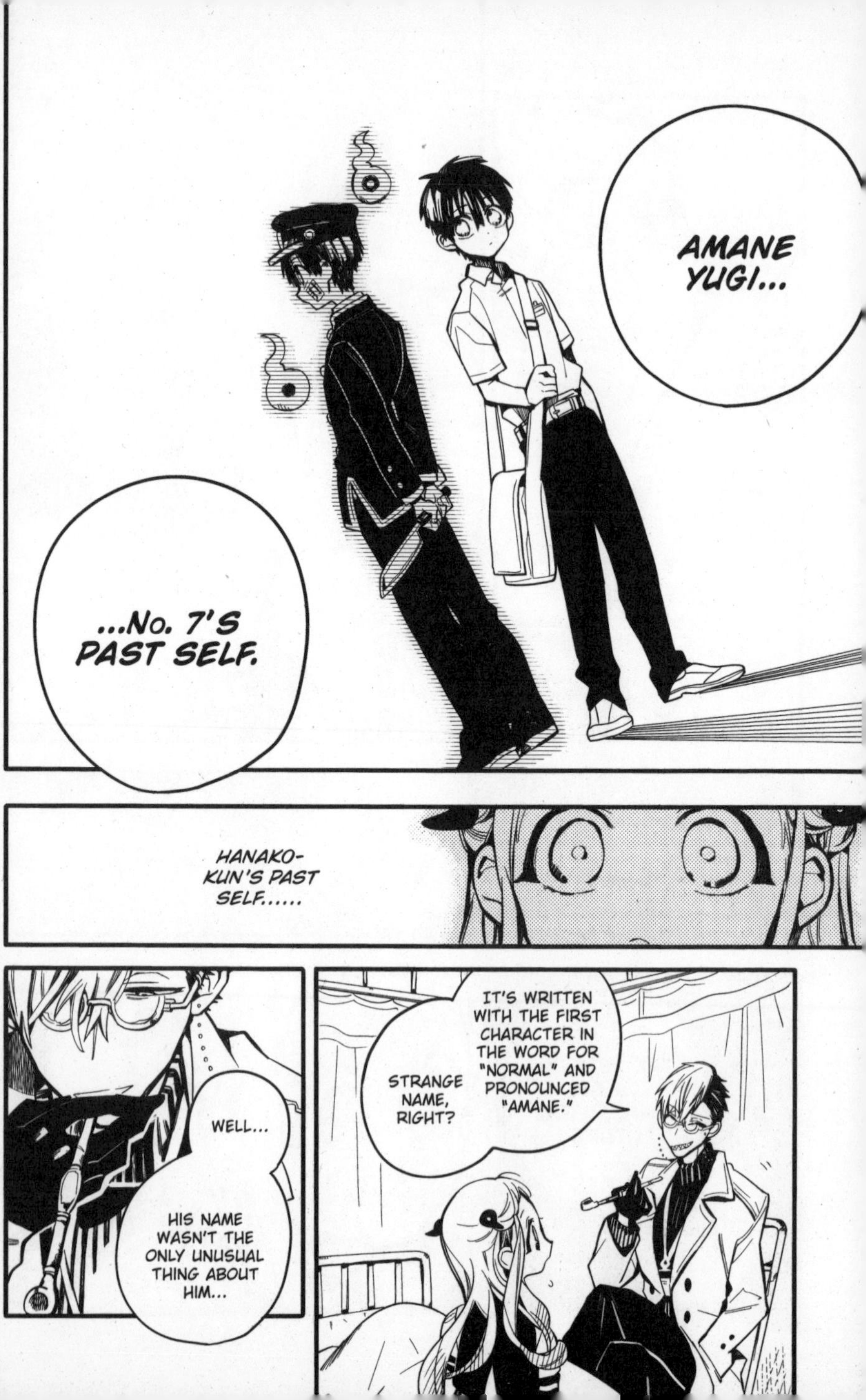
AMANE YUGI...
...No. 7'S PAST SELF.
HANAKO-KUN'S PAST SELF......
IT'S WRITTEN WITH THE FIRST CHARACTER IN THE WORD FOR "NORMAL" AND PRONOUNCED "AMANE."
STRANGE NAME, RIGHT?
WELL...
HIS NAME WASN'T THE ONLY UNUSUAL THING ABOUT HIM...

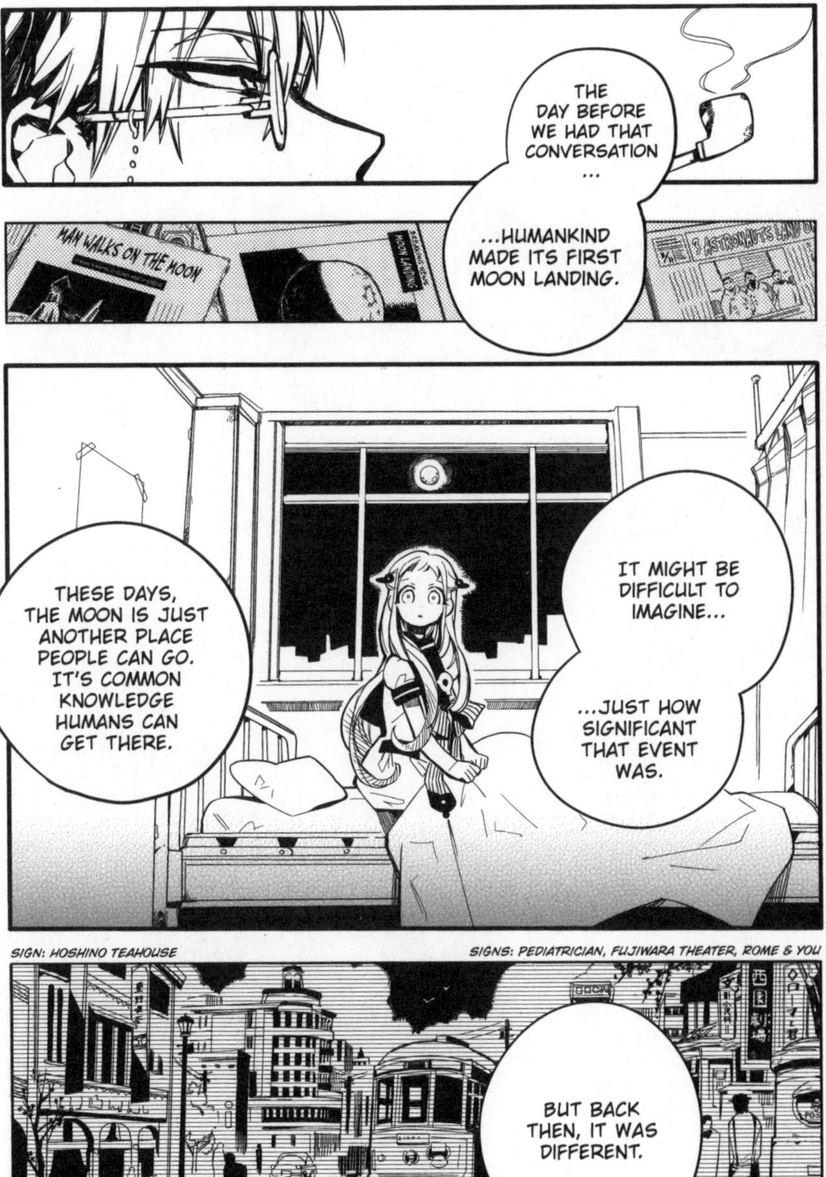
THE DAY BEFORE WE HAD THAT CONVERSATION ...
...HUMANKIND MADE ITS FIRST MOON LANDING.
3 ASTRONAUTS LAND ON
BREAKING NEWS
MOON LANDING
MAN WALKS ON THE MOON
IT MIGHT BE DIFFICULT TO IMAGINE...
...JUST HOW SIGNIFICANT THAT EVENT WAS.
THESE DAYS, THE MOON IS JUST ANOTHER PLACE PEOPLE CAN GO. IT'S COMMON KNOWLEDGE HUMANS CAN GET THERE.
SIGNS: PEDIATRICIAN, FUJIWARA THEATER, ROME & YOU
SIGN: HOSHINO TEAHOUSE
BUT BACK THEN, IT WAS DIFFERENT.

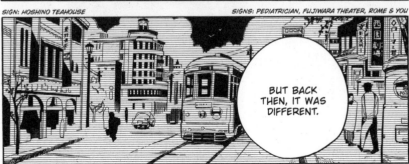

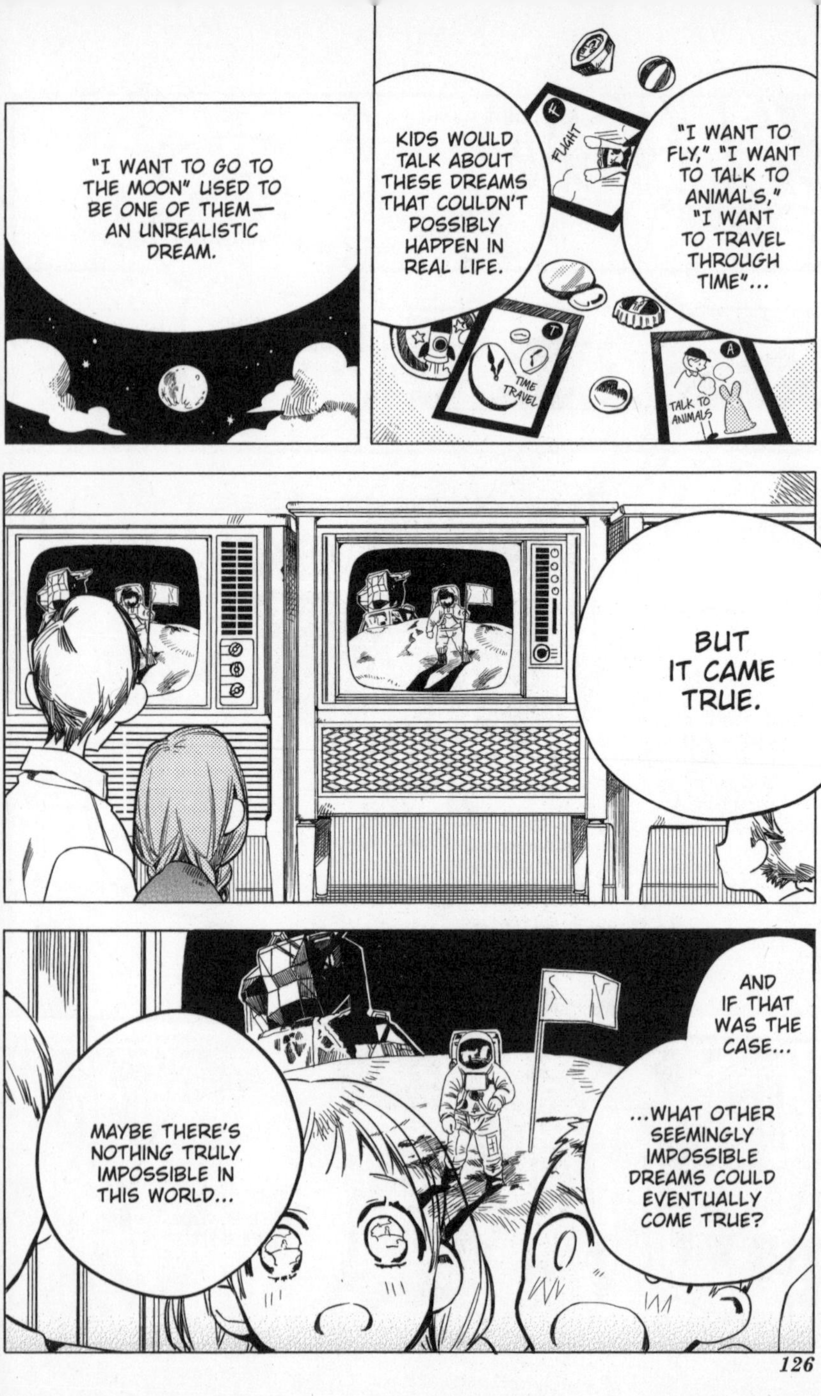
KIDS WOULD TALK ABOUT THESE DREAMS THAT COULDN'T POSSIBLY HAPPEN IN REAL LIFE.
FLIGHT
"I WANT TO FLY," "I WANT TO TALK TO ANIMALS," "I WANT TO TRAVEL THROUGH TIME"...
TIME TRAVEL
TALK TO ANIMALS
"I WANT TO GO TO THE MOON" USED TO BE ONE OF THEM— AN UNREALISTIC DREAM.
BUT IT CAME TRUE.
AND IF THAT WAS THE CASE...
...WHAT OTHER SEEMINGLY IMPOSSIBLE DREAMS COULD EVENTUALLY COME TRUE?
MAYBE THERE'S NOTHING TRULY IMPOSSIBLE IN THIS WORLD...

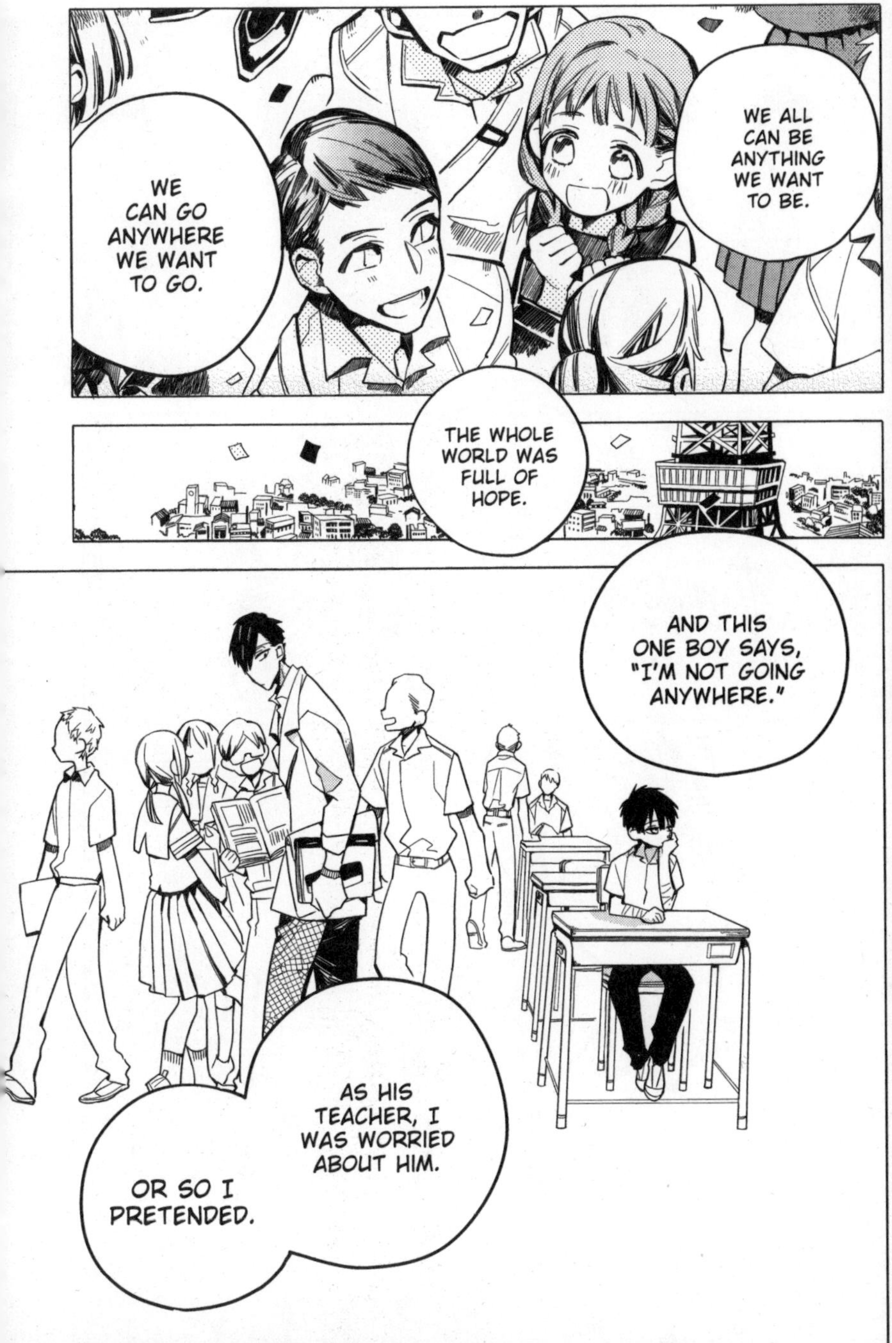
WE ALL CAN BE ANYTHING WE WANT TO BE.
WE CAN GO ANYWHERE WE WANT TO GO.
THE WHOLE WORLD WAS FULL OF HOPE.
AND THIS ONE BOY SAYS, "I'M NOT GOING ANYWHERE."
AS HIS TEACHER, I WAS WORRIED ABOUT HIM.
OR SO I PRETENDED.

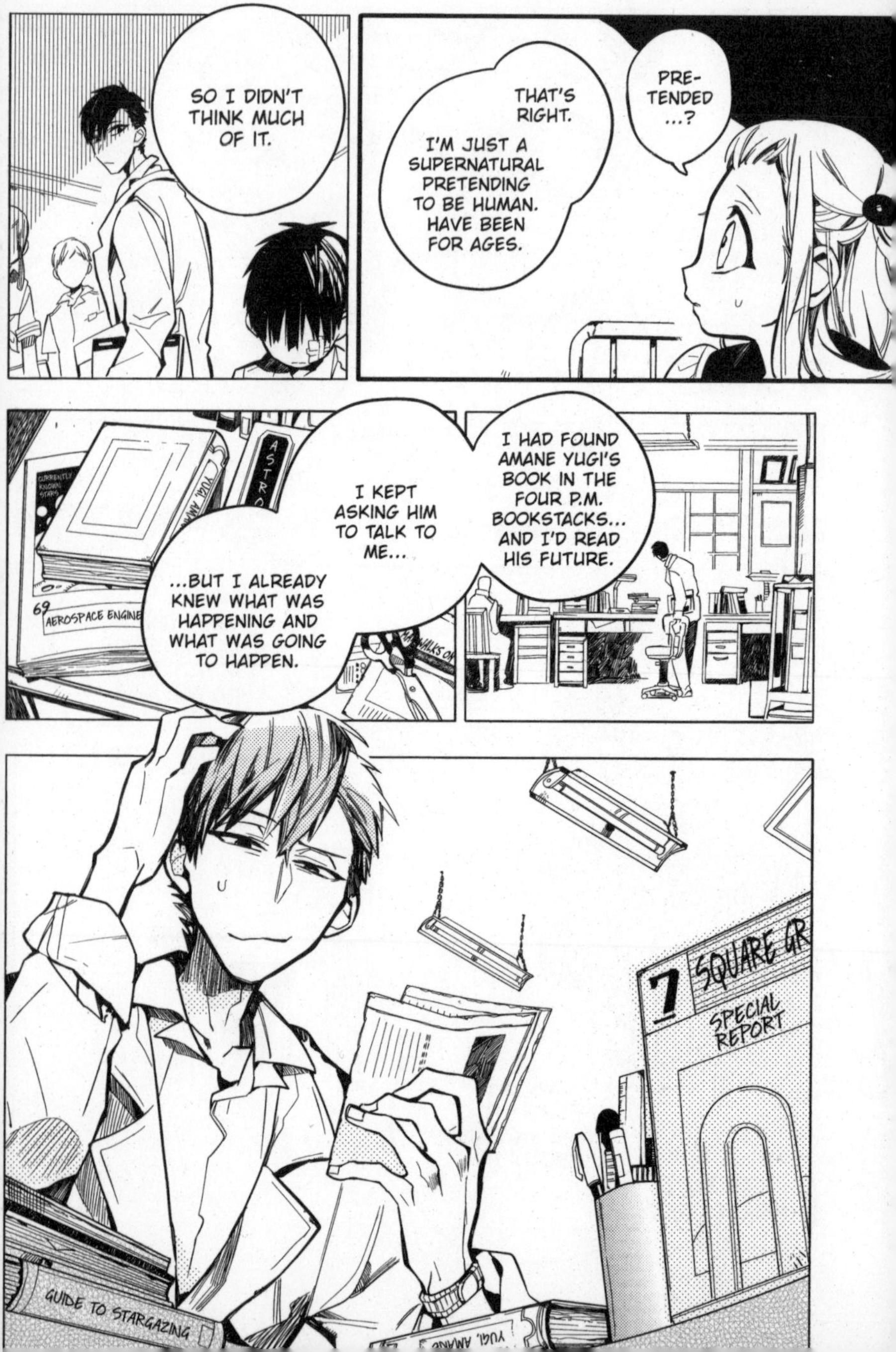
PRE-TENDED ...?
THAT'S RIGHT.
I'M JUST A SUPERNATURAL PRETENDING TO BE HUMAN. HAVE BEEN FOR AGES.
SO I DIDN'T THINK MUCH OF IT.
I HAD FOUND AMANE YUGI'S BOOK IN THE FOUR P.M. BOOKSTACKS... AND I'D READ HIS FUTURE.
I KEPT ASKING HIM TO TALK TO ME...
...BUT I ALREADY KNEW WHAT WAS HAPPENING AND WHAT WAS GOING TO HAPPEN.
ASTRO
69
AEROSPACE ENGINE
7
SQUARE GR
SPECIAL REPORT
GUIDE TO STARGAZING

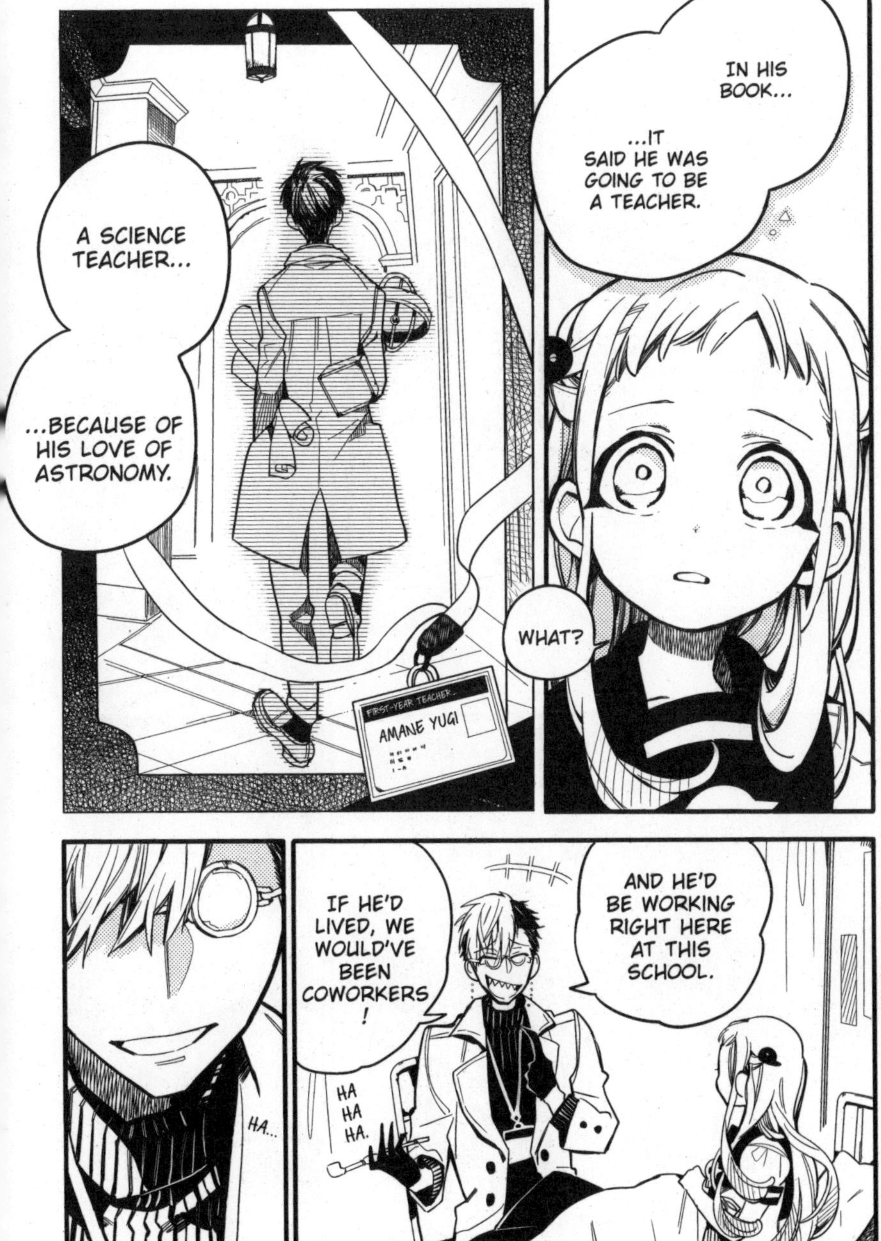
IN HIS BOOK...
...IT SAID HE WAS GOING TO BE A TEACHER.
WHAT?
A SCIENCE TEACHER...
...BECAUSE OF HIS LOVE OF ASTRONOMY.
FIRST-YEAR TEACHER
AMANE YUGI
AND HE'D BE WORKING RIGHT HERE AT THIS SCHOOL.
IF HE'D LIVED, WE WOULD'VE BEEN COWORKERS!
HA HA HA.
HA...

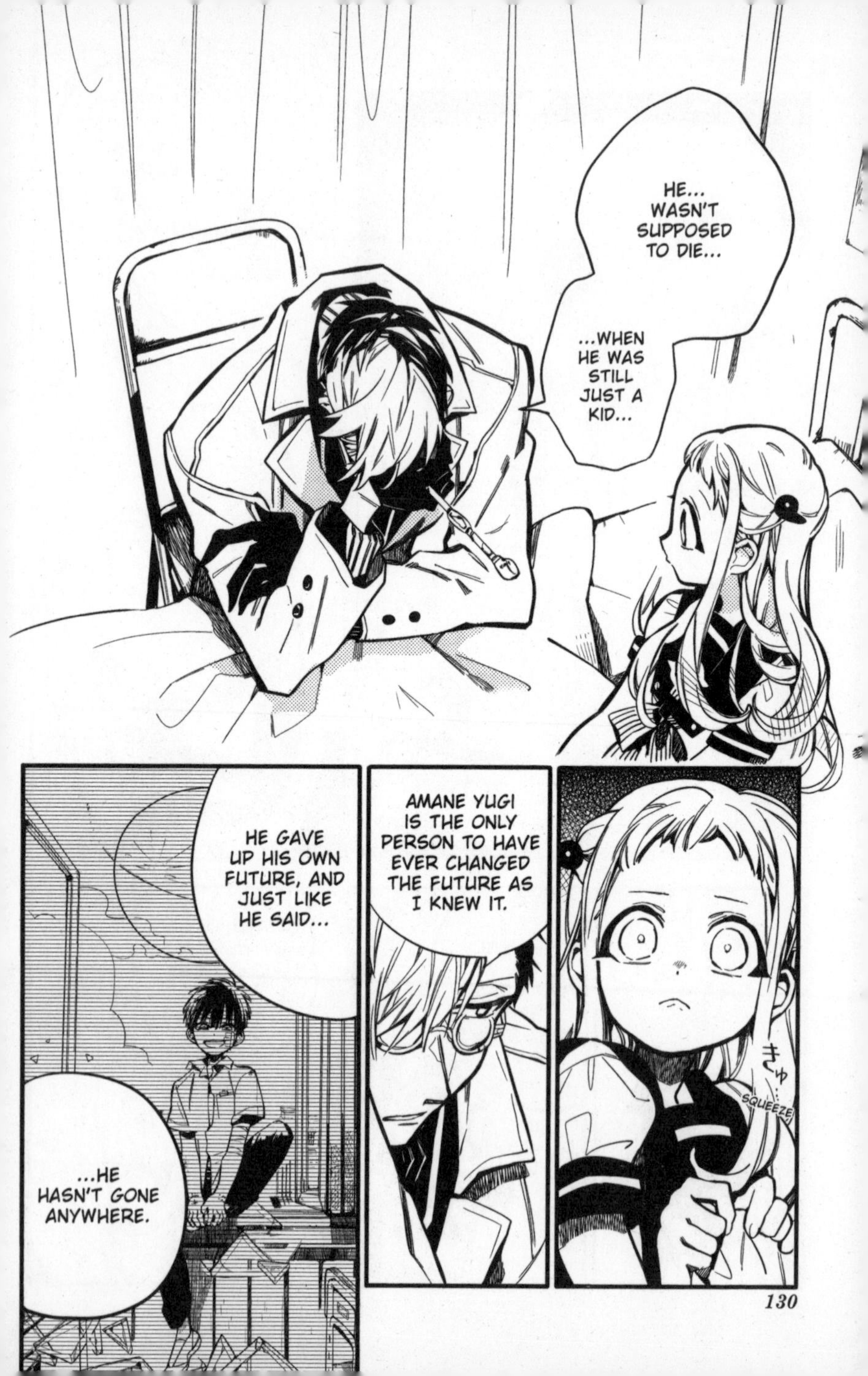
HE... WASN'T SUPPOSED TO DIE...
...WHEN HE WAS STILL JUST A KID...
きゅ
SQUEEZE
AMANE YUGI IS THE ONLY PERSON TO HAVE EVER CHANGED THE FUTURE AS I KNEW IT.
HE GAVE UP HIS OWN FUTURE, AND JUST LIKE HE SAID...
...HE HASN'T GONE ANYWHERE.

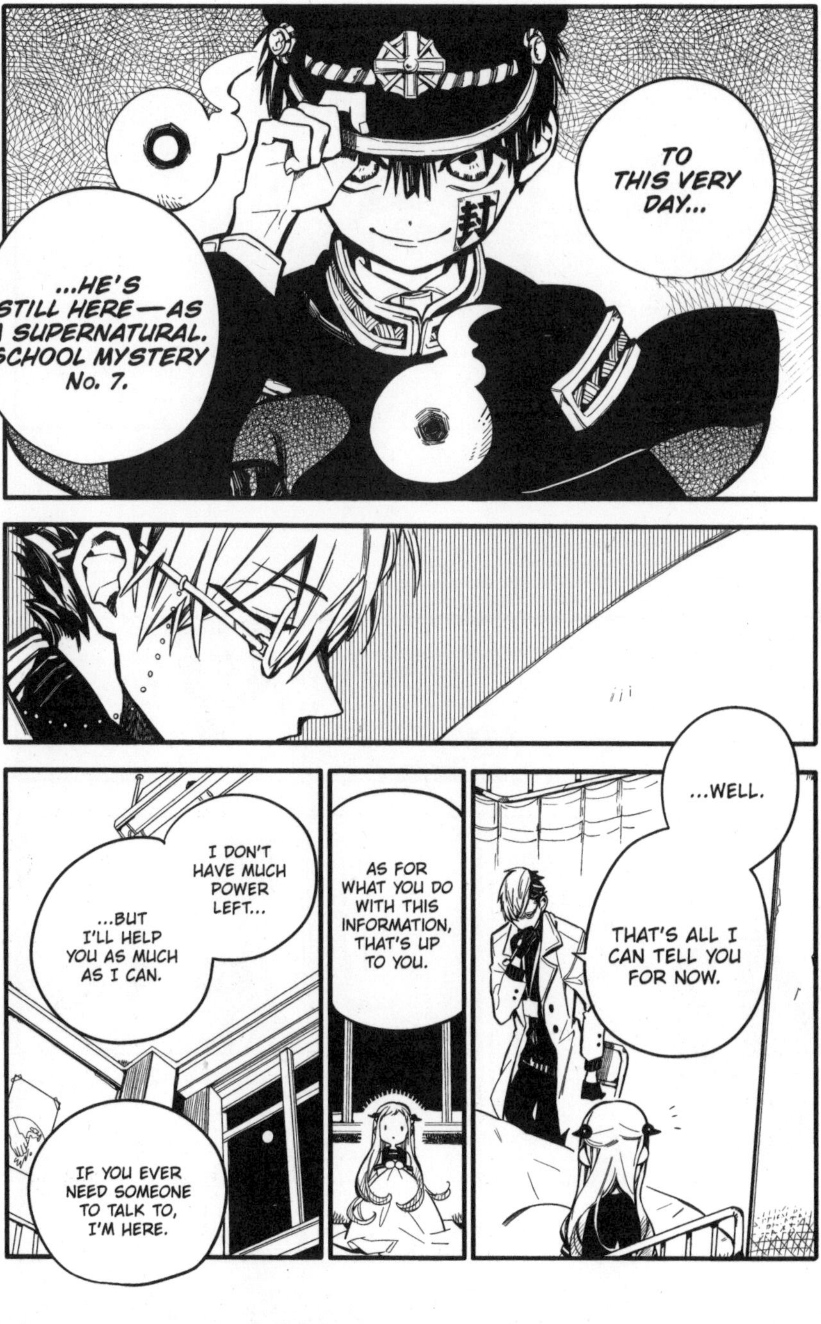
TO THIS VERY DAY...
...HE'S STILL HERE—AS A SUPERNATURAL SCHOOL MYSTERY No. 7.
...WELL.
THAT'S ALL I CAN TELL YOU FOR NOW.
AS FOR WHAT YOU DO WITH THIS INFORMATION, THAT'S UP TO YOU.
I DON'T HAVE MUCH POWER LEFT...
...BUT I'LL HELP YOU AS MUCH AS I CAN.
IF YOU EVER NEED SOMEONE TO TALK TO, I'M HERE.

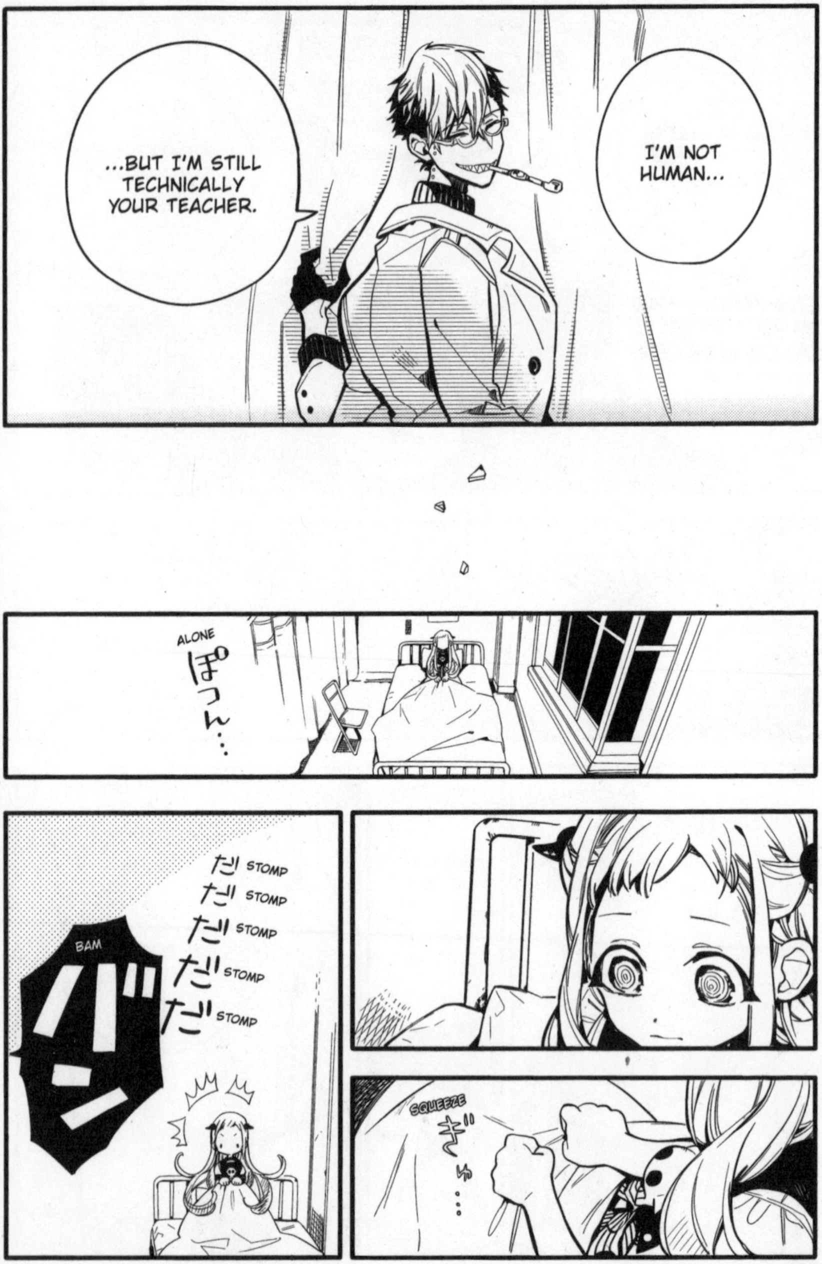
I'M NOT HUMAN...
...BUT I'M STILL TECHNICALLY YOUR TEACHER.
ALONE
ぽつん…
SQUEEZE
ぎゅ…
だだだだだ
STOMP
STOMP
STOMP
STOMP
STOMP
BAM
バン

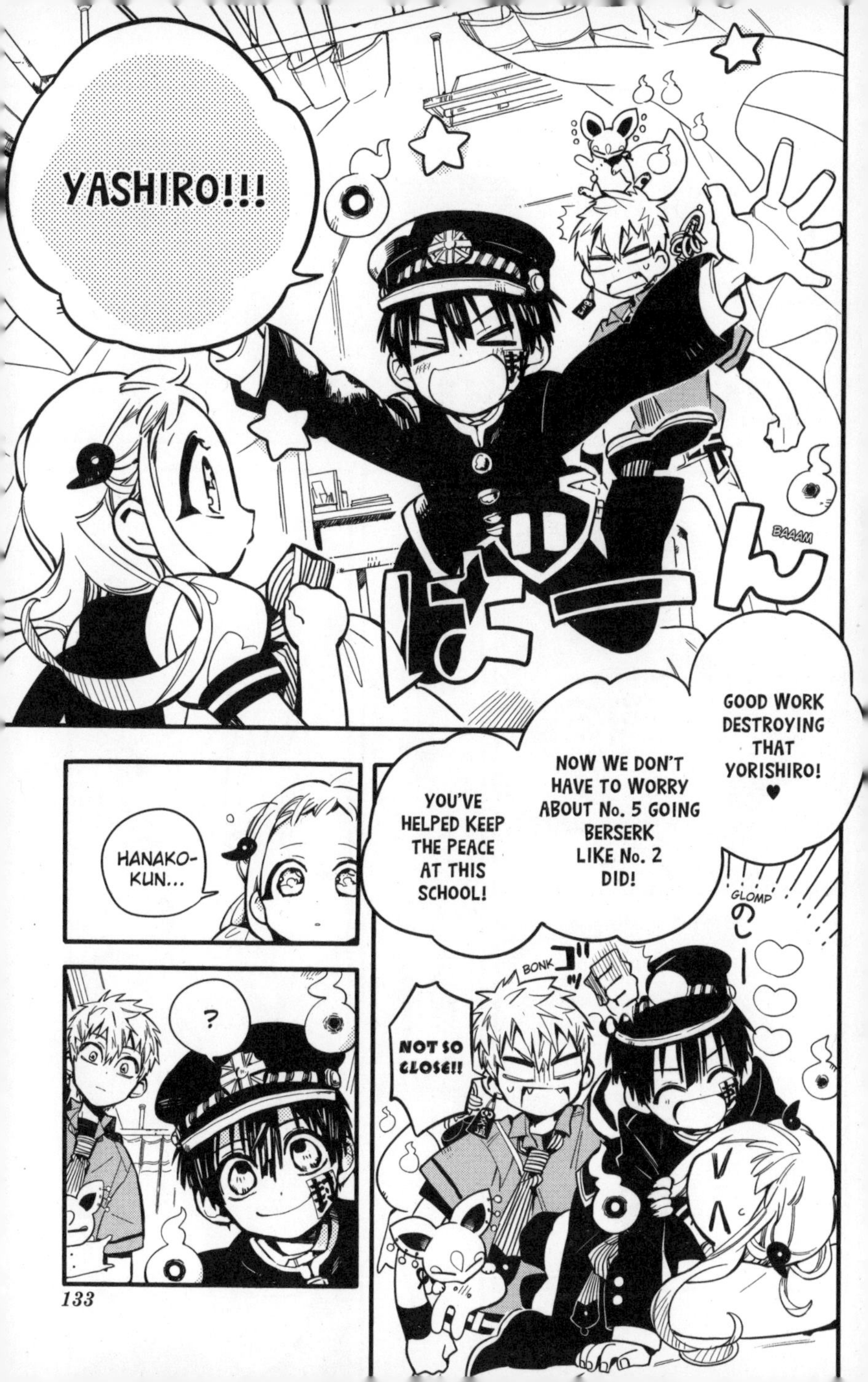

YASHIRO!!!
BAAAM
GOOD WORK DESTROYING THAT YORISHIRO! ♥
NOW WE DON'T HAVE TO WORRY ABOUT No. 5 GOING BERSERK LIKE No. 2 DID!
YOU'VE HELPED KEEP THE PEACE AT THIS SCHOOL!
GLOMP
BONK
NOT SO CLOSE!!
HANAKO-KUN...
?

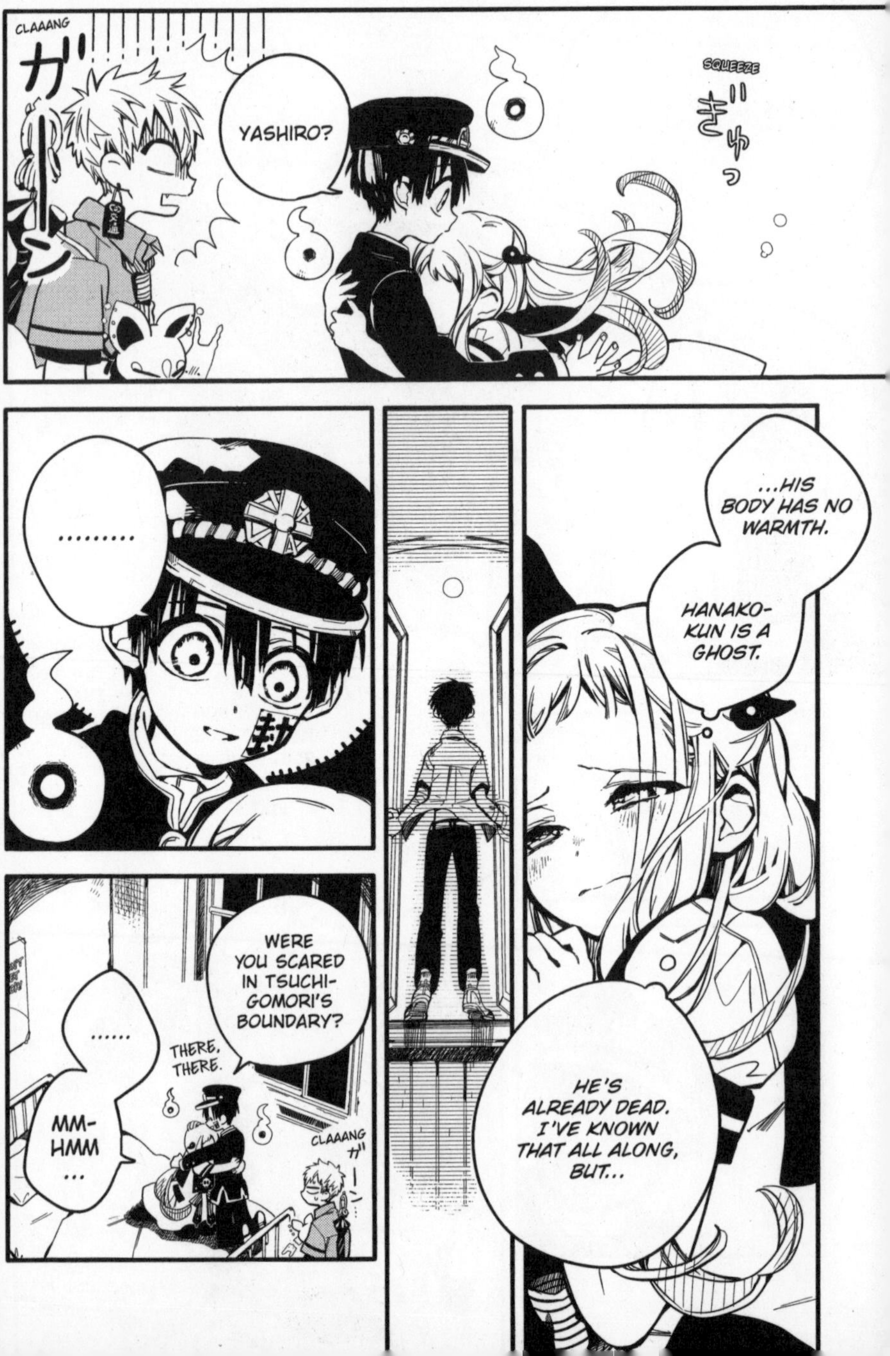
SQUEEZE
ぎゅっ
YASHIRO?
CLAAANG
ガ
...HIS BODY HAS NO WARMTH.
HANAKO-KUN IS A GHOST.
HE'S ALREADY DEAD. I'VE KNOWN THAT ALL ALONG, BUT...
....
WERE YOU SCARED IN TSUCHI-GOMORI'S BOUNDARY?
THERE, THERE.
......
MM-HMM ...
CLAAANG
ガー

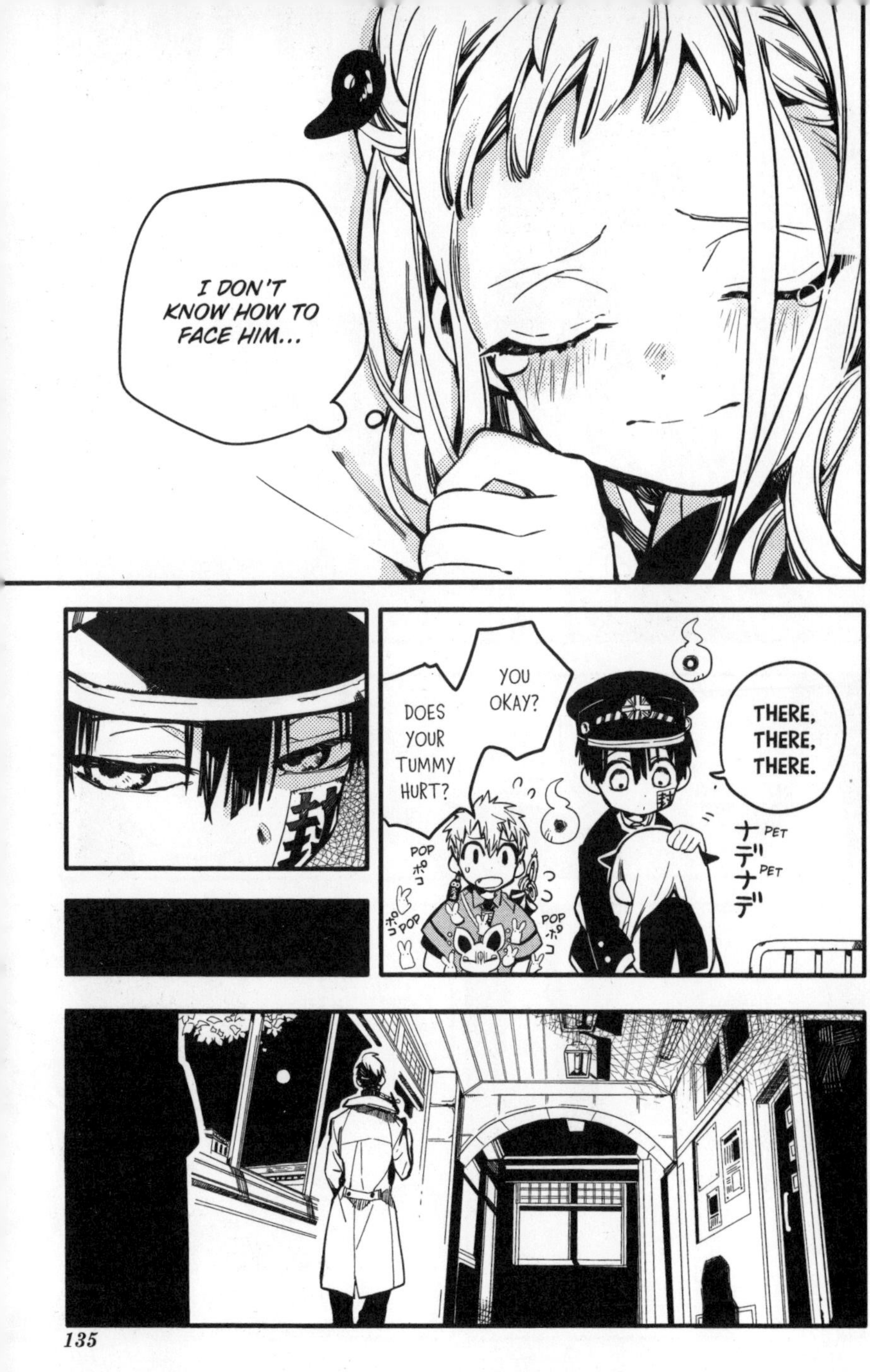
I DON'T KNOW HOW TO FACE HIM...
THERE, THERE, THERE.
ナデナデ PET PET
YOU OKAY?
DOES YOUR TUMMY HURT?
ポコ POP
ポコ POP
ポコ POP

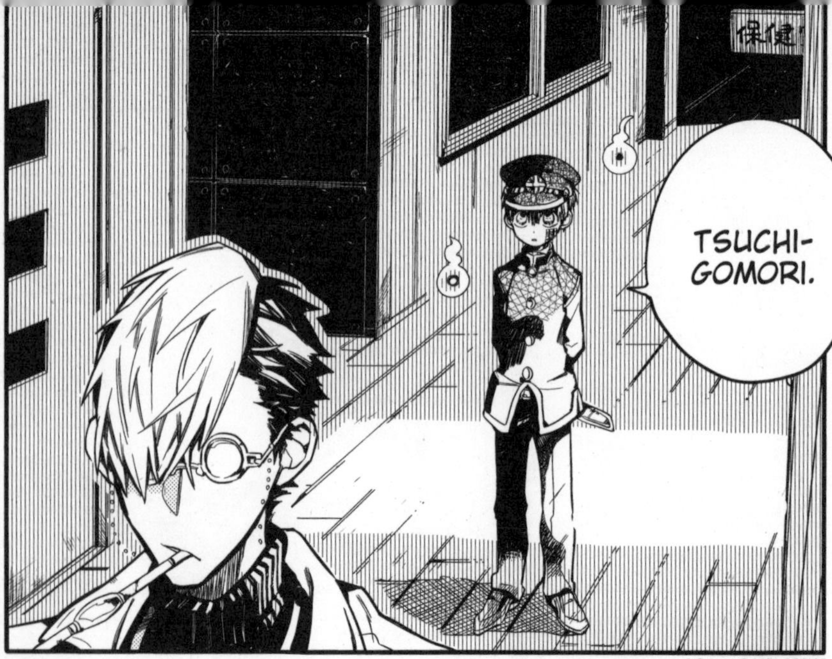
TSUCHI-GOMORI.

SIGN: NURSE'S OFFICE

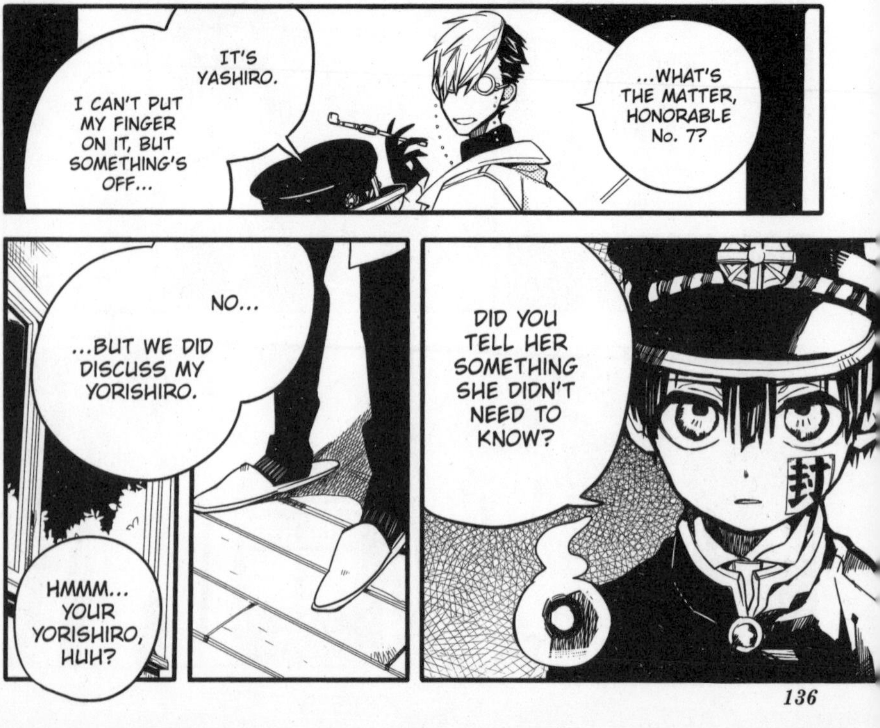
...WHAT'S THE MATTER, HONORABLE No. 7?
IT'S YASHIRO.
I CAN'T PUT MY FINGER ON IT, BUT SOMETHING'S OFF...
DID YOU TELL HER SOMETHING SHE DIDN'T NEED TO KNOW?
NO...
...BUT WE DID DISCUSS MY YORISHIRO.
HMMM... YOUR YORISHIRO, HUH?

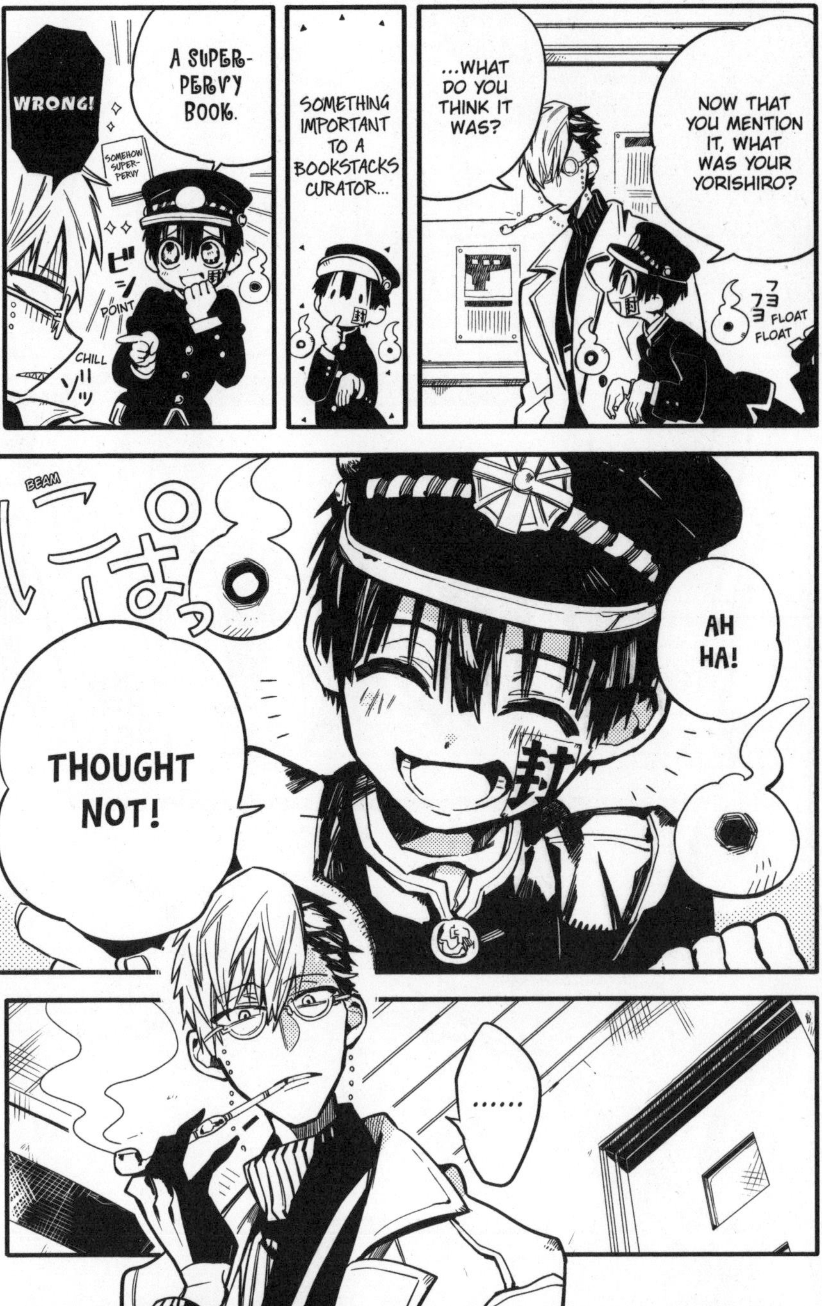
NOW THAT YOU MENTION IT, WHAT WAS YOUR YORISHIRO?
...WHAT DO YOU THINK IT WAS?
フヨフヨ FLOAT FLOAT
SOMETHING IMPORTANT TO A BOOKSTACKS CURATOR...
A SUPER-PERVY BOOK.
SOMEHOW SUPER-PERVY
ビシ POINT
WRONG!
ゾッ CHILL
にぱっ BEAM
AH HA!
THOUGHT NOT!
......

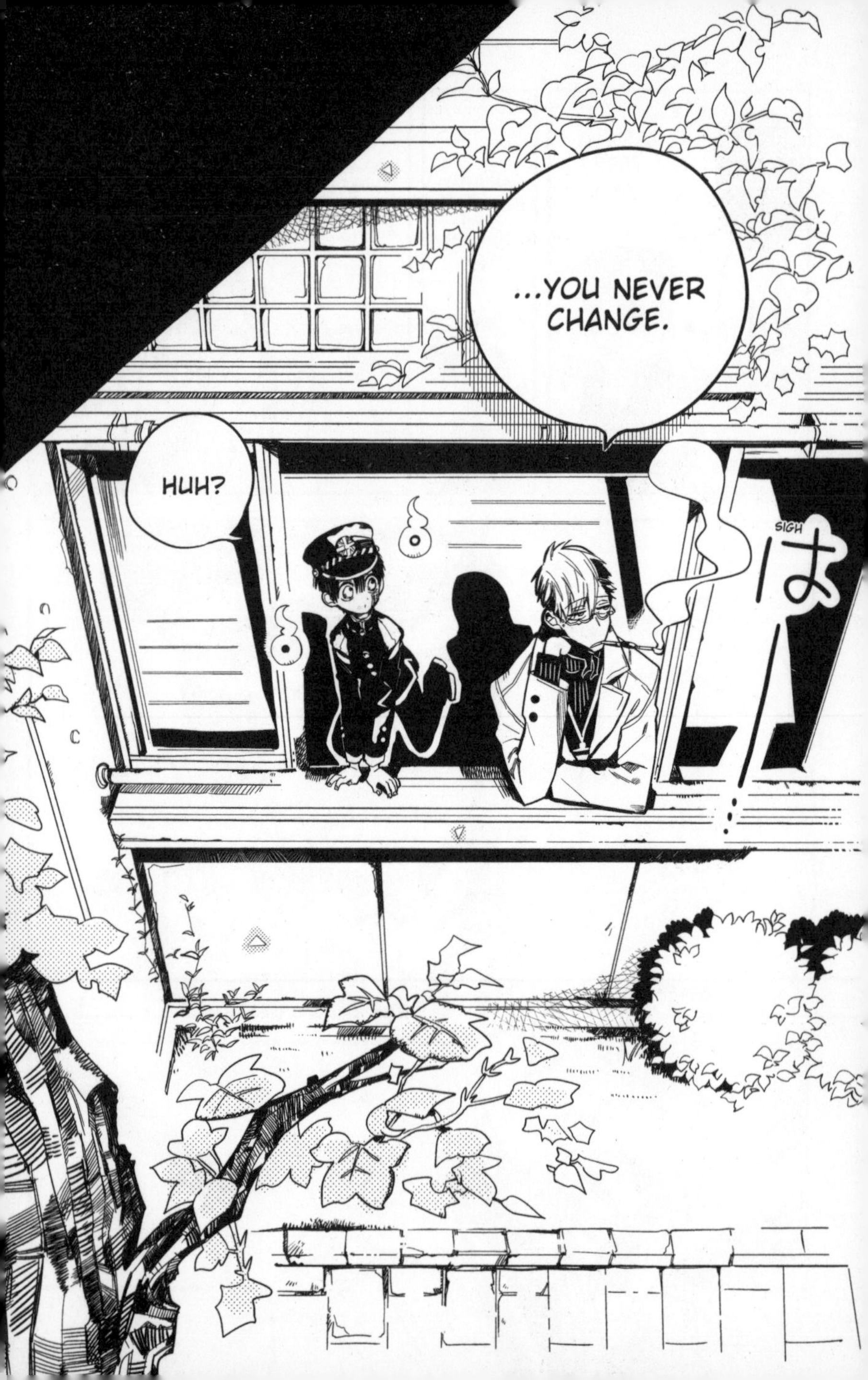
...YOU NEVER CHANGE.
HUH?
SIGH
は

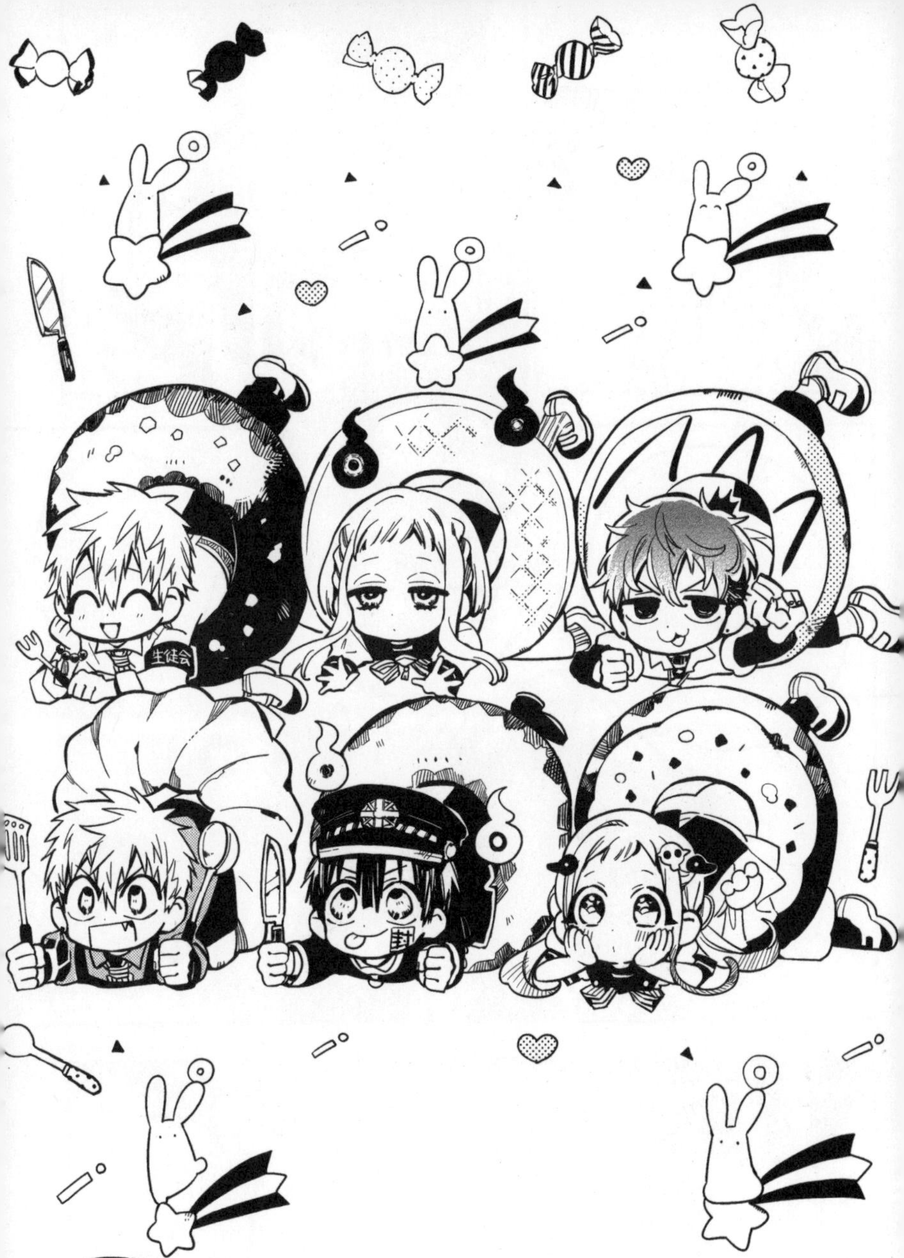
生徒会

SPOOK 15

THE DONUTS

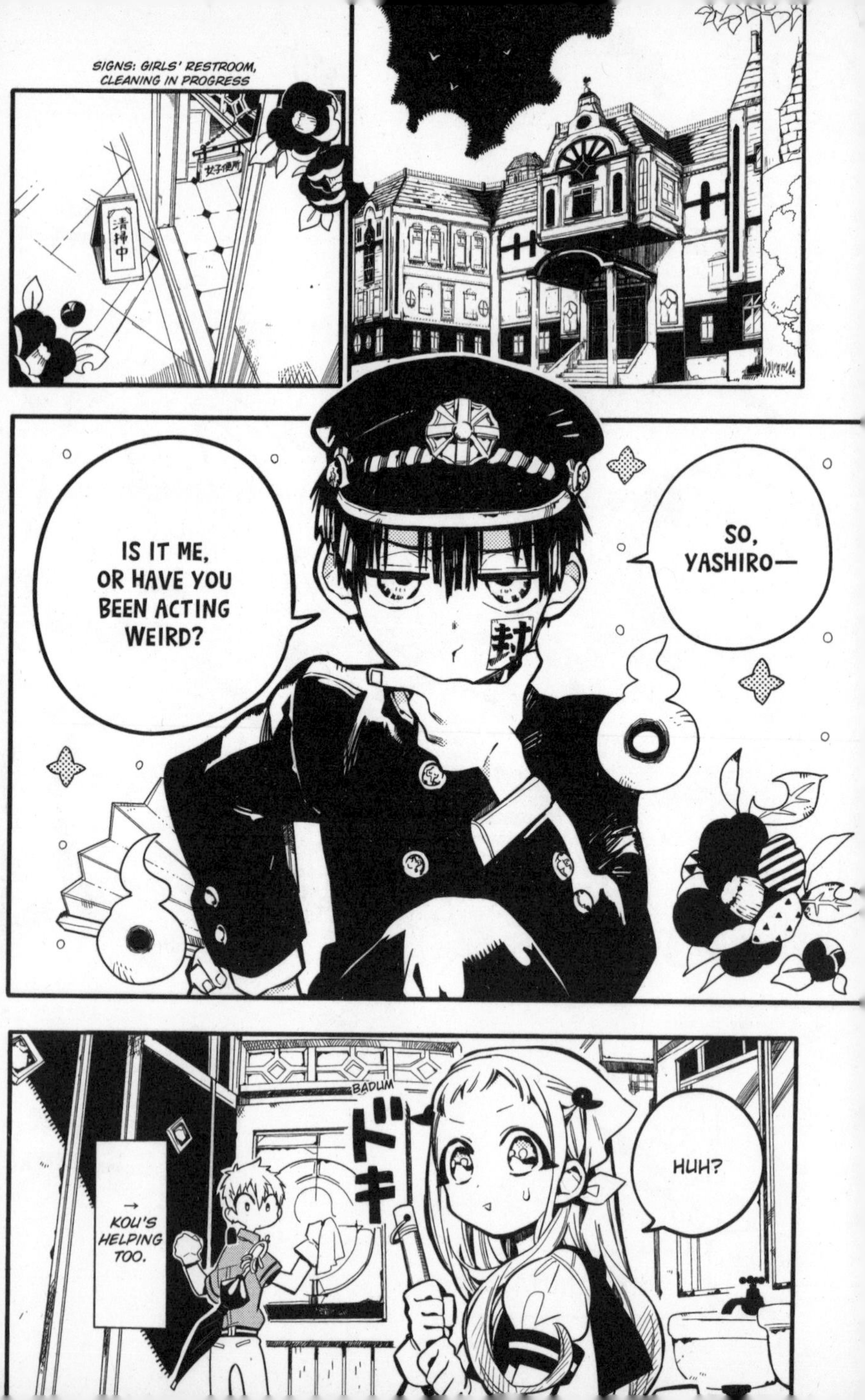
SIGNS: GIRLS' RESTROOM, CLEANING IN PROGRESS
SO, YASHIRO—
IS IT ME, OR HAVE YOU BEEN ACTING WEIRD?
HUH?
BADUM
ドキ
→ KOU'S HELPING TOO.

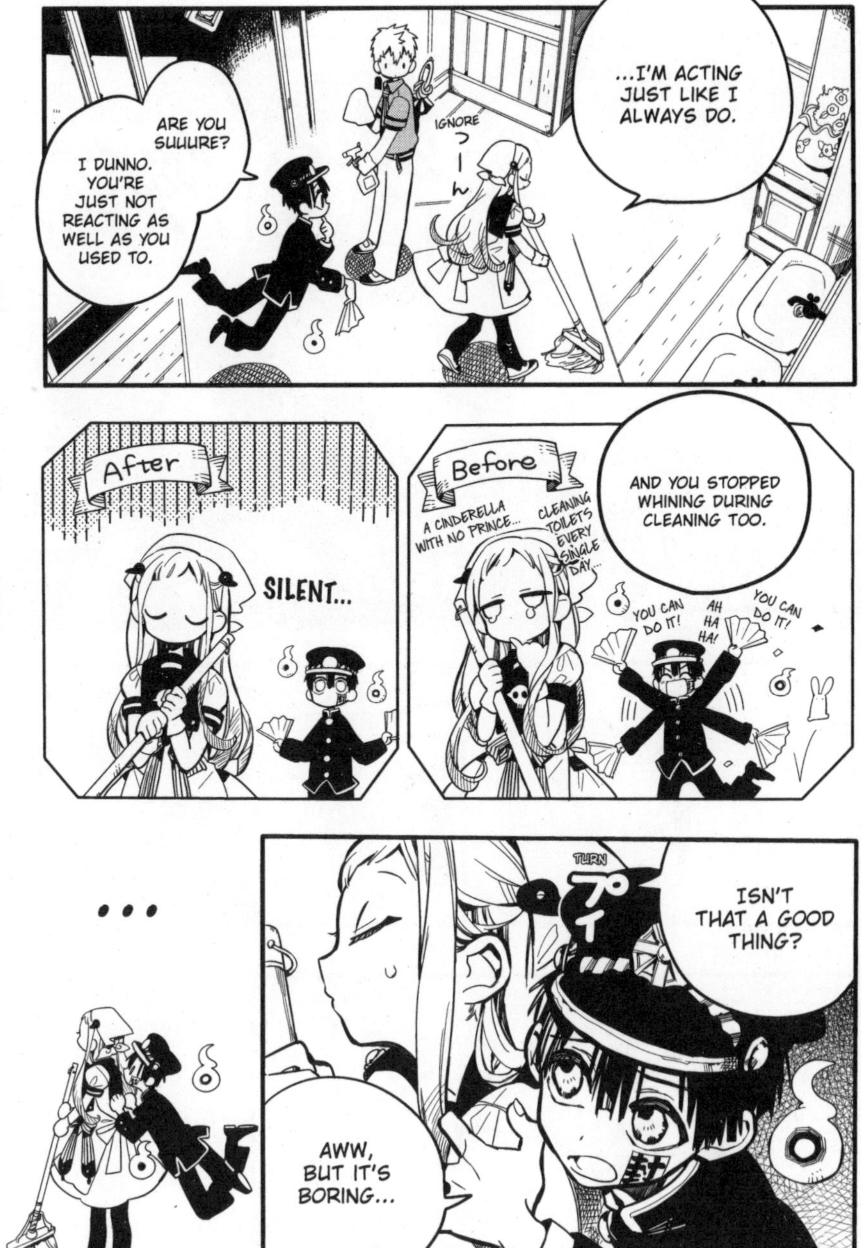
...I'M ACTING JUST LIKE I ALWAYS DO.
IGNORE
つーん
ARE YOU SUUURE? I DUNNO. YOU'RE JUST NOT REACTING AS WELL AS YOU USED TO.
AND YOU STOPPED WHINING DURING CLEANING TOO.
Before
CLEANING TOILETS EVERY SINGLE DAY...
A CINDERELLA WITH NO PRINCE...
YOU CAN DO IT!
AH HA HA!
YOU CAN DO IT!
After
SILENT...
TURN
プイ
ISN'T THAT A GOOD THING?
AWW, BUT IT'S BORING...
• • •

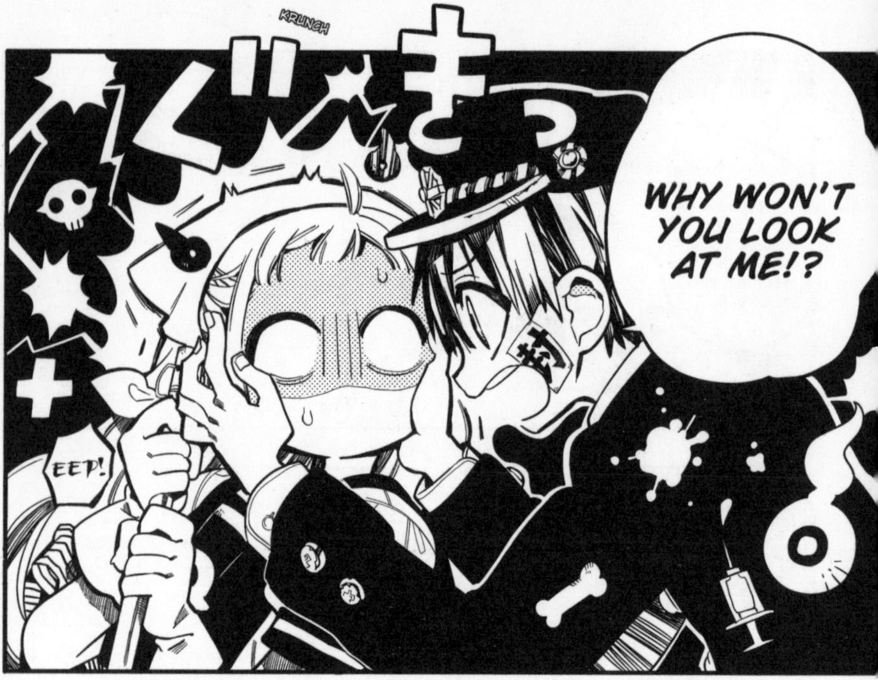
WHY WON'T YOU LOOK AT ME!?
KRUNCH
EEP!

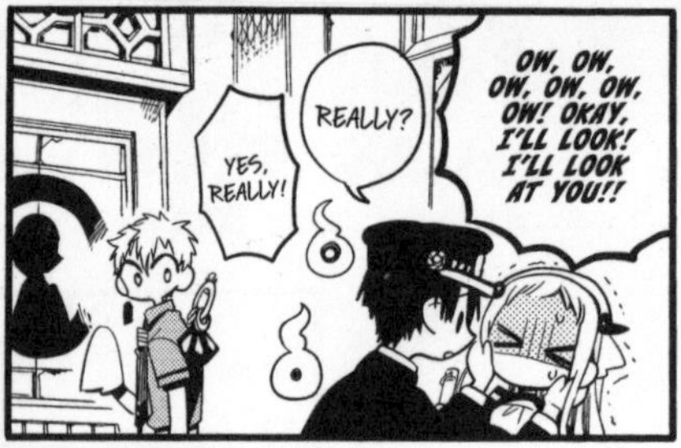
OW, OW, OW, OW, OW, OW! OKAY, I'LL LOOK! I'LL LOOK AT YOU!!
REALLY?
YES, REALLY!

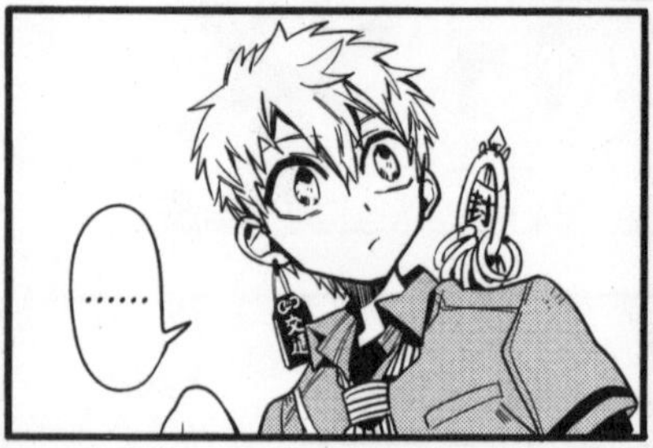
......

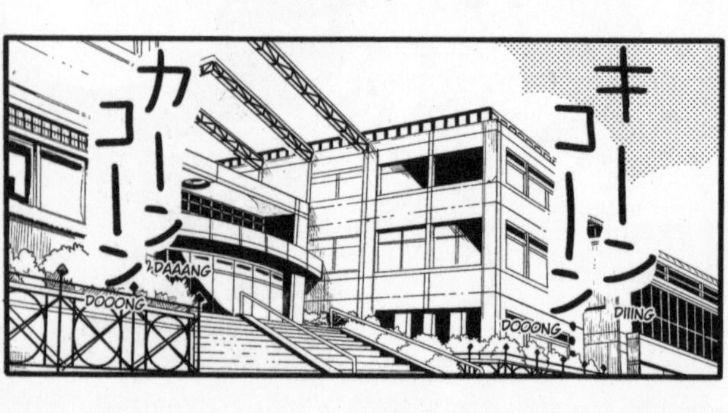
DIIING
DOOONG
DAAAANG
DOOONG

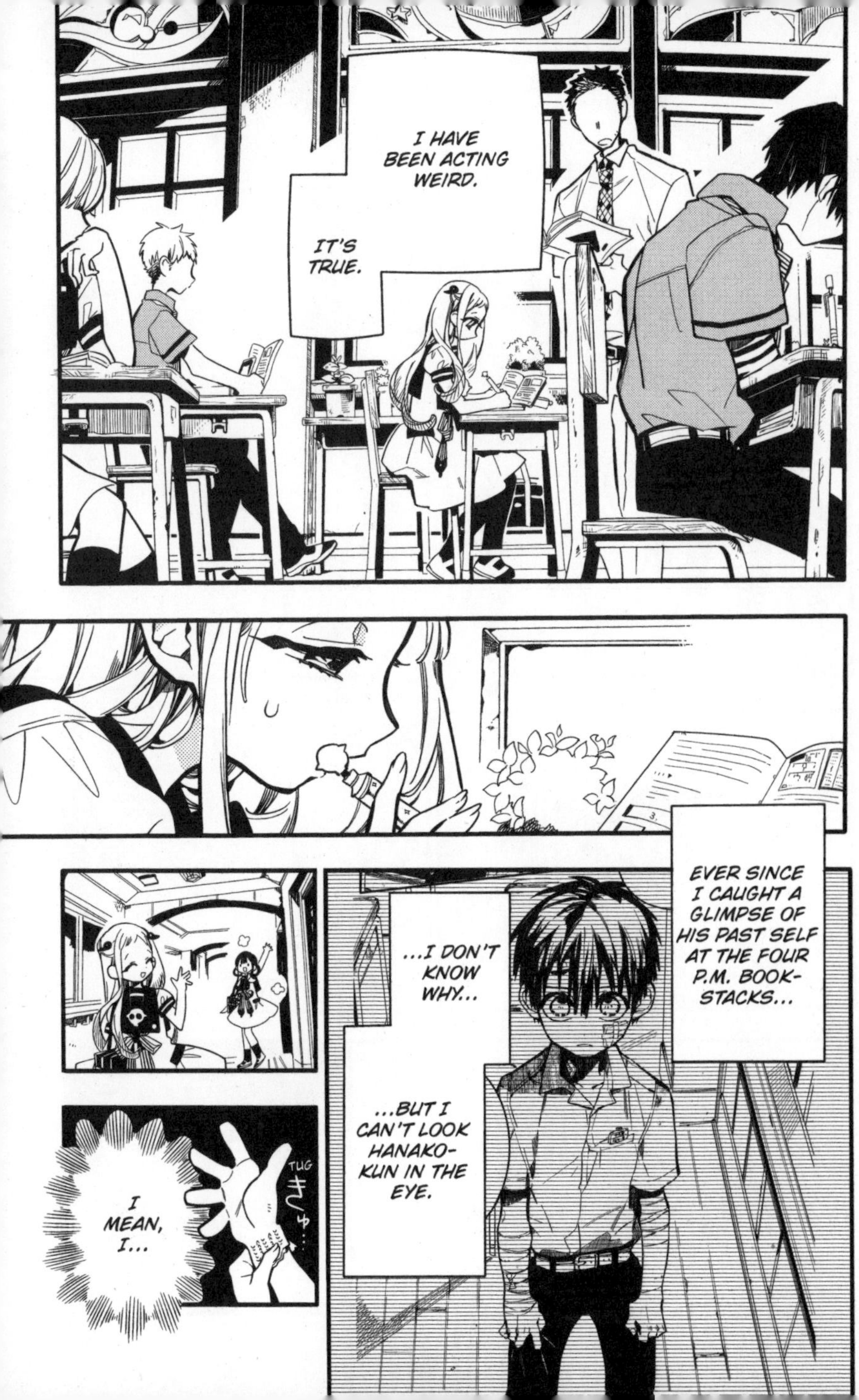
I HAVE BEEN ACTING WEIRD.
IT'S TRUE.
EVER SINCE I CAUGHT A GLIMPSE OF HIS PAST SELF AT THE FOUR P.M. BOOK-STACKS...
...I DON'T KNOW WHY...
...BUT I CAN'T LOOK HANAKO-KUN IN THE EYE.
TUG
I MEAN, I...

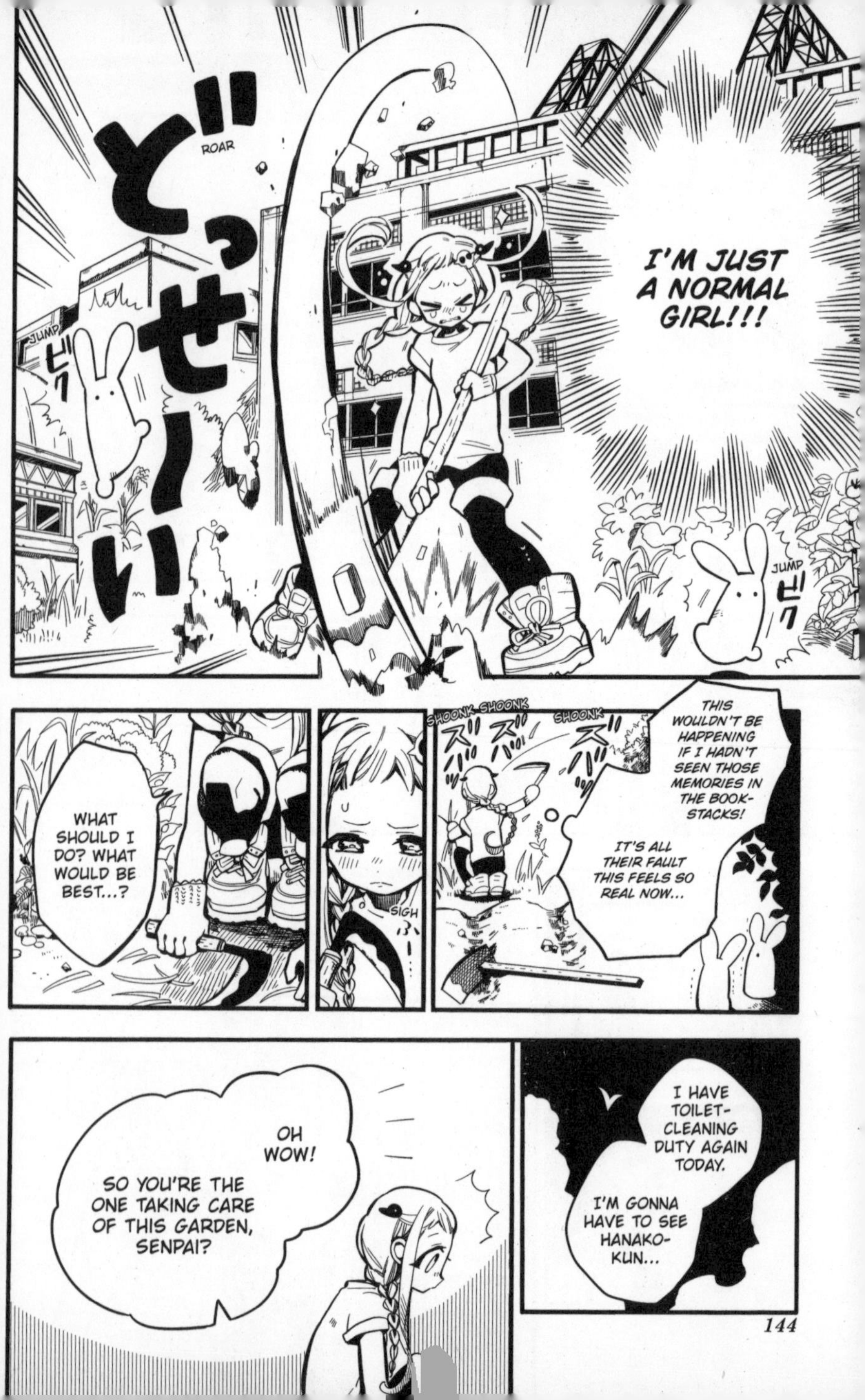
どっせーい
ROAR
I'M JUST A NORMAL GIRL!!!
JUMP
JUMP
SHOONK SHOONK
SHOONK
THIS WOULDN'T BE HAPPENING IF I HADN'T SEEN THOSE MEMORIES IN THE BOOK-STACKS!
IT'S ALL THEIR FAULT THIS FEELS SO REAL NOW...
SIGH
WHAT SHOULD I DO? WHAT WOULD BE BEST...?
I HAVE TOILET-CLEANING DUTY AGAIN TODAY.
I'M GONNA HAVE TO SEE HANAKO-KUN...
OH WOW!
SO YOU'RE THE ONE TAKING CARE OF THIS GARDEN, SENPAI?

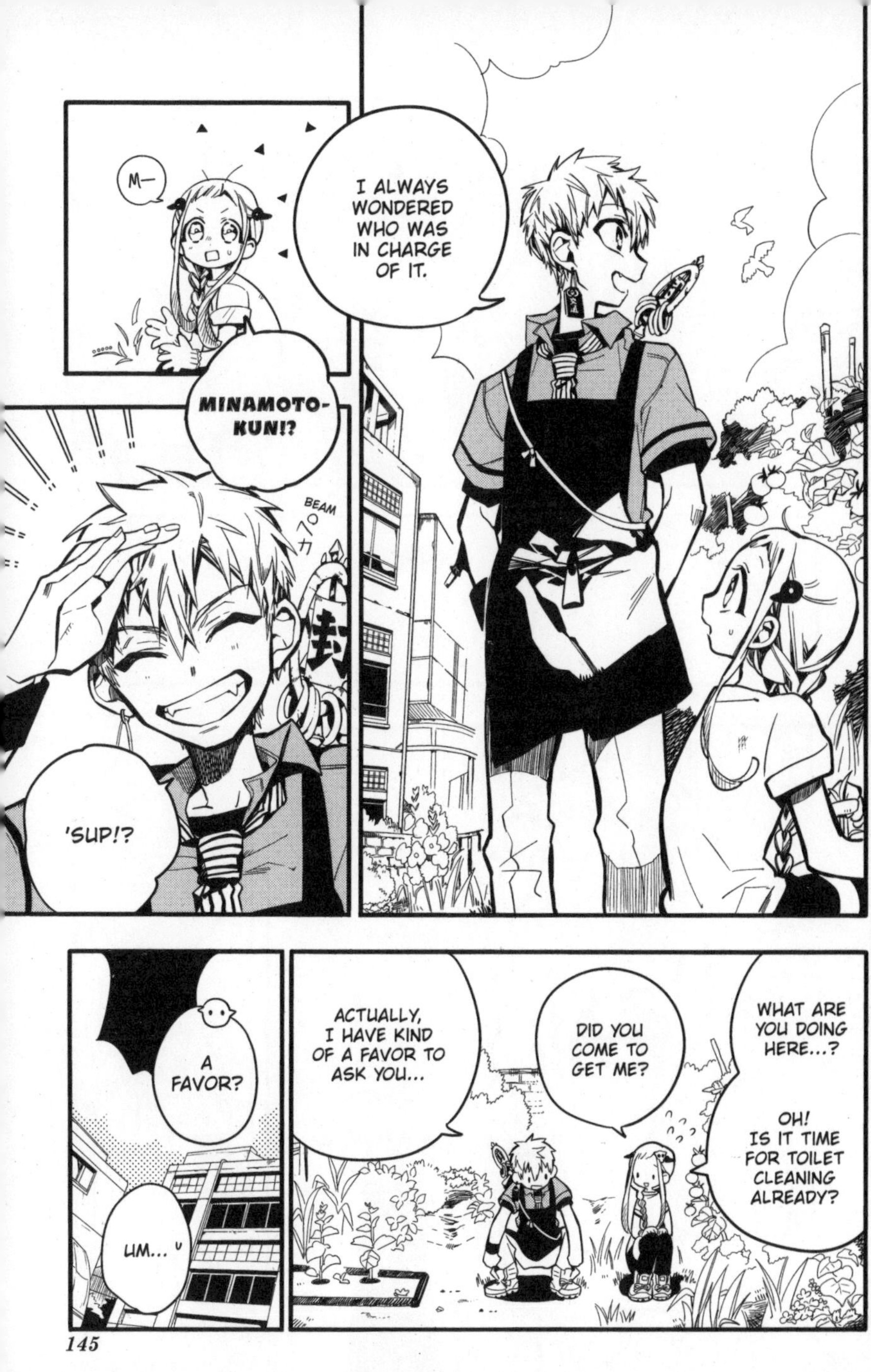
I ALWAYS WONDERED WHO WAS IN CHARGE OF IT.
M—
MINAMOTO-KUN!?
BEAM
ペカ
'SUP!?
WHAT ARE YOU DOING HERE...?
OH! IS IT TIME FOR TOILET CLEANING ALREADY?
DID YOU COME TO GET ME?
ACTUALLY, I HAVE KIND OF A FAVOR TO ASK YOU...
A FAVOR?
UM...

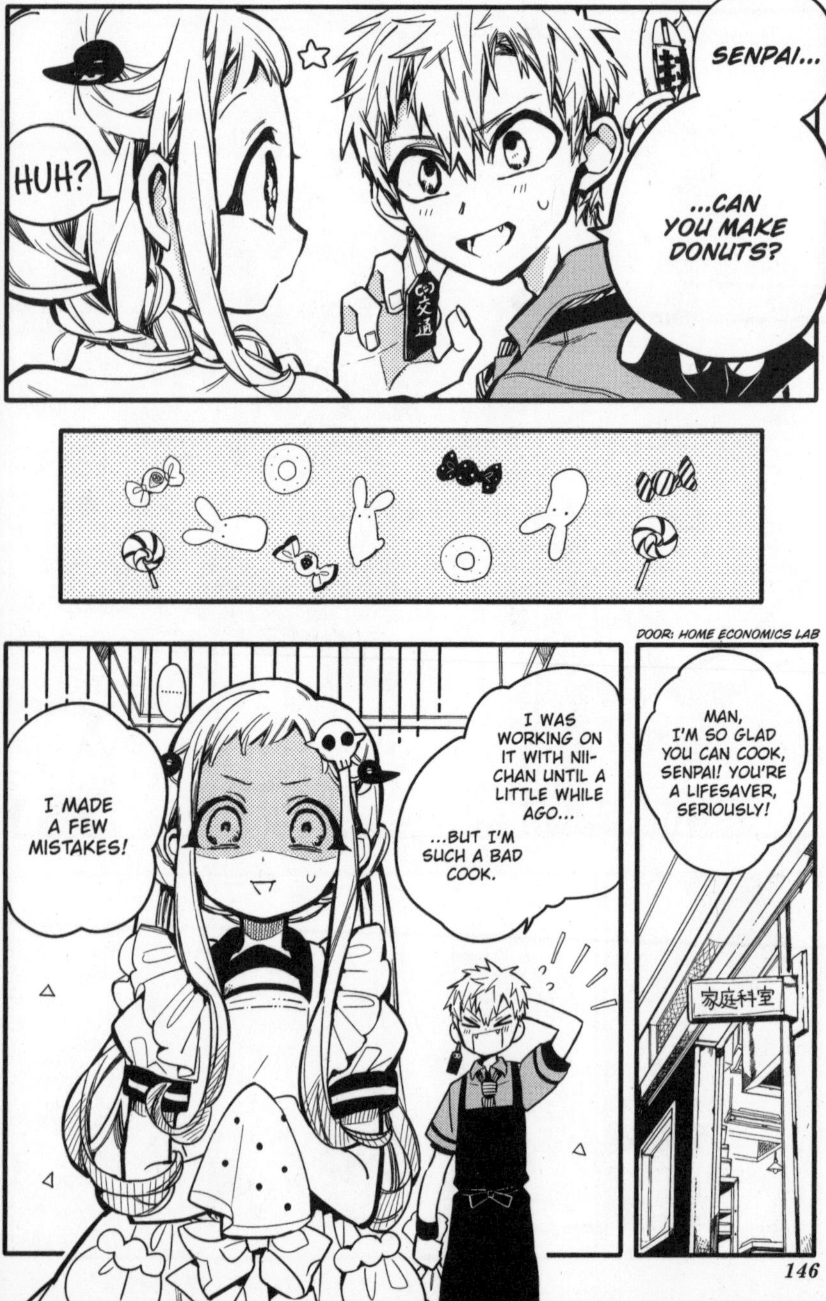
SENPAI...
...CAN YOU MAKE DONUTS?
HUH?
DOOR: HOME ECONOMICS LAB
MAN, I'M SO GLAD YOU CAN COOK, SENPAI! YOU'RE A LIFESAVER, SERIOUSLY!
家庭科室
I WAS WORKING ON IT WITH NII-CHAN UNTIL A LITTLE WHILE AGO...
...BUT I'M SUCH A BAD COOK.
......
I MADE A FEW MISTAKES!

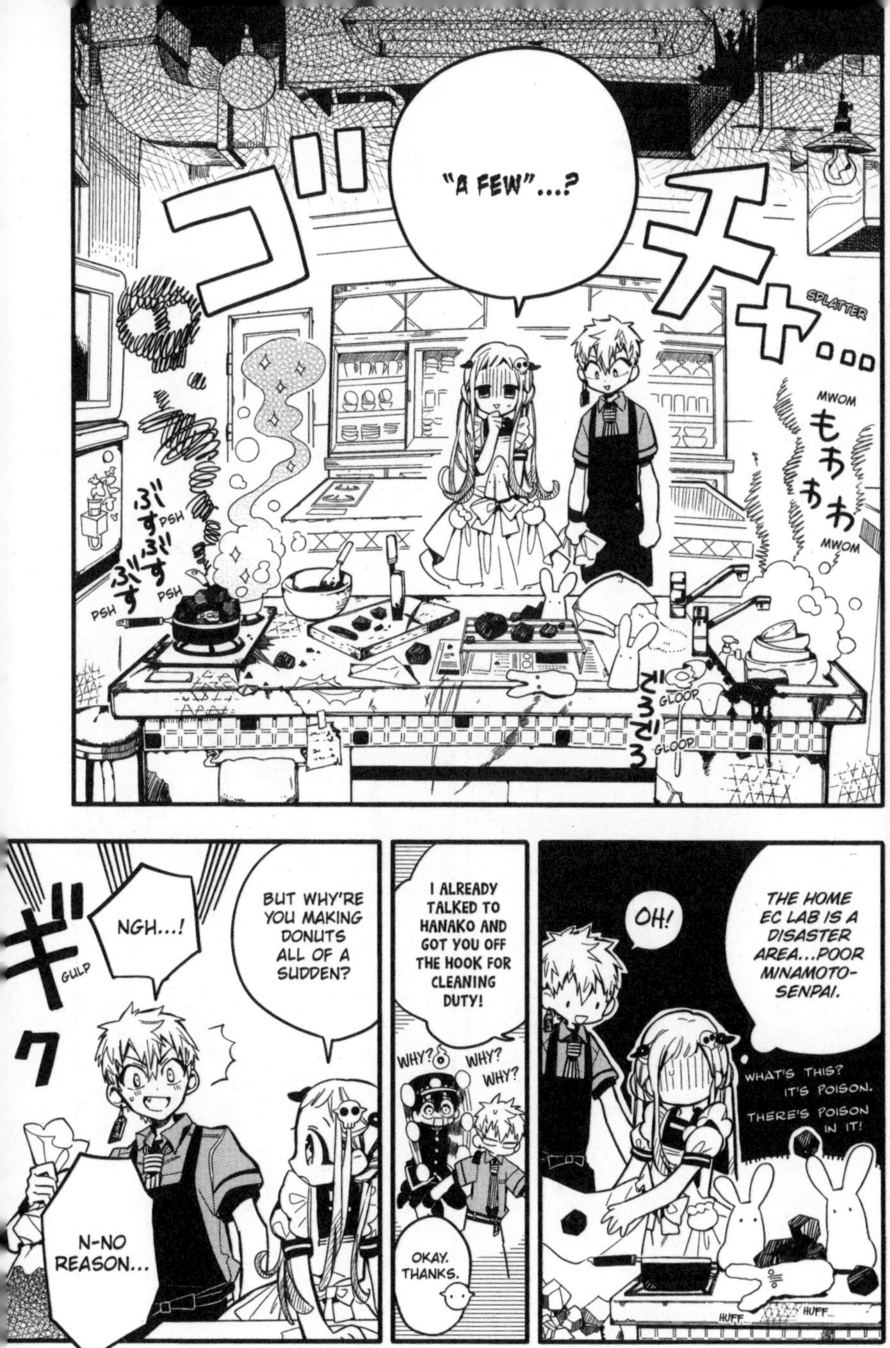
"A FEW"...?
SPLATTER
MWOM
MWOM
PSH
PSH
PSH
GLOOP
GLOOP
THE HOME EC LAB IS A DISASTER AREA...POOR MINAMOTO-SENPAI.
OH!
WHAT'S THIS? IT'S POISON. THERE'S POISON IN IT!
HUFF...
HUFF...
I ALREADY TALKED TO HANAKO AND GOT YOU OFF THE HOOK FOR CLEANING DUTY!
WHY?
WHY?
WHY?
OKAY. THANKS.
BUT WHY'RE YOU MAKING DONUTS ALL OF A SUDDEN?
NGH...!
GULP
N-NO REASON...

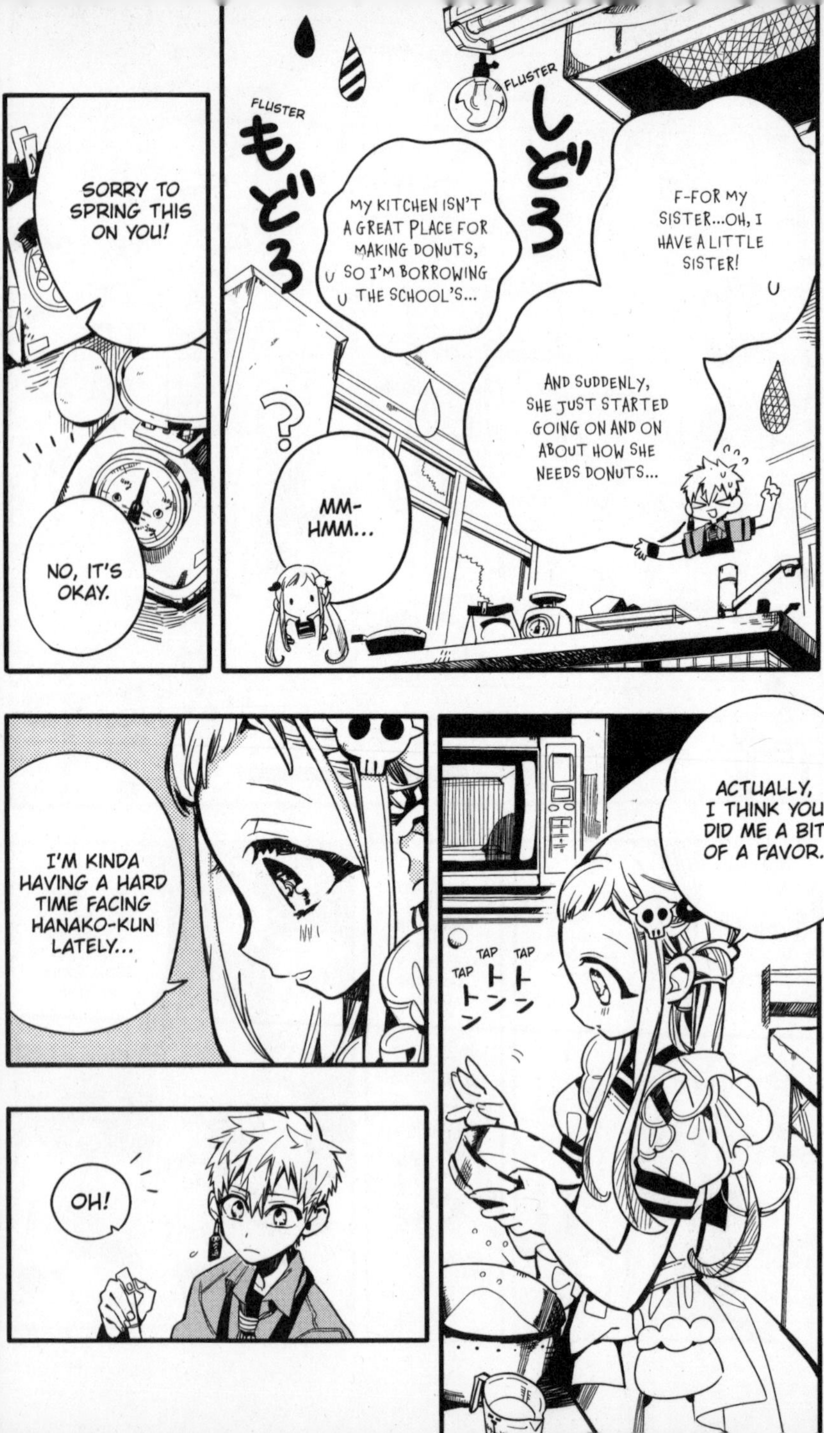

FLUSTER
しどろ
F-FOR MY SISTER...OH, I HAVE A LITTLE SISTER!
FLUSTER
もどろ
MY KITCHEN ISN'T A GREAT PLACE FOR MAKING DONUTS, SO I'M BORROWING THE SCHOOL'S...
AND SUDDENLY, SHE JUST STARTED GOING ON AND ON ABOUT HOW SHE NEEDS DONUTS...
MM-HMM...
SORRY TO SPRING THIS ON YOU!
NO, IT'S OKAY.
ACTUALLY, I THINK YOU DID ME A BIT OF A FAVOR.
TAP TAP TAP
トントントン
I'M KINDA HAVING A HARD TIME FACING HANAKO-KUN LATELY...
OH!

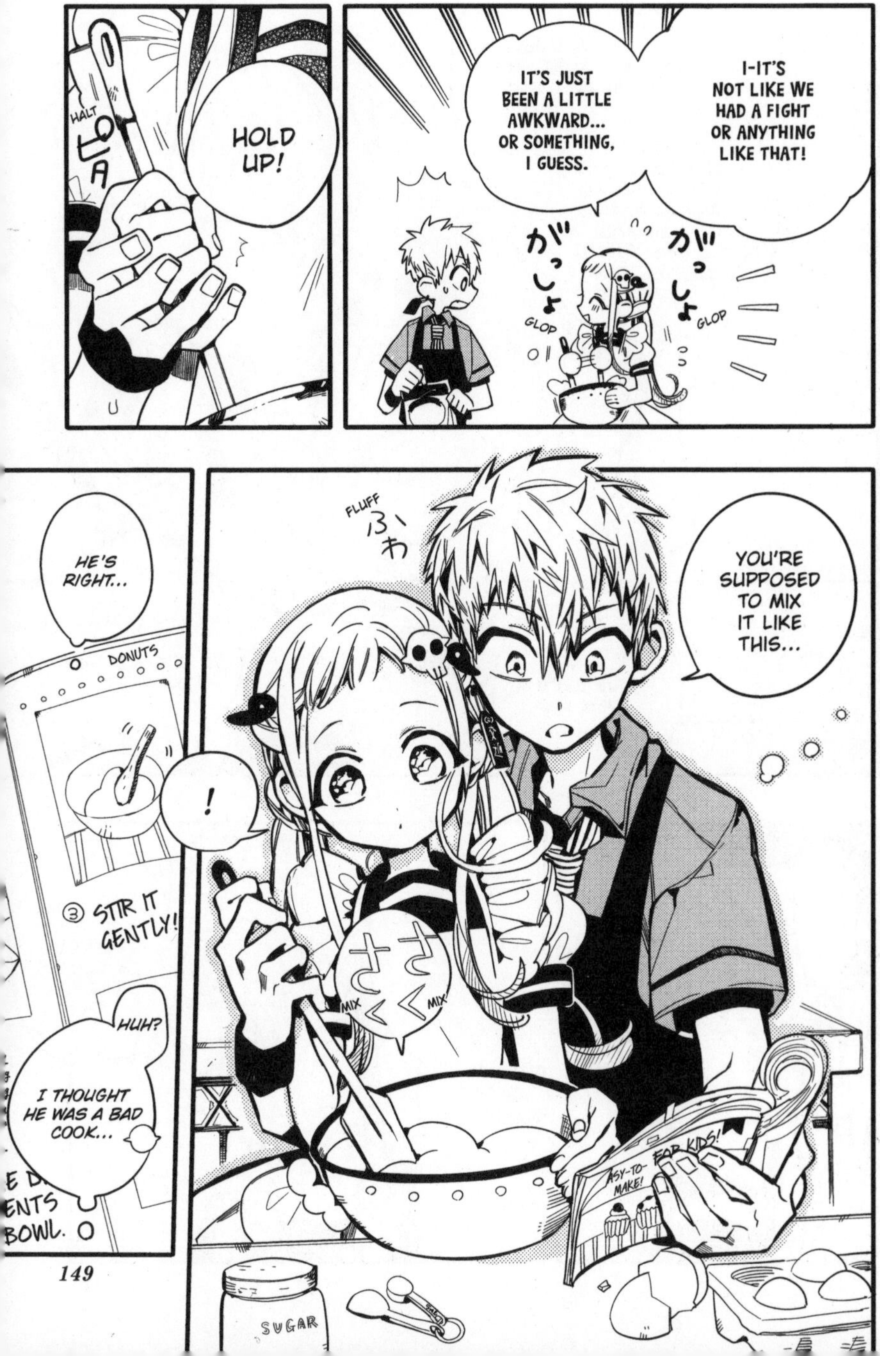
I-IT'S NOT LIKE WE HAD A FIGHT OR ANYTHING LIKE THAT!
IT'S JUST BEEN A LITTLE AWKWARD... OR SOMETHING, I GUESS.
GLOP
GLOP
HALT
HOLD UP!
YOU'RE SUPPOSED TO MIX IT LIKE THIS...
FLUFF
!
MIX
MIX
FOR KIDS!
SUGAR
HE'S RIGHT...
DONUTS
③ STIR IT GENTLY!
HUH?
I THOUGHT HE WAS A BAD COOK...

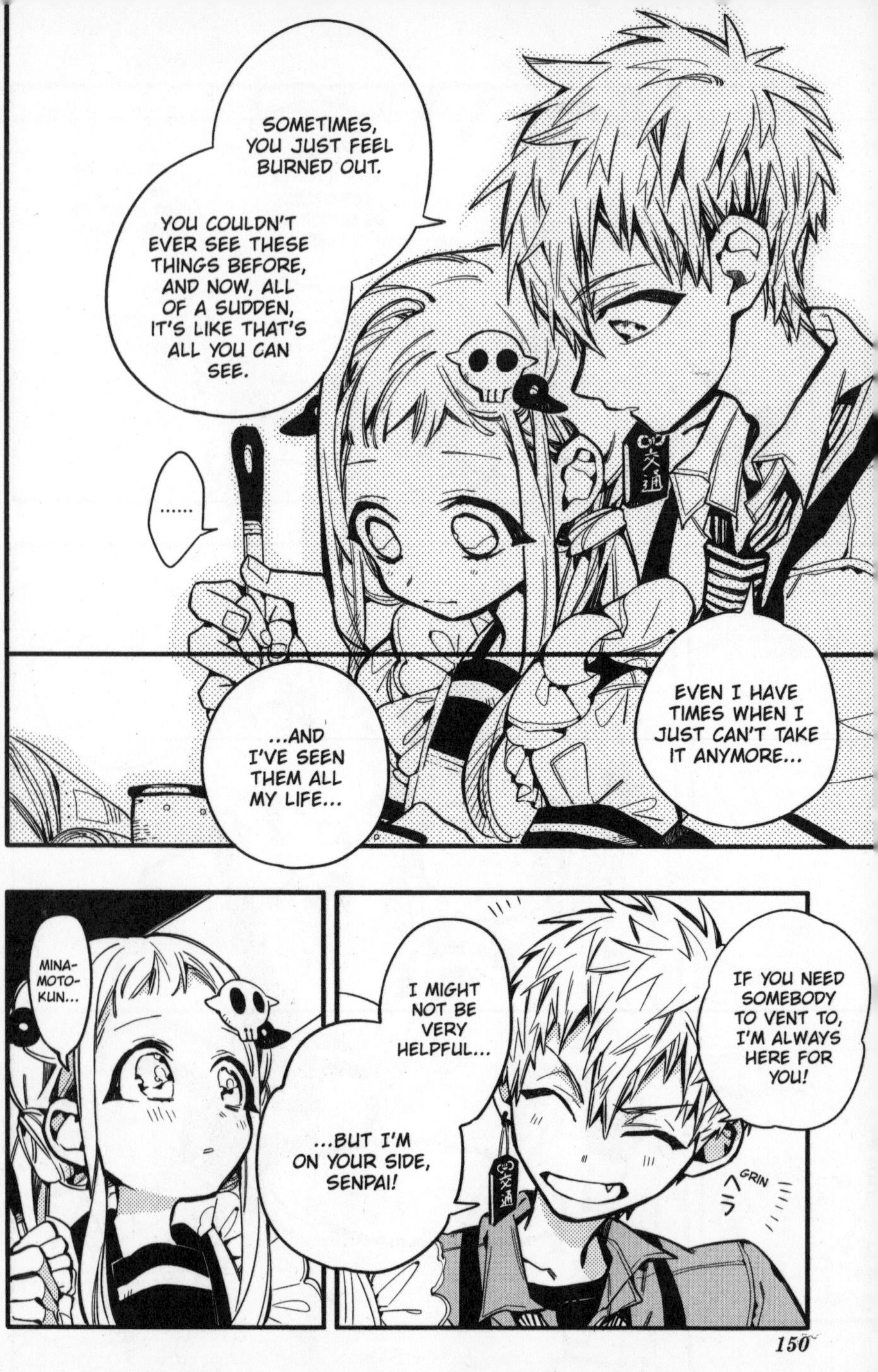
SOMETIMES, YOU JUST FEEL BURNED OUT.
YOU COULDN'T EVER SEE THESE THINGS BEFORE, AND NOW, ALL OF A SUDDEN, IT'S LIKE THAT'S ALL YOU CAN SEE.
......
EVEN I HAVE TIMES WHEN I JUST CAN'T TAKE IT ANYMORE...
...AND I'VE SEEN THEM ALL MY LIFE...
IF YOU NEED SOMEBODY TO VENT TO, I'M ALWAYS HERE FOR YOU!
I MIGHT NOT BE VERY HELPFUL...
...BUT I'M ON YOUR SIDE, SENPAI!
GRIN
MINA-MOTO-KUN...

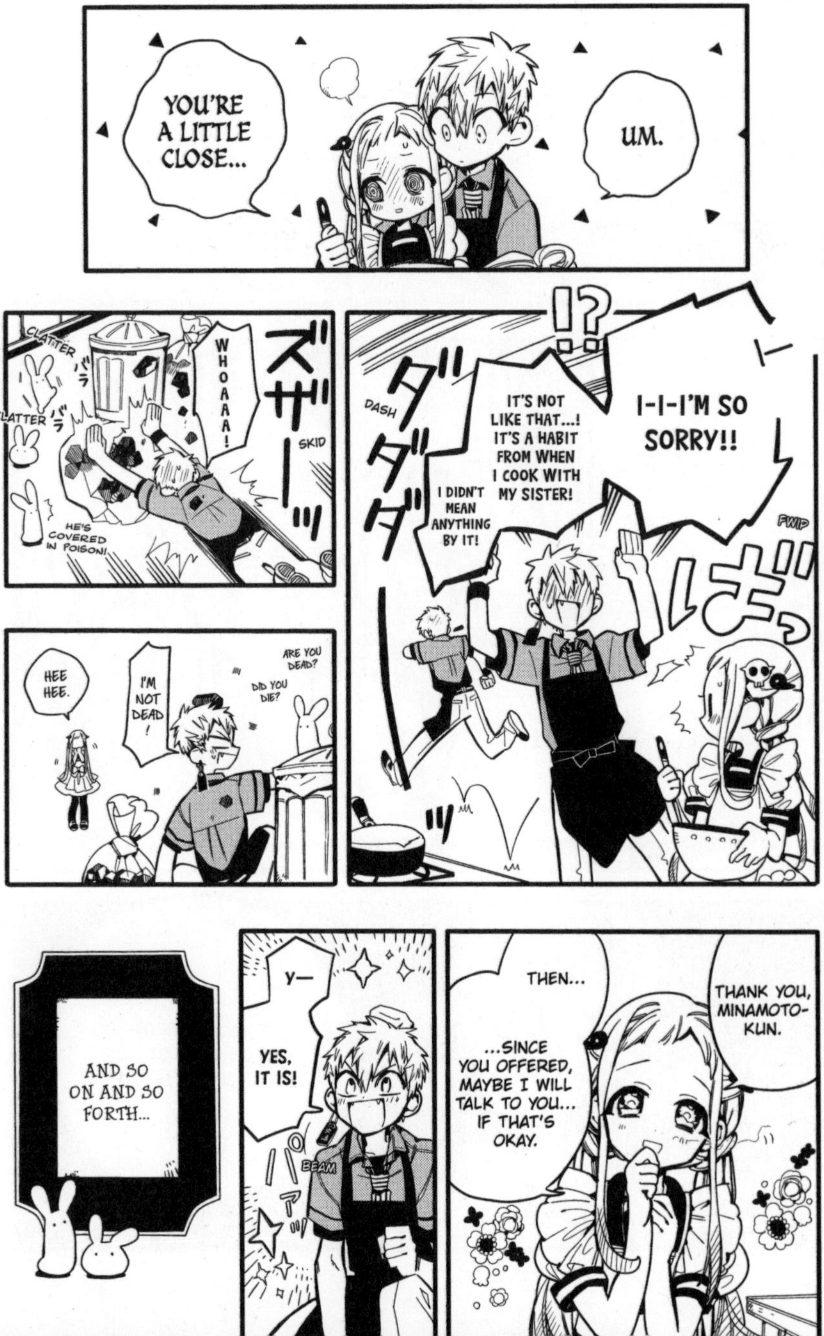
UM.
YOU'RE A LITTLE CLOSE...
!?
I-I-I'M SO SORRY!!
FWIP
IT'S NOT LIKE THAT...! IT'S A HABIT FROM WHEN I COOK WITH MY SISTER!
I DIDN'T MEAN ANYTHING BY IT!
DASH
SKID
WHOAAAA!
CLATTER
CLATTER
HE'S COVERED IN POISON!
ARE YOU DEAD?
DID YOU DIE?
I'M NOT DEAD!
HEE HEE.
THANK YOU, MINAMOTO-KUN.
THEN...
...SINCE YOU OFFERED, MAYBE I WILL TALK TO YOU... IF THAT'S OKAY.
Y—
YES, IT IS!
BEAM
AND SO ON AND SO FORTH...

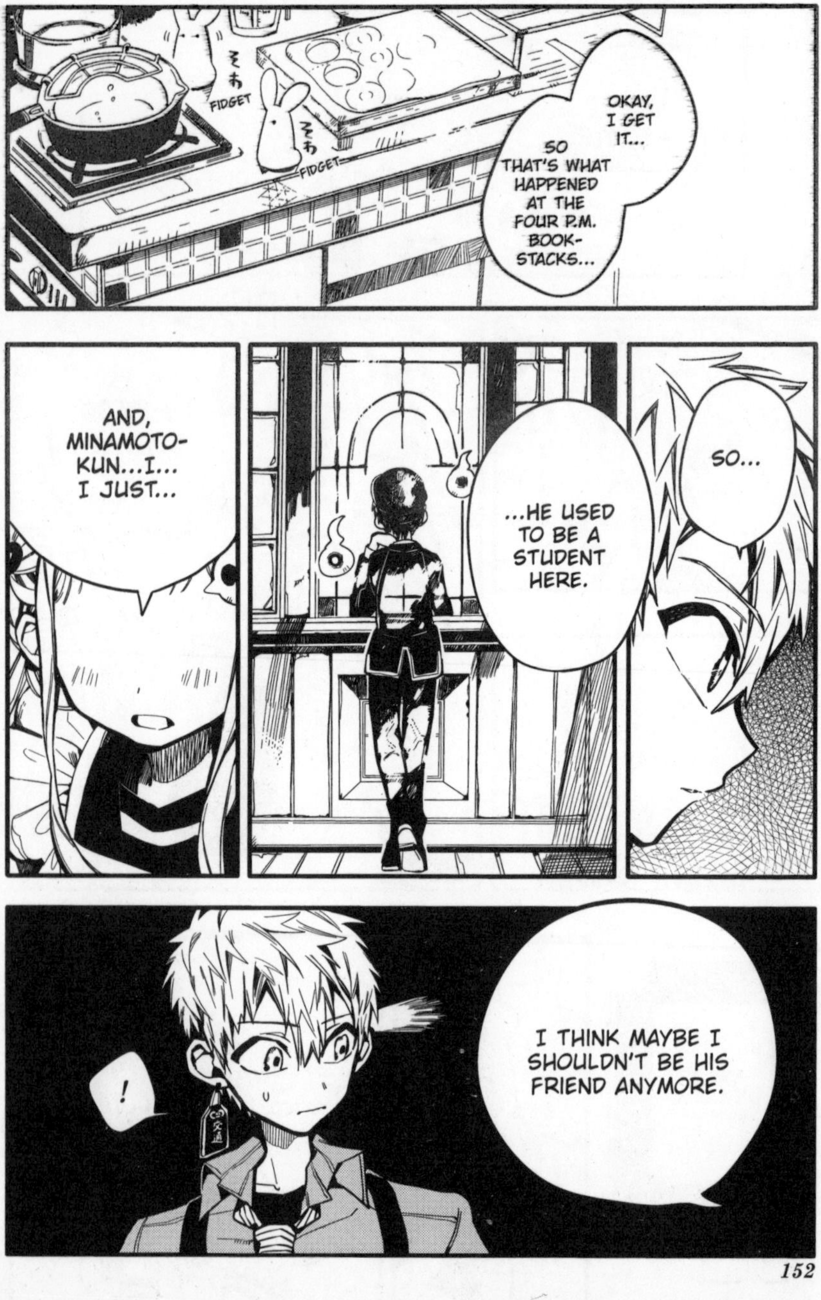
OKAY, I GET IT...
SO THAT'S WHAT HAPPENED AT THE FOUR P.M. BOOK-STACKS...
FIDGET
FIDGET
SO...
...HE USED TO BE A STUDENT HERE.
AND, MINAMOTO-KUN...I... I JUST...
I THINK MAYBE I SHOULDN'T BE HIS FRIEND ANYMORE.
!

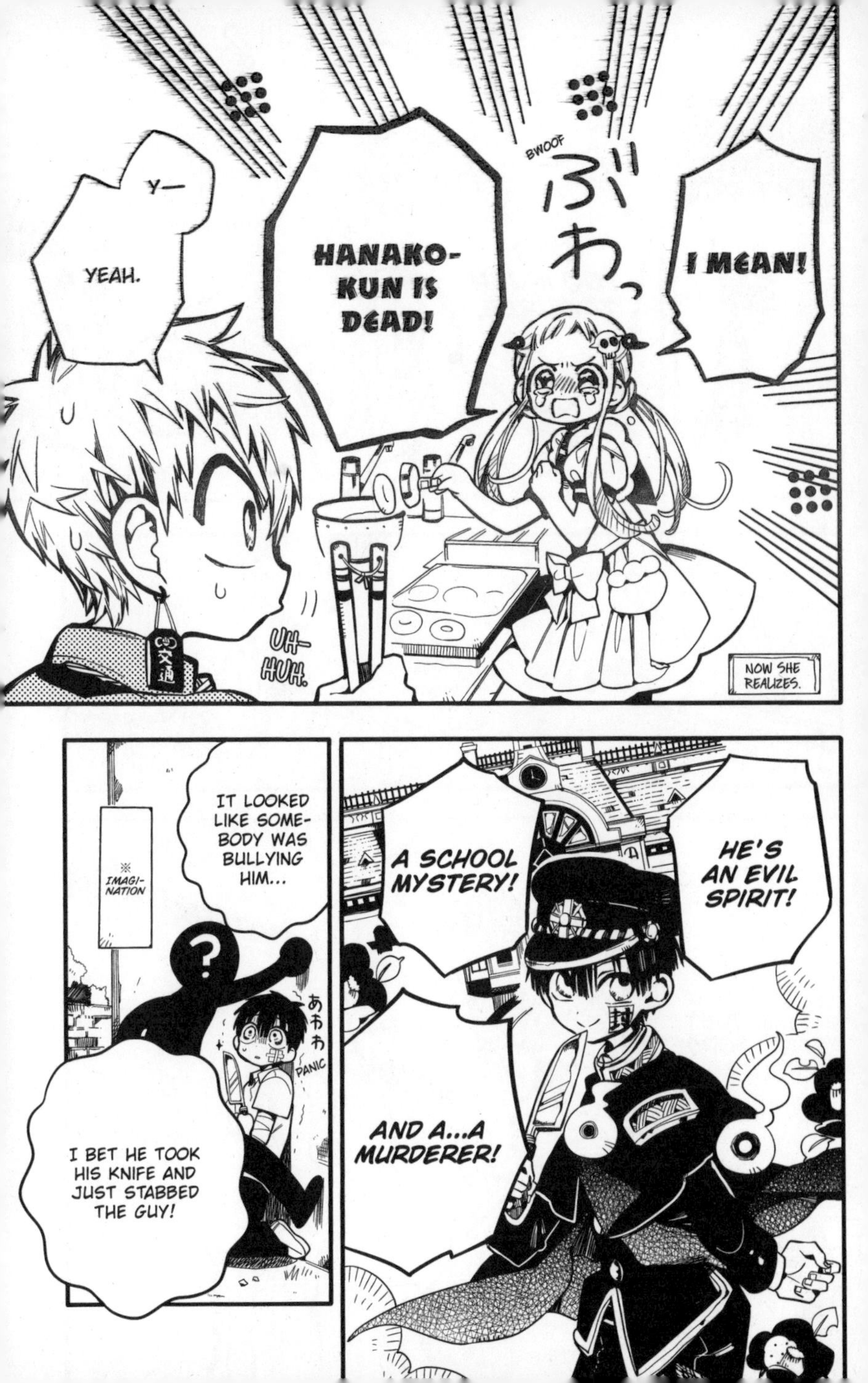
I MEAN!
BWOOF
ぶわっ
HANAKO-KUN IS DEAD!
Y—
YEAH.
UH-HUH.
NOW SHE REALIZES.
HE'S AN EVIL SPIRIT!
A SCHOOL MYSTERY!
AND A...A MURDERER!
※IMAGINATION
IT LOOKED LIKE SOMEBODY WAS BULLYING HIM...
PANIC
I BET HE TOOK HIS KNIFE AND JUST STABBED THE GUY!

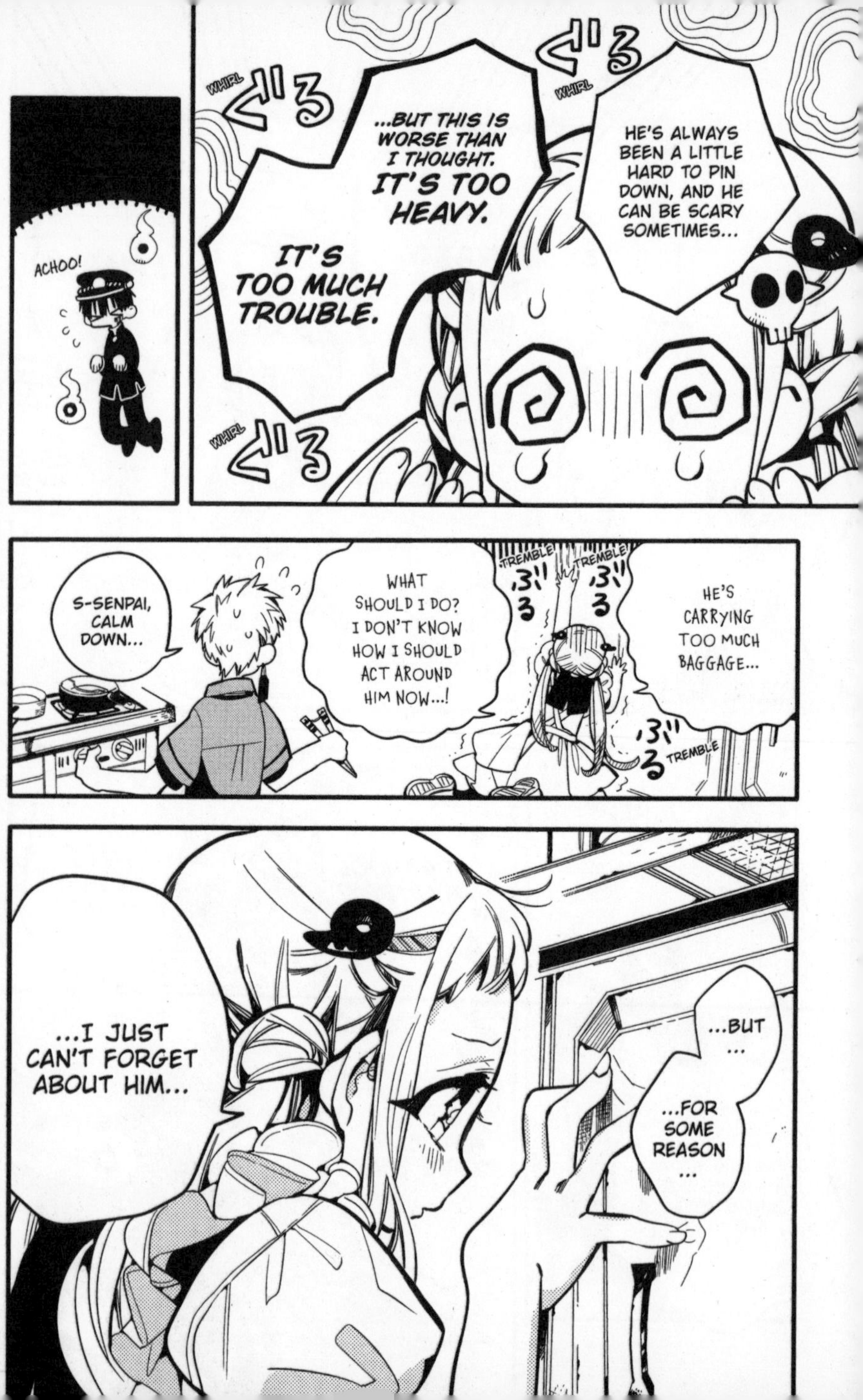
WHIRL ぐる
WHIRL ぐる
HE'S ALWAYS BEEN A LITTLE HARD TO PIN DOWN, AND HE CAN BE SCARY SOMETIMES...
...BUT THIS IS WORSE THAN I THOUGHT. IT'S TOO HEAVY.
IT'S TOO MUCH TROUBLE.
WHIRL ぐる
ACHOO!
HE'S CARRYING TOO MUCH BAGGAGE...
TREMBLE ぶる
TREMBLE ぶる
TREMBLE ぶる
WHAT SHOULD I DO? I DON'T KNOW HOW I SHOULD ACT AROUND HIM NOW...!
S-SENPAI, CALM DOWN...
...BUT ...
...FOR SOME REASON ...
...I JUST CAN'T FORGET ABOUT HIM...

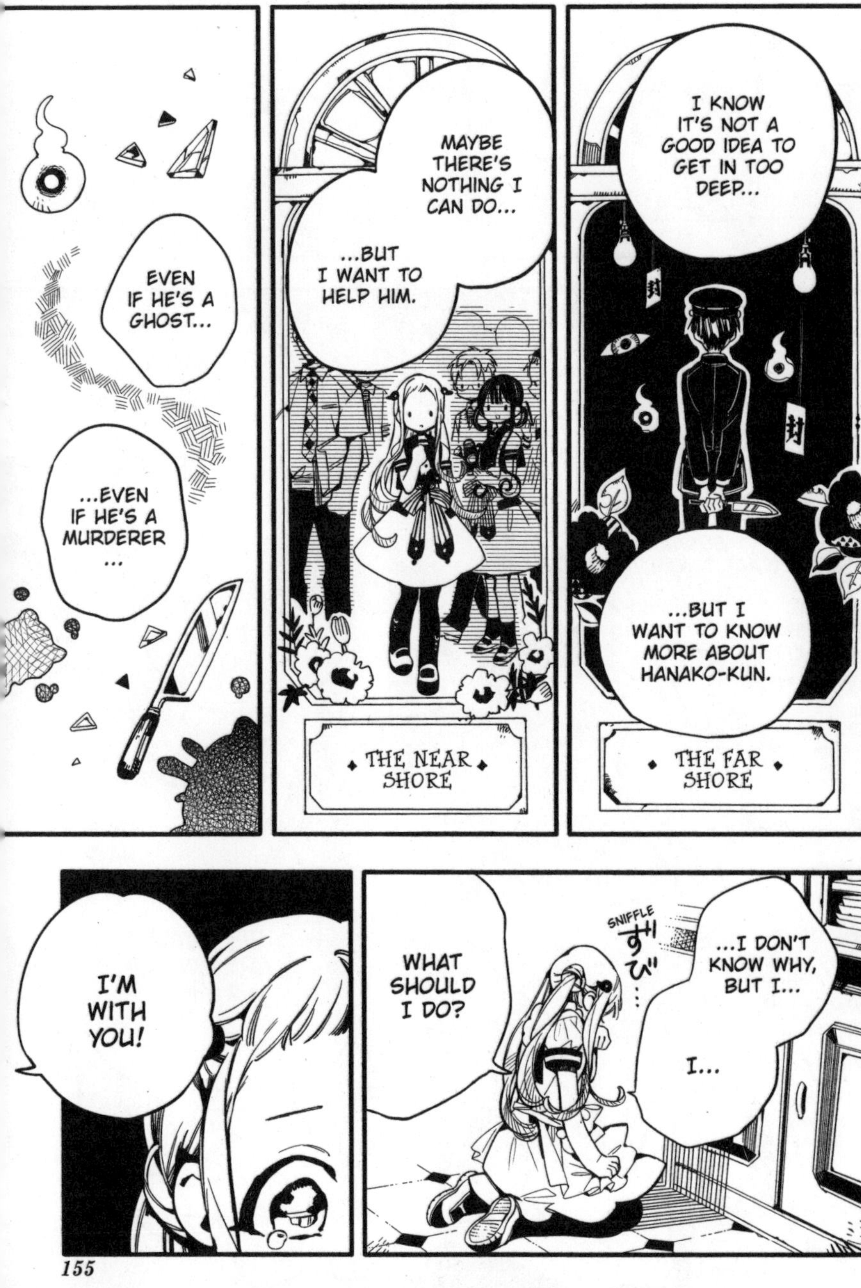
I KNOW IT'S NOT A GOOD IDEA TO GET IN TOO DEEP...
...BUT I WANT TO KNOW MORE ABOUT HANAKO-KUN.
THE FAR SHORE
MAYBE THERE'S NOTHING I CAN DO...
...BUT I WANT TO HELP HIM.
THE NEAR SHORE
EVEN IF HE'S A GHOST...
...EVEN IF HE'S A MURDERER ...
...I DON'T KNOW WHY, BUT I...
I...
SNIFFLE
ずび…
WHAT SHOULD I DO?
I'M WITH YOU!

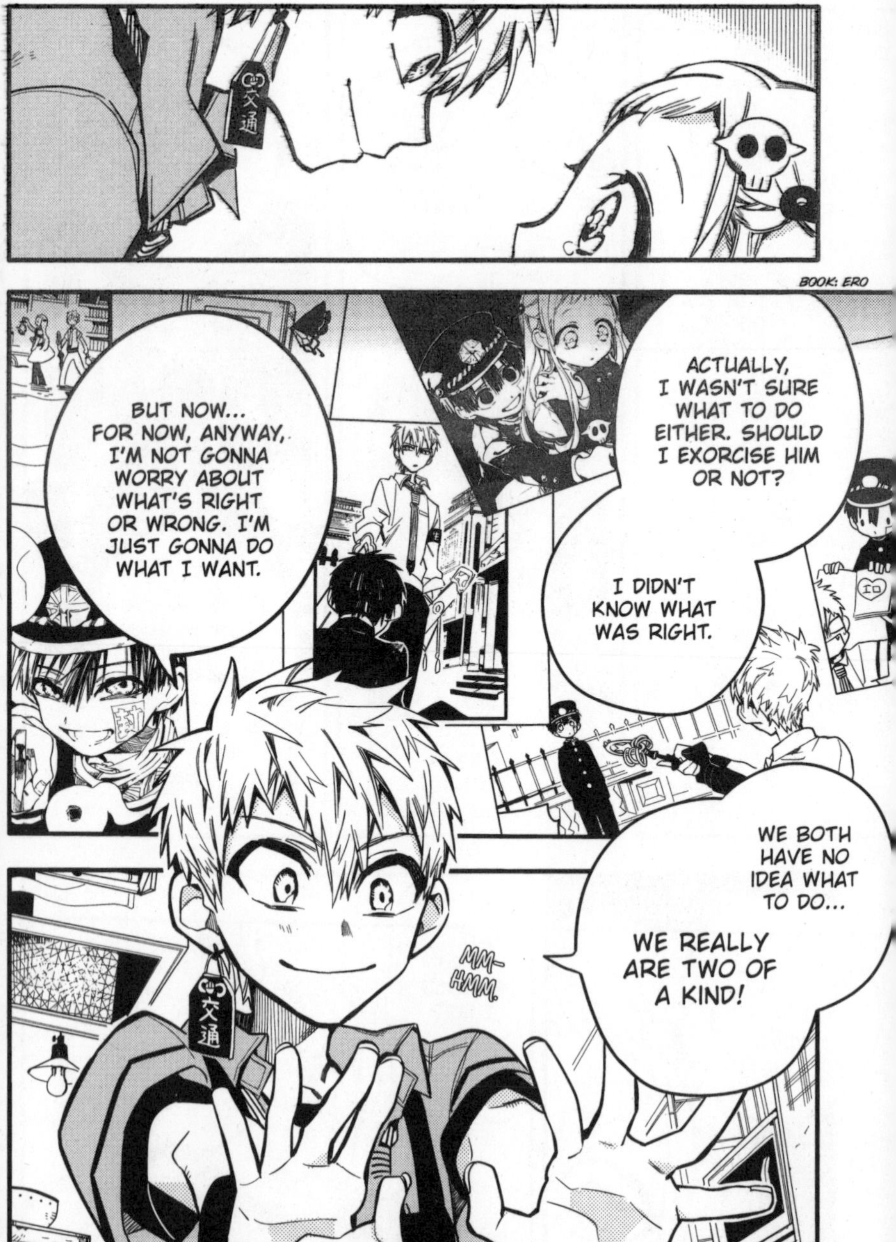
BOOK: ERO
ACTUALLY, I WASN'T SURE WHAT TO DO EITHER. SHOULD I EXORCISE HIM OR NOT?
I DIDN'T KNOW WHAT WAS RIGHT.
BUT NOW... FOR NOW, ANYWAY, I'M NOT GONNA WORRY ABOUT WHAT'S RIGHT OR WRONG. I'M JUST GONNA DO WHAT I WANT.
WE BOTH HAVE NO IDEA WHAT TO DO...
WE REALLY ARE TWO OF A KIND!
MM-HMM.

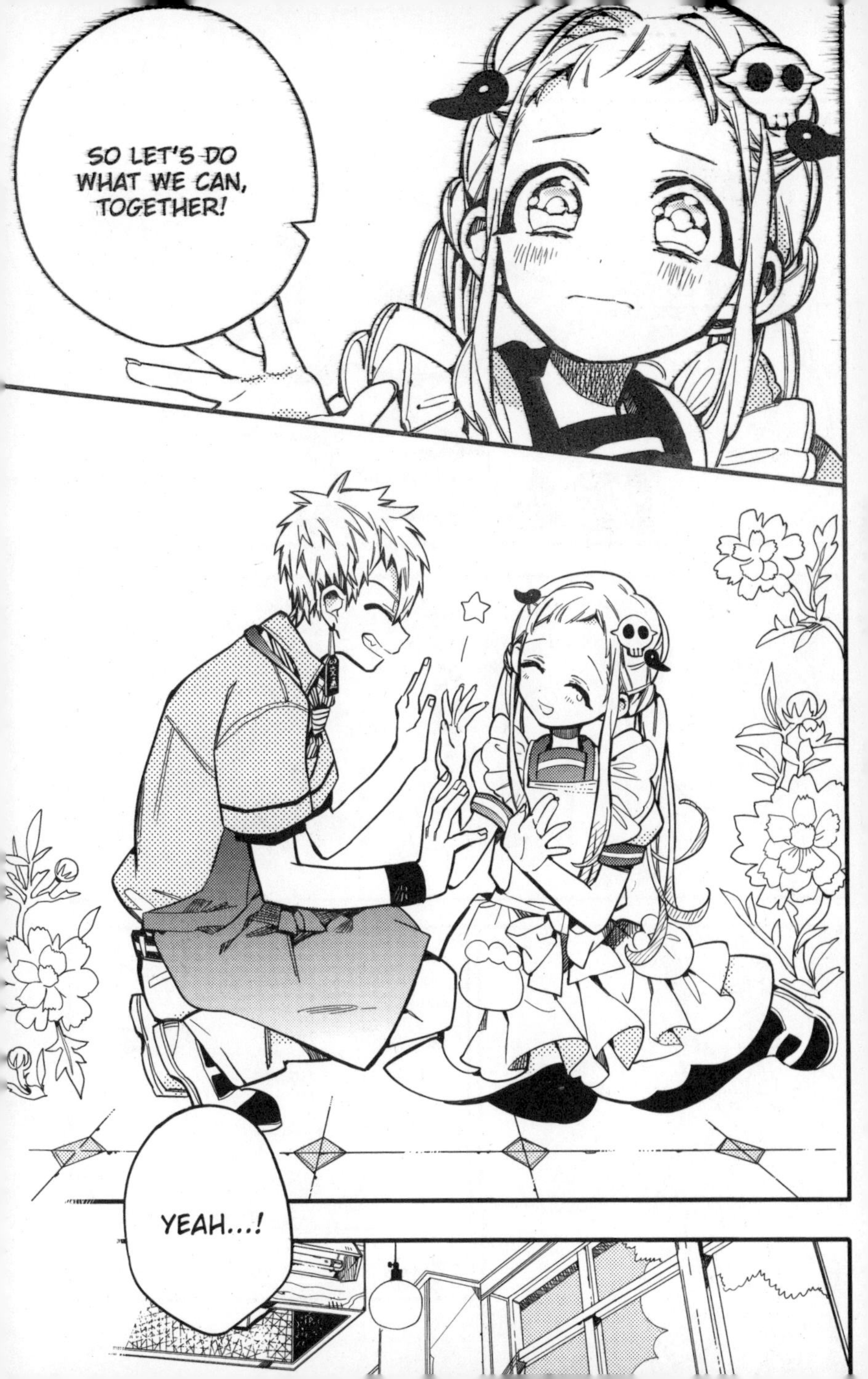
SO LET'S DO WHAT WE CAN, TOGETHER!
YEAH...!

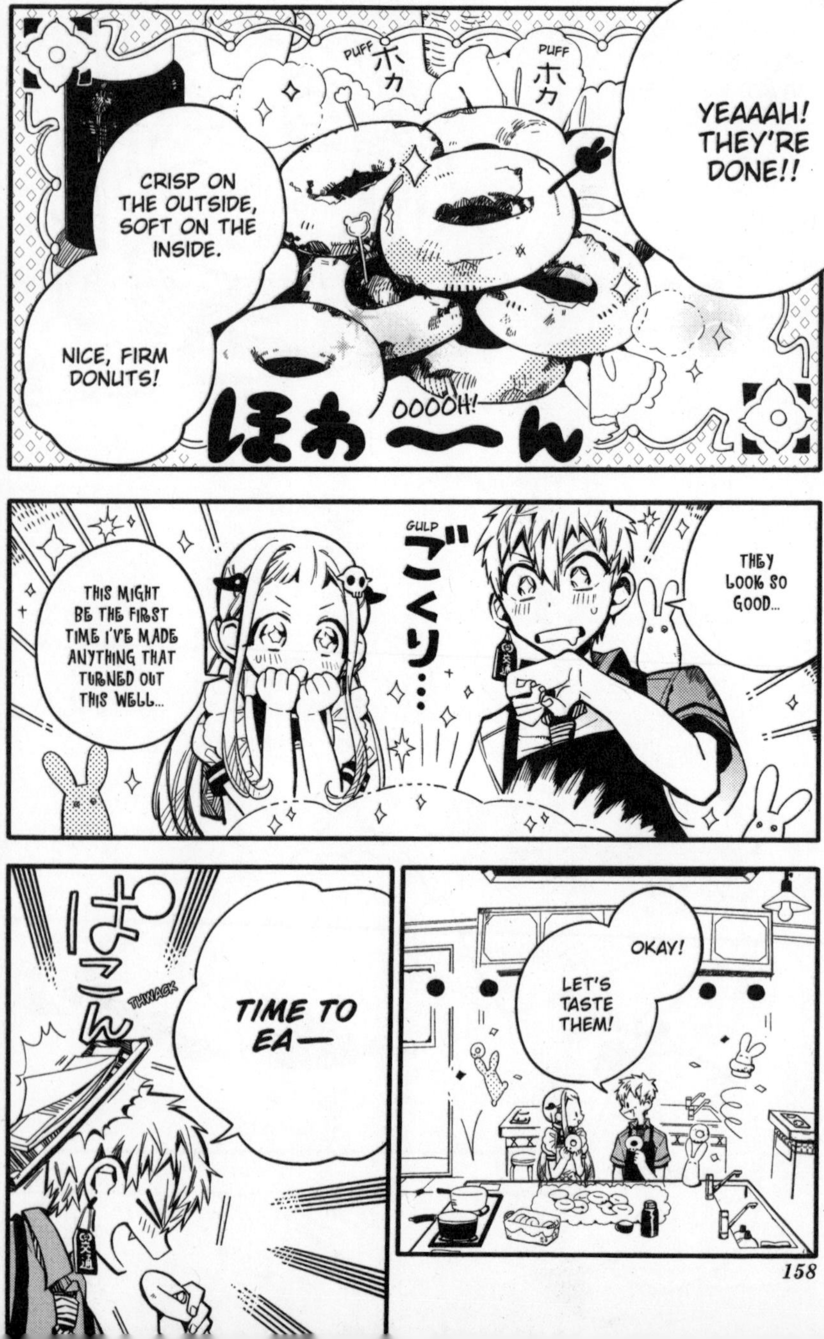
YEAAAH! THEY'RE DONE!!
PUFF
PUFF
CRISP ON THE OUTSIDE, SOFT ON THE INSIDE.
NICE, FIRM DONUTS!
OOOOH!
THEY LOOK SO GOOD...
GULP
THIS MIGHT BE THE FIRST TIME I'VE MADE ANYTHING THAT TURNED OUT THIS WELL...
OKAY!
LET'S TASTE THEM!
TIME TO EA—
THWACK

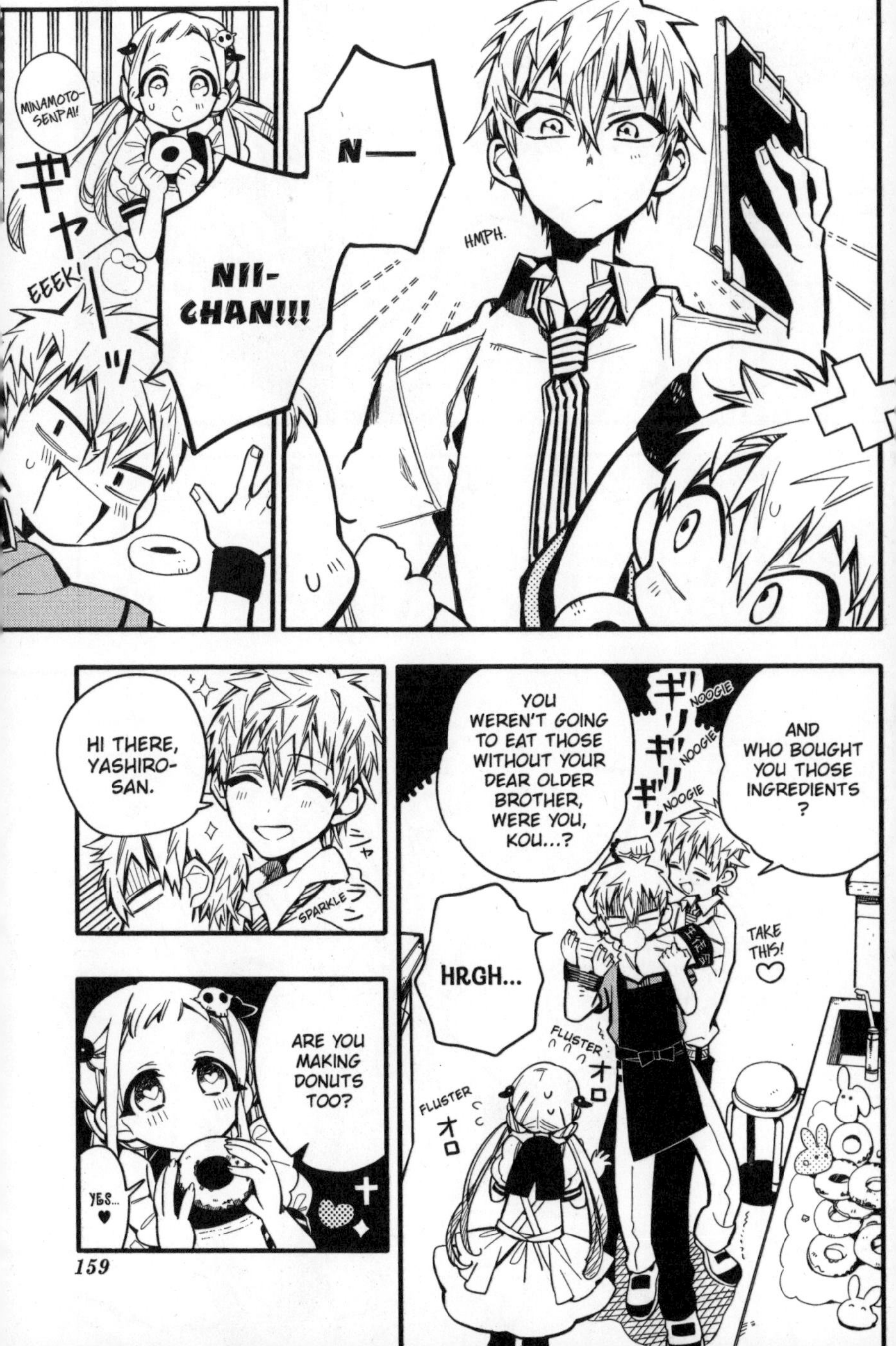
HMPH.
N——
NII-CHAN!!!
EEEK!
MINAMOTO-SENPAI!
AND WHO BOUGHT YOU THOSE INGREDIENTS?
YOU WEREN'T GOING TO EAT THOSE WITHOUT YOUR DEAR OLDER BROTHER, WERE YOU, KOU...?
NOOGIE
NOOGIE
NOOGIE
TAKE THIS!
HRGH...
FLUSTER
FLUSTER
HI THERE, YASHIRO-SAN.
SPARKLE
ARE YOU MAKING DONUTS TOO?
YES...

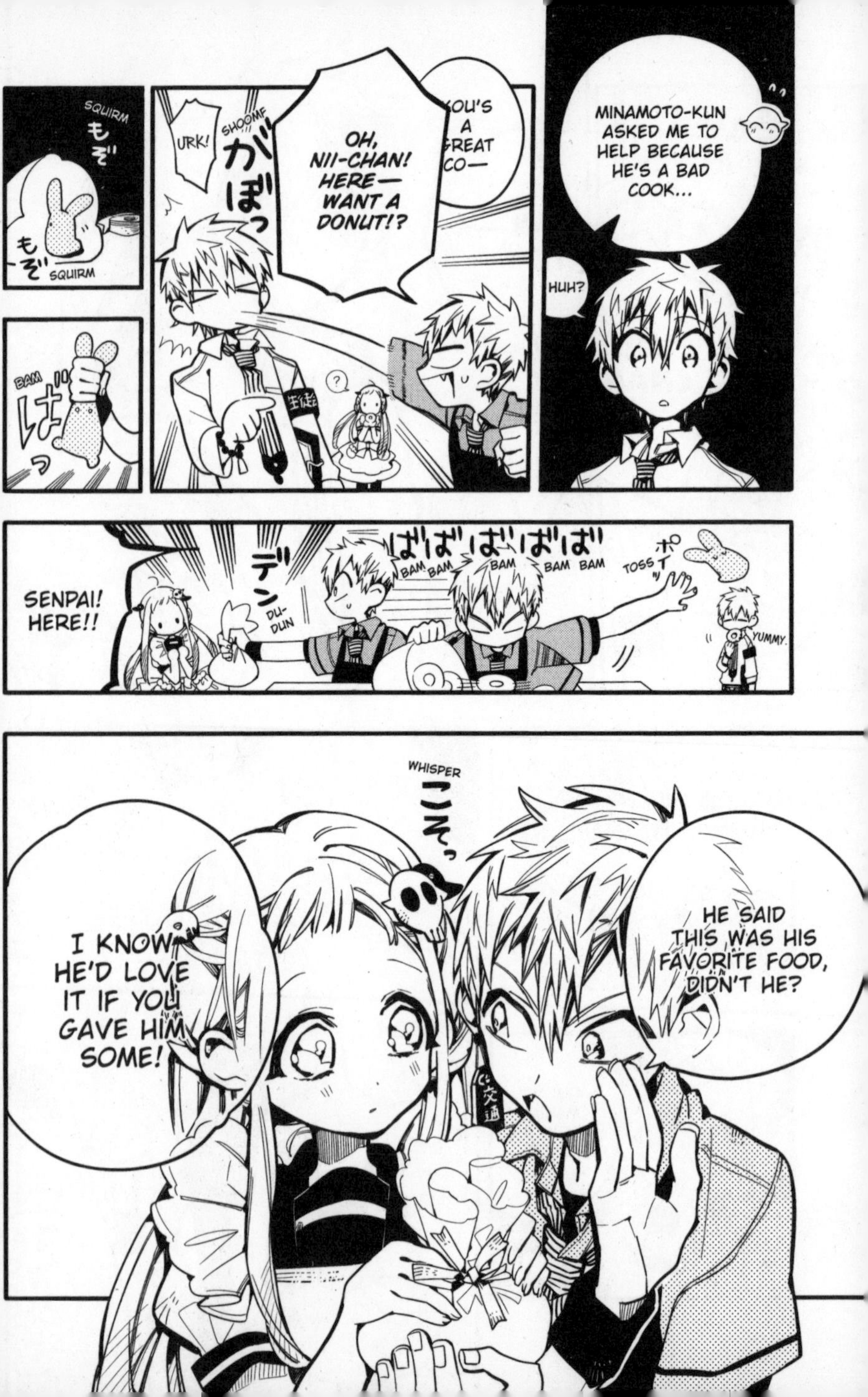
MINAMOTO-KUN ASKED ME TO HELP BECAUSE HE'S A BAD COOK...
HUH?
YOU'S A GREAT CO—
OH, NII-CHAN! HERE— WANT A DONUT!?
SHOOMF
がぼっ
URK!
?
SQUIRM
もぞ
もぞ
SQUIRM
BAM
ばっ
ばばばばば
BAM BAM BAM BAM BAM
ポイ
TOSS
デン
DU-DUN
YUMMY
SENPAI! HERE!!
WHISPER
こそっ
HE SAID THIS WAS HIS FAVORITE FOOD, DIDN'T HE?
I KNOW HE'D LOVE IT IF YOU GAVE HIM SOME!

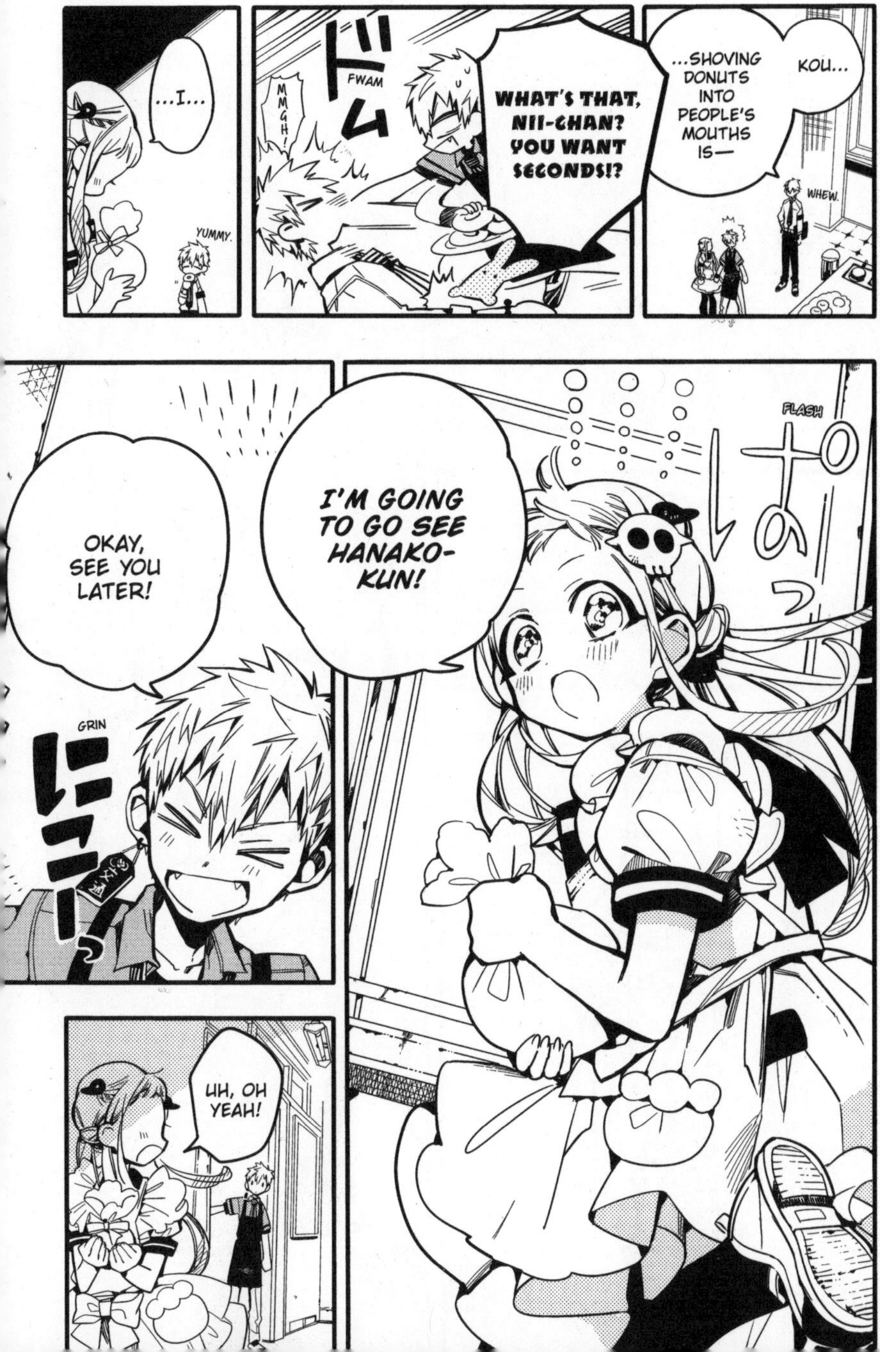
KOU...
...SHOVING DONUTS INTO PEOPLE'S MOUTHS IS—
WHEW.
ドム
FWAM
MMGH!
WHAT'S THAT, NII-CHAN? YOU WANT SECONDS!?
...I...
YUMMY.
はっ
FLASH
I'M GOING TO GO SEE HANAKO-KUN!
OKAY, SEE YOU LATER!
にこー
GRIN
UH, OH YEAH!

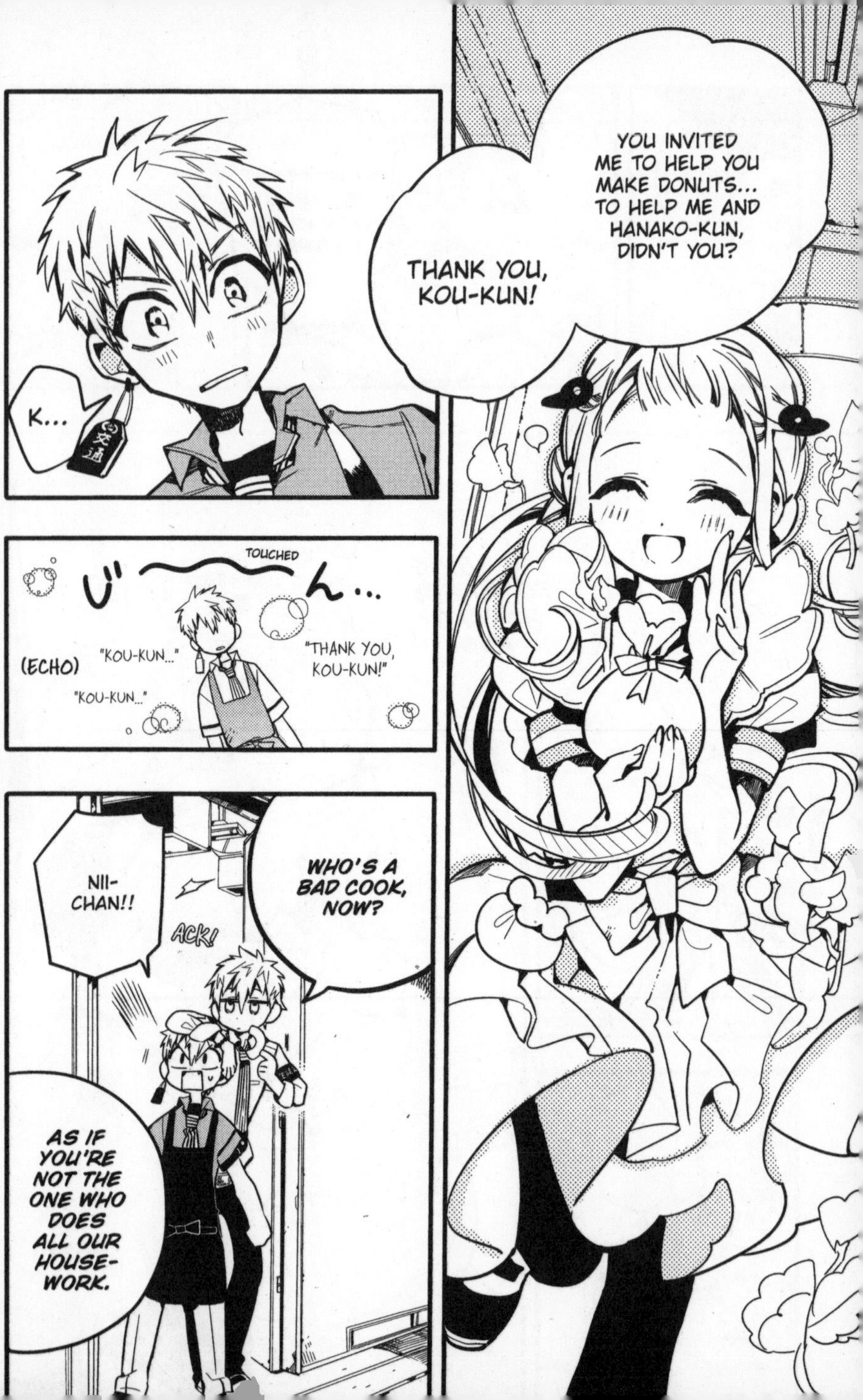
YOU INVITED ME TO HELP YOU MAKE DONUTS... TO HELP ME AND HANAKO-KUN, DIDN'T YOU?
THANK YOU, KOU-KUN!
K...
TOUCHED
"THANK YOU, KOU-KUN!"
"KOU-KUN..."
(ECHO)
"KOU-KUN..."
WHO'S A BAD COOK, NOW?
NII-CHAN!!
ACK!
AS IF YOU'RE NOT THE ONE WHO DOES ALL OUR HOUSE-WORK.

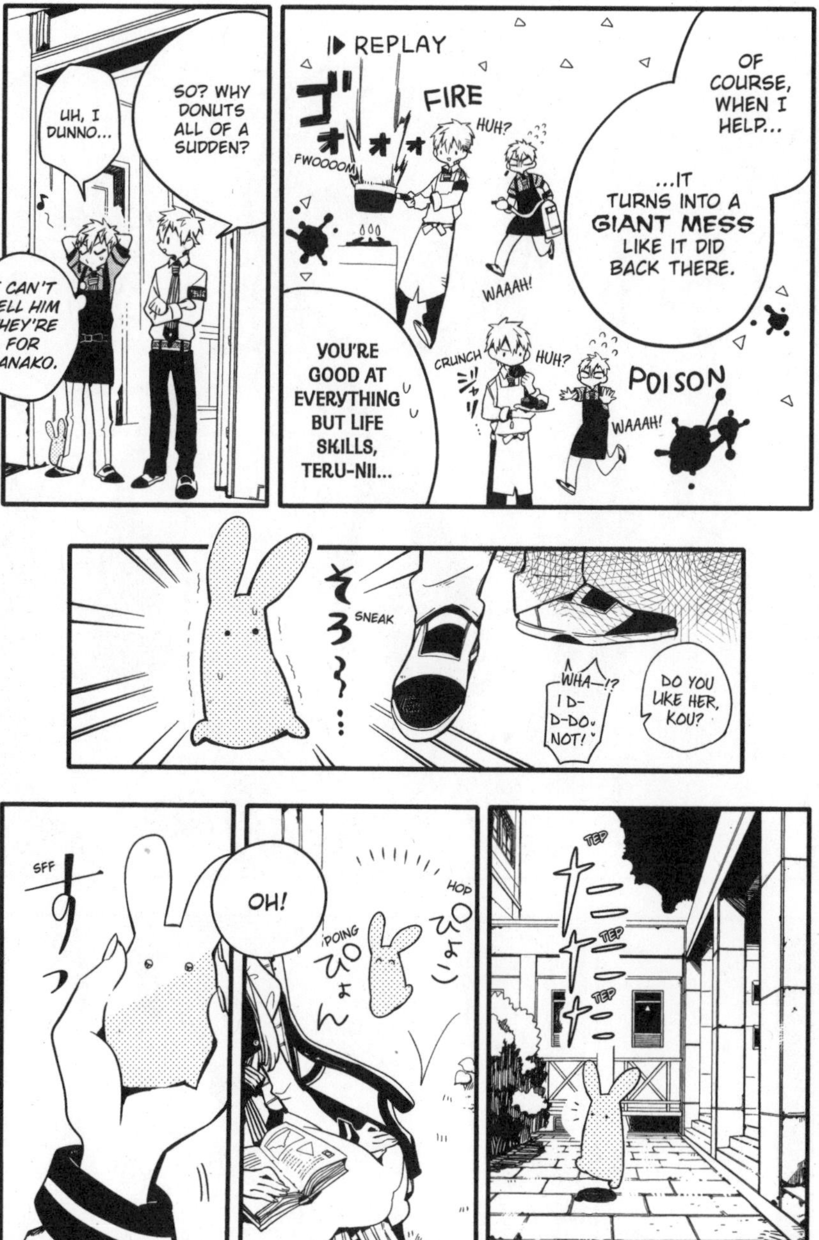
OF COURSE, WHEN I HELP...
...IT TURNS INTO A GIANT MESS LIKE IT DID BACK THERE.
REPLAY
FIRE
ゴォォォ
FWOOOOM
HUH?
WAAAH!
YOU'RE GOOD AT EVERYTHING BUT LIFE SKILLS, TERU-NII...
CRUNCH
HUH?
POISON
WAAAH!
SO? WHY DONUTS ALL OF A SUDDEN?
UH, I DUNNO...
I CAN'T TELL HIM THEY'RE FOR HANAKO.
DO YOU LIKE HER, KOU?
WHA—!?
I D-D-DO NOT!
そろ~...
SNEAK
TEP
TEP
TEP
OH!
HOP
POING
SFF

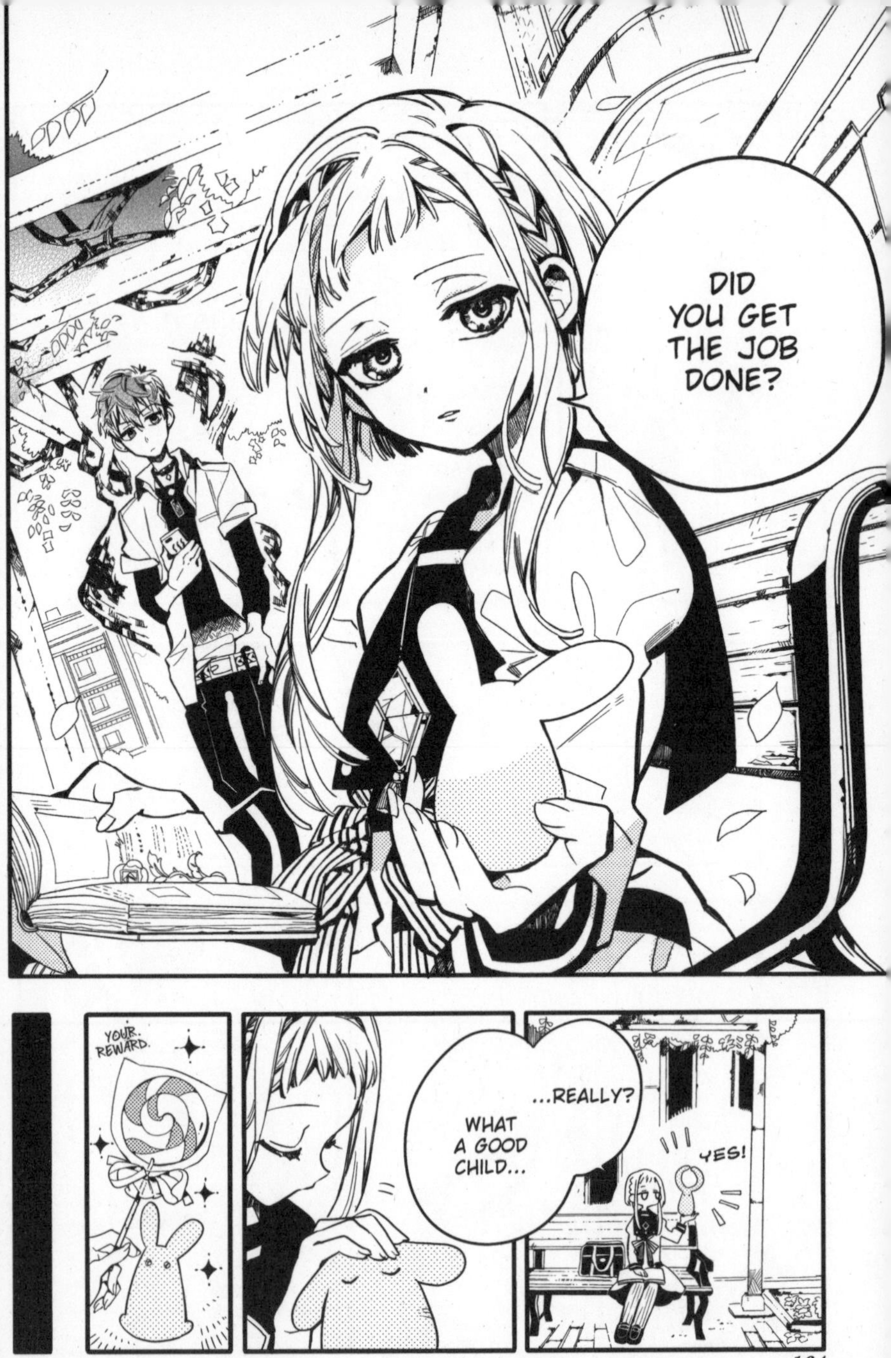
DID YOU GET THE JOB DONE?
YES!
...REALLY?
WHAT A GOOD CHILD...
YOUR. REWARD.

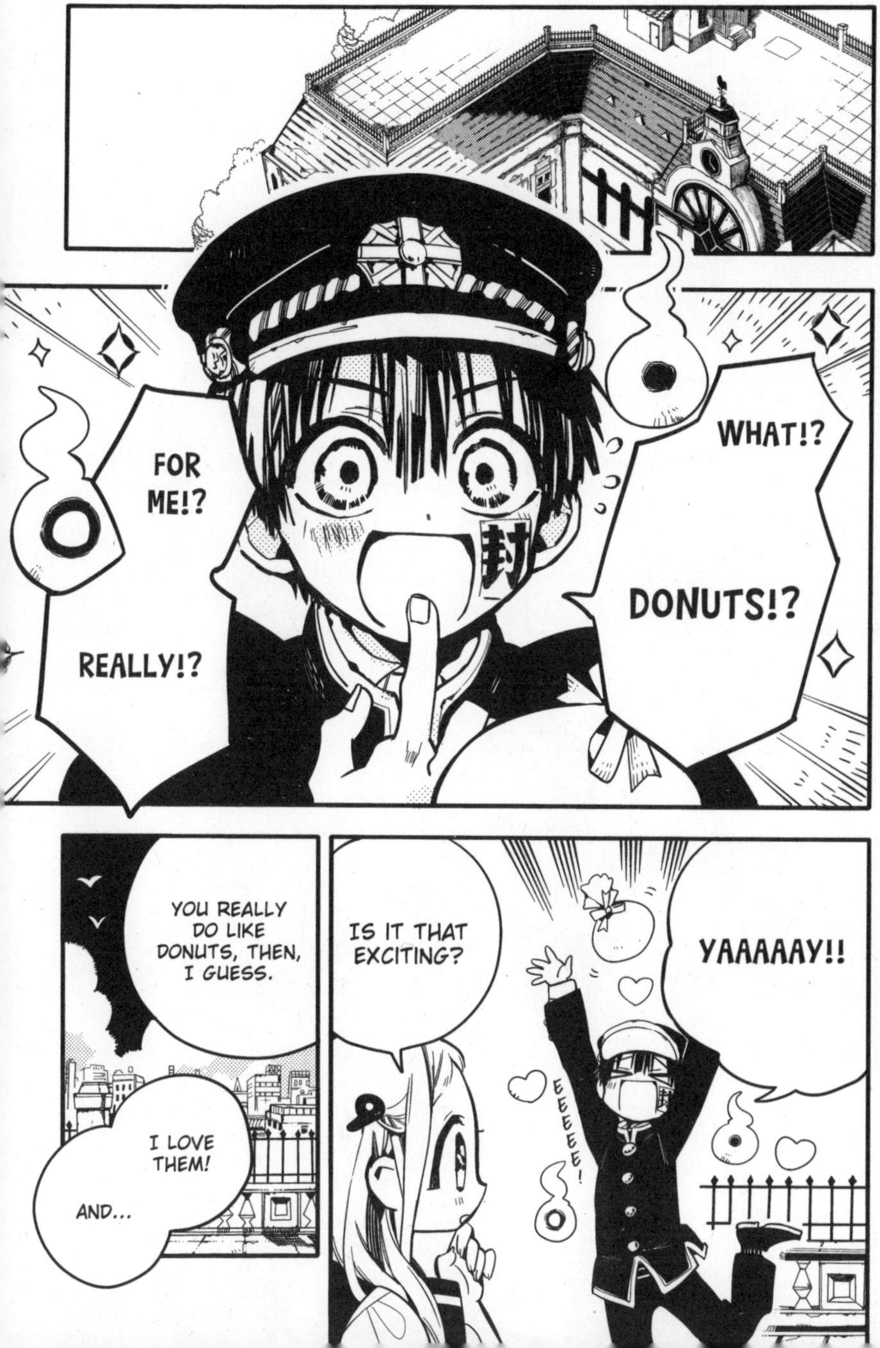
WHAT!? DONUTS!?
FOR ME!? REALLY!?
YAAAAAY!!
EEEEE!
IS IT THAT EXCITING?
YOU REALLY DO LIKE DONUTS, THEN, I GUESS.
I LOVE THEM! AND...

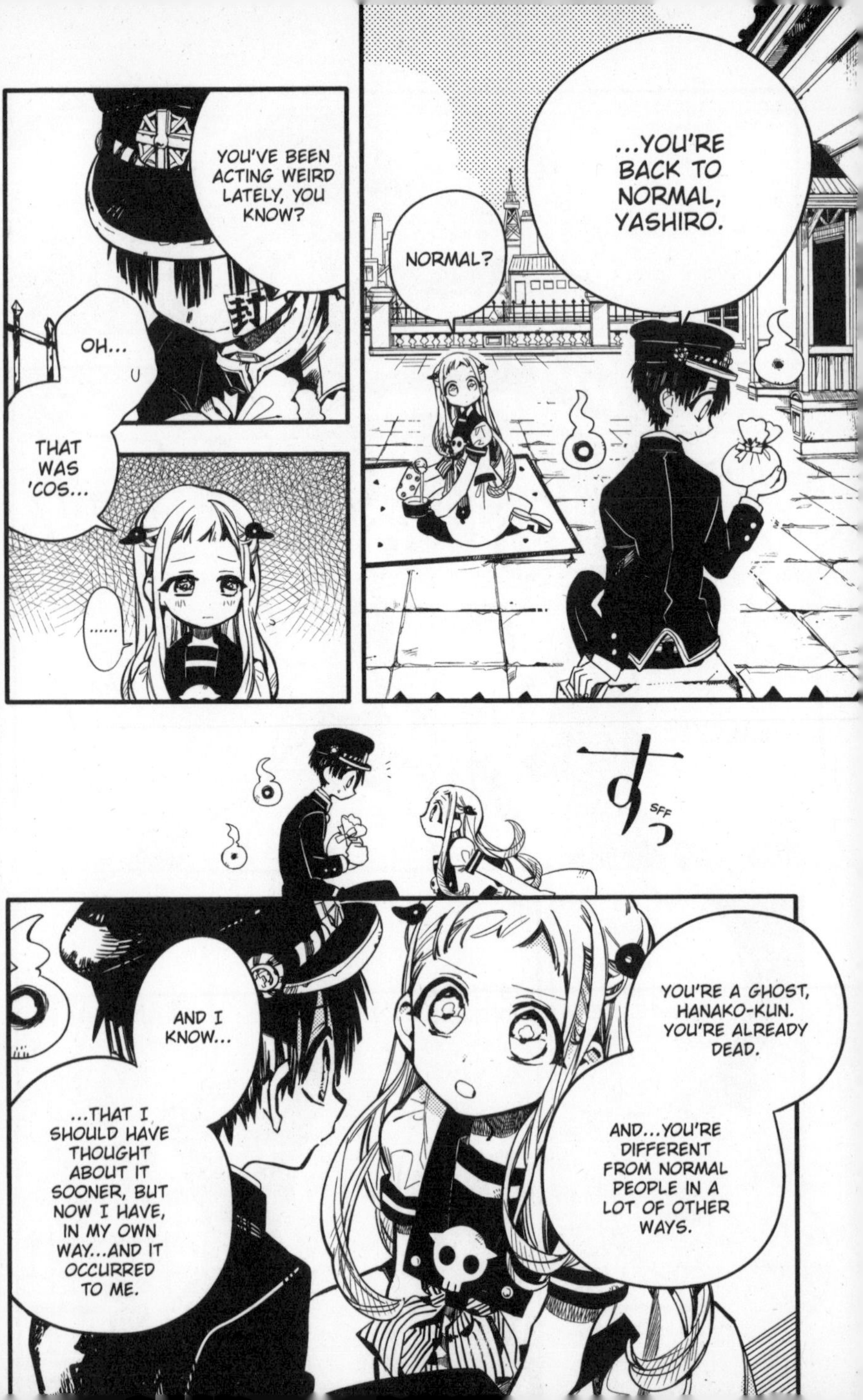
...YOU'RE BACK TO NORMAL, YASHIRO.
NORMAL?
YOU'VE BEEN ACTING WEIRD LATELY, YOU KNOW?
OH...
THAT WAS 'COS...
......
すっ
SFF
YOU'RE A GHOST, HANAKO-KUN. YOU'RE ALREADY DEAD.
AND I KNOW...
AND...YOU'RE DIFFERENT FROM NORMAL PEOPLE IN A LOT OF OTHER WAYS.
...THAT I SHOULD HAVE THOUGHT ABOUT IT SOONER, BUT NOW I HAVE, IN MY OWN WAY...AND IT OCCURRED TO ME.

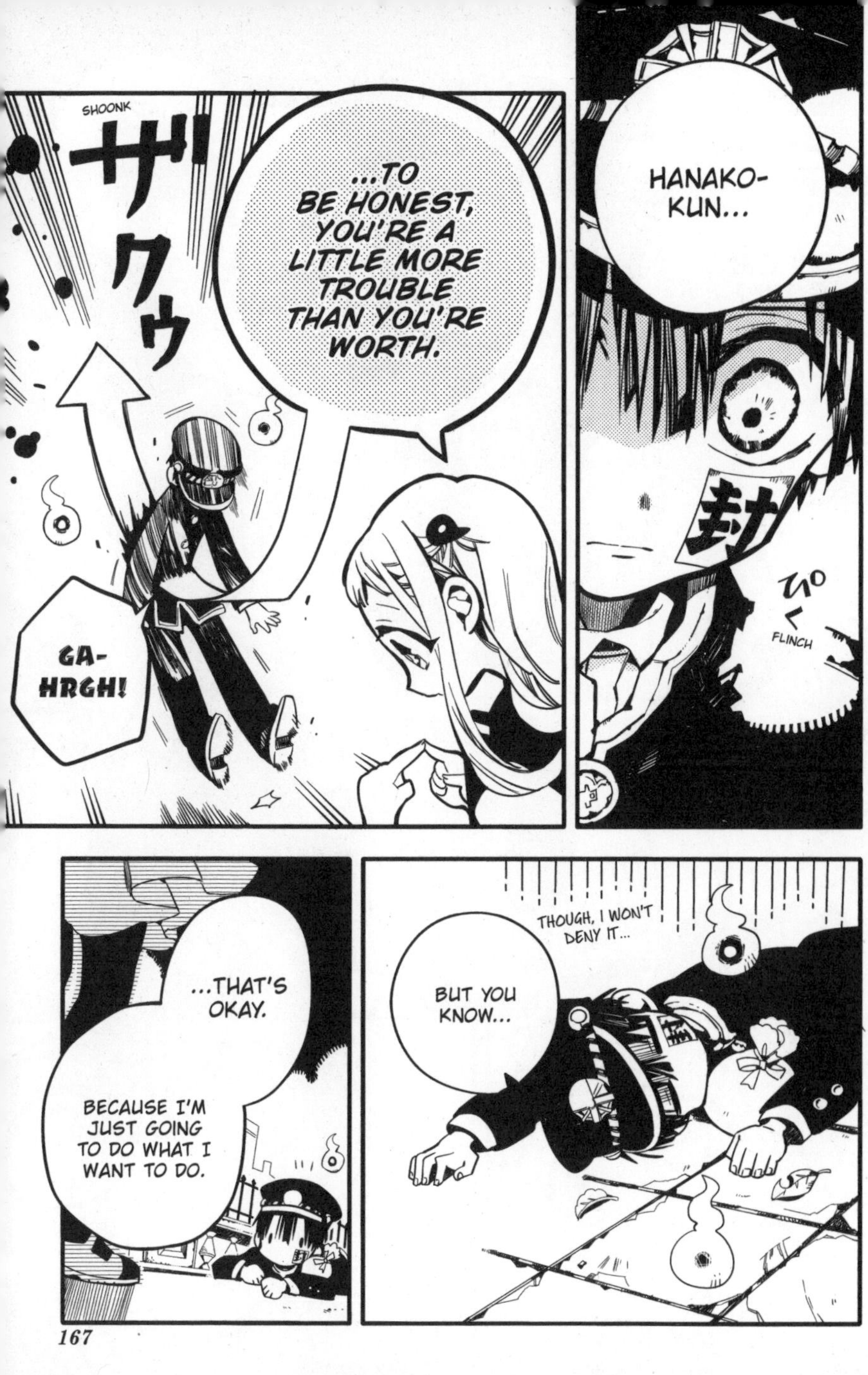
HANAKO-KUN...
ぴく
FLINCH
...TO BE HONEST, YOU'RE A LITTLE MORE TROUBLE THAN YOU'RE WORTH.
ザクゥ
SHOONK
GA-HRGH!
THOUGH, I WON'T DENY IT...
BUT YOU KNOW...
...THAT'S OKAY.
BECAUSE I'M JUST GOING TO DO WHAT I WANT TO DO.

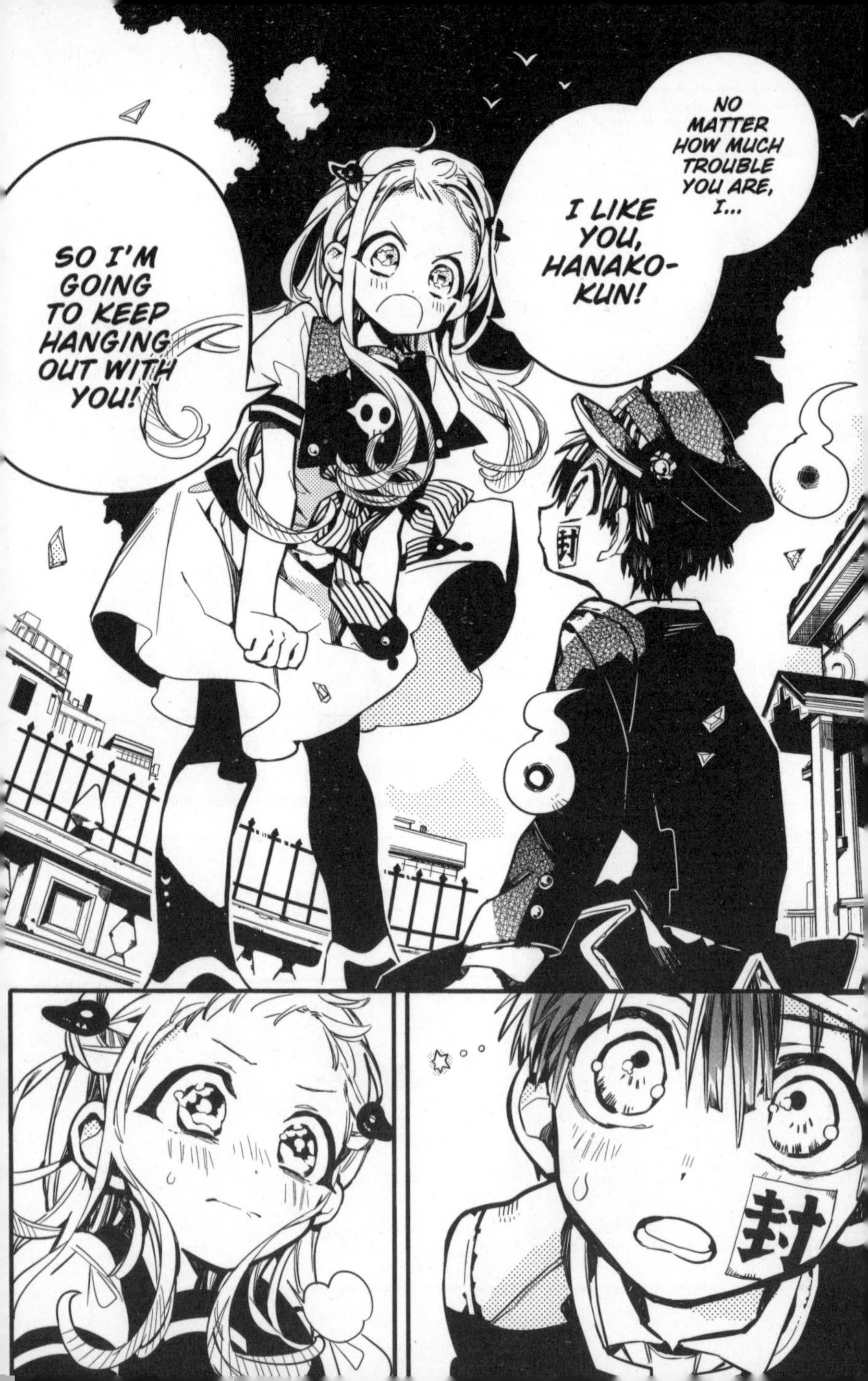
NO MATTER HOW MUCH TROUBLE YOU ARE, I...
I LIKE YOU, HANAKO-KUN!
SO I'M GOING TO KEEP HANGING OUT WITH YOU!

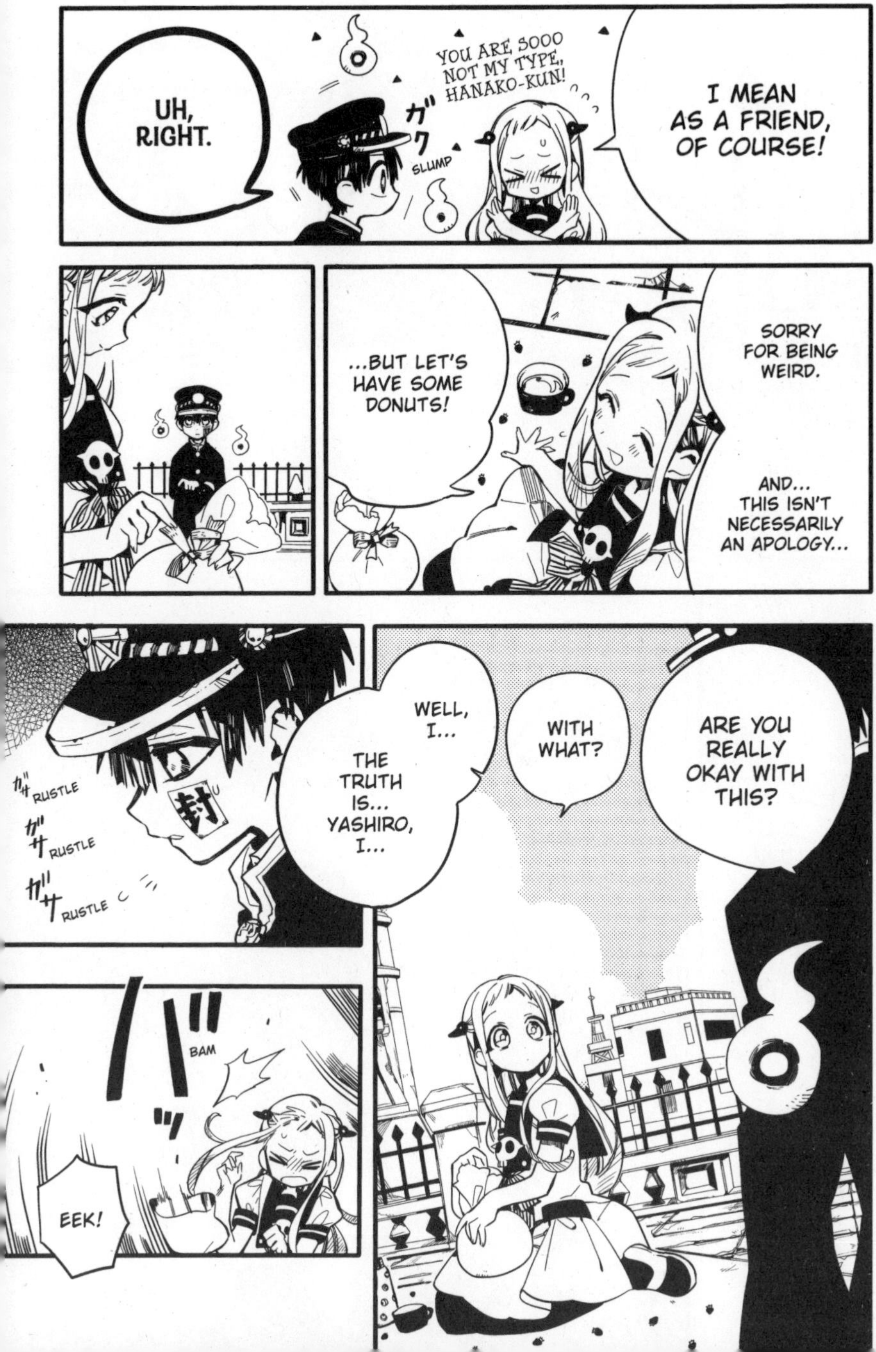
I MEAN AS A FRIEND, OF COURSE!
YOU ARE SOOO NOT MY TYPE, HANAKO-KUN!
ガク SLUMP
UH, RIGHT.
SORRY FOR BEING WEIRD.
AND... THIS ISN'T NECESSARILY AN APOLOGY...
...BUT LET'S HAVE SOME DONUTS!
ARE YOU REALLY OKAY WITH THIS?
WITH WHAT?
WELL, I...
THE TRUTH IS... YASHIRO, I...
ガサ RUSTLE
ガサ RUSTLE
ガサ RUSTLE
バッ BAM
EEK!

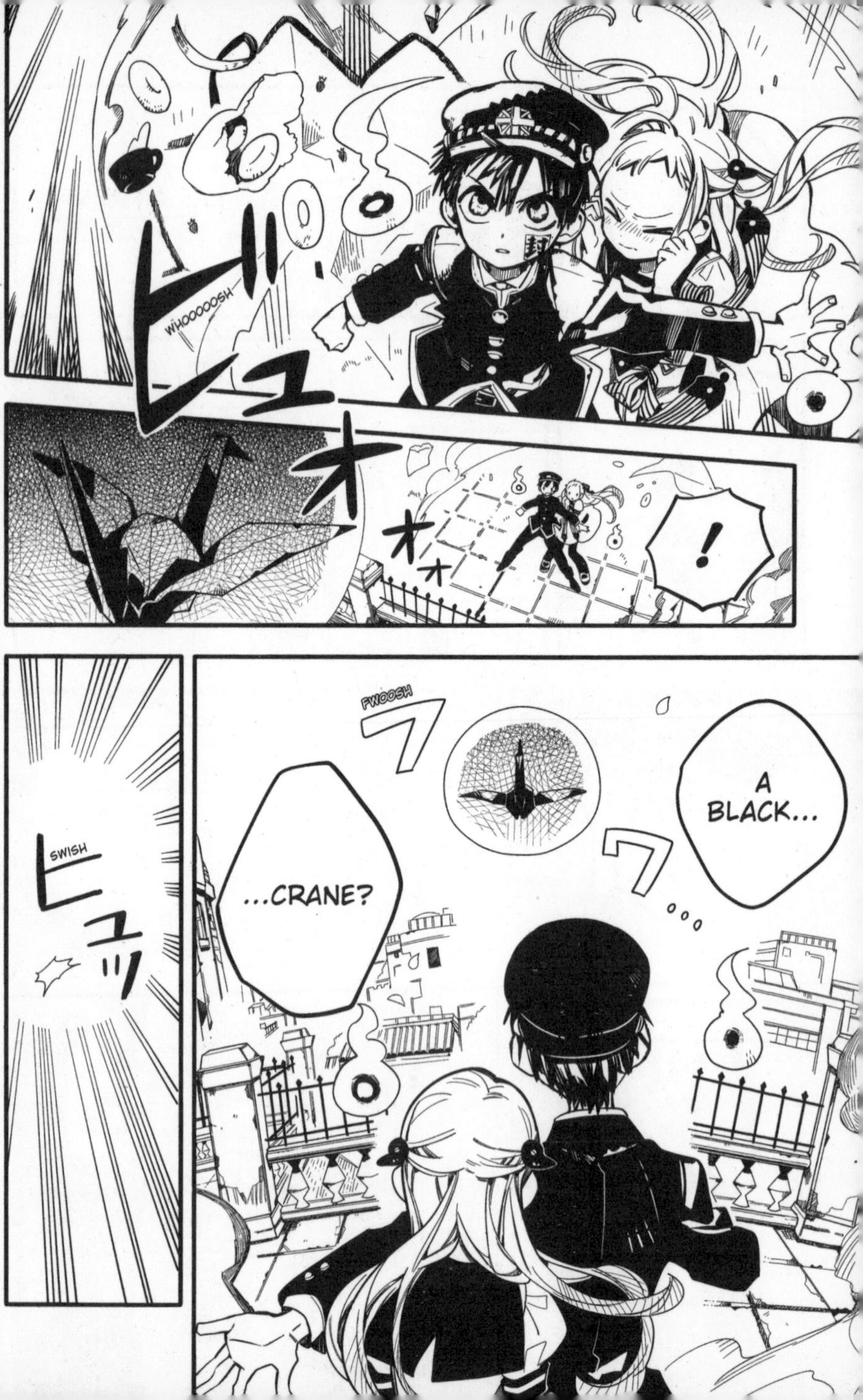
WHOOOOOSH
!
FWOOSH
A BLACK...
...CRANE?
SWISH

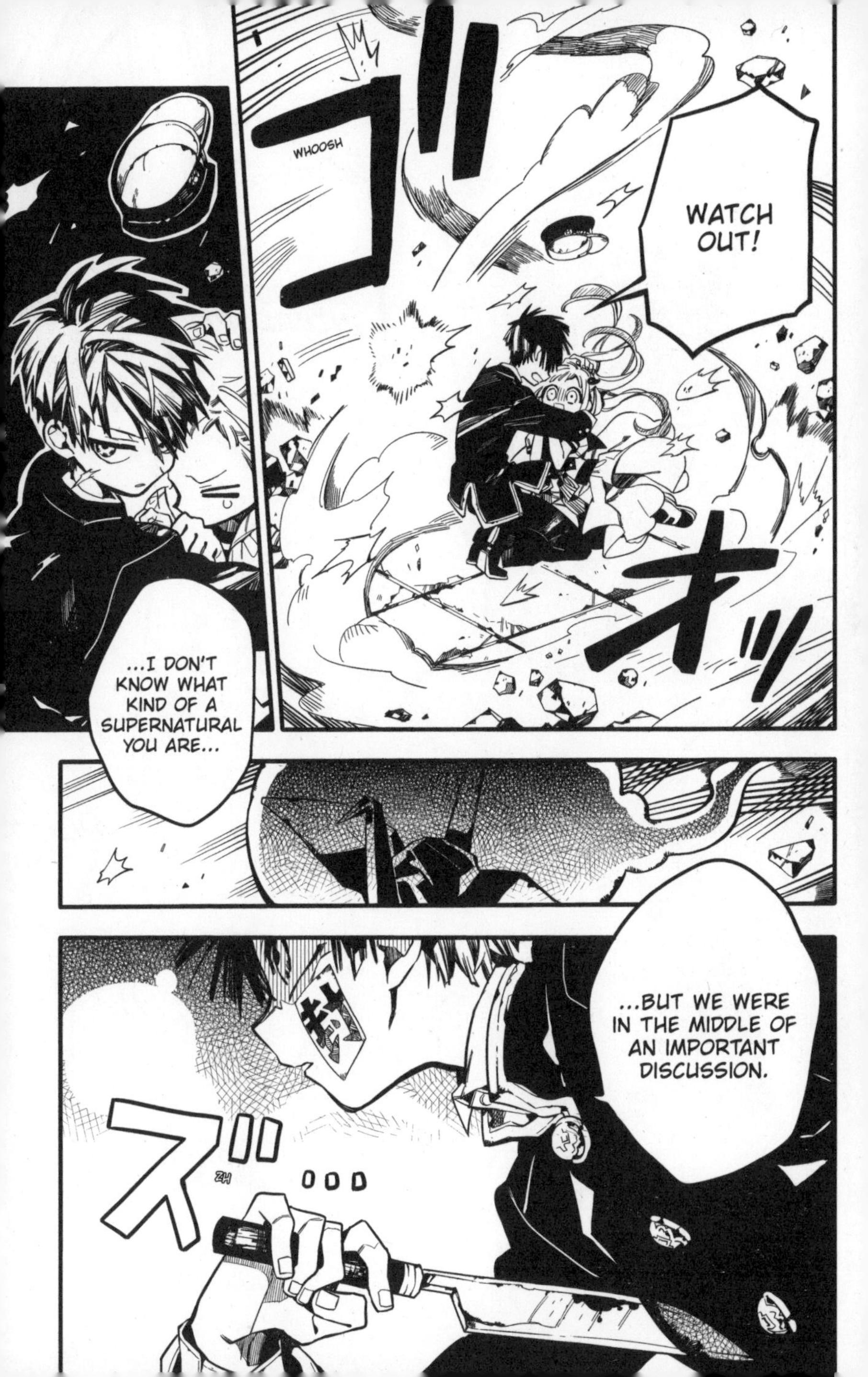
WATCH OUT!
WHOOSH
...I DON'T KNOW WHAT KIND OF A SUPERNATURAL YOU ARE...
...BUT WE WERE IN THE MIDDLE OF AN IMPORTANT DISCUSSION.
ZH
ooo

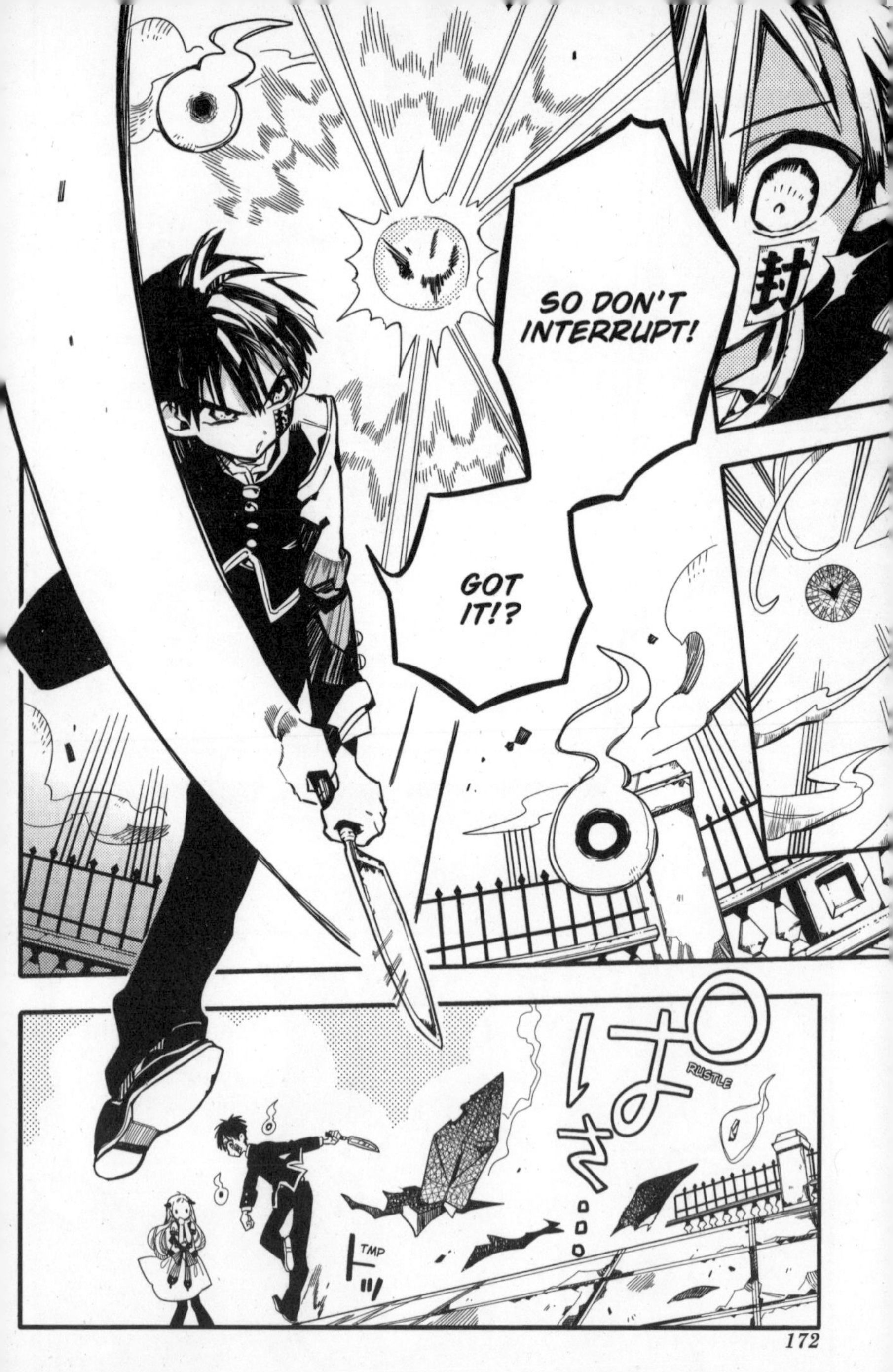
SO DON'T INTERRUPT!
GOT IT!?
封
ぱさ…
RUSTLE
ドッ
TMP

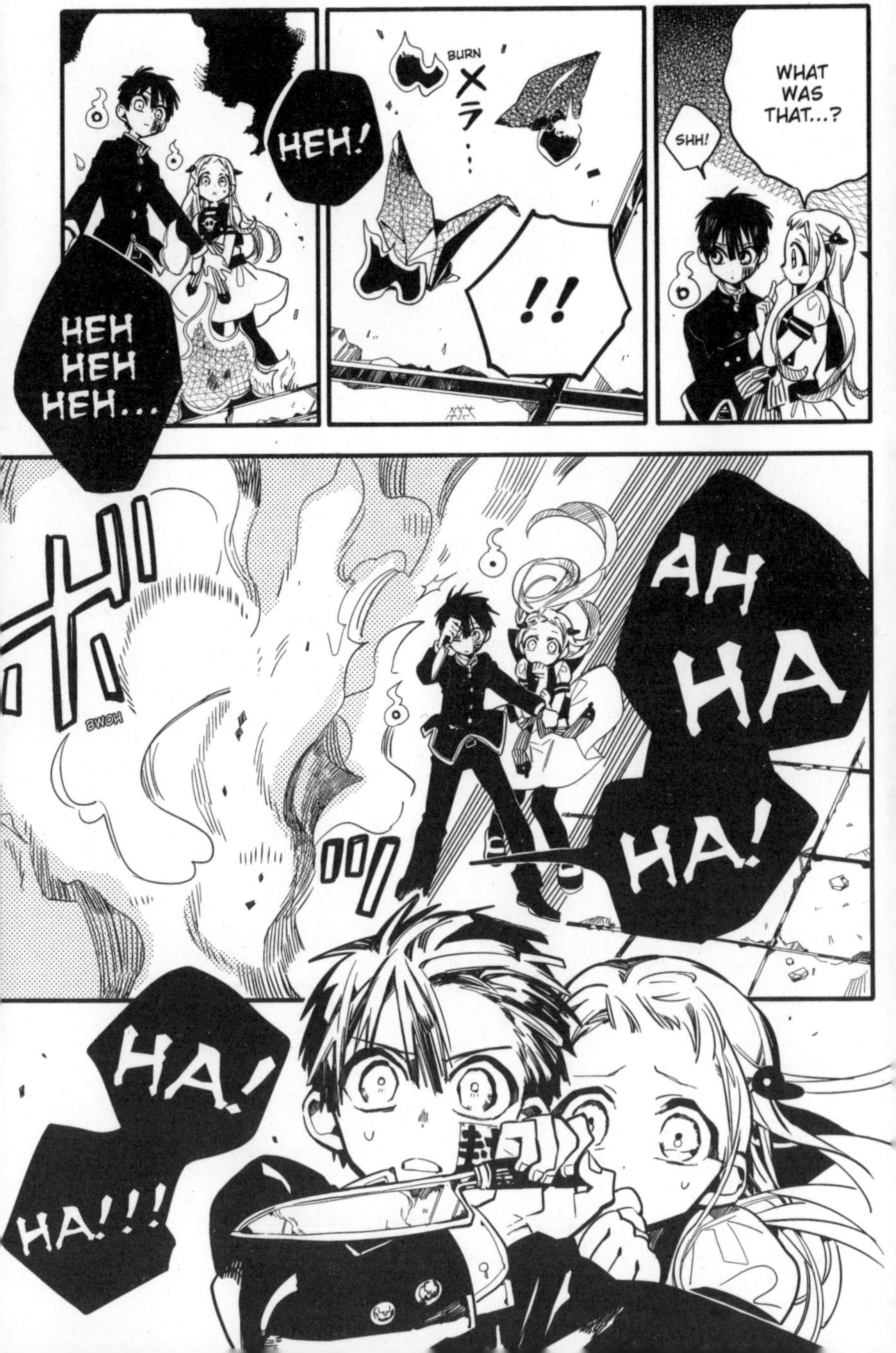
WHAT WAS THAT...?
SHH!
BURN
メラ...
!!
HEH!
HEH HEH HEH...
AH HA HA!
BWOH
HA!
HA!!!

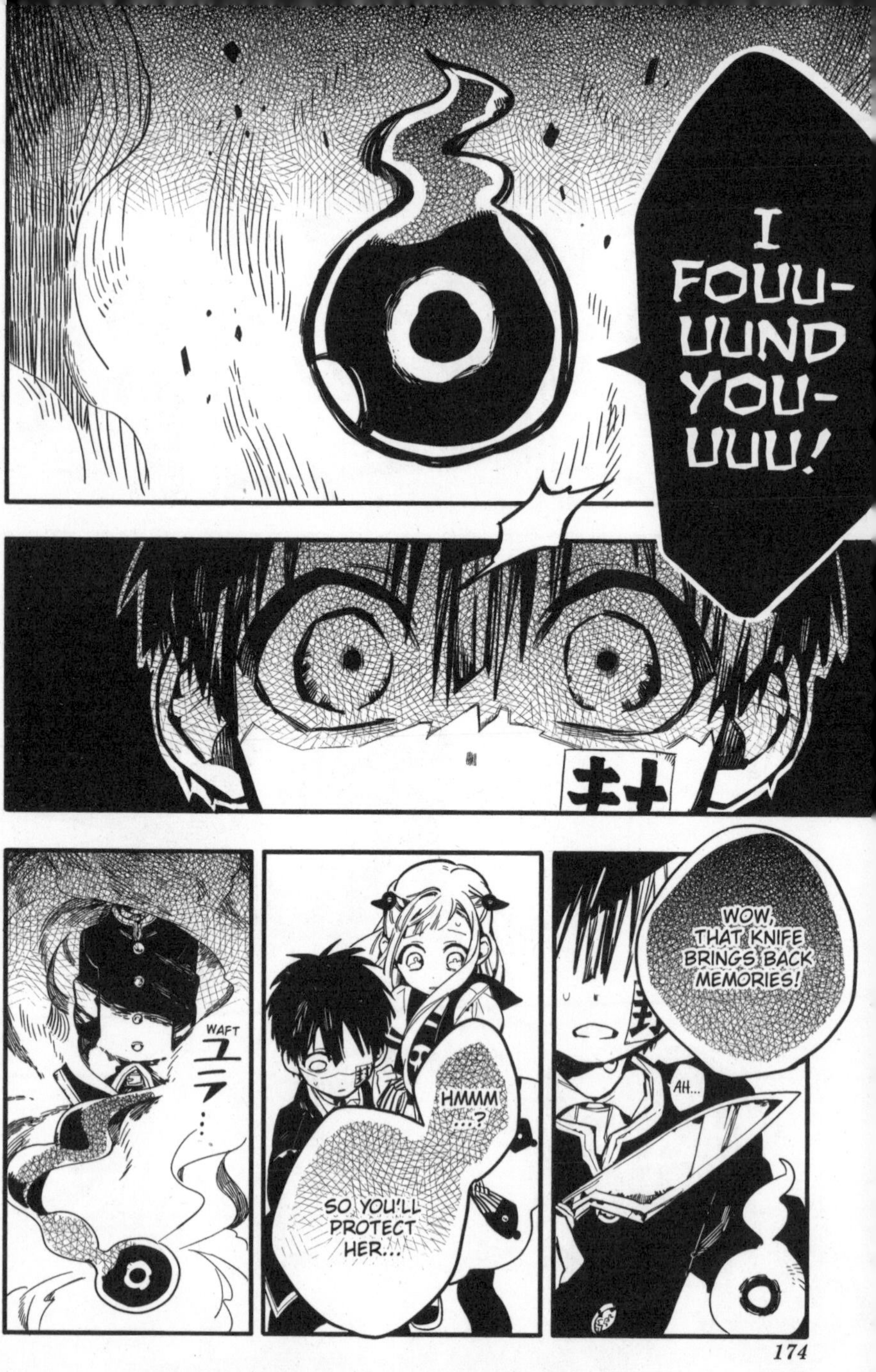
I FOUU-UUND YOU-UUU!
封
WOW, THAT KNIFE BRINGS BACK MEMORIES!
AH...
HMMM ...?
SO YOU'LL PROTECT HER...
WAFT
ユラ...

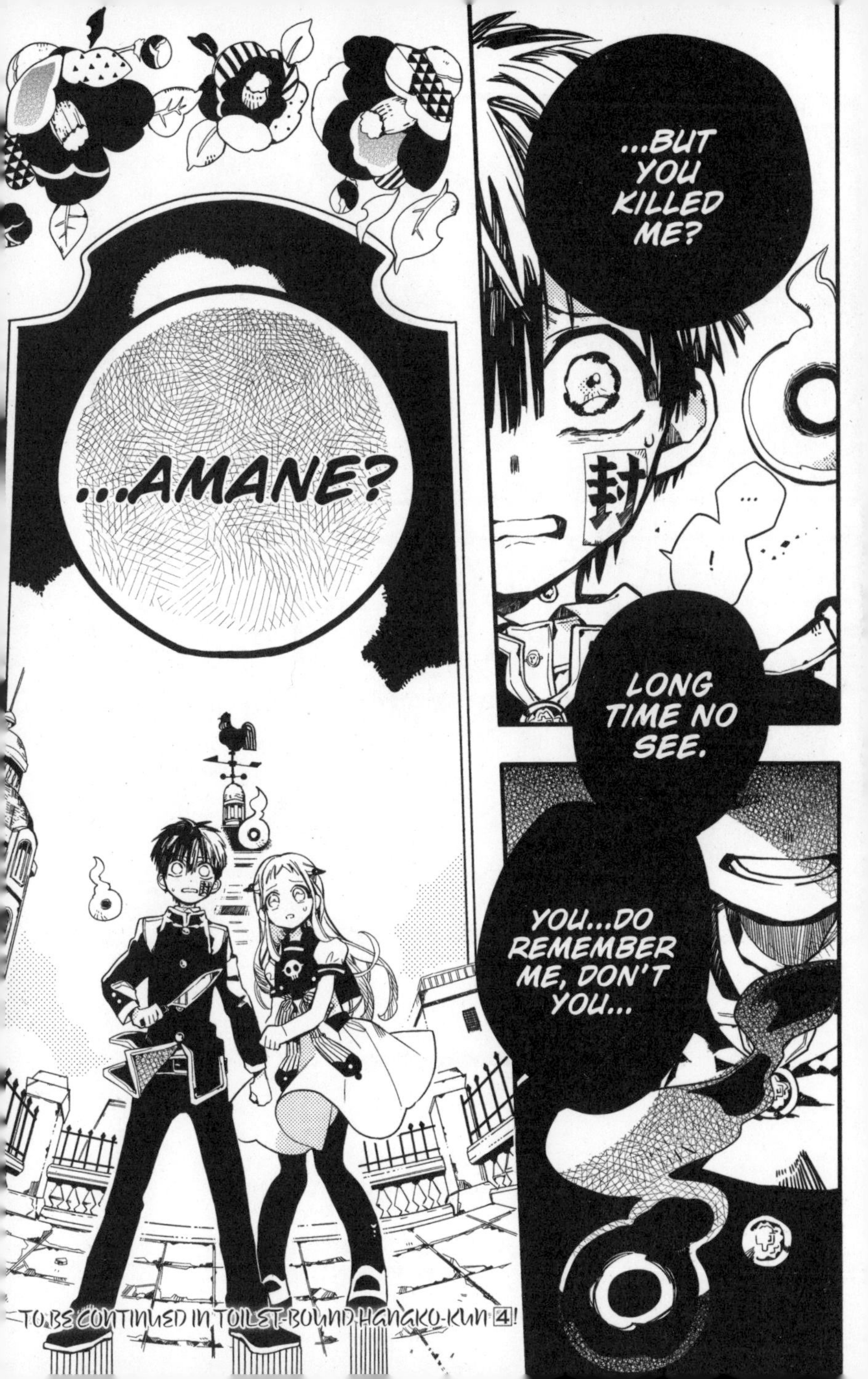
...BUT YOU KILLED ME?
...
LONG TIME NO SEE.
YOU...DO REMEMBER ME, DON'T YOU...
...AMANE?
TO BE CONTINUED IN TOILET-BOUND HANAKO-KUN 4!

OUTTAKE FROM SPOOK 15

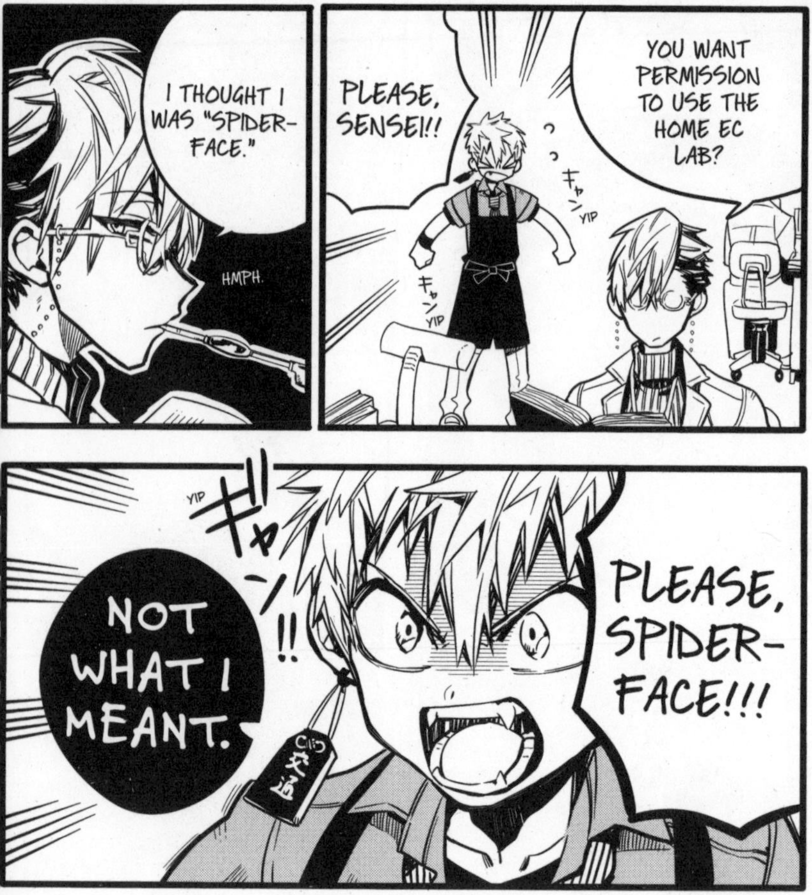
YOU WANT PERMISSION TO USE THE HOME EC LAB?
PLEASE, SENSEI!!
YIP
YIP
I THOUGHT I WAS "SPIDER-FACE."
HMPH.
PLEASE, SPIDER-FACE!!!
YIP
NOT WHAT I MEANT.

Send fan letters here:
yenpress@yenpress.com,
or to Yen Press,
150 West 30th Street, 19th Floor
New York, NY 10001

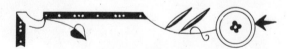

TRANSLATION NOTES

Common Honorifics

no honorific: Indicates familiarity or closeness; if used without permission or reason, addressing someone in this manner would constitute an insult.

-san: The Japanese equivalent of Mr./Mrs./Miss. If a situation calls for politeness, this is the fail-safe honorific.

-sama: Conveys great respect; may also indicate that the social status of the speaker is lower than that of the addressee.

-kun: Used most often when referring to boys, this indicates affection or familiarity. Occasionally used by older men among their peers, but it may also be used by anyone referring to a person of lower standing.

-chan: An affectionate honorific indicating familiarity used mostly in reference to girls; also used in reference to cute persons or animals of either gender.

-senpai: A suffix used to address upperclassmen or more experienced coworkers.

-sensei: A respectful term for teachers, artists, or high-level professionals.

Page 23

The kanji used for the number five in the Four P.M. Bookstacks is archaic and seldom used in modern Japanese.

Page 47

Literally meaning "earth spider," *tsuchigumo* is the name of a supernatural creature from Japanese folklore. It's basically a giant spider.

Page 64

Echinococcus is a parasite commonly associated with foxes.

Page 68

An exchange diary, or *koukan nikki*, is a diary shared between friends or lovers. Each person sharing the diary will take turns writing down their thoughts or feelings, knowing full well other people will read it — kind of like Facebook without the Internet. Like Facebook, all of the writer's friends who are in a position to read the "feed" can comment on posts/entries. In the case of lovers, only the couple will see the entries, but this diary is even more private than that, as she is playing the role of both writers.

Page 71

Setsubun is a Japanese festival to welcome spring. During this time of year, it is customary to cast out demons in order to welcome a peaceful new season. This has led to a tradition of having people wear an *oni* demon mask; others will throw beans at them to "exorcise" them.

Page 79

Hijiki is a nutritious sea vegetable eaten in Japan.

Page 85

The word *kannagi* refers to a servant of the gods, usually a woman. It may come from the phrase *kamu nagi*, "to soothe the gods," as her role is to appease the gods and prevent their wrath from harming the people around them.

Page 101

Cicadas are seen as emblematic of summer in Japan, so their buzzing in the second panel of this flashback is a cue to help the reader understand what time of year it is supposed to be.

Page 103

The complete version of the quote on this calendar reads "At first, there is no path—yet when many pass one way, a road is made," which is the last line of the 1921 short story "My Old Home" by Lu Xun. The story is about a man who returns to his childhood home and realizes his relationships with his former friends and neighbors have always been tainted by imbalances of status and wealth. The last line is a prayer for future generations to build a better society that is now frequently used in Japanese graduation ceremonies and the like. However, the abridged version used on the calendar (*chijou ni michi wa nai*) drops the "at first" and translates more literally as "there is no path through this world," hinting at Hanako's fascination with the limitless freedom of the moon and foreshadowing his "decision" at the end of the flashback.

Page 112

380,000 kilometers is about 236,000 miles.

Page 164

Instead of saying "yes," the Mokke actually uses the word *maru* (circle) and makes one with its ears, which is the equivalent of a check mark in English.

Toilet-bound Hanako-Kun 3

AidaIro

Translation: Alethea Nibley and Athena Nibley
Lettering: Jesse Moriarty

JIBAKU SHONEN HANAKO-KUN Volume 3 ©2016 AidaIro / SQUARE ENIX CO., LTD.
First published in Japan in 2016 by SQUARE ENIX CO., LTD. English translation rights arranged with SQUARE ENIX CO., LTD. and Yen Press, LLC through Tuttle-Mori Agency, Inc.

English translation © 2017 by SQUARE ENIX CO., LTD.

Yen Press
150 West 30th Street, 19th Floor
New York, NY 10001

Visit us at yenpress.com • facebook.com/yenpress • twitter.com/yenpress • yenpress.tumblr.com • instagram.com/yenpress

First Yen Press Print Edition: May 2020
Originally published as an ebook in December 2017 by Yen Press.

Yen Press is an imprint of Yen Press, LLC.
The Yen Press name and logo are trademarks of Yen Press, LLC.

The publisher is not responsible for websites (or their content) that are not owned by the publisher.

Library of Congress Control Number: 2019953610

ISBN: 978-1-9753-1135-3 (paperback)

10 9 8 7 6

TPA

Printed in South Korea

WITHDRAWN